DOCTOR WHO

THE QUANTUM ARCHANGEL

CRAIG HINTON

For Julian and Christian Richards, Adam and Samuel Anghelides, and Robert Stirling-Lane.
The next generation.
May you find the friendship and love that we have.

Published by BBC Worldwide Ltd,
Woodlands, 80 Wood Lane
London W12 0TT

First published 2001

ISBN 0 563 53824 4

Printed and bound in Great Britain by Mackays of Chatham
Cover printed by Belmont Press Ltd, Northampton

I'll be revenged on the whole pack of you.
Malvolio - *Twelfth Night*

His sins will find their punishment in due time.
Rassilon - *The Five Doctors*

And thus the whirligig of time brings in his revenges.
Feste - *Twelfth Night*

The Quantum Mechanics

Gods...

She had been there for an eternity. Then again, what was eternity to an Eternal?

Stars could burn and die, galaxies could collide, timelines could converge and collapse... but Elektra would wait, wait out her long silent vigil in the depths of the darker strata. Elektra knew that she would be undisturbed there.

The darker strata, the deepest levels of the time vortex, were ignored by all - the Eternals, their cousins the Chronovores, the mysterious Time Wraiths with their insane appetites, the Swimmers mindlessly pressing against the multiversal boundaries... All the Transcendental Beings shunned the darkness, preferring the upper levels or the Six-Fold Realm itself. But the dim, turbid streams of the darker strata were the perfect place for an Eternal who didn't want to be found.

And Elektra most certainly did not want to be found.

Like all the Transcendental Beings, the Eternals had existed since before the universe had formed - an eternity in the most literal sense. Abandoned by their parents, they had been left to forge their own path - but it was a path that Elektra rejected. Not for her the endless hunt for lesser beings to fulfil her life; not for her the need for ephemeral thoughts and desires to give purpose to her existence. No - Elektra knew what she wanted.

But what Elektra wanted was forbidden, forbidden by the Ancient Covenants that bound the Transcendental Beings.

Because Elektra wanted fulfilment.

Once, long ago, within the abyssal confines of the darker strata, she had found that fulfilment. And she would do again, so very, very soon.

Because, for the first time since the remnants of the big bang had hung in the vortex like veils of preternatural fire, since the Transcendental Beings had found themselves in their new home, Elektra had found one simpatico to her needs and her wishes...

As if in response to her reverie, the dark of the abyss began to stir. It began to curdle into patterns of time, space and reality, new regions of space-time bubbling down through the substrates to the closed reaches of the darker strata, permitting a heavily built figure of fire and ice to penetrate Elektra's oubliette, his wings outstretched in greeting. Elektra responded, creating a spiral spectrum of turbulence in colours that could only be seen in the time vortex, and then only by gods.

But Elektra was a god, and so was her consort.

Prometheus.

As he approached, his mind began to burn within hers as hers did within his, minds of unimaginable complexity and reach... but also minds of imagination, a concept that their fellow Eternals and Chronovores simply couldn't comprehend.

For theirs was a marriage that screamed in the face of the Ancient Covenants.

She was of the Eternal caste: those who drifted mindlessly, seeking out other imaginations, other lives, to lead and to leech from. Occasionally, if the boredom grew too great, they would be drawn to the Games, where the Council of Guardians or the less aloof old gods would organise tournaments and entrapments for them, but most of their time was spent looking for others - for those who led real lives - who could fulfil that great longing that was the Eternals' curse. But not Elektra. As far as she knew, she was unique - the only Eternal who lacked the great longing for external fulfilment.

But there was another longing, another need... one that required succour from another who could meet her on her own plane. Not one from the brotherhood and sisterhood of the Eternals, but from another source...

The dark caste of the Chronovores.

Segregated at birth, they had been consigned to exile just because they failed to meet the standards of the council. Damn the Ancient Covenants! She looked at Prometheus, radiant, magnificent... She found it hard to reconcile that with the covenant description of the Chronovores.

According to the council's ruling, the Chronovores were nothing but vampires: subsisting on the primal energies of the Six-

Fold Realm, only truly living by drawing the life essence from the moments of choice, where they could thrive on the what-ifs and the what-might-have-beens, keeping this cosmos alone in the multiverse. An empty existence, a life of loneliness.

Just like the Eternals.

But not Elektra and Prometheus. Not them. As he approached her through the murk of the darker strata tendrils of thought stroked the outer edges of her mind. Reinforcing her belief in him. Reinforcing her.

Elektra and Prometheus. Eternal and Chronovore. They had broken the rules, because they were the future. And their forbidden needs and desires would forge that future. With his imagination and her primal strength they would lead their estranged families to a common ground, to a place where all the Transcendental Beings could live together with the races spawned by this universe. The humans, the Gallifreyans, the Daleks... they would all have their part to play.

As would those Transcendental Beings that had stolen away into the hidden places, regions of the multiverse that were even more remote than the darker strata, beings that had seen the universe as a challenge to be conquered, a people to be raped, an artefact of so high a price that they would destroy everything to possess it. The Great Intelligence, the Nestene Consciousness, the Animus... Especially the darkest and greatest of the Old Ones, Nyarlathotep: after what he had done, Elektra had a special place in Hell reserved for him.

All of them, hiding and waiting like spiders in their vile webs. They would be the enemy.

That was her driving purpose. Such evil needed to be fought, and, for that, Time would need a champion. A champion that Elektra and Prometheus would give their wonderfully united universe, a champion that grew within her.

Their child.

Avatar.

Their child would be the being who would unite all of sentience under one banner, whose dual heritage would show that this new universe was to be shared for the betterment of all.

A mission led by Elektra and Prometheus.

Elektra, my love.

He was with her now, his body conjoining with the radiant aura which surrounded her. Eternals and Chronovores were built from matrices of exotic particles, resonating superstrings that gave them power and majesty, and Elektra gasped as those matrices intertwined. But their feelings... were there particles for that? If there weren't, then Elektra and Prometheus would create them.

The moment approaches, my love. Our child will be magnificent. Prometheus' wings enfolded her, allowing them both to feel the embryonic consciousness within her communicating with them on a level that was almost impossible to detect. But they could detect it. And Elektra could tell that their child's epiphany was imminent. An epiphany for the universe. A new universe, overseen by Elektra and Prometheus. They would be the parents of a new dawn, a new era...

Thoughts of the future and their unborn child were thrown aside as the Stygian gloom of the darker strata was suddenly illuminated by a brilliance that defied description. For the first time since the Big Bang had lit the vortex, the darker strata were dark no longer. They were filled by a light that was even darker.

They had found them. Even in the darker strata, they had found them.

Elektra and Prometheus may have been gods, but there were greater gods. Beings at the very pinnacle of existence, at the summit of the cosmic hierarchy.

The Guardians.

Elektra had never seen anything like it in her long, so very long, life. And she knew that few others in the universe had either.

Thankfully.

The entire Council of Guardians, six burning figures of wrath and vengeance, of power and unimaginable majesty. A Six-Fold-God.

A Six-Fold-God for a Six-Fold Realm.

YOU HAVE TRANSGRESSED THE ANCIENT COVENANT, they said, six voices as one. YOU HAVE BROKEN THE VERY LAWS OF THE CONTINUUM.

YOU WILL ALL BE PUNISHED.

Elektra and Prometheus remained silent: there was nothing to say, nothing to do. Together, the Guardians could bend reality, fashion space and time to their whims. To them, a Chronovore and an Eternal were insects - less than insects.

And then Elektra realised what they meant - what they intended to do. She screamed her defiance, her cries tearing through the vortex, powerful enough to shred matter down to the quark level. But to the Council of Guardians it was nothing more than a summer breeze.

They had decided. Now they would act. Without further discussion they handed down their sentence.

Prometheus was the first to be punished for his sins. Acting in metaconcert, the Council of Guardians was the most powerful force in the universe. In many respects they were the universe. Effortlessly, they took Prometheus' timeline and unravelled it, string by superstring, back and back. Elektra could do nothing; even if she had dared to defy the council, its massed energies were freezing her in stasis. She could only observe as her lover, her partner, her mate, was unpicked from the fabric of space-time.

She could feel Prometheus' mind convulsing in agony, reaching out for her in a single long moment of need, before he ceased to exist. Before he ceased to ever *have* existed. The time vortex turned inside out as it came to terms with its fundamental nature being disturbed, before finally calming down into the blackness of the darker strata.

Painfully, Elektra's attention turned from the nothingness that had been one half of her life, anger igniting within her. Even though Prometheus had never been, his memory - his seed - would live on within her. Avatar. Even the Guardians could not rob her of that.

CALM YOURSELF. YOU WILL NOT BE HURT.

YET.

IT IS THE CHILD WE WANT.

No! Not the Avatar.

She was still screaming as the First Phalanx of the Eternals, her family, descended from their hiding places and took her away.

They say she never stopped screaming.

. . . and Monsters

Murder was too small a word for it.

'You've killed them,' Mel whispered, turning away in distress. She looked at the Doctor through tear-blurred eyes. 'All of them.'

The shutters closed over the image on the scanner with a nonchalance that belied the utter carnage that lay outside. Billions of people were now dead or dying beneath the sickly, scintillating green of a poisoned sky, their once-verdant planet nothing more than a ball of radioactive slag hanging in space.

The clear blue waters that had once girdled it were stinking brown liquid graves, brimming full with the bobbing corpses of all marine life; the fruitful garden belt was blindly glazed with the obsidian residue of countless nuclear ground-zeros; the stately avenues of trees that had lined the capital city were nothing but charred fingers, grasping for a hope that no longer remained. Maradnias wasn't quite dead, but only the last rites remained.

Even now, Mel wasn't sure how it had happened. She and the Doctor had arrived on the planet full of hopeful optimism, confident of averting the possible civil war that had threatened to disrupt it. The Doctor had commented as they materialised that the civil war was never going to be more than a small-scale affair, a mere bagatelle in his cosmic crusade; he just felt that it was his responsibility to stop even those few deaths. But now? What had gone wrong on Maradnias?

She turned from the blind scanner and stared at the Doctor through moist eyes. His tall figure, incongruously dressed in that tasteless red-and-yellow jacket, was bent over the hexagonal central console but the strain was clear, even from behind. His broad shoulders were slumped, his head of curly blond hair was bowed in defeat, despair... But those were purely human emotions. And the Doctor wasn't human, Mel had to remind herself. However human he looked, however human he acted, the Doctor was anything but. Mel was, and although the last thing the Doctor wanted was an interrogation she couldn't help herself:

she had to know. With the ghoulish interest of someone watching a car crash, she felt the words slip from her mouth.

'What happened?'

The Doctor didn't look up from the console as he answered, his voice low, sepulchral. 'I miscalculated,' he muttered to the monitors and keyboards. 'I didn't realise how strong the anti-Federalist faction was, or that they'd be idiotic enough to use their nuclear stockpile. I -'

Mel couldn't let him continue. Not any more. 'You miscalculated?' she exclaimed. 'This isn't an exercise in mental arithmetic, Doctor!' The tears were still flowing, but her sorrow was subsiding into uncharacteristic anger. 'Billions of people have died because of you; billions of innocent lives - all gone, all because you miscalculated!'

This time, he did turn round and Mel was momentarily silenced by the tears that were streaming down his face. 'Don't you think I feel it too, Mel?' he bellowed, thumping his chest. 'Don't you think I'll carry the blame for this for the rest of my lives?' The weight of the entire universe was carried on his voice, threatening to make it crack, threatening to make the Doctor crack. But Mel didn't care - it was no less than he deserved.

In spite of the Doctor's obvious distress, unexpected venom coloured Mel's next words; feelings that had been bottled up for months now spilling over without restraint, without a care as to their effect. 'No, Doctor, I don't. Who knows what Time Lords feel? What you feel? You go on about the Daleks, the Cybermen, the Vervoids - creatures that you blame for spreading untold misery and destruction. But if you ask me, you *want* the universe to be filled with evil!'

The Doctor reeled back at the intensity of Mel's words, but she didn't even slow down. The words needed to be said, if only for own her sake. 'Those creatures only seem to exist to justify your own crusade. If it wasn't for them, you'd have no moral high ground to preach from, would you? And that wouldn't suit the Doctor, great and glorious righter of wrongs, would it?' She span on her heels and moved towards the internal door, but her outburst couldn't be contained, even in retreat. She stopped in the open doorway, her back to the Doctor. The words still needed to be said and she turned to face him, her eyes blazing.

'Well, you're just as bad! No, you're worse. At least they admit what they're doing, and don't try to justify... no, to whitewash it like you do.' She pointed at the closed scanner. 'A billion people are dead because you thought you could play God, Doctor, and I'm sick of it. Find another disciple.'

Her courage failing, Mel ran from the console room, the heels of her shoes clattering down the sterile corridor. The Doctor made no move to follow her; instead he reached out and activated the scanner, gazing impassionately at the fatally wounded surface of Maradnias.

Mel had just reached the door to her room when she heard the noise, echoing through the white-walled, roundelled corridors.

It was the Doctor.

Screaming.

Screaming.

It wasn't until he slammed his fist on the lever and closed the great doors that he realised the screams he could hear were coming from his own mouth. Taking a deep breath he willed himself to fight the pain, reminding himself that he had suffered far, far worse in his many lives. But that was of little reassurance - every nerve fibre burnt with the effects of the blast, every inch of his skin was blistered and blackened.

Forcing his charred fingers to obey him, he operated the controls, watching as the time rotor begin to rise and fall as his TARDIS was once more enfolded in the protection of the time vortex. At last he was safe.

Stepping back from the ebony control console, the Master slipped into the shadows of a nearby chair trying to marshal his thoughts. As business deals went, that hadn't been one of his more glorious successes: his... employers had seen through his ruse, and had double-crossed him, just before he could pull the same stunt on them. But it was time to consign it to experience, to put it behind him and carry on with his quest. Because his quest was far more important than grasping at tiny morsels of conquest. His quest now was quite literally a matter of life and death.

Slowly, tentatively, he reached into himself, seeking out the almost depleted pockets of energy that still remained, looking for the burning embers of the Source of Traken that still smouldered within his adopted body, its waning glory only slightly bolstered by the Numismaton Gas of late-lamented Sarn. But it just wasn't enough for him.

Since stealing both the Source of Traken and the body of one of that benighted world's inhabitants, the Master was no longer the desiccated husk of hatred and revenge that he had been. Whereas his current injuries would once have forced a regeneration, now he simply bathed himself in the unutterable goodness of Traken, corrupting that purity to his own ends. Part of him still missed the Time Lord heritage he had mortgaged for this new form of immortality, but that was sentiment, and the Master had no time for such callow, weak emotions. However, despite the added support of the Numismaton Gas, the Source of Traken burnt dimly now, and his overriding concern was to find a replacement before his body, his soul, his very existence simply crumbled into nothing, so much ephemeral dust to be blown away by the time winds.

Mentally fanning the Source's embers, he began to effect repairs to his burnt and broken body, eking out the remaining energy down nerves and sinews, repairing flesh and bone. Unlike the wild explosion of a regeneration, this was more calculated, more painful... but more controlled. None of the wastefulness of a regeneration, where even the healthy tissue was sacrificed in favour of the new matrix that the limbic gland enforced, a genetic coding decreed by his Time Lord physiognomy. With his powers, he could mould his new body, choose his physical form -

- the impact that rocked the TARDIS knocked him from both his regenesis and his chair, at the same time throwing him on to the polished black floor and halting the physiological repair.

His body crying out in pain, the Master dragged himself upright, trying to reach the console to ascertain what was going on, to try to control it.

He didn't make it.

The next jolt hurled him against a black, roundelled wall; he managed to fall forward and grab the edge of the console, biting back the scream that rose within him as his burnt flesh cracked and wept with the effort. But there was no time for pain: locking it away, his eyes scanned the read-outs... and he looked in disbelief at what they were telling him. His TARDIS was under attack!

But how was that possible? Those bumbling crystalline fools may have been able to injure him, but their asinine Dynatrope certainly didn't have access to the sort of technology that was currently shaking his TARDIS to pieces. To affect a TARDIS in flight demanded time technology of the highest order, and there were mercifully few races in the cosmos who could wield such powers. Mercifully few rivals, that was.

The Time Lords, certainly, but this brazen attack wasn't their way at all. No, they hid behind agents, lies and half-truths - direct action was anathema to them. And besides, hadn't the new High Council been only too happy to see the back of him once he had been released from the limbo atrophier in the Matrix?

The Daleks? Rassilon alone knew, they had every reason to want him dead but he hadn't felt their evil lurking on the sidelines and, despite everything, he still trusted his instincts. The Cybermen? The Sontarans? He shook his head. Those pathetic races with their stolen, half-hearted time technology? Bastardised DARDISes and feeble osmic projectors?

So who was it? He examined the readings more closely. And froze. He'd been looking in totally the wrong direction.

It was a mistake he knew he was going to regret.

The energies which were now beginning to tear his TARDIS apart weren't coming from the planet he had just left. They weren't even coming from the time vortex. They were coming from the deepest levels of reality, from the primal substrate that underpinned the universe - and that could only mean one thing.

The Master gulped back his fear.

He boosted power to the defences, surrounding his ship with a nigh-impenetrable force field, one stolen from a Farquazi time cruiser in the 300th segment of time and far more resilient than a TARDIS's standard defences. There, that should do it. He stepped back as the console room filled with the reassuring burbling and twinkling of the energy barrier, as it enwombed his TARDIS and protected it. There, safe now -

The Master fell backwards, only managing to roll and protect himself at the very last second, as a gout of flame erupted from the console. The time rotor's movements became unsteady and laboured, and the regular hum of the TARDIS became uneven and raspy. That last hit had penetrated a Farquazi shield - Impossible! Even a head-on assault from a Dalek time fleet couldn't dent that! As he got to his feet and staggered back to the console a horrible theory was taking shape. Whoever was wielding this magnitude of temporal energies wasn't using technology. There was something natural behind this, it was more like being swatted by some unimaginable power... Oh no... He didn't have to wait long for the confirmation. The word burnt in his mind like fire in the abyss.

Kronos.

His suspicions had been correct. Panic began to grip his hearts.

As flies to wanton boys. The Time Lords saw themselves as gods, but there were greater ones than them, gods who could treat them and their vaunted technology as nothing more than irritations to be swatted. Not the Guardians: to preserve the structure of reality, their hand could never be detected. But there were others, beings that inhabited the deepest, darkest depths of the vortex. And once, a very long time ago, the Master had enslaved one of them, bent it to his will.

Kronos, greatest of the Chronovores.

Even as the words lanced into his mind, the Master knew he was no longer alone. The dark shadows of his TARDIS were burning with preternatural fire, flames which coalesced into a figure that was almost too bright to look at. Like some vicious firebird, it hovered over him, its radiance banishing the TARDIS's permanent gloom.

Hear me, Lord of Time. The words both hung in the air and burnt into the Master's mind. *We are a vengeful people. Our reach is infinite and our patience is eternal. For your actions, we* will *have vengeance.*

And the vengeance of the Chronovores is terror beyond imagining.

The visitation ended, the firebird exhausting itself, the console room darkening into shadows once more. But they were no longer the safe and friendly shadows that the Master welcomed. They were compromised. Tainted. Corrupted.

With difficulty the Master began to compose himself, but his tormentor had one more surprise. Before the Master could do anything, his TARDIS was hit by a force so great that it even made the Cloister Bell chime, warning of the imminent destruction of his Ship. Hanging on to the console with his charred weeping fingers, the Master could only wait as his TARDIS was flung across eternity, a hurtling blur through the vortex, its outer surface pixelating as the stresses overwhelmed the chameleon circuit.

And within? For the first time in centuries, the Master was scared. Terrified. Against the power of a vengeful god, what could a simple Time Lord do?

The Piecemeal Construction of Small Gods

Chapter One
Total Eclipse of the Heart

It took a long time before Mel could even begin to calm down. And an even longer time to work out how she was going to approach the Doctor. A long time.

It wasn't going to be easy, she decided.

Feeling a measure of peace, she sat down on the peach duvet that covered her bed and sighed, releasing the last of the tension - or rather, enough for her to carry on with what she had to do. As she sighed she examined her reflection in the full-length mirror that rested against the roundelled wall, feeling hideously overdressed in the sequinned organza ball gown she had worn for the governor's ill-fated banquet.

Had the horror and carnage she had experienced taken their toll on her? She looked exactly the same: five feet one, slim, well proportioned with a shock of curly red ringlets. Just as she had done when she had first stowed away on the TARDIS, all those years ago. Healthy living and a clear conscience... wasn't that the reason she had once given as to why she hadn't aged much?

She looked into her own eyes, and immediately made herself a liar. There was a darkness there, an emptiness. Just the beginnings, but the beginnings of a descent she simply couldn't let happen to her.

Mel knew what she had to do, even though it was one of the most difficult decisions she had ever had to make. But she didn't have a choice - not if she valued her own peace of mind. No, more than that: her own sanity. Taking a deep breath, she got off her bed, opened the door and strode purposefully down the empty white corridor towards the console room.

The Doctor didn't appear to have moved since she had last seen him: he was still standing over the console, his broken spirit betrayed by his slumped posture. Mel knew that what she was about to say would only make matters worse, but it had to be done. There were some things that just simply couldn't be left unsaid.

She had once entertained the notion that the Doctor was nothing more than an extraterrestrial little boy with good intentions; his mood swings, his violent temper, his overgrown ego nothing more than manifestations of his underdeveloped psyche. The worlds and times they had visited had simply been the Doctor's playpen.

It was an easy mistake to make.

Little boys didn't make mistakes which cost billions of lives. Little boys didn't commit acts of mass murder by mistake. Little boys didn't hold the fate of the universe in their hands.

'Doctor?' she whispered. Her stomach churned with conflicting emotions: anger, fear, regret. But there was no going back. Not now. Not after Maradnias.

He slowly turned his head towards her, and she was horrified to see the transformation. His eyes were hollow, sunken and haunted; his once fruity expression was cold, lifeless. Mel's earlier words had obviously sunk in, but she had made her mind up; no displays of grief were going to sway her from her decision.

'Mel, I...'

She shook her head, warding off his apologies and explanations. She had heard them all before, and they would only make what she had to do even harder. She put her hands up, almost as if that would deflect the Doctor's pleas.

'Set the coordinates for Earth, Doctor.'

'Earth? Why Earth?'

The faintest flicker of his usual *joie de vivre* crossed his face, the briefest of colours in the monochrome of his despair. 'Mel, there's an entire universe out there!' he protested, throwing his arms open wide. 'A veritable atlas of wonders, just waiting for us to visit. What about the halls of Mount Aeternis, where the air is like nectar and the food is prepared by the gods themselves? Or the Rainbow Pillars of Hercules on the Rim of Twilight, overlooking the very edge of reality?' His desperation was embarrassingly obvious, but Mel couldn't allow herself to buckle under it. It was far too late for that.

'Earth, Doctor,' she repeated instantly. In response, the Doctor's expression was crestfallen; the little boy had had his sweets taken away from him. For a moment, her resolve faltered. 'Please?'

He frowned. 'Are you trying to tell me something?'

At last! 'I've had enough, Doctor. More than enough.'

He moved towards her, his hands unsure whether to move from his sides to comfort her, to reassure her... 'If you mean Maradnias...' His hands stayed at his sides.

She gave a pained smile. And kept her distance. 'It's more than just Maradnias...' She cast her hands around the multidimensional interior of the TARDIS, part of her realising that she would never see it again. But nor would it remind her of the pain her travels had caused her. 'I'm a middle-class girl from Pease Pottage, Doctor... I'm not meant to be travelling around the galaxy and going on day trips to the Big Bang!'

'But Mel...' implored the Doctor. Her expression gave him no respite. He trailed off, his face falling by the second.

Mel leant against one of the roundelled walls and sighed. 'When I was at university, I had every intention of becoming a computer programmer with one of the big multinationals... you know that.' Of course he did - he'd been there, she remembered.

'But it didn't work out that way. And then you blundered into my life... that business with SénéNet happened, and then all of this.' She held her hands out towards him, almost in supplication. 'I'm not cut out for this sort of life, Doctor.'

His puzzled expression made it clear she wasn't getting through to him. Couldn't he see that some people just weren't supposed to be time travellers? 'I need to get my life in some sort of an order. I want to go home.'

The little boy was holding back his tears. 'You're leaving me?'

At last! 'I have to, Doctor!' she yelled, more forcefully than she would have liked. 'I can't cope with this any more!' Then, more softly. 'I just want to go home.'

'Home,' he repeated, a strange twist of emotion in his voice. 'I had one of those, once. Once, a long time ago.' And then the emotion drained away as his hands darted over the console, as if he were playing some complex musical instrument. 'Pease

Pottage, 1986?' he asked coldly. 'That is your home, isn't it?'

Bitter, Doctor - very bitter, she thought. But she was forced to admit that he was right: now that she had forsaken the TARDIS Pease Pottage was her home.

Had been her home, Mel reminded herself. Now she had to think about where she was going to go, but Pease Pottage wasn't at the top of the list: what was left there for her any more? Especially after what she'd been through. Because she wasn't the innocent little computer programmer who had stowed aboard the TARDIS: she had seen civilisations rise and fall, exotic life forms from across the galaxy... horror beyond imagining. She had seen things that no normal person could have seen without going mad.

She hadn't gone mad. Not yet. But she needed to get away, needed normality, before she did lose it. But what counted for normal nowadays?

Then it came to her. A vivid, photographic memory of a recent visit to Earth at the very end of the twentieth century, a reunion... Mel suddenly realised that she knew the whereabouts - and whenabouts - of many of her old university colleagues. And, having already visited Earth in 1999, she knew enough about the web of time to know that it made sense for her to settle down there some time after that. Rejoin main carriageway, as it were.

Her mind made up, she gazed into the forlorn face of her erstwhile mentor.

'No, Doctor,' she said sadly, the emptiness in his eyes seriously attacking her certainty. 'Put me down just after we were last there. Near the university. There are a few friends I saw again at that reunion that I can get in touch with.'

The Doctor began to protest, but obviously thought better of it. 'If I remember the geography correctly, that's somewhere in West London, isn't it? Isleworth?' He managed to make the innocuous suburb sound like the deepest pits of Hell. Perhaps it was, but it was better than the hell that she would feel staying here in the TARDIS.

Mel nodded. 'I'll wait in my room until we land. I... I need to collect my thoughts. And my things.'

The Doctor raised an eyebrow. 'Whatever,' he muttered, before turning his back on her and fussing with the console.

Realising that there was nothing more to say, Mel walked out of the console room, knowing that collecting her thoughts was impossible. The best she could do was put them into some sort of order. She strode purposefully down the corridor, cataloguing her feelings. She wanted to leave the Doctor. She wanted a home that didn't meander through time and space and perpetually land in the middle of trouble.

Above all, she wanted absolution from the horror she had seen on Maradnias.

But who did she still know well enough to stay with, twenty years out of time? Mel's mind raced as she tried to remember her old friends, with all their plans and their dreams at that reunion at the end of 1999. It wasn't that much of a problem for a girl with an IQ of 162 and a photographic memory. The candidates assembled themselves in Mel's mind like a list of missing persons on *CrimeWatch*. Some she remembered from the reunion; some she retrieved from her oh-so-accurate memory as she followed the tracks. But they were all equally vivid.

Julia Prince had told her that she was about to go on a four-year placement to the university's twin seat in Italy as part of her job at West London - although Mel just didn't want to think about what Rome would make of her clothes sense - and Leonor Pridge had been flying out to Rio to begin a modelling contract. Well, with the best will in the world, even if Leonor and her cosmetic surgery had been in the country she would hardly provide the stability that Mel craved. Too flighty.

Then there was the stunning Chantal Edwards, all blonde hair and designer labels. An obvious choice, she thought wryly. Mel dismissed the flirty, overdressed Chantal out of hand: she needed an anchor, and Chantal was about as anchored as a feather cushion in a hurricane.

The faces continued to roll past in her mind: Wesley, Teresa, Fran, Toby, Vicky, Karl...

Of course!

During Mel's last year at West London University she had shared a room in halls with someone who fulfilled all her the requirements. Level-headed, caring, understanding...

Anjeliqua Whitefriar.

With the recollection of the name, all the attendant memories came tumbling down like dominoes. For a second, vivid nostalgia overwhelmed Mel as she remembered the good old days at university, the dinner parties (on the cheap, of course) with Anjeliqua and their best friends Paul and Arlene, as the four of them sorted out the world, putting it to rights as only they knew how. If Mel had known that she would eventually have been responsible for sorting out the galaxy... imagine the after-dinner conversations they would have had then!

Mel realised that she was now at the door to her room. It was a door like every door in this mad, lovable place that she had called home - white and roundelled - but she knew it was hers and hers alone, knew this from the familiarity she had shared with the TARDIS from day one, a presence that sat within her mind like an old friend. A friend she was abandoning, a familiarity that she knew had to come to a sad, final end.

She swallowed, pushing open that door, forcing herself to accept that this was the last time she would see this room, see the knick-knacks and paraphernalia she had accumulated over the years... Closing the door behind her, she leant against its cool white surface and took a deep breath before stepping into what had once been hers.

Trying to ignore the knot that was tightening in her stomach, she picked up the red cone of a party hat from the dressing table, a celebration of 31 December 1999 and all that had happened on that fateful day. Then there was the rugged sphere anointed with cones - a disconnected Quark processor unit from their terrifying run-in with the Quarks and the giant wasps. The holoempathic image of Troy, his cheerful bearded face and effervescent personality resonating in her mind. And the scintillating green trapezium of a Dalek logic crystal sitting next to her make-up.

Wonderful memories, true - but she didn't need holoempathic images and Quark heads. And she definitely didn't need Dalek logic crystals. She had those memories, and she had her memory. And that was where all this bric-a-brac was going to be consigned.

She did remember, she would remember, and that was all that was important.

This was her past. It most certainly wasn't her future.

Mel just knew that she didn't want to become like the Doctor - a time-travelling jackdaw with a magic box full of the past. She wanted to start living her life again, being herself - finding out what Melanie Bush would have been if she hadn't hooked up with the Doctor and his meanderings. Renewing her determination, she grabbed her holdall from the top of the wardrobe and started to pack.

Packing for her future.

The Master forced his eyes open, trying to ignore the pain as the blistered flesh tore, leaking bitter, bitter tears down his scarred face.

Being knocked unconscious by the temporal acceleration hadn't given him the chance to immerse himself fully in the healing pool of the Source of Traken, and now the fleeting initial effects had worn off... with all that that entailed. Once again, he was forced to deal with the familiar side-effect: the acceleration of his decay and devolution, his inevitable, final end. Within his ink-black suit staggered the withered, emaciated creature that was all that remained of his Time Lord body, Tremas's form long rotted and gone.

His life now. The humans that the Doctor loved, those same humans that the Master adored for their malleability, believed in Hell, in Satan - indeed, it was a belief that the Master had turned to his own advantage on more than one occasion. The Time Lords had different gods and very different devils. And a very different hell. But were they so different in the end? Indeed, was the Master so evil that even Hell would reject him? No. It was nothing to do with good and evil. Only power - his power. Dismissing his fears he pulled himself to his feet, his festering eyes, set within the ravages of a once handsome Time Lord face, peering through the murk of his console room at the glittering read-outs from his console.

Even through those ravaged eyes he could tell where he was.

Despite everything, his symbiotic link with the TARDIS was still working. The Rassilon Imprimatur was his birthright - even the Time Lords couldn't take that from him. He knew with an absolute certainty that his TARDIS was adrift, lying powerless on the blue shift: the very edge of the universe. The end of everything. Beyond this point, the laws of physics were being written by another hand. Exotic particles responded to bastard forces under an utterly alien set of rules. No place for a TARDIS... or its ravaged Master.

Or was it? Exotic particles...

With painful steps, he reached the console and began to plan his escape. And his own revenge.

Mel checked that she looked OK for twenty-first century Earth. Cream slacks, white shoes, a white blouse and a dark blue jumper, the arms tied around her neck. Perfect. She gave her room one last look before she picked up her holdall, leaving the Quark head and the Dalek logic crystal behind. In the TARDIS - where they belonged. The holoempathic image... well, she might have a photographic memory, but there were times when she forgot to put the film in. The perfect representation of Troy's face fell into the holdall, cushioned by Mel's favourite jumper.

Now she had everything she needed to start her new life. Apart from... Mel couldn't help but pick up the stuffed owl. A present from someone who would understand... understand that it was time to leave.

She touched the cool white wall and said goodbye. And, deep within her mind, she heard a voice. Rich, fruity... not unlike the Doctor's.

Goodbye, Melanie Bush. Like the others, you too will be missed.

Holding back the tears Mel closed the door for the last time, and tried to look forward. Forget the TARDIS, forget the Doctor, forget travelling through time and space. It was time to put down roots. She smiled as she thought of Anjeliqua. Perhaps they could celebrate her return with a dinner party? Yes, that was it: a dinner party. And they could invite Paul and Arlene! Ah yes, Arlene, calmly putting down Paul's often outrageous behaviour with nothing more than a shrug and a pointed look at the ceiling.

There was very little that could faze Arlene Cole.

'You bastard!' yelled Arlene, looking up from the inset monitor, her dark face contorted in anger. 'After all the work I put into this alignment, you've recalibrated the Array!' She stood up, knocking her chair over with a reverberating clang. 'Why the hell did I bother?'

Paul, who had been sauntering through the white and chrome expanse of the TITAN Array with a cup of instant cappuccino from the coffee machine in the anteroom, stopped in his tracks. This tall, elegant black woman, still attractive even in her lab coat, was many things - his research partner, his best friend, his fiancée - but in this mood she was his worst enemy.

And saying nothing was the best defence in this situation.

Mainly because he knew he was in the wrong.

Arlene was standing in front of him within seconds, her face inches away from his. Paul could smell the coffee on her breath, her trademark perfume... but the look of loathing in her eyes was almost enough to make him recoil.

'I haven't slept for four days, Paul!' she shouted. 'Four days! What do you think I've been doing every night while you've been away at that symposium? Washing my hair?' She turned her back on him and threw her hands in the air. 'That was the most complex set of penetration criteria we've ever attempted. And for what? It's all ruined.'

'I can change them back,' said Paul. But he knew this was a lame reply. Calculating the penetration criteria wasn't simply a question of maths and physics. Paul, Arlene and their mentor, Stuart, had had to invent entirely new methods of scientific inquiry for the TITAN Array. Criteria which were correct now, at this precise moment in time, wouldn't be correct a second time. The Uncertainty Principle, Planck's Constant and a whole host of other esoteric factors meant that each attempt to explore the fundamental nature of reality was a one-off. With TITAN, the microscopic factors which dictated the fine stitching of the fabric of reality were magnified into the macroscopic world. It wasn't like programming a computer - nothing so mundane. It was like playing a musical instrument, a Stradivarius or a Steinway. No two performances were exactly the same.

And Arlene's one-off performance had been well and truly screwed up this time.

'I'm sorry,' he stuttered. 'I thought -'

'Thought? Thought?' Arlene started to laugh. 'For someone who's supposed to be one of the most intelligent men on this planet, you show a frightening lack of common sense.' Shaking her head, she stormed out of the Array heading for the anteroom.

Paul didn't - couldn't - follow her. Because he had to admit that she was right. When he had got back from the physics symposium in Copenhagen - a day early, due to the fact that (a) there was nothing being discussed that was of any interest to him whatsoever, and (b) he had spent most of the week attempting to avoid that old fraud Winterdawn hurling himself around the Copenhagen conference centre in his souped-up wheelchair - he hadn't gone to the flat; instead, he had come straight to the university - to the TITAN Array, hoping to see Arlene, to surprise her. But she was nowhere to be seen - and from what she had just told him, he guessed she had been taking a rest after her epic stint at the Array. If only he had gone to the flat!

Standing in the centre of the marble cathedral of the Array, he had looked around, bored, only to see that the master console was still live.

He hadn't meant to change anything. He'd only wanted to see what Arlene had been doing. He had just taken a quick look at the penetration parameters for this evening's TITAN run, the one scheduled for 8 p.m. But then he hadn't liked what he'd seen: there was something just not quite right about the wave envelope.

Call it intuition, call it a gift, but Paul could feel the equations in his mind, feel their shapes, their rhythms. He could feel how they interacted with the basic fabric of reality - the whole purpose of the TITAN Array - and the penetration surface that Arlene's criteria defined just didn't feel as if it would work. The right equation set was like a key fitting in a lock - and Paul knew that

Arlene's key simply wouldn't unlock Calabi-Yai space: their ultimate goal. And so he had sat down at the master console, and started to tinker. The Planck-length compensation factor didn't tally with the Kikkawa-Yamasaki models that he and Arlene had constructed, so he adjusted it; the Kaluza-Klein variance seemed too high, so he reduced it to more manageable levels. For nearly an hour Paul had tweaked and refined his fiancée's equation set until he was happy - until it felt *right*.

And then he had got himself a coffee...

But Arlene wasn't his assistant. She was his partner, in all the ways that she possibly could be, that anyone could be. What had he been thinking, just discarding all her work like that? It was unprofessional, it was rude... it was downright insulting!

But... Paul was professor of temporal physics at the University of West London, and one of the most respected physicists in the world. There wasn't anyone on the planet who could do what he could, who knew what he knew. Staring at the cold froth of his coffee, Paul thought of his dear friend Aaron Blinovitch - but that young Russian bear's theories were closer to witchcraft than science, especially where his downright nonsensical limitation effect was concerned. Even the Whitaker Archives, released by the Government after thirty years, showed nothing to back up the rumours that Whitaker had created a working time machine. As for the Newton Institute at Wootton in the Seventies? Well, Emeritus Professor Stuart Hyde wasn't giving anything away - Paul had spent enough money on getting the old man drunk on cider and whiskies and orange to prove it. And as for Winterdawn's attempts... Well, Paul wasn't going to give him any credit. The man was an intellectual thief with the integrity of an earwig.

So, at the end of the day... Paul Kairos was unique. Unique, because he was the man who was going to give the world the universe.

But he wasn't going to do it on his own. He couldn't do that to Arlene: he owed her too much. She deserved her chance on the Array, whether he thought she was wrong or not.

He checked his watch: 6.45 p.m. They had been planning

another run at 8 p.m, and both the generator time and access to the Grid had been booked from 7.30. Paul pursed his lips: it would a shame to waste it all...

He knew he had time to re-create her parameters - that was simply a question of physics and mathematics. All he had to do was revoke Werner Heisenberg's Uncertainty Principle, tell Max Planck he was mistaken and tear up every physics textbook in the university library.

It was the least that he could do for Arlene.

Paul sat down at the master console and started to re-create Arlene's settings. Perfectly. Flawlessly.

Like a concert pianist.

A chime from the console indicated that the TARDIS had landed, but the Doctor didn't even make the effort to look round at her or communicate the information. He simply stared at the monitors and read-outs, silent, impassive.

Standing in the doorway to the console room, her holdall in her hands, Mel didn't know what to think. It was the end of an era: despite the fact that she knew that she couldn't stay, leaving him felt terrible.

It felt like desertion.

What if the Doctor needed her? What if her departure would lead to even worse things? But Mel wasn't equipped to answer those questions: she was a simple human being, and she wanted - needed - a simple life. She just couldn't stay.

She broke the sepulchral silence of the console room. 'I take it we landed OK?' No response. Right, if he wanted it that way... 'I'll be off, then,' she added flatly.

The Doctor remained silent: his only response was to pull up the red lever that allowed the great doors to open. Mel lifted up the holdall and made for them. Before she could get there the Doctor looked up at her, and the depth of sorrow etched into his face, and the darkness of his eyes, made her momentarily reconsider her decision. This wasn't a Time Lord - this was that lost little boy, desperate for someone to chase the monsters away. He handed her a small blue velvet pouch.

'Here. You might need this.' His voice was cracked and broken. Without thinking, she took the pouch and threw it into the holdall.

No. If you don't leave now, you'll never leave. Tearing her gaze from the pathetic figure clutching the console, she strode through the open doors, through the darkness of the dimensional interface into the warm summer night.

It's over.

Mel gave a final glance back at the TARDIS settled incongruously in the drive of a house in Osterley, the rich suburb-within-a-suburb of Isleworth. What would the Doctor do now, she wondered? Would he simply pick up another willing victim like her, or would he learn the error of his ways?

But it was no longer her problem, was it? Turning away from the reassuring blue shape of her former home, Melanie looked around for the turning she needed to take to find Anjeliqua's flat. Hoping that it still was Anjeliqua's flat - it had been thirteen years since Mel had known for certain that her old friend lived there - she determined the route and set off.

And froze, dropping the holdall on to the pavement.

From behind her the raucous groaning briefly echoed around the cul-de-sac, drowning out the traffic noise from the A4. Mel span round, just in time to see the faded blue outline of the TARDIS finally evaporate, its roof light the last thing to dissolve into the August twilight.

Somehow, deep, deep down, she hadn't expected him to leave. The weight of realisation finally hit her: she was alone, at least thirteen years after she had left with the Doctor, with no idea what to do. For a second, it threatened to overwhelm her. But she had made her decision. She was home, firmly rooted in terra firma. She was in London, on Earth, not fighting monsters on the edge of time and space. She was home. So why did it feel so dreadful?

Ignoring her heavy heart, Mel picked up the holdall and set off for Anjeliqua's flat, deliberately ignoring the golden retriever that barked at her.

At 7.30 p.m Arlene stubbed out her cigarette, left the rest room

and headed towards the TITAN Array. As she walked down t
deserted corridors of the Chapel Institute of the University
West London much of her anger had subsided. But she wasn
going to let Paul get away with it. She knew that, intellectually, h
was superior to her - in terms of his knowledge of tempora
physics, he was superior to everyone. But that was accepted
between them: it was how their relationship worked.

Paul's broad-brush approach had achieved much - the TITAN Array was simply the latest in a series of successes that had given him a shelf-ful of scientific awards, including the Nobel Prize before he had hit twenty-five - but his attention to detail left a lot to be desired. That was where Arlene's skills came in. She dotted the 'i's, crossed the 't's and joined the dots after Paul's butterfly imagination had fluttered off to pastures more interesting. It was a methodology that worked for both of them - until those (admittedly rare) occasions when Paul did something as bloody-minded as this.

Four nights of coffee, Pro-Plus and cigarettes - all for nothing. She'd even given up rehearsing with her band for a fortnight - how was that for dedication? Only to see Paul throw it all in the bin.

Reaching the secure entrance to the TITAN Array, Arlene held her smart card to the sensor, waited for the click, then pulled the heavy white door open. And stopped.

Paul was hunched over the master console, but that was nothing unusual: TITAN was his baby, and he cared for it almost as much as he cared for Arlene - if not more, she ruefully admitted. What was strange was the noise.

The fact that there was any.

Normally, the TITAN Array was completely silent: subatomic particles and fundamental forces aren't exactly known for being rowdy. But during the build-up to a test run, TITAN drew on the entire output of the Chapel Institute's generators. And the capability to power all of London three times over comes at a price: a throbbing hum that you feel in your bones.

Like now. The marble walls and floor, the fifty-foot high chrome lattice of the Array - all of it was vibrating at its resonant

, was Arlene. And that could only mean one thing. verything that had happened between them, Paul was d with another run! And after their previous argument nothing less than a slap in the face. She hurried over to er console, her Doc Marten boots clumping on the ing marble floor.

'Now look here, mister!' Arlene put her hand on Paul's shoulder – none too delicately – and pulled him round in his chair, enjoying the scared bemusement on his chubby, goatee-bearded face. He deserved it. 'What do you think you're...' She trailed off as she caught sight of the main monitor in front of him. One of the Q-Solaris windows was showing the wave envelope that would be used in tonight's run.

Her wave envelope.

'I don't understand...'

Paul shrugged her off, stood up and grasped her shoulders in turn. 'We're going with your parameters. I re-created them.'

'But that's not possible,' she whispered. Her parameters – however important they were to her – were nothing more than a set of coaxing guidelines, polite attempts to persuade the universe to behave the way she and Paul wanted it to. Once the waveforms and equations were created within the artificial intelligence at the heart of the TITAN Array, that was it – they could never be used again. The Uncertainty Principle, all-powerful at the quantum level, was writ large within the Array: it mattered at a macroscopic level. Arlene had configured the Array with her parameters, and Paul had changed them. End of story. As far as Arlene knew, there was no possible way that he could have re-created them without changing the laws of physics.

But he had re-created them.

For her.

Taking a deep breath, Arlene gave a nervous smile. 'I'm not even going to ask.' Sometimes that was the best way with Paul. For all she knew, he had just discovered some little-known corollary to Heisenberg and was now putting it to the test.

Paul grinned. 'I think that's very wise. Shall we start? We've got full generator access, and we have 820 petahertz processing power from the Grid for the next five hours.' With that, he sat at the master console and indicated for Arlene to take the other chair, as if he'd done nothing more complex than make a cup of tea.

Arlene shrugged. She'd got used to the idea of Paul as a genius years ago. Now it looked like she was going to have to accept that he had godlike powers. All in a day's work, she decided, as she started checking the read-outs. But she still couldn't help but be puzzled.

Never had the sound of the TARDIS dematerialising sounded so harsh, so accusatory, the Doctor decided as his vessel entered the time vortex. But what could he have done? Run out of the TARDIS and begged her to come back? Got down on bended knee and promised to mend his ways? No, not the way that Mel felt.

He pressed the pause control, leaving the TARDIS hovering in the portion of the vortex adjacent to Earth. It wasn't necessary to be a mind-reader to sense the depth of her feelings, of her hurt... The Doctor groaned. There were times when he had been exactly that... but now? It was if other people's feelings were invisible to him, other people's souls impervious.

A bitter smile. Once, Mel had protested at how unfair it all was. But, as always, the Doctor had had an answer: 'The universe rarely is. That's why I'm here.'

Not any more. He just couldn't be here any more.

So, where now? Another period in Earth's history? Or another planet, one which would be a surprise to him? He shook his head. How could he do anything without the constant fear of making a mistake, or doing to another world what he had done to Maradnias? Another memory, this time Peri: *I used to think that you were different. That you cared for justice, truth and good.* How much justice, truth and good lay in the radioactive wastes of Maradnias?

Overriding guilt and confusion were freezing him into inaction – a brace of emotions that were completely alien to him. The Doctor wanted silence, he just wanted to be on his own. But not in the TARDIS, not where every roundel would remind him of his failure, of his complicity in genocide. Even the cloister room was too steeped in memory. How could he be on his own within the transcendental interior of his oldest friend, its mind constantly reaching out to him? He didn't want the TARDIS's pity!

No, it was a time for solitary reflection, and a time for him to start to understand his place in the universe. That nagging call of solitude had been with him since his last regeneration, begging him to consider how a single Time Lord could make a difference to the cold, unfeeling cosmos out there. Begging him to understand the sacrifices he would need to make to champion his cause.

Champion... Frowning, he considered those worlds which could offer him the luxury of reflection, and began to tap out staccato requests to the TARDIS database. The image of the turbulent vortex on the scanner screen vanished, to be replaced by a scene of utter tranquillity - simple wooden huts on a rolling plain of emerald grass. Tall pale figures strolled between the huts, dressed in basic beige robes, their heads bowed in contemplation. It was Darron, where he had spent decades during the latter part of his second incarnation learning the psychic techniques of the Mind Monks, the most serene people in the cosmos. So how could he contaminate their purity with the blood that stained his soul?

Another tap-tap-tap on the console, and the picture now showed the desolate hermitage of Titan 3, a barren expanse of rocks and boulders. It was possibly the most remote planet in the galaxy, so far below the plane of the ecliptic that no one ever came closer than a hundred thousand light years. No visitors - usually - no stray thoughts, nothing. The ultimate retreat. No, too lonely. Amidst that particular solitude, the Doctor knew that he would go insane. And an insane Doctor hardly bore thinking about...

He refused to go there, both mentally and physically. A wave of nostalgia overcame him as the picture changed once more. Unobtrusive lamps mounted on the carpeted walls showed off sheer opulence to its best advantage: the whole place glittered, and everything that didn't glitter simply glowed.

Tempus Fugit, the greatest restaurant on Pella Saturnis, ice world of the Hroth... and the Doctor's home for five years. But what would Pfifl and Laklis say if they knew of the blood on his hands? Their adopted son a mass murderer? No, there was one other sanctuary, tap-tap-tap...

The soaring towers and minarets of Gallifrey itself, the lesser towers of the Capitol pupping around the emerald dominance of the Panopticon, all sealed beneath an impenetrable dome: the grand isolation of the Time Lord homeworld. It was somewhere the Doctor had turned his back on centuries ago... and every successive return had been a nightmare.

Yet deep below the junior senate block lay the famed polygonal Zero Room. Built in Time Lord prehistory by the Other himself, it would give him the rest-cure that he craved. Cut off from external distractions, yet enwombed by the Time Lord intelligentsia, it would be the perfect place to recuperate, to leave the cold, hard cosmos behind.

Hard facts hit him like a bucket of cold water. How could he return home? How could he face the disapproval and accusation of his peers after the events on Maradnias? He had narrowly escaped being found guilty of genocide during that kangaroo court on the CIA space station, and on that occasion he had been innocent. But this time... His guilt was clear. The blood was still wet.

And in that moment of self-doubt his thoughts quickly strayed from the courtroom to the dark figure of the learned court prosecutor...

The Valeyard.

The man - no, the creature - that had been appointed by a corrupt High Council to try him for his supposed crimes had been him, had been the Doctor. But a Doctor from the Doctor's own future, the distillation of all that festered inside his soul across all his incarnations poured into one foul vessel. The fear of becoming that had hovered over the Doctor's life like some black mocking raven ever since he had left the space station so very many years ago. He had done everything to avoid that future from coming to pass, but to no avail. He had tried to keep away from Earth - from Mel - only to find himself there and to be tricked into taking her on board the TARDIS. He had tried to avoid the region of space and time that contained the *Hyperion III* - only to respond instinctively to the commodore's distress call and deliberately commit genocide by destroying the Vervoids.

And now... he had destroyed Maradnias. Was his descent into the Valeyard inevitable? Was that haughty, mocking, arrogant being his ultimate destiny? He remembered a line from his defence: 'And you took it upon yourselves to act like second-rate gods.' So what had he done on Maradnias? He had interfered, he had committed genocide once again: all the charges that the Valeyard had thrown at him. He was guilty, and no court - even the august reverence of the High Tribunal - would think otherwise.

So how could he return to Gallifrey now?

An urgent bleep from the console brought him gratefully back to the present. Something untoward was happening, and his frown deepened as he read the graphs and figures on the monitors. According to the three traces, the Earth was virtually on fire with temporal energies.

So: nothing new there, then.

Noting the date - 2003 - the Doctor was able to disregard two of the traces: one was dear old Blinovitch - or dear young Blinovitch, depending on how his unstable timeline was doing - still pottering around in St Petersburg with his theories and Heath Robinson equipment, while the other was undoubtedly that oleaginous LeFabvre with his purloined theories and stolen equipment, destined to come to a very sticky end.

The other one was very familiar as well - yet from where? It wasn't a TARDIS, that was certain. Although the Earth was a honey pot for his fellow renegades, the planet was currently clear of any of their trademark artron energy traces. But this one was familiar...

The Doctor slammed the console in anger as he finally recognised it. Visiting Time Lords were one thing, but this was something quite, quite different: the other reading was not of Time Lord origin. It wasn't even of extraterrestrial origin. It had been developed on Earth.

And that made it the Doctor's business. Setting the coordinates for the time trace, he groaned when he saw the location, which simply served to confirm his suspicions. But he had no choice.

Because if what he was seeing was what he thought it was, none of them had much time - in the worst possible sense of the word.

Beyond the dark side of the moon, the Master's TARDIS - disguised as a cloud of ionised vapour and shielded from detection by technology that would have staggered the Time Lords even at the pinnacle of their scientific prowess - drifted in the void.

Within its darkly transcendental interior the Master pored over the console, ensuring for one final time that everything was perfect. In relative terms it had been months since his encounter with the Chronovores; months in which he had painstakingly prepared his defence, his revenge... and his rebirth.

At the edge of creation he had gathered the exotic materials he would need, transforming his TARDIS into a ramscoop for the purpose; and, while the TARDIS had been storing these particles in magnetic bottles next to the dynamorphic generators, he had finally been granted the time to repair the damage to his physical form. But it had been difficult, so very difficult. Despite the boost that had come from the Numismaton Gas, the Source of Traken was now virtually exhausted. The effort needed to rebuild himself had been more than he had ever imagined, draining his strength, his will, his very soul... The Master was well aware that this was the last time he could rely on the Source of Traken.

Which made what he was about to do all the more important.

Renewed - for the last time - there had been another clandestine visit to Gallifrey: in and out without those pompous fools ever suspecting a thing. After their grand overreaction to the Sleepers from Andromeda - and what a pantomime that had been! - the Master had expected at least a token attempt to beef up security, but no: his TARDIS had slid through the quantum and transduction barriers without a care, materialising in its usual spot, deep below the Capitol where he had complete access to the Matrix and all its secrets.

Stepping out of his TARDIS, which was blatantly undisguised in its default form as a plain white box, he remembered the first time he had plundered his people's secrets...

Just beyond the range of the planetary detection system, a

localised space-time event curdled the laws of physics for a few moments. Finally the quantum foam of the continuum stabilised, but space was no longer empty.

Suspended in the void, immune to detection, the Master's TARDIS had finally come home.

To Gallifrey.

The Master checked the complex assembly of components attached to various parts of his control console and nodded: bought, stolen and fought over on a hundred worlds, the end result of this technology would shield him from the inquisitive eyes of his former brethren on Gallifrey. The osmic projector, bought from a rogue Sontaran on Veltriis 4; the DARDIS core, stolen from Skaro itself; a vortex cloak, discovered in the ruins of the Gubbage Cone Throneworld on the edge of the Great Attractor... all brought together by his genius in temporal engineering, all designed to keep his presence secret.

However, getting thus far would not suffice: the Master needed to reach Gallifrey itself. He glanced at the table that stood next to the console: a dull golden circlet sat there, surrounded by discarded tools - the equipment necessary to breach an excitonic network.

A quiet bleep issued from the console, informing the Master that the scan of Gallifrey's defences was complete: the Rutan analysis engine had seen to that. Satisfied, he slammed his fist down on the vortex primer, hurling his TARDIS down the single weak point in Gallifrey's ramparts. According to the Rutan device there was a weakness, a fracture caused by a chance interference pattern in the tenth dimension between the quantum and the transduction barriers. It was slight - nothing that could be exploited by an attacking enemy - so nothing that could possibly concern the Time Lords, assuming that they even noticed it. Unless that enemy was piloting one of the Time Lords' own TARDISes.

Camouflaged by the array of defensive devices, the Master's TARDIS deftly slipped through Gallifrey's defences, darting through the time vortex until it reached the entry point he had defined.

And then, unannounced by the alarms and alerts that usually accompanied unauthorised materialisations in the Capitol, the Master's TARDIS faded into existence, appearing as an ancient pillar gothically cloaked in the dust and decay that surrounded it, one more ruin amongst many.

Picking up the circlet, the Master opened the door and stepped out of his TARDIS. The air was dank and stale, but that wasn't surprising: the Master had materialised about half a kilometre below the foundations of the Capitol, within the ruins of the first Capitol that had stood on the site tens of millions of years ago. The whole area had been wiped from the Time Lords' consciousness, the loss of the early building an embarrassment, a reminder that with great power comes great responsibility.

But the Master did not adhere to that philosophy. The Time Lords' great power should be used to ensure harmony, to assure complete obedience... with such obedience the universe would be united as never before. And yet the Time Lords sought only to nurture, to encourage. And lately, to ignore. That wasn't enough for the Master: he knew, with the certainty that comes with the absolute confidence of true superiority, that this bred only weakness.

Which was why he was here. To take the Time Lords' knowledge and power and put it to the use for which it was truly intended.

Moving purposefully over to a low, grime-covered console, the Master extracted a cloth from his pocket and wiped away the dust of billennia before pulling a small crystal block from his pocket and placing it on the flat surface. The result was immediate: the console lit up, displays flashing, strings of read-outs glinting in every colour, old High Gallifreyan script and symbolic logic scrolling across the monitors. The Master smiled and stroked his greying goatee beard. After all this time the console still worked! Wryly, he doubted that the Time Lords enacting their ancient charades far above him would have the faintest idea how to operate this machine, let alone build something similar.

But activating the console had been the easy part. The difficulty would be in using it. Because failure would mean death... his mind incinerated. Failure would leave him a drooling cretin, dribbling and babbling among the cadavers of his people's past. Carefully he placed the circlet over his head, adjusting it so that it sat correctly. Then, taking an involuntary deep breath, he laid his hands on the console's telepathic circuits, one living mind reaching out to a multitude of dead ones.

And accessed the Matrix.

He felt his mind being drawn into the endless, timeless amplified panatropic net that comprised the Matrix, a bottomless ocean of thoughts and memories. It would be so easy to let go, to allow himself to be immersed in the Matrix for ever... But although that would grant his mind immortality, his empty, soulless body would quickly perish. No, the Master knew what he was looking for, and would not allow himself to become distracted. He waited impatiently for the psychic landscape to stabilise around him, eager to seize his prize and get away.

Cloaked with cyber-psionic technology that made the excitonic circuitry of the Matrix look like an abacus, hidden from the baleful eyes of the Time Lords, the Master got his bearings. From his meticulous studies, he was prepared for the fact that the Matrix looked different to each Time Lord who entered it. What he wasn't prepared for was what his subconscious had in store for him. It was a necropolis, an impossibly endless horizon of mausoleums and gravestones, of funeral pyres and juggernauts, orbiting death stations and spirit-crystal monuments - thanatic memories of a thousand worlds.

It felt like home.

Striding through the serried headstones, under the shadows of the death satellites, the Master examined each one in turn. Each monument, each grave, contained a secret. But there was a particular set of secrets that the Master needed, that he craved.

Dark knowledge.

The circlet on his brow was more than just a copy of the Matrix terminal worn by the Time Lord president; the Master's version should allow him to read and transmit the information to his TARDIS's databanks. And now he was about to put it to the test: he had found the first of his chosen targets. Kneeling by a black marble headstone, he satisfied himself that it would be of value and transferred it to his TARDIS. Then another headstone, and another; the Time Lords' darkest secrets were being plundered from beneath their very noses. Gravestone, funeral pyre, death satellite - each one offering him immeasurable glory... The Master's ecstasy was beyond compare.

The doomsday weapon on Uxarieus; the psychic parasites of Bellerophon; the frozen gods of Volvox; the Earth's sleeping races; the mechanics of the Source of Traken; the location of the Nestene homeworld; the hidden beauty of the Midnight Cathedral; the secret name of the last of the Daemons... all of it his. All of it.

Now intoxicated by the influx of information, the Master didn't hear the alarm the first time its tocsin rang out. Nor the second - the deathworms were such a fascinating life form - but the third chime caught his attention.

They had found him.

Accessing the last secret - the mysterious Crystal of Kronos and its relationship with the Chronovores - the Master quickly inserted the program he had prepared into the Matrix. Then he withdrew his mind and removed the circlet.

The program was simple in purpose, but unimaginably complex in design and execution: it would enable the Master to slip through the Time Lords' defences without having to rewire most of his console. It would permit him to plunder the dark secrets of the Time Lords whenever he wanted, wherever he wanted.

Amidst the alarms and cacophony that were audible even deep underground, and imagining the chaos above him, the Master stepped back inside his TARDIS. With a final look back at the wasted promise of the Time Lords, he closed the doors. Seconds later, his TARDIS was gone, with nothing to suggest that it had ever been there.

That was so many, many years ago. Since then, the Master's mind had returned to the Matrix time and again, using its arcane knowledge to reinforce his power base. Dry facts and desiccated data became knowledge, conquest and dominion as he strove to rework the universe in his own image. The ice world of Spiridon and its army of Daleks? The political machinations of the Amentethys? The Proculus and their vile offspring, the Scerbulus? The Martian GodEngine, there for the asking?

This time was different. This time, he could no longer rely on his remote access to the Matrix. The secrets he required were buried within its deepest fortresses, fortresses that required a more direct approach.

Which was why he had returned to Gallifrey one more time.

The Matrix was a psychic mausoleum, ten million years of Rassilon's destiny entombed within the telepathic lattices of a million dead Time Lords, empowered by the artron energy of the prime Eye of Harmony. The sum total of all knowledge, patrolled by the dead.

But the Master chose to ignore the ghosts that haunted the cyber-psionic circuitry, the spectres that lurked within the artron pathways. He didn't need their distractions: he knew exactly what he was looking for. In the past, it hadn't been necessary to hurry; he had had all the time in the universe. But on this occasion it was different: the Chronovores were out there, watching, waiting... and he had run out of time.

Speeding through the excitonic circuitry he found his way to the mental crypt he had spotted centuries ago. Then, the knowledge it contained had been esoteric, useless; now, it was his lifeline.

Thirteen million years ago, on the planet Kirbili at the edge of the Pegasus Tract, the inhabitants had discovered something; something important. Not to them - they wiped themselves out a couple of centuries later during a facile argument, having never even put the technology into practice. But the information had been harvested by the Time Lords, transmitted to the Matrix, stored away in their deepest vaults and subsequently forgotten for billennia.

Until now.

Using mental incantations and cyber-psionic spells that instantly broke through the encrypted words which protected the data, the Master had seized the information in a moment and carried it back to the infinite repository of his TARDIS - the forgotten knowledge of the Kirbili, and the perfect instrument for his revenge...

And now he was a quarter of a million miles away from the final piece of his jigsaw puzzle: a very large piece called TITAN.

The piece that would allow him to seize godhood.

Stuart Ian Hyde, Emeritus Professor of Physics at West London University, looked around his study and sighed: nothing to show for anything but the accumulated crap of three decades. Leather-bound copies of his researches, all pointless. Half-hearted awards for simply not being dead yet. Piles of journals by academics half his age, hammering home everything that he hadn't achieved.

Stuart had been hoping to retire soon, but how could he? How could he retire when young Kairos was so close to cracking it, cracking the secrets that had been revealed to him nearly thirty years ago before they were snatched away? How could he retire before his one last chance to bask in someone else's reflected glory?

He picked up the silver-framed photograph on his desk and stared back into his past. It showed him as a bright, hopeful graduate, his mentor Doctor Ruth Ingram at his side, ready to take on the universe. What Stuart hadn't counted on was the universe taking him on. How could he have guessed that the charming Greek professor who had stepped in to take over after Professor Opfer's unfortunate and unexpected death had been anything but a visiting academic from Athens University? How could he have known that Professor Thascales had been not a Greek scientist but a renegade member of an omnipotent time-travelling alien race?

At that point, Stuart Hyde's optimism had died. At twenty-five - the age another Greek scientist, Paul Kairos, had been when he won the Nobel Prize - Stuart had realised that whatever he and Ruth achieved there would be others who got there first. What was the point in striving to find the secrets of the universe when there were... creatures... out there to whom the deeper mysteries of time were nothing more than bedtime stories for children?

His career had progressed, true. After the incident at the Newton Institute in Wootton his very notoriety had assured him a place on a post-grad course. But it had hardly been the meteoric rise everyone had predicted when he had been a shining star at Cambridge. Instead, Stuart - now only too painfully aware of his oh-so-human limitations - had become a methodical plodder, floating to the academic surface bit by bit as soon as he had accumulated enough academic bubbles to get him there.

But what was the point? It wasn't as though he could discover something that hadn't already been discovered aeons ago, was it? Thanks to UNIT and the Official Secrets Act, he was forced into silence, while parasites like Winterdawn were stealing the information from under his very nose with Government approval. Thank God he could remember most of the work he and Ruth had done - even if Ruth was now seconded to some stupid project over in Paris with LeFabvre - and that Paul was carrying it out. TITAN was the son of TOMTIT, and Stuart was the stepfather. Whatever that was worth.

He sighed as he replaced the photograph, and checked the ormolu clock on the mantelpiece. It was just after eight: more than enough time to get into town and indulge himself. Dinner at La Bella Donna, a bottle or two of Croze Hermitage... Stuart Hyde pulled himself out of his chair feeling every second of his fifty-five years. As he stood up he caught a glimpse of himself in the mirror, and it didn't make him feel any better: his hair was white, and cut short; he had grown a beard - and that was white as well. His eyes, once deep and expressive, were now dark and empty.

Thanks to this bout of introspection, that Croze Hermitage was looking more and more inviting.

His reverie was broken when the door to his study was suddenly flung open. He looked round to see a wild-eyed stranger, his expression verging on the maniacal, in the doorway.

'You stupid, stupid man!'

Stuart had never seen him before. He would have remembered a tall, thickset man with a shock of curly blond hair, dressed in a Joseph's coat of red and yellow. This was a complete stranger - and Stuart really ought to press the security alert. But something stopped him.

Something told him that he had known the man all his adult life. He began to fashion a response, but before he could utter a single word the stranger let rip.

'Didn't that incident with TOMTIT teach you any lessons, you microcephalic numbskull?' he yelled, his multicoloured jacket trailing behind him like some rainbow cloak. He leant over the desk, shoving his face into Stuart's. 'Time isn't some sort of laboratory experiment for you to play about with. The fabric of reality is a delicate thing, man!' he spluttered. 'It's a chain of circumstance and chance which underlies everything! Your experiments are tantamount to sticking a pin in a balloon - just to see what's inside!'

He looked different. He sounded different. And yet... Stuart frowned. Could it be? The hairs began to stand up on the back of his neck as the truth sank in.

After all these years of dreaming - of praying! - for the chance to meet another of these aliens, to discuss the higher meanings that lay beyond space and time, one was here. Standing in front of him, as bold as brass, accusing him of crimes that, thanks to this race of cosmic policemen, he could never commit...

Stuart had simply had enough. 'You really are a hypocritical bastard,' he stated. 'What the hell do you think you're doing, bursting in here after all you did! For a godlike being, you show an alarming lack of omnipotence.'

The man recoiled. 'How dare I? How dare I?' He shook his head in disbelief. 'How dare I? Hyde - you're tampering with reality here. What do you think you're doing?'

Stuart picked up his jacket from the chair. 'I'm going to dinner, Doctor. Would you care to join me? Because if you do, I know just the place.'

Chapter Two
Holding out for a Hero

Arlene looked at her watch and sighed. It was gone midnight and she was absolutely exhausted – yet another night without sleep. But she and Paul were making real progress here… weren't they? She shook her head. Whatever the results, she really needed to go to bed.

'Paul?'

Paul turned from the master console with a quizzical look. 'Mmm?' Mmm – Paul's favourite word, it would seem.

'Well? Did it work?'

A typical TITAN run could take four or five hours. Unfortunately, since it wasn't designed for George-Lucas-style special effects, there wasn't really any way of telling whether it had worked. And since Paul had spent most of the last four hours hunched over the master console, occasionally scratching his beard and uttering the odd 'Mmm', Arlene was none the wiser.

Paul's face fell, assuming the look of an abused puppy, his deep brown eyes full of sadness. 'I'm sorry, Arlene – we're still not quite there.'

Arlene sighed. Yet another failure. Perhaps she should just call it a day and throw herself into her singing. At least that was one area where she was better than Paul!

'Hey!' Paul stood up and hugged her. 'It doesn't matter. We've got unlimited funding and unlimited time,' he whispered into her ear. 'And we're getting closer – I know it.'

Arlene moved her head and kissed him. 'Let's call it a night. I'm shattered.'

Paul nodded. 'We'll run through the penetration envelope with Stuart tomorrow. Perhaps we'll spot something.'

'Good idea.' She checked her watch once more – 12.15 a.m. 'If Stuart's got any sense, he'll be fast asleep by now.'

* * *

'That is marvellous. Absolutely bloody marvellous,' said Stuart Hyde in his rich, throaty voice, as he placed his just-emptied wine glass on the green and white tablecloth, just next to the empty plate that had once been covered with grilled lobster in garlic oil. 'Far better than marmalade sandwiches and Moroccan Burgundy, don't you think?'

Entranced by the food (carbonara, of course), drink (a glorious Croze Hermitage) and company (the multifaceted Stuart Hyde), and deliberately distracting himself from darker matters, the Doctor decided to agree. There was a choice of emergencies, and he had to choose: save himself or save the Earth. And he knew the answer. There really was no alternative.

There never was.

As he took another sip of the Croze Hermitage - the 1935 and an all-time classic - he realised that it had been nearly four years since he had last sampled the delights of La Bella Donna; in real terms it had been scarcely less.

Four years. Four years to forget the sybaritic pleasures of the best-kept secret in the West End: a members-only restaurant down Hanway Street, a tiny curved side street joining Oxford Street and Tottenham Court Road. Four years - give or take a year - to forget that he had had been introduced to its charms by Dame Anne Travers, just before her untimely death.

Four years? Was that all it took a Time Lord to cleanse his soul?

No, that way leads to... With determination, he raised his glass of Croze Hermitage and toasted Anne's memory. 'Absent friends,' he said, pleased that Stuart clinked his glass against his. Dame Anne... such a waste.

'Perhaps this one act goes some way towards making up for that,' she had whispered. If only it could have. If only it could make up for much, much more...

And now it turned out that Stuart Hyde was also a member of La Bella Donna. Small universe. Small number of plots, Aristotle had said to him one evening, over a goblet of delicious honeyed wine. *Too small. I just hope history really isn't going to repeat itself.*

The Doctor had no choice but to return his attention to the

here and now. He had to choose between emergencies. There were more important considerations that were even greater than a night in one of the best restaurants in the universe.

Even greater considerations? Yes, much greater. As great as the time traces blazing from the Chapel Institute of West London University. But as much as the Doctor wanted to leap in and ask questions directly, it was obvious that this wouldn't get him anywhere. Stuart Hyde had been wounded, his personality severely bruised. And although the Doctor suspected he knew the reason, he also knew that Stuart wanted to talk.

Which was the least he owed him.

Thirty years ago Stuart Hyde had been lab assistant to a lab assistant, helping his colleague Doctor Ruth Ingram in experiments to transmit matter through interstitial time - Project TOMTIT. But TOMTIT had been a blind, a cover for a far more sinister experiment: Professor Thascales, the suave genius responsible for TOMTIT, had been anything but a visiting academic from Athens University. He had been the Doctor's arch-nemesis, the Master, bent on yet another of his twisted schemes.

It was true that TOMTIT was capable of moving solid objects through the interstices of reality, taking advantage of the granularity of space-time. But that was nothing more than a side effect, the unique selling point that 'Professor Thascales' had used to drain hundreds of thousands of pounds from the Newton Institute budget. In truth, the project was much, much more: its true purpose was to breach the Crystal of Kronos, a multidimensional prison containing a godlike being - Kronos, greatest and most fearsome of the Chronovores.

Hiding on Earth after yet another of his mad schemes had forced him to lie low for a while - double-crossed by the Voords, indeed! - the Master had taken advantage of the scientific pioneering of Stuart and Ruth and betrayed them. TOMTIT had released Kronos, that was true. But Kronos was a vengeful god and his freedom had destroyed Atlantis and almost cost the Doctor, his assistant, Jo Grant, and the Master their lives.

And, for a time, it had cost Stuart Hyde his youth. The name Chronovores described these beings accurately: they indeed ate time. They fed on timelines: the timelines of people, of planets, of entire realities... and Stuart had been unlucky enough to have been a light morsel upon which Kronos fed after his release, his twenty-five-year-old frame ageing to his dotage within seconds.

He had recovered. But somehow the Doctor doubted that that was the experience which had scarred him so deeply. Something else had hurt him, hurt him badly enough to leave him embittered, even after thirty years.

Unfortunately, the Doctor's recollection of events following the defeat of the Master were hazy. Very soon afterwards, he had been given back his freedom by the High Council of the Time Lords and he had left UNIT to clear up the mess the Master had caused. Over the last couple of years, however, he had come to learn that UNIT's definition of clearing up left an awful lot to be desired.

'What happened?' he asked quietly. 'What happened after the Master?'

Stuart shrugged. 'The same thing that I imagine happens after any breach in national security. A lot of men in dark suits turned up, confiscated everything pertaining to TOMTIT, and vanished.'

The Doctor stared into the dark ruby surface of his wine for a second before looking up and subjecting Stuart to the same penetrating gaze. 'I meant to you.'

'Oh, I carried on in academia, Doctor. With Ruth's patronage one research post led to another; I obtained my doctorate and took a series of chairs at various universities: Reading, Sussex, Luton, Warwick. Ending up as Emeritus Professor of Physics at West London.' He raised an eyebrow. 'Quite a career, eh?'

He was feigning nonchalance, but the Doctor knew it went a lot deeper. He frowned: somebody like Stuart Hyde should have been sitting comfortably at CERN, or replacing Anne Travers as scientific adviser to the Cabinet after her death. Even scientific adviser to UNIT, for goodness sake. But a professor at a university? 'Your experience, Stuart? Surely that must have counted for something?'

Stuart twirled his wine glass in his hand. 'Experience?' He slammed the glass on the table. 'What experience? Ruth and I thought we were developing a technology that would change the world, Doctor. Instantaneous transmission of matter. All transportation problems solved. No more food shortages. Interstellar travel beckoned... but what did we have to do with it? At the end of the day, it was your friend who developed TOMTIT, not us.'

Friend? Once, long ago, the Master *had* been his best friend. The Doctor, the Master and the others of the Deca, the ten Time Lord acolytes who had thought that they would make a difference, who had thought that they could change the universe.

In many ways, they had.

But how could the Doctor consider someone who could rob a perfectly decent human being of his self-confidence, his self-respect - his pride - a friend?

He leant forward and gazed into Stuart's eyes. 'Stuart, listen to me. There was a very good reason why the Master came to Earth to find help in releasing Kronos.'

'Because of Atlantis,' Stuart snapped back. 'That was the link.'

The Doctor shook his head. 'Didn't you learn anything from that incident? As far as Kronos is concerned, time and space are irrelevant. The Crystal of Kronos has been hidden on millions of worlds since the dawn of time: the Master could have just as easily gone to the planet of the Daleks!' Seeing Stuart's blank look, he carried on. 'As you know, the Master and I are both Time Lords - members of a race that developed time travel millions of years ago.'

Stuart's eyes widened. 'Millions of years ago? So why aren't you gods?'

'Because we tried to be,' said the Doctor sadly. 'On countless worlds, we thought we knew best. And on countless worlds, we saw the consequences of our actions. On Minyos we helped them to split their world in two in a nuclear war. On Klist we taught them to reverse evolution. And on the starlit ring of Plastrodus 14 we sent an entire civilisation totally, utterly mad.' The Doctor took a deep swig of his wine. 'The Time Lords of Gallifrey are capable of amazing things, Stuart. But we have our faults and our weaknesses. We are arrogant, we are capable of... questionable acts.

'We're not gods, Stuart. But we soon recognised that there was a race out there that was capable of godhood.'

'A race more powerful than the high and mighty Time Lords?' Stuart sneered.

'Yes,' said the Doctor. 'You.'

'Hah!' Stuart snorted. 'Don't patronise me, Doctor.'

Time to talk out of class. 'Perish the thought. Humanity is an amazing species, Professor Hyde. I have watched your race crawl from the primordial swamp to inhabit the galaxy. I have watched mankind fight against the most overwhelming odds to survive; I have watched it take on the worst this cosmos can manage and win. I have also watched how my people regard your race, Stuart: with a mixture of fear and envy. I also know that at the very end of time...' He broke off. If he said any more, he was at risk of doing a 'there are some things mankind is not meant to know'. But there was no choice: he was going to have to do a 'there are some things mankind is not meant to know'. What were the Time Lords going to do? Put him on trial again? Was there another Valeyard waiting in the wings, ready to prosecute him?

'Humanity is one of the few races in the universe which has an instinctive understanding of time travel, Stuart. Stattenheim and Waldorf put together a working blueprint of a TARDIS in the sixteenth century, while Lassiter and Monroe encroached upon Time Lord technology in the eleventh millennium.' He smiled at the memory. 'Throughout history, humanity will keep on stumbling upon time travel, and my people will try to stop that understanding - constantly, indefatigably. Although whether the Time Lords are acting out of jealousy or out of fear is another question. And finally your race wins, and inherits our mantle, just before the final end of this universe.'

Stuart's gaze dropped to his empty wine glass. 'Why are you telling me this, Doctor? To make me feel better? Because if you are, it isn't working.'

The Doctor was forced to admit partial defeat: clearly, the Master had dealt a bitter blow to Stuart's pride in his own achievements, and there was little chance of the Doctor's repairing that over a three-course meal. But it was worth a try.

'If you must know, yes,' he stated, slamming his hands on the table and causing the maitre d' to look round. 'The Master needed your ingenuity - that human ingenuity that the majority of Time Lords lack - to release Kronos. Without you and Ruth, TOMTIT would never had been built. That's what I've been trying to tell you, man! He couldn't have managed it on his own - he lacks the imagination. Only you and Ruth could have done it.'

Stuart gave him a wry look. 'Despite everything, Doctor, I believe you.' He grinned. 'I do believe you. But that still doesn't explain why you're here.'

'Why am I here?' The Doctor raised an eyebrow and smiled. He'd won! Now for the hard part. 'I'm here because I think you've been a very naughty boy.'

Mel turned over and over beneath the thin sheets of the hotel bed, unable to sleep. Whether that was to due to the humid August night or the thoughts that flared in her mind, she didn't know, and didn't care.

It seemed that Anjeliqua had moved out of her flat a couple of years ago and the new occupant didn't have a forwarding address, although he did think she was still working at the university. Which was quite lucky, since Mel had discovered that she was actually in 2003 - the Doctor couldn't even get that right! Then again, late by three years... she knew she should be grateful that it wasn't three centuries!

Walking away from the flat she had realised that she was in a bit of a quandary. Having decided to leave the TARDIS, she had been convinced that the world - her world - would accept her readily; unfortunately, that didn't appear to be the case. And since it wasn't all going to be handed to her on a plate, she was going to have to take matters into her own hands.

Mel's impeccable memory had reminded her that there was somewhere to stay ten minutes up the Great West Road - the Osterley Hotel. With its bar favoured by the oh-so-mature students of West London University and the underage schoolboys of Isleworth Grammar School, staying there seemed her best strategy until she could contact Anjeliqua - or, indeed, anyone from her past. So she lugged her holdall up the busy A4 until she reached the squat white buildings of the hotel.

Checking in - grateful for the Doctor's gift of what amounted to over £5,000 - she had thought of her room on board the TARDIS, with its creature comforts. But there wasn't a hotel on Earth with a holographic TV and a library of every book ever written, nor was there one with a zero-G jacuzzi or a food machine that could replicate any meal in the known universe. Mel was going to have to settle for satellite TV and an *en suite* bathroom - and get used to it.

As she plumped up her pillow and tried to clear her mind, she began to question her decision. Despite everything... was the Doctor all right?

Images of Paul, Arlene and Anjeliqua swirled around for a few minutes, intercut with the ruins of Maradnias and an old, broken Time Lord, before sheer exhaustion overcame her and she finally fell into a deep yet fitful sleep.

After another hour in La Bella Donna, skirting around the real issues, the Doctor realised that he was no closer to understanding what was going on. There was the odd clue, the occasional snippet of information, but nothing concrete. Thankfully, Stuart appeared to be in the mood to carry on talking - and drinking - and had suggested that they retire to his flat for a nightcap. The Doctor had readily agreed.

Stuart's flat in Great Titchfield Street - twenty minutes walk down a still busy Oxford Street from La Bella Donna - was compact yet homely, with a huge kitchen: apparently Stuart had swapped the bedroom and the kitchen around when he had first moved in, since the bedroom had been bigger. He had obviously grown into a bon viveur, if the well-stocked fridge and cupboards were anything to go by. The kitchen also contained a very generous supply of all manner of alcoholic beverages.

Soon after he had settled into this body the Doctor had discovered that he once again liked the odd tipple. His Fifth incarnation, up there on his rented high moral ground, had been virtually teetotal, but the Sixth Doctor relished both the taste and effects of alcohol. True, his Gallifreyan metabolism could overcome the effects in a trice, but it was still highly enjoyable getting drunk. Sometimes, it was good to get away from it all.

As he was now, slumped in one of Stuart's capacious armchairs like some multicoloured scatter cushion.

'Another, Doctor?' Stuart Hyde was brandishing a very large vodka and tonic, ice and a slice. The Doctor's fifth, with Stuart not far behind. 'The evening's young!'

'Don't mind if I do,' said the Doctor, slurring as he took the proffered glass, his taking of it matching Stuart's haphazard delivery. A lie - but the truth was he needed to know about the time trace and getting Stuart off guard like this, although underhand, was probably the best way. Especially given how crucial it was to find out about the trace.

Whatever the technology in the university was it was almost identical to TOMTIT, but slightly more sophisticated: some of the rough edges that TOMTIT's time trace had exhibited - those edges that had caused time distortion when the device was in operation - had been cleaned up. But it was definitely 'son of TOMTIT', as Stuart had described it to him. But how could that be if C19 - the Government's black ops and dirty tricks department - had 'retrieved' all the hardware and information about TOMTIT for safe keeping at the Vault, like it was supposed to do? Then again, it wasn't exactly unknown for the Vault's alien technology to fall into the wrong hands, was it? The Doctor thought of SénéNet - and then thought of Mel, and decided not to pursue that particular line of memory.

The fact was, someone at West London University was delving into time travel in such a manner that the Doctor had to stop them. The reason wasn't the notion of mankind developing time travel - he'd be damned if he was going to become a proper little Time Lord at his age, and TOMTIT was nursery school stuff as far as those stuffed shirts on Gallifrey were concerned - it was the fact that the culprit was doing it in such a way that they might very well attract the attention of beings who would think nothing of destroying the Earth to stop them. Although the Time Lords didn't usually employ such heavy-handed techniques, the

Doctor's experiences with Ravalox had made him wary of his own people. But he knew that it wasn't them he should really worry about.

There were others for whom restraint was a dirty word. Such as the Chronovores. They would recognise the signature time-trace of TOMTIT... and the Doctor doubted they would be overjoyed to realise that someone was employing the same technology that had enslaved one of their own. And the vengeance of the Chronovores was terrible to see. *Remember Atlantis*.

'So', said the Doctor, placing his glass on the coffee table, 'what has your protégé been doing? Kairos, wasn't it?'

Stuart nodded. 'Boy's a genius, Doctor. Knows more about temporal physics than I ever could.'

'So how did he learn about TOMTIT?'

Stuart hesitated for a moment, but it was obvious that his pride in Kairos' achievements was going to win through. And it did.

'Paul was the brightest student I had ever taught, Doctor. Before long, it was very obvious that there was nothing more I could tell him about temporal physics. I chose to remove him from the class and tutor him privately. Before long, he was teaching me.'

'And so you chose to confide in him as well,' said the Doctor. 'You told him about TOMTIT - which, I ought to add, is in direct violation of the Official Secrets Act that UNIT made you sign.' Not that it had ever worried the Doctor.

Stuart laughed, a deep, throaty cackle. 'Do you really think I was bothered, Doctor? Yes, I told Paul about TOMTIT. But I did more than that - I showed him it.'

'What?' Once again, the spectre of C19 loomed. 'But how is that possible? Everything -'

'Everything pertaining to TOMTIT was appropriated by UNIT's murky little friends. Is that what you were going to say, Doctor?'

The Doctor could only nod.

'Perhaps they weren't as thorough as they thought they were.' A sly smile crossed Stuart's face. 'Or perhaps they thought the box of tricks they were wheeling out of the door actually was TOMTIT, rather than a hastily put together contraption of broken motherboards and fused transistors.'

The Doctor couldn't help but laugh at the man's audacity. 'You mean...'

Stuart nodded. 'TOMTIT is sitting in a store cupboard at the university, Doctor.' His expression hardened. 'Whether I created it or not, TOMTIT was mine and Ruth's. And I'd have been damned if I was going to give it to those goons in suits!'

'But Paul's not using TOMTIT, is he?'

'Oh no, Doctor. For Paul, that was just the starting point. The boy reverse-engineered back to first principles and built something far, far superior.' His eyes lost their focus, as if he were staring beyond the confines of his flat. 'He built the TITAN Array.'

With that, Stuart collapsed back in his chair and started to snore rather loudly. The Doctor realised that Stuart's eyes had become unfocused because he was drunk.

Taking a sip from his vodka and tonic, while clearing the alcohol from his system at the same time, the Doctor was intrigued. What was the TITAN Array?

A beautiful August morning. The birds were singing in Osterley Park, the sky was cloudless and the sun was bright but not overpowering. Mel had to admit that, despite her troubled night, she felt a million times better. As she stepped out of the hotel into the sunlight, her time with the Doctor had lost its edge. She realised that she was quite looking forward to always knowing what planet she woke up on.

The university was about ten minutes' walk down the Great West Road, a leisurely saunter during which she could enjoy the beginnings of a new life. Mel adjusted her Oakley sunglasses and picked up her holdall. She couldn't wait to see Anjeliqua again.

'As far as I'm concerned, you can go and screw yourself.' Anjeliqua Whitefriar sat back in her leather chair and gave a patronising smile. As director of intellectual property marketing, her job was simple: to take the patents, proposals and products of the various departments at the university and make money out of them. And the wheedling stick insect in front of her wasn't offering her anything she could bring to market. An intelligent toaster, indeed!

'Ms Whitefriar –' the stick insect bleated.

'Go. Now. Before I snap you in half, you pathetic little man.' With that Anjeliqua started reading the latest edition of *Computing*, waiting for the satisfying thud of the door shutting.

Anjeliqua looked up and grinned. I love my job, she thought not for the first time. She glanced at her wafer-thin Dell laptop and checked her e-mails. More obsequious requests for funding, more far-fetched ideas which would never see the light of day... Nothing that would boost the not inconsiderable coffers of the university.

Not that Anjeliqua was particularly worried: sales of the Whitefriar Lattice were going though the roof, and thanks to her lucrative contract with the university – 0.01 per cent – she was already a multimillionaire. If she was totally honest, her job was nothing more than a hobby, something to occupy her time. And a wonderful opportunity for her to throw her not inconsiderable weight around.

Her phone trilled at her. 'Whitefriar,' she snapped, irritated at the interruption. But as soon as she heard what her PA had to say, her sour face beamed.

Melanie Bush?

'Morning, Stuart. I took advantage of your superb kitchen and rustled us up some eggs Benedict. Hope you don't mind. It's waiting in the living room.' A prod in the chest. 'Hurry – don't want the hollandaise sauce to get cold, do we?'

Stuart opened his eyes and tried to focus them. For a second, he couldn't work out why there was a man in an iridescent black-and-white waistcoat with a vivid purple polka-dot cravat standing over him. Then he remembered.

The Doctor.

'Be with you in a couple of secs, Doc,' he murmured.

'Just make sure you are,' said the Doctor. 'We've got a long day ahead of us.'

Once again, Paul let out a series of mewling squeals as he thrashed about in the bed, before his cries finally died away.

Arlene was still totally exhausted - there was no way she could have had a good night's sleep with Paul lying next to her in his present state, the sheets soaked with sweat. As she extracted herself from the duvet and smoothed down her pyjamas, she had to admit to herself that she was worried. For the last couple of weeks, Paul's sleep had been fitful at best. She knew they were both working hard, but this was more than simply overwork - Paul had something on his mind, but he refused to confide in Arlene.

She knew she was going to have to live with it.

With a final glance at Paul, now sleeping peacefully, she padded into the kitchen to make breakfast.

In his white Pink shirt, his charcoal Paul Smith suit and the burgundy Armani tie he had found in his wardrobe, the Master felt underdressed. But it would have to do. His fruitful morning, constructing another identity for himself, was more important than his appearance. Almost.

It was second nature to him: Magister, Keller, Thascales, Estram... intricately woven lives that he had made his own. And this time was no different. Moments after his TARDIS had infiltrated the various computer systems that codified the inhabitants of both this benighted city and the rubble of Belgrade, the Master was picking up his new birth certificate, his national insurance number, his Serbian passport... all the little bits of paper and strings of numbers that defined human beings in the twenty-first century. All perfectly replicated by his TARDIS.

As he filed the new credit card in his pigskin wallet, he couldn't help but grin. He was no longer the Master. He was now Branko Gospodar, a businessman from Serbia. A man who had an appointment at West London University with a certain Anjeliqua Whitefriar.

'Mel!' Anjeliqua leapt from behind her desk and embraced her. 'It's so good to see you!'

Mel responded to the hug in kind, but there was something not quite right about all of this. Was she being paranoid, or just sensible? There was something... different about Anjeliqua. Something unpleasant.

'Where have you been?' Anjeliqua cried, after barking an order for coffee and herbal tea down her phone. 'I knew that you were at the reunion - Chantal told me, surprise, surprise. I so wanted to make it, but business got in the way - always does, I'm afraid. I saw in the Millennium negotiating terms for a new network for the university with an oily French computer magnate, sitting in a hotel room overlooking the Seine.'

'Sounds wonderful,' said Mel, remembering the events of her own Millennium.

'It was, when he could keep his hands to himself. Saved nearly three and a half million pounds for the university.' Anjeliqua indicated a chair. 'Have a seat.'

As Mel sat down she still couldn't overcome her unease. Anjeliqua looked the same - slightly dumpy, long straight brown hair falling down her shoulders and back, the same old-maid dresses - but there was an edge to her. A nasty edge.

'So, where have you been?' Anjeliqua repeated. 'After the reunion you just seemed to vanish. When I got back from Paris I asked Julia and Chantal, but they didn't know.'

This was the difficult bit. 'I went travelling again - I decided to see the world.' *This world and countless others*. At that point the door opened. A handsome young man entered, bearing a laden tray.

Anjeliqua indicated the table between herself and Mel, and subsequently ignored him. 'Well, I have to say, travelling's been good for you - you don't look any older than you did at university.'

'Healthy living and a clear conscience,' Mel answered, well aware that she had used the line before. What else can I say? 'Anyway, I'm back now.'

Anjeliqua grabbed her hand. 'I'm glad.' She eyed the tray. 'Camomile all right?'

Impressed by Anjeliqua's memory, she nodded. 'That would be wonderful.'

As Anjeliqua poured she gestured around the room, hung with pictures - if they weren't reproductions, they were worth hundreds of thousands... 'What do you think about the office? Not bad for someone who got a third in compsci, is it?'

Mel had to admit the room was impressive, but the trappings were irrelevant. This wasn't the Anjeliqua that she had been at university with, and she wanted to know why.

'So,' said Mel, sipping her coffee. 'What do you do, exactly?'

Anjeliqua grinned. 'I keep this place running, Mel - from a financial point of view - now that the Chapel bursary has dried up.'

Ashley Chapel... Mel's thoughts about him were unprintable, even for her. The idea that that person had had his claws in her old university... But Anjeliqua was still talking.

'I find the research projects which I think are viable, and arrange for them to be brought to market.' She narrowed her eyes. 'Surely you must have heard of the Whitefriar Lattice?'

Mel shook her head.

'You really have been travelling, haven't you? I didn't think there was anywhere on this planet that hadn't heard of it,' Anjeliqua said with clear disbelief. 'The Lattice is part of virtually every electronic device around.'

'I have been to some pretty remote places,' said Mel, trying to sound apologetic. She searched her memory. 'Is it a bit like the micromonolithic circuit?' Four years ago, the same claim was being made for that. By Ashley Chapel.

Anjeliqua smiled. 'Dear old Ashley's toy? Yesterday's technology, Mel. The Whitefriar Lattice is a revolutionary device which has made the transistor completely obsolete - and the micromonolithic circuit is nothing more than a glorified transistor. The Lattice manipulates photons at a quantum level. No more clumsy heat sinks and fans - today's processors can operate at speeds that were once physically impossible.' She reached round to her desk and picked up what appeared to be a mobile phone. 'This PDA has the processing power of a desktop PC from two years ago. And in a year, something this size will be capable of quantum computing - an entire new generation of technology.'

All very impressive, thought Mel, but it did sound as if Anjeliqua were reciting a marketing brochure rather than actually understanding what she was talking about.

'And don't forget that seventy-eight per cent of the Grid runs on the Whitefriar Lattice', she added, 'bringing unlimited processing power to everyone.'

The Grid - the Doctor had explained that one to her, trying to lighten up the journey away from the planet of the Sporrads and their vicious and unnatural ways. Some revolutionary technological advance in the year 2001 meant that it had soon been possible to take advantage of all the spare processing power of all the computers linked to the internet. Every last gigahertz of idle time, every spare gigabyte of storage from every computer, could be pooled into a dissociated cloud of processing power and memory, available as easily as electricity or gas.

Was the Whitefriar Lattice the advance that had made it all possible? Was Mel's old roommate the technological visionary who had changed the world? And if so, how?

'So when did you invent it?' asked Mel, amazed that her old friend, someone who had struggled through the technical parts of their computer science degree, could have come up with something so revolutionary. She wasn't prepared for the cruel, calculating, spiteful look that darkened Anjeliqua's face.

'Invent it? Me?' Anjeliqua laughed. But it wasn't a pretty laugh. It was a cackle, verging on a shriek.

She handed over a small clump of foamy metallic wire. The words 'Whitefriar Lattice' were clearly visible in small white letters on the nodes interspersed in the wire. 'Mel, my percentage of the Whitefriar Lattice has made me one of the richest women on this planet. I have homes in four countries, and more lovers than you could ever believe.' She sipped her coffee. 'But can you really see me getting my hands dirty? I hardly know how to wire a plug! Our dear old friend Paul invented it, of course.'

Mel frowned. 'Paul? Our Paul?'

'If you mean Paul Kairos, then yes.'

So Paul was the visionary! But if Anjeliqua was this rich, where was Paul in the equation? Indulging his passion for rare American comics? Married to Arlene and living in a castle somewhere? Anjeliqua's next words put paid to all of that.

'Unfortunately, under the terms and conditions of his contract here, poor Paul didn't get a penny.' She pursed her lips. 'He doesn't even get to go down in history.' She sipped her coffee. 'Unlike me, of course.'

That was the point at which Mel realised how Anjeliqua had changed. She was no longer the happy-go-lucky student, game for a laugh, letting her hair down at dinner parties. Something had happened, something so fundamental that it had drained all the good from her, filling her up with bitterness, spite and hate.

What in God's name had happened to her?

Before Mel could get to the bottom of it, a bleep issued from Anjeliqua's PDA. She checked the tiny screen before looking up. 'I'm sorry, Mel, but I'm going to have to cut this short. I've got another meeting in five minutes - some low-level dignitary from the former Yugoslavia wants to write me a very big cheque.' She picked up a card from her desk and handed it to Mel. 'Give me a ring later, in about two hours, say? Perhaps we can have lunch?'

Mel found it hard to reconcile this Anjeliqua - eager to rekindle their friendship - with the woman who had shown such glee in getting one over on Paul. And even harder to reconcile it with the Anjeliqua she had known at university. Given that Mel's plans had hinged upon staying with her, everything now appeared to be fraying at the edges. For a second, she thought about the Doctor - half-way across the galaxy by now, fighting the good fight. But who was at his side?

But Mel had made her bed. For better or for worse, she had to accept that she was never going to see the Doctor again.

The taxi pulled up outside the high-energy physics block of the university - the grandly titled Chapel Institute - and Stuart and the Doctor got out. Stuart was still feeling a little delicate, but decades of drinking himself into oblivion gave him a familiarity with the condition and the experience to overcome it. Usually - unless he had an overexcitable Time Lord in tow. He reached into his pocket and pulled out a solid silver hip flask - a present from Ruth Ingram - and took a long swig of whisky.

'I have to say that I'm really looking forward to this,' said the

Doctor, rubbing his hands together. 'Can't wait to see what it does.'

'Young Kairos will be only too pleased to explain, Doctor,' said Stuart as he signed his companion in at reception and handed over a smart card. 'To be honest, it's more difficult getting him to keep his mouth shut!'

As they reached the door that led to the TITAN Array Stuart gently pulled on the Doctor's arm. 'Just a word of warning, Doctor. As well as telling him about TOMTIT, I also told him about your lot - the Time Lords. Perhaps you ought to be prepared for a less than favourable reaction.'

The Doctor shrugged. 'I'm sure my natural charm will be sufficient to win him over, Professor Hyde. Lead on.'

Stuart couldn't help but grimace. If only he could be as confident.

The smartly dressed man in the doorway, his hair slicked back, his mouth framed by a black goatee, gave her a warm smile of greeting. But somehow the smile didn't quite reach his eyes... those very, very deep eyes... Anjeliqua tore herself away.

'Mr Gospodar,' she said crisply, inviting him to take a seat. She was impressed: even now, four years after the Kosovo war and the return of democracy, she knew that things were still unstable in Belgrade. So it was quite difficult to reconcile the images of queues for food she had seen on Sky News with the immaculate attire worn by her guest. Then again, given the flourishing black market in his country, perhaps the charcoal Paul Smith suit shouldn't have come as a complete surprise. Indeed, if he was going to give her even half the sum that had been discussed over the phone, his clothing was a reassurance.

'Madame Whitefriar, it is very good of you to see me at such short notice.' His accent was thick, but not impenetrable. If anything, it was rather sexy. Gospodar took her hand and kissed it. 'I know that you are a very busy and very important woman, but I believe that what I can offer you will be to our mutual advantage.' He waited for Anjeliqua to sit down before taking a seat.

'Mr Gospodar, I have to say that details you provided were rather… sketchy.'

The Serbian nodded sagely. 'And for good reasons. I am authorised by my government to negotiate a contract with your university for the provision of certain… equipment that we believe will be vital in the reconstruction of our country.'

'Equipment?' Anjeliqua's job involved the licensing of patents, rather than actual box-shifting. If this charming stranger wanted equipment, he was sadly barking up the wrong tree. 'Are you sure you have the right person, Mr Gospodar? I think you might be mistaken.'

'I do not think so, dear lady.' He stared into her eyes, those endless black pools drawing her in. 'I believe that I have come to just the right person.' He reached out and took her hand in his, squeezing gently. Anjeliqua didn't - couldn't - resist. 'For us to work together, however, I must be sure that you trust me. You do trust me, Anjeliqua?'

Of course she didn't! She had only met the man minutes ago. But somehow she found it difficult to protest.

'You see, my dear, I can offer you something beyond money. Beyond anything that you could possibly comprehend.

'I can offer you power.'

Had his accent changed? Anjeliqua went to pull away - from his hands, from his eyes - but she couldn't. No - she didn't want to. It was as if this strange Serbian's mind was within hers, exploring her memories, her thoughts, her desires…

There was no trace of an accent when he continued. 'You see, I am the Master. I am the Master and you will obey me. You *will* obey me.'

At that moment, Anjeliqua knew that there was nothing that she wouldn't do for him. For her new Master.

The Doctor was unsure what to expect as Stuart opened the door to the TITAN Array: the thirty years since he had last seen him had seen some of the most rapid advances in human technology in that race's entire history: the Internet, the Grid, the Whitefriar Lattice…

TOMTIT had been a collection of boxy units filled with printed circuits and some very dodgy wiring, 1970s technology trying to reach for Time Lord understanding. The master terminal - what a term! - had been in the main part of the lab, while the slave terminal, powered by the Newton Institute's primitive nuclear reactor, had been in a lead-lined anteroom. All very parochial.

The TITAN Array was anything but.

The room was a cube, fifteen metres a side, the walls, floor and ceiling smooth white marble - it was more like the Tate Modern than a scientific research institute. The illumination came from what looked like purple neon tubing set into all twelve edges of the room, giving everything a crisp, antiseptic appearance - something that was bolstered by the pervasive tang of ozone that accompanied all high-energy experiments.

But that was just the room. It was what the room contained that impressed the Doctor.

At the very centre, eight metres above them, hung a translucent, pulsing sphere of ruby crystal, three metres across, held in place by eight thin steel rods. Each rod reached outwards from the centre until it hit the corresponding corner of the room, where a metallic web of circuitry held it in place. It was like standing inside a huge cat's cradle of chrome and crystal.

On closer inspection, the Doctor realised that what he had first taken for neon lighting was actually even more circuitry, linking the eight vertices of the room together; knotted ropes of luminous glassy fibres. And the nature of the illumination suggested that Kairos was using some kind of accelerated black-light conversion technique - very advanced. Indeed, perhaps slightly too advanced for 2003.

A single, thicker rod ran from the sphere to the floor, where eight parallel conduits connected it to a shining chrome console about 4.5 metres from the doorway in which the Doctor stood. Two figures were leaning over the console: a thickset man in his late thirties with short hair, olive skin and a beard, and a taller, elegant black woman, her hair in a bun. They were disagreeing quietly. Stuart coughed politely, alerting them to his and the Doctor's presence. They turned round in unison.

'Stuart!' The man came bounding up enthusiastically, the woman gliding behind him. 'I was hoping you'd pop in - there's something we wanted you to check over for us.'

'Maybe a bit later, Paul.' He gestured towards the Doctor. 'I'd like you to meet someone.' He paused and the Doctor could sense the tension, the apprehension, in Stuart's voice. 'This is the Doctor.'

'The Doctor?' Paul frowned for a second, before realisation dawned on his face. 'The Doctor? The one who...'

Stuart - and the Doctor - nodded.

Paul sighed. 'You bastard.' As that polite epithet rung in the Doctor's ears Paul turned on his heel and returned to the chrome console, pointedly ignoring both the Doctor and Stuart.

Stuart shrugged. 'I did warn you, Doc. Leave this to me.' He walked over to the console, the Doctor in tow.

'Please, Paul - listen to me,' Stuart insisted. But his protégé was having none of it. The woman was keeping out of the way, the Doctor noted. Very wise.

'Why should I?' Paul's face was twisted with a mixture of emotions: anger, jealousy... and concern. Concern for Stuart and what he had suffered at the hands of the Time Lords, the Doctor guessed.

'Just think what we could have done if he'd decided to share his precious knowledge with us, rather than just dangling it in front of you and Ruth.'

The Doctor shook his head: he was going to regret this, but it was time to get involved. He stepped forward. 'Professor Kairos, you have to understand. It wasn't the time travel that was the problem, although my people do have a tendency to be a little... protective, where that is concerned. It was Kronos! Surely your mentor has told you about that creature? What it was capable of?'

'That was years ago,' said Paul. 'Years.'

'Years? What is time to the Chronovores?' the Doctor snorted. 'We're talking about beings billions of years old!'

'How is that possible?' It was the woman. 'I'm Paul's partner, Doctor: Professor Arlene Cole. Professional and personal,' she added, shaking his hand. 'Life couldn't develop that long ago. The physical nature of the cosmos was inimical to life at that time.'

'Human life. Life based on cold hard matter, yes. But the Chronovores aren't made of baryonic matter.'

Paul raised an eyebrow. 'Living nonbaryonic matter?'

The Doctor waved a multicoloured sleeve at the TITAN Array. 'And why not? I thought you were a genius? In their natural form the Chronovores exist as six-dimensional polymorphic lattices of photinos and chronons, bound by superstrings.'

'Nonsense,' yelled Paul.

The Doctor groaned. 'Human life is made from the remnants of Population II stars - star-stuff. The Transcendental Beings are made from the very fabric of time itself - time-stuff. Now do you understand how dangerous all of this is?'

Paul snorted. 'I've never heard such overblown claptrap. Has Stuart actually explained what the TITAN Array does?'

The Doctor had to admit that, until this point, he had simply assumed that TITAN was a glorified TOMTIT: a high-class matter transmitter. Perhaps it was time to find out more. 'Actually, Professor Kairos, he hasn't. Would you care to elucidate?'

Paul laid his hands on the chrome console. 'The Trans-Interstitial Time Analysis Network - TITAN - isn't like TOMTIT, Doctor, although I did base it on some of TOMTIT's principles. We're taking advantage of the granular nature of time, just as TOMTIT does, but for an entirely different reason.

'We're trying to touch the face of God.'

'Paul - stop being so melodramatic,' said Arlene, giving his right hand an affectionate pat. 'Doctor, basically TITAN is the biggest microscope ever made. We're trying to penetrate Calabi-Yau Space - does that mean anything to you?'

'Indeed it does!' Perhaps there was a chance that these humans would actually understand!

But before he could say anything further, Stuart took up the story - the Doctor suspected he was feeling left out. His rich voice took on the manner of a university lecturer. Which, of course, he was.

'When the universe was created, dimensions started to solidify out of the primal chaos. But five got there first - the three spatial dimensions and two of time.'

The Doctor couldn't bite his tongue any longer. They might be a trinity of professors, but the Doctor had learnt this in elementary class at the Academy! Holding his hands up in protest, he remembered one of his primers: Rassilon's *Guide to the Multiverse*, volume 3. The one without the pictures.

'At the risk of sounding like a high-and-mighty Time Lord, I *am* a high-and-mighty Time Lord. And to quote one of my elementary texts in the matter: "And in the aftermath of Event Zero, eleven dimensions did fight for existence. Five were triumphant - together they did become the three dimensions of space, and the two dimensions of time through which we travel. But the remaining six dimensions did still exist: although beaten, although denied their dominance, they curled and curdled amongst themselves to become a six-fold universe, separate yet conjoined.

'"They formed a realm all their own - a universe in which the Transcendental Beings could thrive and prosper without interference from the lesser beings. A realm protected by the Great and Ancient Covenant.

'"Although we and the Transcendental Beings share the time vortex, the Covenant divides us. But the Six-Fold Realm is denied us by the Covenant, and it is a Covenant that we dare not transgress." You see, even the Time Lords have kept away from what you call Calabi-Yau Space. We simply left it alone, as most sensible races have done!'

'Until now,' said Paul. 'The aim of the TITAN Array is to reach into Calabi-Yau Space, to examine it... Doctor, this is man's greatest achievement!'

'Man's greatest folly, more like.'

'Advancing human knowledge!' Paul yelled back. 'Or does that offend your Time Lord sensibilities?'

'This is nothing to do with that - and I wish you would get it through that thick skull of yours that I am not some kind of a galactic policeman! Paul - Calabi-Yau Space is more than just a scientific curiosity - the Transcendental Beings call it the Six-Fold Realm. It's their home! With TOMTIT, you were simply knocking on the door. With TITAN, you're inviting yourself in and making a cup of tea! The creatures that live there are beyond your comprehension - they're beyond mine, come to that! Leave - well - alone.'

Paul shook his head. 'With TITAN we can examine the fundamental nature of reality, Doctor. Surf the quantum foam, examine superstrings first-hand, map the topology of Calabi-Yau Space... Doctor, this is our chance to understand our place in the universe.'

The tenacity of human beings was one of their greatest gifts... but it was also one of their most annoying faults. The Doctor remembered an apposite quote. '"For there was Time Before this; and there was Being before this; and there was Space before this. And there were Things Damned in that place, and there were Things Remarkable." And that's from the *Book of the Old Time*! We're dealing with the Things Damned, Paul!'

'I'm sorry, Doctor, but that is total bollocks!'

Was there no way to make them understand?

'Understand this, Paul. The moment you enter Calabi-Yau Spaceyou will light a beacon. A beacon that the Chronovores will pounce upon!' The Doctor turned his back on them in disgust. 'And at that point, your place in the universe will be nothing more than fodder for the Chronovores!'

'Doctor?' It was Arlene, the blessed still point in the room, it seemed. 'You said earlier that these creatures lived in something called the time vortex. What has that got to do with Calabi-Yau Space?'

Finally, an intelligent question! The Doctor turned round in his chair. 'The time vortex is the second temporal dimension - it's the region through which TARDISes travel, the region that TOMTIT creates a gap through to enable matter transmission. When the dimensions froze out of the void it became inexorably linked to Calabi-Yau Space. The Chronovores may live in the time vortex... but they eat and feed in what you call Calabi-Yau Space. You're trespassing on their feeding grounds!'

Arlene looked over at Paul. 'If the Doctor's right, perhaps we ought to rethink what we're doing.'

Paul laughed. 'Have you forgotten how these Time Lords played with Stuart? What they did to him? They just don't want us to learn their secrets. I'm going ahead with the run.'

The Doctor sighed. He didn't like it, but at least he would be around to pick up the pieces. He just hoped that that would be enough.

Now that he had control of Anjeliqua, the Master had sunk back into his Gospodar persona. Perfect Serbian manners and a very different face: holographic image-inducing was far better than the old mask routine. 'I understand that you have a very gifted young scientist at your university. A Professor Kairos. Is that correct?'

She nodded. 'Paul? He's responsible for the TITAN Array.'

The Master was impressed by Anjeliqua – it was rare to find such a malleable, obedient mind. The perfect tool for what he needed to do.

'And that would be the experiment designed to penetrate Calabi-Yau Space?'

The bitterness was clear in her voice. 'Waste of money, if you ask me. But yes, that's the experiment.'

'I would like to see this... this TITAN Array, Madame Whitefriar. Would that be possible?'

'I'm sure I can arrange it.' She looked at her watch. 'Actually, he's due to do another run about now. I know, because I had to sign off access to the Grid. Over one exahertz of processing power... do you know how much that costs?'

'Dear lady, I can assure you that the university will be very well rewarded for its assistance. Very well rewarded.'

This woman was motivated by two things: a desire for money and a desire for revenge. Her avarice was understandable: a useful vice shared by so many of her fellow human beings. But the bitterness was something else. Even the low level of mind control the Master was using could sense the intensity of her feelings towards this Paul Kairos. But there was something... unnatural about it. Something abnormal. A block in her mind.

'Come along,' she was saying. 'The next run starts in five minutes, and I'm sure you don't want to miss it.' With that, she was virtually out of the door.

The Master smiled. If the TITAN Array was even half the

machine that his initial scans had indicated, it was an even more perfect tool for his revenge than dear Anjeliqua.

The deep thrum of the university generators once again vibrated throughout the marble cube of the TITAN chamber. Arlene and Paul were fussing around the control console, adjusting settings, fine tuning penetration parameters, checking readings and muttering to each other under hushed breaths.

To Stuart, it was as if he was young again: he and Ruth preparing TOMTIT for another run. A faint trace of envy momentarily crossed his mind, but how could he be jealous of Paul? The boy was a genius, and deserved to succeed. Stuart couldn't helping thinking, though: would he and Ruth have won the Nobel Prize, had the Master not intervened?

'Approaching full access to the Grid: 950 petahertz now available,' said Arlene, raising her voice about the vibration of the generators. '970, 990... one exahertz, 1.1... full access, Paul!' she yelled.

'And full power from the generators, if you hadn't guessed,' Paul replied. 'Preparing to realise wave envelope.' His hands danced over the chrome of the console, a dazzling blur reflected in the silver surface. 'Wave envelope beginning to form; realisation in five, four, three, two, one - we have realisation!' he announced.

As he spoke, the ruby of the TITAN core began to fluoresce, red radiance playing over the white walls of the chamber like some demonic shadow play. Stuart moved closer to the console, trying to catch a glimpse of the readings, to see if this latest experiment was working. He was too involved to hear the door to the chamber open and close behind him.

'All systems go, I see.'

At the sound of the wheedling voice, Stuart turned round. 'Anjeliqua - what do you want?' The woman had an annoying habit of cropping up just where she wasn't wanted, such as at funding meetings. And here. She was accompanied by a swarthy-looking fellow in an expensive suit who was watching the Array's performance in rapt awe.

'Might I remind you, Professor Hyde, that my department funds this game of smoke and mirrors? I have every right to observe what you are spending my money on.'

It was funny how Anjeliqua considered the university's money to be her own. To think that this woman had been one of his worst pupils - and now she was telling them all what to do.

'Who's this?' asked Stuart. He nodded towards the elegantly dressed stranger. 'Might I remind you, Anjeliqua, that the TITAN Array has level one security clearance?'

'My name is Branko Gospodar, Professor Hyde.' The accent was heavy - Eastern Europe? The man held out his hand. 'I have heard much of you and your protégé, Professor Kairos.' He smiled - which gave Stuart the creeps. 'I am preparing to invest a considerable sum in this university. Before I did so, I wanted to see its crowning glory.' He stepped forward and approached the master console. 'A fascinating device, Professor Kairos. Fascinating.'

'Thank you,' said Paul.

The man caught him with a brutal uppercut, sending him flying across the chamber. He then began to alter the settings on the console, his hands darting across the chrome surface as if he knew what he was doing...

Stuart attempted to pull him away, but the man gave him a shove in the chest that left him winded on the floor, then continued to tap away, even as Arlene grabbed his shoulders to no avail. A sickening sense of *déjà vu* came over Stuart. Surely it couldn't be *him*?

Within moments, the results of the man's actions were alarmingly obvious. The regular pulsing of the TITAN core became erratic, almost painful, as the red deepened from ruby to blood, washing across the walls. It was as if time itself had been wounded.

The Doctor almost knocked Anjeliqua out of the way as he tried to reach the stranger but seemed to falter, to slow, until he had stopped in his tracks, poised in an impossible position. Stuart suddenly realised that he too was immobilised. It was as if time were standing still.

With a churning feeling in his stomach, Stuart realised that it was. And it was something he had felt before. Thirty years ago.

Out of the blood-red TITAN core, a brilliant luminance began to form, brightening and brightening until the red was gone, washed away by the terrible incandescence. Stuart found it impossible to pull his eyes away as it gained definition, the fuzzy blur concentrating and resolving into a massive firebird, its wings swooping above them. A deafening shriek filled the chamber as the firebird proclaimed its magnificence.

It was a sight that Stuart had hoped never to see again.

The Chronovores had returned.

Chapter Three
It's All Coming Back to Me Now

It had taken the Doctor scant seconds to work out what was happening. Even before the malevolent firebird formed out of the TITAN core, he could feel its approach like a fire in his blood: the unmistakable torsion in the fabric of time as something unholy tried to tear through, manifesting itself as the hairs on the back of his neck standing on end. Normally, like all Time Lords, his special relationship with time made him immune to the collateral effects of a Chronovore visitation. But he too was frozen in place, unable to move more than his eyes.

Unlike the man operating the controls. The face, frowning with concentration, was unknown, but the Doctor instinctively knew who he was dealing with. Someone who would have no problems creating a localised field to override the Doctor's natural temporal grace. Gospodar, indeed. Serbian for... Was he running out of languages now?

The Master.

Hadn't the fool learnt anything? The Chronovores were uncontrollable, beings of fire and ice and unutterable cruelty. Summoning one up on twenty-first century Earth threatened the very web of time!

The Doctor strained, but to no avail. He could only watch as the Master played the TITAN controls, obviously attempting to do what TOMTIT had failed to do. Tame the untamable.

And it was clear that he was having as little success. The Chronovore was growing larger and larger, its hellfire wings dominating the chamber. Within seconds, it would burst from the room, an eruption of spite that would soon tower over London, and then Britain... the Doctor had a brief vision of the firebird clutching the Earth in its hellish talons. *The Things Damned*. There had to be something he could do!

Discontinuity.

The Doctor blinked as movement returned to him, aware that time had passed without his knowledge: something that, as a Time Lord, made him feel quite queasy, a bit like someone forgetting whether they had turned the gas off or not.

But there were more important things to think about. Of the Master and the other woman there was no sign - what a surprise: he must have admitted failure and hightailed it out of there, creating the temporal discontinuity to cover his escape. But the Chronovore was still hanging above them like an angel of death, its wings beating a cadence of lost chances and unfulfilled opportunities, its song a soul-rending screech.

If TITAN was based on TOMTIT there was only one possible defence - it just depended on whether Stuart had correctly judged Paul's genius. But it was their only chance. The Doctor almost fell on to the console, trying to take in the location and function of the controls. It didn't take him long.

'Paul - set up an interference pattern! Try to entangle the Chronovore inside it while I involute the waveform and send it back!'

Even though Paul was obviously still in shock from the temporal effects of the Chronovore's manifestation, he followed the Doctor's orders, glancing at the monitors to check his own progress as he started to run interference.

Meanwhile, the Doctor was attempting to calculate a counterharmonic to the waveform, its involute, designed to cancel out the tunnel the Master had set up between the real world and the dark secret at the heart of Calabi-Yau Space: the Lux Aeterna.

As he waited for the Array's quantum computer to work though twenty thousand variables in eleven dimensions, he spared a quick look behind him. Arlene was hugging Stuart and shaking like a leaf: understandable. But they were all still alive - and their correct ages. The Doctor returned his attention to the console. 'How's it going?' he shouted to Paul above the shrieking.

'Almost there... Yes!' Paul slammed his hand down on a set of keys. At the same time the Doctor completed his own waveform and sent it hurtling down the tunnel the Master had created, collapsing it and cutting off the immediate danger.

The effect on the Chronovore was immediate. Its shriek turned from triumph to pain, a cacophony of death, of life, and of all the unspeakable moments in between. As the firebird thrashed around the chamber, visibly shrinking, its brilliance began to fade, its existence retreating into the ruby sphere of the TITAN core. With a final, agonised wail the creature dwindled into nothing.

For the next few moments, everything was blessed silence as the Doctor and Paul deactivated the TITAN Array, the red glow of the core dimming to nothing. Finally the Doctor was able to let out a sigh of relief.

'Is everyone all right?' he said.

Arlene's face was tear-stained, but her voice was steady. 'That was... one of those creatures, wasn't it?'

'A Chronovore, yes. But not Kronos, thankfully.'

'How could you tell? I would have thought one time-eating monster looked the same as any other,' said Stuart sarcastically.

'Because, Professor Hyde, that one was still a baby. A baby on guard duty.' The Doctor shook his head. 'Surely this must have shown you the folly of all of this? Thanks to the Master and his machinations, this apparatus has just surpassed its parameters by several orders of magnitude and accessed the Lux Aeterna. And I very much doubt that the Chronovores are going to be too impressed by that!'

Stuart Hyde held up his hand. 'Hang on, Doc - bit of knowledge overload there. Are you saying that man with Whitefriar was the Master? It certainly didn't look like him.'

'And I don't look like I did, Stuart. Perhaps he's regenerated again, although I suspect he's playing around with his wretched holograms. But it has to have been the Master - unless this university is full of people who know how to recalibrate the TITAN Array in mid-session.'

'But that's not possible,' said Arlene. 'Even Paul can't do that.'

Paul gave a hollow laugh. 'I'm a bit different from a Time Lord, Arlene. But you're right.' He looked at the Doctor. 'Our quantum computer - it drives the formation of the penetration envelope -

won't permit that sort of operation: it isn't built that way.'

'Then I suggest we take a closer look at your quantum computer. You might be in for a bit of a surprise.' The Doctor strode over to the square chrome cylinder that stretched from floor to ceiling in the right-hand corner of the chamber, the other three following. A discreet grey badge marked it as a Deutsch 3270 Quantum Server. 'So, Paul: what's your analysis?'

Paul ran his fingers over the touch screens on the cylinder for over a minute, checking and double-checking the quantum logic diagrams that flashed across them. When he turned to look at the others his face was drawn in puzzlement.

'This isn't the same machine. I mean, physically it is, but the Q-Solaris operating system and the software processors have all been changed. Upgraded! I doubt that a machine like this will exist on the planet for another ten years. It's incredible!' The admiration dripped from his words.

'The Plath have been using quantum computers for the last ten thousand years,' said the Doctor quietly, remembering their perfidy on Earth quite clearly. 'The Lurlak for even longer.' He returned to the master console. 'The technology's out there, I assure you. The Master upgraded your computer on the fly to allow the TITAN Array to open a gateway to the Chronovores. And I would wager that he was successful.'

'So why has the Master returned here if we're all so primitive?' asked Stuart. 'Surely there's a race out there that has perfected this technology?' He indicated the Array.

The Doctor sat the wrong way round on one of the swivel chairs. 'As I said, he needs human ingenuity. And all the other races that have tried to access the Lux Aeterna stand as warnings - their stars turned supernova, their planets lifeless...' He tried not to think of Maradnias. Instead, he couldn't help but think of something far, far worse. It couldn't be... could it? Surely even the Master wouldn't dare attempt that? This went far beyond his normal schemes of megalomania. This was suicide on a cosmic scale! But all the clues fitted...

The Doctor's voice was like the grave as he continued, virtually ignoring the others while he basically thought out loud. 'To simply activate TITAN might not have been enough for him. One Chronovore - even the baby one that manifested here - could have enacted the Chronovores' revenge and destroyed TITAN and most of London, but that isn't enough for him. The Master's gone far, far further this time. He's used TITAN's more advanced facilities - including the software upgrade to your quantum computer - to penetrate deep within Calabi-Yau Space-'

'We did it!' screamed Arlene. 'TITAN works!' She hugged Paul, who couldn't help smiling proudly. Even Stuart was grinning. How was the Doctor going to impress upon these humans the danger that they were in?

'But at what cost?' he continued. 'TITAN has just sent a warning shot into the heart of the Lux Aeterna. And with that, the Master has probably signed this planet's death warrant.'

Stuart whistled through his teeth. 'Anyone fancy a drink?'

Arlene ignored him. 'What is this Lux Aeterna?' she asked. 'You keep mentioning it, but I've never heard of it.'

The Doctor's voice was very, very quiet. 'And it would have been better if you never had.'

The knots of Calabi-Yau Space, existing at every point in the four familiar dimensions of space-time as well as throughout the time vortex, were inaccessible to the majority of races in the cosmos. Even the most advanced of them treated it as an abstract set of solutions to some esoteric quantum equations.

Which was just as well.

Because where those six stunted dimensions crossed the other five of the space-time continuum and the time vortex, they created a point singularity which tapped directly into the fundamental energies that underlay the universe: the seething primal force of the quantum foam. At the heart of each microscopic knot was a point no larger than a quark, but with the potential energy of a quasar. And each of these points linked together across space and time to create an eleven-dimensional lattice of unimaginable power that framed and defined the cosmos.

A lattice that the Time Lords - to their cost - knew as the Lux

Aeterna. The eternal light. The food source of the Chronovores.

While timelines and parallel universes were a feast for the Chronovores, such banquets were few and far between; for them, sustenance came from the Lux Aeterna. By the Ancient Covenants forged in Event One, the Big Bang, the four dimensions of space-time were forbidden to the Chronovores; they were unable to leave their twin domains of Calabi-Yau Spaceand the time vortex unless summoned. But if a being in what they called the Higher Place were to open such a path for them, those covenants were breached and the Chronovores would be freed.

A being from the Higher Place such as the Master.

'The Master has not only alerted the Chronovores to the existence of TITAN, he has forged an opening for them which the rules of time permit them to use. Thanks to Paul and myself, that channel is now closed, but if you use the TITAN Array again that channel will reopen. A channel that will allow every single Chronovore to pass through into our universe.'

'How many of them are there, Doctor?' asked Arlene. 'Can we defend ourselves?'

The Doctor shook his head. 'If they come through en masse there will be enough of them to lay waste to this entire cosmos. And I have a horrible feeling that bringing them all through is part of the Master's plan.'

'As you can see, my dear, they are extremely resourceful.' The Master and Anjeliqua were watching the events occurring in the TITAN chamber on the scanner in the Master's TARDIS: a multidimensional time machine which was apparently inside one of the green cleaners' cupboards lined up against the whitewashed walls of the university basement. Anjeliqua hadn't questioned it for a second.

The Master was continuing, his voice like a honey-dripped razor blade. 'Even when the danger is self-evident, they continue their lethal experiments. Kairos and his associates will bring disaster upon us all!'

'But you will find a way to beat them, won't you?' There was no way that she was going to allow Paul Kairos to hurt her any more - not after all he'd done. And she certainly wasn't going to let him hurt her new Master.

The Master turned to her. He was no longer disguised by his image-inducer; if anything, his true appearance was far more attractive than that of Branko Gospodar. And somehow his very presence was reassurance enough that all of this - the strange black control room that was bigger on the inside, the Master's changing face, firebirds and time machines - was perfectly normal.

'Anjeliqua, they are all playing into my hands: Paul, Stuart, Arlene... even the Doctor. They think they have defeated me, but they have already given me what I need to save us all.' He tapped some keys on the hexagonal black console. 'Behold!'

The scanner showed both Paul and the Doctor typing away on the chrome master console.

'They have shown me how to control the Chronovores.' She guessed that the Master was referring to the parameters the Doctor and Paul had entered to vanquish the firebird. 'That is the first stage. The next stage... well, we need a little diversion for that one.'

Anjeliqua smiled. Allied to the Master, she could finally bring Paul down.

Mel was tired of phoning Anjeliqua and getting her voice-mail. In fact, she wasn't even sure she wanted to spend any more time with her: Anjeliqua simply wasn't the same person she had known all those years ago! Finishing off her mineral water and tofu pitta, she carefully cleared the table and dumped her rubbish in the bin, before leaving the university's cafeteria. Though goodness knew where she was going to go, what she was going to do, or what was going to happen. She just didn't know what to expect.

She most certainly hadn't expected to see the Doctor.

As she walked down the corridor the doors at the far end were flung open to reveal him in intense, and very loud, conversation with an older man whom she vaguely recognised - wasn't that Professor Hyde? - and two people she had known extremely well:

Paul Kairos and Arlene Cole. She slipped into a stairwell and waited.

What were they doing, talking to the Doctor? By now his TARDIS should have been years and light years away. What was he still doing on Earth? Hoping she would change her mind? Or was he interfering again?

Whatever he was up to, Mel had to find out.

'Doctor?' She stepped out of the stairwell and confronted him.

'Mel!' He grabbed her and swung her around. 'How good to see you!' His face was beaming.

To Mel, unfortunately, it felt as if he had completely forgotten about Maradnias. 'Doctor,' she replied calmly. 'How are you?'

The Doctor frowned. 'How am I? How am I? How am I! Mel - the Master's here! He's trying to release Kronos again - or some such perfidy. You have to help us!'

Ignoring him, she looked over at Paul and Arlene - they looked so much older than Mel felt - and broke into a grin. 'It's good to see you both again.' She turned her back on the Doctor and walked over to them.

'And you too, Mel,' said Paul, grasping her hand. 'But how do you know the Doctor?'

Mel glanced at the Doctor... and saw the look in his eyes. 'I... I travel with him,' she answered.

Arlene gently pushed Paul to one side. 'It's great to see you,' she said. 'Are you staying long?'

Another sideways look at the Doctor. 'I haven't decided yet,' she muttered.

The Doctor sidled up to her. 'Mel - despite everything - something's happening here. Something bad. I've got to stay and help.'

Mel was sure how to react. Seeing the Doctor again was wonderful, she had to admit. But there were still so many issues unresolved between them - issues that weren't going to be resolved in a corridor in West London University. 'Doctor - I've got some things to sort out. I need some time...'

He gave her a sad, lonely look. 'Time,' he muttered. 'If only that was all it took...'

'We're just going for a spot of lunch, Mel.' It was Professor Hyde. 'Perhaps you'd like to join us?'

Typical of the Doctor to hijack her reunion. Well, she wasn't going to have it. 'I've got some work to do in the library,' she countered. 'But I should be free later.'

'Excellent, excellent,' said Stuart.

'See you later, Mel,' said the Doctor sadly - hopefully.

'Sure,' she answered, as the little group headed towards the students' union. 'Sure.'

Why did seeing the Doctor make her feel so bad?

It was a shame that Anjeliqua was so necessary to his plans, the Master decided: the woman was such a tiresome bore, a bloated sack of bitterness and spite without any redeeming features such as cruelty or sadistic panache.

Her complete and utter devotion to him had been flattering at first - most victims of his hypnosis tended to fight back subconsciously, and it was an effort to keep them in line - but now she was becoming an irritation. No backbone: she had submitted to his will so very easily... He frowned. Perhaps too easily. Could he trust Anjeliqua? Trust her totally? Because, for his plans to succeed, he needed to trust someone completely. And after all that had happened to him over the centuries trust was now a virtually alien concept to the Master.

He sank back into his chair in his study and stroked his beard. He had sent the woman back to her office, on the ruse of collecting the blueprints for the TITAN Array. Not that he needed her to do that: he had surmised most of its operations from his brief stint on the controls, and if he had wanted detailed plans his TARDIS could rip them from the university mainframe in nanoseconds - which it had done a few moments after Anjeliqua had left. In truth, he had simply wanted some time on his own. Time to think.

Sipping a fine cognac and puffing on a Cuban cigar, the Master considered his options. And pondered the blueprints.

There was no doubt that the TITAN Array worked, nor that it was based on TOMTIT - that much was obvious. Indeed, Hyde himself had been in the TITAN suite. But Kairos was obviously a gifted temporal scientist in his own right. The Master had come to Earth to find TOMTIT, but what he had found was infinitely superior: a quantum computer replacing paracybernetic circuitry; helmic regulators to maintain the stability of the channel; a stator-rotor assembly... He had to admit that he was actually impressed. This level of technology was far in advance of what he would have expected at this period of Earth's history. But it was perfect for what he had in mind.

The Chronovores had sworn revenge and the Master knew that, short of never entering the time vortex again, he would always be at risk. And he had no intention of exiling himself on a single world in a single time. He had seen how po-faced and sanctimonious that had made the Doctor.

So there was only one alternative. The Chronovores would have to be wiped out, exterminated. All of them. For that, he would need to gather them all in a place where he had the advantage, and where he would have the power to destroy them.

And the showdown was going to be here, on Earth, in the region that the Chronovores called the Higher Place.

The Master continued to analyse the blueprints, looking for a way to make TITAN serve him. He needed it to reopen the channel, but that was only part of it. While the Chronovores were swarming in he would needed to extend the channel, further and further, straight into the heart of their precious Lux Aeterna. Then he would use a combination of his TARDIS and TITAN to generate a web of force fields: these would protect him from the Chronovores' wrath for the scant seconds required for him to take what he needed, but - just as importantly - it would cut them off from their food source.

The Lux Aeterna. The power of the Chronovores.

His very survival.

With the Lux Aeterna saturating every cell of his body, invigorating and renewing them, the Master would solve both of his problems in one fell swoop. The Chronovores, weakened by their isolation from their food source, would be no match for his newly augmented powers. And with the energies of the cosmos itself flooding through him, he would be free to commit the greatest act of genocide the universe had ever seen.

The absolute, total destruction of a race of Transcendental Beings. Even the Time Lords had never managed that!

And once the threat of the Chronovores was no more, he could luxuriate in the incandescence of the Lux Aeterna, renewing his body, finally casting off the cadavered remains of his Time Lord one. No longer would he be forced to rely on the dwindling sparks of the Source of Traken, to beg for scraps to continue his life; the Lux Aeterna would give him power and immortality. He would no longer be made of base matter - he would be the stuff of gods.

He truly would be the Master.

'You really cannot mean that, Paul.' The Doctor slammed his glass on to the bar and groaned. He, Paul, Arlene and Stuart had retired to the tutors' bar, an establishment on the sixth floor of the students' union which was reserved for PHDs and their friends, although friendly was not a word Stuart would have used to describe it at this time.

Paul and Arlene - and indeed Stuart himself - were actually in a celebratory mood, despite all that had happened. Even though it had taken the Master's intervention they had finally penetrated Calabi-Yau Space - the TITAN Array was fully operational!

But somehow the Doctor didn't share their jubilation.

'Doctor - it works!' Paul insisted. 'I designed TITAN to analyse the fundamental nature of matter, and that's what it's doing. Why can't you understand that?'

The Doctor thrust his face in Paul's. 'I understand that very well, Paul. Why can't you understand that you are threatening the entire galaxy? If the Chronovores -'

'The Chronovores?' Paul laughed in the Doctor's face. 'All I know about the Chronovores is what Stuart's told me and that *son et lumière* performance in the suite. For all I know, you and that madman could have been in cahoots!'

'Me? Me? Me!' The Doctor jumped to his feet. 'From what I've gathered, you'd be better off looking closer to home, Professor Kairos. Such as at your director of marketing, perhaps?'

'You can leave her to me,' said Arlene, a trace of relish in her voice. 'I owe her one.'

Stuart decided it was time to wade in before things got completely out of hand. 'Doctor, Paul, Arlene: listen to me. We're approaching this all the wrong way. The Doctor is right about the Chronovores - believe me. But I'm sure there must be a way to adjust TITAN to avoid them. Doctor?'

The Doctor scrunched his mouth up in concentration. Long seconds... and then he nodded. 'I'll give it a try. But if Paul disobeys my instructions...'

The threat of the Chronovores was one thing. But the threat of an angry Time Lord... Stuart shuddered. He put his hand on Paul's shoulder. 'I'll make sure Paul does just what you tell him, Doc.'

Mel reached the university library and handed over her card to the stern-faced librarian. Although, in real time, it was seventeen years since she had last been a student, she had taken the precaution of having the card updated the last time she had been there: the librarian didn't even give her a second glance.

As much as she longed to see Paul and Arlene again, she still didn't feel comfortable seeing the Doctor - especially with him looking so enthusiastic. Didn't he feel anything about what had happened? Anyway, he could go off and play his little games. She had work to do.

Sitting in one of the booths, she began her search. Something had happened to Anjeliqua - and Mel was determined to find out what it was. Although the library's systems were separate from those of the university itself, Mel felt sure it wouldn't be too difficult to go from one to the other: it wasn't as if she hadn't done it before, was it? Her nose wrinkling in concentration, she started to hack.

The Master had laid the blueprints on a circular table and was scribbling equations on a notepad when Anjeliqua returned.

'I've brought the blueprints you asked for...' Her voice trailed off when she saw copies of them on the table. The Master looked up at her and smiled that smile.

'As you can see, my dear, I was actually able to save some time by accessing them directly through my TARDIS. I apologise for your wasted effort. But it has given me a chance to think, to plan... And I believe I can see how we should proceed from this point. If you would give me a couple of seconds to complete these calculations?'

Anjeliqua had to admit that she was a bit put out, but in the scheme of things... well, if it gave her a chance to finally get her revenge on Paul it was all worth it. The end always justified the means.

The Master had returned to his calculations. 'E equals MC to the fourth power...' he muttered.

'Cubed.'

'What?'

'E equals MC cubed.' Anjeliqua might not have been the genius that Paul was, but she still remembered her temporal physics courses. E equals MC cubed in the time vortex.

'Not in the hexadimensional physics of Calabi-Yau Space, you ignorant...' He shook his head. 'Ms Whitefriar, please accept my apologies. The strain of these calculations is taking its toll. Indeed, I have to confess that this enterprise is proving to be a little beyond me. I require assistance.'

Anjeliqua wasn't used to people talking to her like that, but decided to let it pass. There was too much at stake. 'I'll do everything I can to help.'

The Master took her hand in his. 'As indeed you have. But I need someone whose talents are in a different field. I need a temporal physicist.'

'Paul?' How could he help them? The Master simply wasn't making any sense.

'Of course not. Nor that bumbling Stuart Hyde. But from what you've told me, Professor Cole would be perfectly suitable for my needs.'

'Arlene would never do anything to hurt Paul. They're getting married at Christmas.'

The Master nodded. 'Which is why she won't know. I have prepared a little surprise which will keep the Doctor and

Professors Hyde and Kairos preoccupied while we carry on unmolested, and for which I need your help, Anjeliqua. Listen carefully...' Anjeliqua looked into his eyes, his deep, timeless eyes...

And knew there was nothing she wouldn't do for her Master.

That was it! Mel glanced away from the LCD display and chewed her bottom lip. Thanks to the personnel files she had managed to access - as well as bank records and other assorted information that hadn't been hidden quite well enough - Anjeliqua Whitefriar's entire professional history was there for the asking: her degree - a third in computer science; her first job as PA to the director of business studies; her promotion to the newly created job of director of intellectual property marketing. Her first year, in which West London University became the most profitable university in the country - thanks to Anjeliqua. All of it perfectly reasonable.

She had obviously been ambitious, but a streak of social virtue ran through everything she did. Marketing of certain technologies refused, simply because she foresaw ecological problems; charitable funds and bursaries set up; an endless list of fund-raising dinners for the needy. Even if Anjeliqua hadn't been a saint, she was very close to being canonised.

And then things changed. Over a single weekend she stopped giving ten per cent of her salary to charity. She resigned from all her fund-raising positions - one the week before she was due to host a dinner where Prince William was the guest of honour. Three of her colleagues mysteriously resigned, amidst allegations of corruption that would appear to have been generated by Anjeliqua herself.

In short, it took precisely two days for Anjeliqua Whitefriar to become a complete and utter bitch.

And one week later, she stole the patent for the Whitefriar Lattice.

As Mel pondered this, another thought appeared on the horizon. One she really should have considered earlier. What had the Doctor said? That the Master was here?

Mel jumped to her feet. Anjeliqua's mysterious personality change, *and* the Master? That was too much of a coincidence. Time to do a little more spying.

Anjeliqua stood in the bathroom looking at herself in the mirror. Of course, since the bathroom lay inside a space-time machine, it was anything but ordinary: the mirror was holographic and the taps dispensed water at the exact rate and temperature the user required.

If only we could patent that, she thought. And then she looked back at her reflection. She knew the Master's word was law, but when she wasn't with him that feeling diminished to the point where she wondered what she was doing. So far, his aims and hers appeared to be running side by side. But there would come a time when they diverged.

And at that point, she was going to have to be ready for him. Sealing that thought in a very strong box in her mind, Anjeliqua returned to the console room.

'Ah, Ms Whitefriar. Feeling refreshed?'

'Perfectly,' she replied. 'What now?'

The Master smiled. 'Now we execute the next stage of my plan. I need you to inject a little humility into the proceedings.'

The Doctor followed Arlene, Paul and Stuart down the corridor, his mind still racing in an effort to understand what was going on. Advanced technology - perhaps too advanced. TITAN accessing the realm of the Chronovores. The Master's presence... He briefly thought about Mel, but instantly knew that he wasn't ready to deal with her yet. Just so long as she kept out of trouble...

He knew he really ought to forbid the professors using TITAN - he should probably dismantle the thing bit by bit to humour his Time Lord peers - but something told him that it was best to let matters take their course. Call it a hunch.

And his hunches were never wrong, were they? Snorting, he caught up with the others.

Mel tried Anjeliqua's office, but her PA explained that she wasn't going to be back. So where else would she be? Anjeliqua had never been one for lunch-time drinking, so the university bars were out of the question. But food was a different matter. Anjeliqua's personality might have changed, but Mel felt sure her appetite hadn't. Lunches tended to be sacrosanct to Anjeliqua.

She headed off to the grill bar. Anjeliqua had never been able to resist chips.

As Anjeliqua left his TARDIS, the Master returned to the blueprints. The device he had in mind - the converter from the lost race of the Kirbili and powered by his store of exotic particles - would have to be attached to the TITAN Array at the precise point where the balance of energies was correct. Too far one way, and nothing would get through; too far the other, and whoever was in the converter would be instantly incinerated.

I will definitely have to get my sums right for this, he thought wryly.

As Mel turned the corner, heading towards the grill bar - assuming it hadn't been moved in the last three years - she was aware that she felt nervous. Not only in case she bumped into the Doctor, although goodness knew how that was all going to resolve itself, but also because she was worried about seeing Anjeliqua again. Now that Mel knew she was involved with the Master, it put a whole new slant on things.

But it had to be done. The Doctor was obviously busy with some other part of the Master's devilish machinations, so it was up to her to do her bit.

Then she saw Anjeliqua. Coming out of a side door, not seeing her. And heading towards one of the research wings of the university.

Mel hurried to catch up, but as she passed the door from which Anjeliqua had emerged she had to do a double take. The door led to the basement! What was Anjeliqua doing in the basement?

Only one way to find out, Mel decided, opening the door. The stairwell was dark, but she had no intention of switching on the light and drawing attention to herself. Gingerly, she made her way down the metal staircase, peering into the gloom. Finally she reached the basement, which was lit by a single, slightly swaying light bulb. There was nothing there apart from a row of six cupboards, presumably for the cleaners.

So what on Earth had Anjeliqua been up to down here?

Moments later, Mel got her answer. One of the cupboards opened and a far too familiar figure emerged. The Master, in a tailored grey suit, checking an ornate watch on his wrist. Very dapper, and certainly up to no good. Mel knew from experience that tackling him directly was an extremely unwise course of action, so she sank into the shadows beneath the staircase and waited for him to depart.

Once she had heard the upstairs door shut she moved over to the cupboards. The Master had appeared from the third one; she tentatively touched the handle and turned it.

It was locked. For a moment, Mel uncharacteristically felt like swearing - she had optimistically hoped that it would be open. Then she remembered: her own TARDIS key. She had forgotten to - no, Mel, be honest, you had decided not to - hand it back. Removing the chain from around her neck, she looked for the lock. She had no idea whether the Doctor's key would open the Master's TARDIS, but she didn't really have many other options. Locating the lock, she inserted the key, turned it... and the door creaked open. Grinning, Mel entered.

Structurally, it was virtually the same as the Doctor's TARDIS: roundelled walls, high vaulted ceiling, central control console. But the atmosphere was very different. Everything was darkness and shadows rather than brilliance. Even the reassuring hum of the his TARDIS had been replaced by a sinister susurration. Mel gulped: the whole place was making her skin crawl. Taking a deep breath, she looked around, trying to see if there were any clues she could take back to the Doctor. Despite everything that had happened, she wasn't going to stand idly by while the Master cooked up another of his evil schemes - especially if it involved Anjeliqua.

Walking over to a nearby table, she examined the huge sheet of paper draped over it. Circuitry, system designs... blueprints of some sort: very advanced, but Mel wasn't exactly stupid. Within a couple of seconds she realised that she was looking at some kind of high-energy device. A device which involved the fundamental nature of space and time, if the wave equations were anything to go by. And she knew of at least one person at the university for whom this would be child's play.

Professor Paul Kairos.

A sudden noise from behind made her spin round. Lights were beginning to flash on the black console while levers and buttons began to move by themselves. At the same time, the great doors closed with a thump. With horrified recognition, Mel knew what to expect next. So she wasn't surprised when the time rotor lit up and began its rise and fall. The Master must have taken off by remote control!

She had no idea how long the flight would last or where she would end up, but she knew the console room was the most dangerous place to be. Looking around, she saw the door to the interior and ran over to it. If she could lose herself in the Master's TARDIS, perhaps there was a chance she would get out of there alive.

As she approached the TITAN suite, Anjeliqua could hear the arguing half-way down the corridor. Paul's voice was instantly recognisable, but the other... rich, fruity and very, very angry. She guessed it was the multicoloured stranger she had seen the last time she had been in the suite. The Master's nemesis, the Doctor.

She opened the door and saw that her guess was correct, although the man had taken off his hideous jacket to reveal a metallic, black-and-white striped waistcoat - not much of an improvement. Much of the master console was now a mass of unravelled Whitefriar Lattice and holographic memory crystals, haphazardly strewn across the floor.

'That simply won't work,' Paul shouted. 'Without the stator-rotor assembly, TITAN just can't generate the force vectors needed to push the wave envelope...' He stopped as he caught sight of Anjeliqua standing in the doorway.

'You!' he yelled. 'You've got some nerve coming back here.' He turned to Stuart. 'Call security. She's not getting away again.'

Anjeliqua stepped into the suite. 'Paul,' she said in her most placatory, pathetic tone of voice. 'Just listen to me for a minute. That's all I ask.'

Paul was obviously unconvinced, but Arlene came from behind Anjeliqua - had she been following her? - and stood next to Paul, taking his hand. 'Paul - give her the minute. What harm can she do?'

'Plenty,' he spat. 'Oh, I suppose you're right. Go on then, Anjeliqua,' he said coldly.

'I know what I did was wrong,' she continued in her best pleading tones. 'I fell under the spell of this Master - he hypnotised me in some way, got me to do things... terrible things.'

'So how did you get away from him?' It was the Doctor. 'Or is this another of the Master's little subterfuges?'

She shook her head. 'No... no... I managed to get away... my mind cleared. I've come here to warn you.'

'Warn us? Warn us about what?' asked the Doctor.

'He's trying to steal the TITAN Array.'

'What?' Paul started to laugh. 'What's he going to do? Walk in here and carry it out of the door? Don't be ridiculous Anjeliqua.'

The Doctor held up an admonishing hand. 'Don't be so hasty, Paul. The Master is almost as resourceful as I am, and I can see ways of doing it. Did he tell you any more about his plans, Ms Whitefriar?'

'His base is near Heathrow Airport - somewhere along the A4. His time machine is there, along with all the equipment he's going to use to steal TITAN.'

The Doctor put his arms around his pet professors. 'If you would excuse us a second, Ms Whitefriar, we have a couple of things we need to discuss. But I'd appreciate your staying here: there might be more you can help us with.'

Of course, Doctor. After that bravura performance, I'm not going anywhere until you take the bait.

'She's lying, of course,' said Paul once they were out of earshot on the far side of the suite, underneath the chrome struts of the Array.

'I have to admit, her story is pretty unlikely,' the Doctor agreed. 'The Master's "hypnosis" is far more than a parlour trick; it's a form of telepathy which isn't that easily broken. Then again, if she's a strong-willed person...'

'That's an understatement,' muttered Paul.

The Doctor glared at him. 'This is no time for personal vendettas - mine with the Master is going to be enough for all of us. Let's apply a little logic to the situation, shall we? Considering that the sum total of your intellects comes close to rivalling mine, I'm sure we can manage, mmm?'

Ignoring the looks the other three gave him, he continued. 'Assume that she's lying: then we'll be walking into a trap. Assume that she's telling the truth: then the Master is there. Assume that she's simply leading us off on a wild goose chase... well, we'll deal with that one later. Whichever way, there's a very good chance that we'll learn more about his plans.'

'Suicide,' muttered Stuart. 'Pure stupidity.'

'I'll stay here,' said Arlene.

'Arlene?' said Paul.

'Look - someone's got to keep an eye on both TITAN and that witch over there, and I can't trust either of you two', she indicated Stuart and Paul, 'to refrain from strangling her. God knows, I'm going to find it difficult enough.'

The Doctor nodded. 'I agree. Arlene - find out if she knows more about the precise location of this secret base; Stuart - phone for a taxi.'

'A taxi? What about your TARDIS?'

'Oh no!' The Doctor waved his hands. 'Assuming it is a trap, the last thing I want to do is go blundering in there with the TARDIS. That could be exactly what the Master expects. Then again, there is something I need from the TARDIS - I'll meet you outside reception in ten minutes. And Paul - there is something you can do for me.'

Mel had achieved her objective: she was well and truly lost. Unlike the erratic logic of the Doctor's corridors, there was no comforting sense of direction here. The Master's TARDIS was a twisted labyrinth of black tunnels and dark satanic hallways, full of the constant whispering that pervaded every corridor and room.

Currently, she was standing in the middle of what appeared to be his TARDIS library. But it was a library of the evil and the arcane, where the godless *Necronomicon* was sandwiched between those terrible works *Liber Inducens in Evangelium Aeternum* and *The Black Scrolls of Rassilon*. Where the infamous *Book of Vile* and its Black Appendix sat next to *The Ambuehl Lores* and the wretched *Insidium of Astrolabus* - all considered to be the most malevolent books in the galaxy. And that was a piece of knowledge Mel would really rather not have known.

The airy openness of the Doctor's library had been replaced by low dark ceilings, heavy, musty drapes and dim gas lamps - it reminded Mel of the Library of Saint John the Beheaded in London, which was where, in an altered reality, she had learnt about the books. And, to be honest, the memory of that particular incident made her feel ill. Almost as ill as the Master's library did.

Every inch of his TARDIS was the absolute antithesis of the Doctor's, and went a long way to explaining their centuries-long vendetta. Opposites: dark and light, good and evil... but was it really that simple? Especially considering Maradnias.

A slight shudder that Mel felt in her stomach - just what I need! - told her they had landed. But, however disturbing she found it, she knew that the library was the safest place to be.

She just hoped that the Doctor, Paul and Arlene were OK.

'All set then?' The Doctor stood on the steps of the university holding a bizarre contraption that looked vaguely phallic. Flat, but phallic. The Doctor obviously saw Stuart's gaze.

'Oh this?' He waved the cream-and-silver device in front of him, showing off the extremely retro dials in the... lower area. 'This, Professor Hyde, is what Jo called a "TARDIS sniffer-outer". It's a time sensor that can measure temporal disturbances down to six decimal places on the Bocca scale, and was clever enough to allow me to locate TOMTIT thirty years ago.'

'Couldn't your TARDIS detect where the Master's TARDIS is?' asked Paul. 'It is supposed to be a time machine.'

'It is a time machine,' the Doctor said pointedly. 'However, the Master's TARDIS bears about as much resemblance to the standard Type 40 as mine does. He's probably got it shielded with all sorts of shenanigans, and I can't really be bothered to spend a regeneration recalibrating the systems. And anyway, there's no point looking for temporal disturbances from here, what with TITAN spewing out so much low-level time spillage. This can detect time disturbances on the fly.' He looked at Paul. 'By the way... you really ought to do something about your shielding - it's beginning to register on the Bocca scale!'

Stuart stepped forward. 'Once the Master is defeated we can rework TITAN and make it environmentally friendly. But we've still got to stop him. Come on Doc, the taxi's here!'

Arlene was sitting in Anjeliqua's office, idly reading an article about Gigabit Ethernet in an old copy of *NETWORK Solutions*. How wonderfully old-fashioned it all seemed. And how terribly unfair that gigabit speeds had been replaced by the virtually infinite bandwidths offered by the Whitefriar Lattice. The technology that Anjeliqua had stolen off Paul.

Paul never talked about it, but Arlene knew him well enough to know that it had hurt him deeply. He had found it hard to believe that someone he had once considered one of his closest friends had turned on him so viciously. It wasn't the money - it was his place in history that she had stolen. He had immediately immersed himself in the TITAN Array, hoping this would enable him to retake his place. And he was always civil to Anjeliqua - indeed, his outburst in the TITAN suite had been quite uncharacteristic.

Unlike Arlene. She didn't like Anjeliqua, she couldn't trust Anjeliqua, but Anjeliqua did appear to be their only lead. It was just a pity that the woman was such a complete bitch. What she had done to Paul was so... so evil that it would be a cold day in Hell before Arlene came even close to forgiving her.

'Oh, Arlene,' said Anjeliqua from behind her desk, in a

nonchalant tone for a prisoner. 'I've got an appointment now. Would you mind?'

Arlene shook her head. 'Anjeliqua, I wouldn't trust you as far as I could throw a neutron star. Either you cancel the appointment or you allow me to sit in on it. It's up to you.'

Anjeliqua's smile was pure poison. 'You're more than welcome to sit in, dear. It could to be to your advantage.'

The door opened, and a smartly dressed man with a goatee beard and slicked-back hair walked in. He went over to Anjeliqua and kissed her hand.

'I gather that this is the fragrant and delightful Professor Arlene Cole, my dear?'

Anjeliqua nodded.

'Excellent.'

Arlene suddenly felt very, very scared. This just had to be the Master, and she was trapped in a room with him. And then she realised – she'd willingly walked into a trap! If the Master was here, what were Paul, Stuart and the Doctor getting themselves into?

She was still wondering this as her mind fell into the Master's – at which point nothing much mattered any more.

The Doctor was sitting in the front seat of the taxi, his device on his lap. Stuart listened as it made the odd bleep while they headed down through Osterley, past Heston and down towards the A4 which bordered Heathrow Airport on the southern side. As they reached the A4 the bleeping grew more and more insistent, much to the fascination of the car driver.

Finally, just as they sped past Hatton Cross tube station, the bleep became a rising whine.

'Stop here!' shouted the Doctor. The driver immediately pulled over to the side of the road.

As they disembarked, the Doctor waved his 'sniffer-outer' around like a Geiger counter – which it basically was, thought Stuart. Time instead of radiation. A spinning ring on a stick had somehow popped up at the end.

'The signal's just over that bank.'

'I still think this is all a bit fishy, Doc,' said Stuart.

'Of course it is,' the Doctor sighed. 'It's a trap, isn't it?'

The Master sat behind Anjeliqua's desk, his two companions staring blankly into space, their minds wandering off at his instructions. Perfect.

The Doctor and those other two troublesome scientists were about to walk into a very entertaining trap, while he was about to build the device that would give him godhood. He double-checked his equations - all present and correct - and then turned his attention to the two women. Utterly obedient, utterly malleable... and totally his.

'Your first task, Professor Cole, will be to reassemble the TITAN Array, before assisting Ms Whitefriar with the converter. Hopefully, the Doctor's half-baked meddling with TITAN can be rectified fairly easily.'

Arlene nodded calmly. Then her personality appeared to return. 'Right, I'll head off to the TITAN Array.' She even started singing as she left the office.

He relit his cigar before sinking back into the soft black leather of the chair. The Master didn't like to lose. And with this much at stake, he'd be damned if he was going to.

Chapter Four
Faster than the Speed of Night

'Oh, how terrifying. A warehouse,' said Paul drolly as they clambered up the grass bank. 'Not exactly a supervillain's hide-out, is it?' The building was big and grey and featureless, with ridged walls and a ridged roof. And with nothing to distinguish it from any of the other warehouses dotted around it. 'I was expecting an extinct volcano at the very least.'

'The Master has been known to base himself in the most unlikely locations, Paul. Don't let his current lack of melodrama mislead you - this place is very probably booby-trapped to the nines.'

'How can we tell, Doc?' asked Stuart, still wheezing from the exertion of climbing up the grassy hillock.

The Doctor held up his sniffer-outer. 'According to this, the warehouse is alive with temporal energies. Not exactly what you would expect from an empty warehouse next to Heathrow Airport, eh?'

'Depends on what they were shipping,' muttered Paul. 'So, what are we going to do? Knock at the front door?'

The Doctor grinned. 'Why not? The direct approach often works - especially when you're walking into a trap.' He strode over to the main gates of the warehouse and threw his arms out wide, trying to locate a CCTV camera.

'I want to announce my presence!'

'Exquisite, my dear, quite exquisite.' The Master was inspecting Angeliqua's handiwork: the transference frame itself was nearly complete - a man-sized construction of titanium-iridium wire - while the programming adjustments to TITAN were taking shape under the excellent management of Arlene. Of course, he could have built the whole lot himself, but that would have denied him part of the fun: stealing people from the game and using them against their own friends... That was what life was all about.

Turning his back on the two women as they toiled away in the corner of Anjeliqua's office, he checked his watch - although 'watch' was rather a misnomer for the full functionality of the wrist unit. Quite apart from the time, it told him exactly what was going on. The Doctor's delightful companion, the energetic Miss Bush, was ensconced in his TARDIS library - did she really think she could have entered his TARDIS with the Doctor's key without his knowledge? - while the Doctor, Hyde and Kairos were arrogantly walking into his trap. Excellent. In a matter of hours, he would finally have won.

He would be a god.

'It's empty,' said Paul. 'Apart from that thing at the end.'

'That thing at the end, as you put it, is a TARDIS,' said the Doctor, examining his tracer. Then he looked up. 'The sheer arrogance of the man.' At the far end of the warehouse stood a stout blue Metropolitan police box, of the type that used to be on the streets when Stuart was young. It was also the shape assumed by something else. Stuart leant over to the Doctor.

'Is it yours?'

'Good grief, no: it's the Master's,' said the Doctor with a trace of disgust. He held up the sniffer-outer and showed Stuart the readings - whatever they meant. 'Mine hasn't got all of these fancy time traces - the Master's obviously been fiddling again. But it's obviously the prize in his pathetic little trap.' He peered at his device again and frowned. 'Now that's odd.'

'It had better be the prize,' said Paul. 'There's bugger-all else.'

Stuart had to admit that his young protégé was right. Apart from some discarded general office bric-a-brac, the warehouse had apparently housed nothing more sinister than cement - given the few forgotten Blue Circle bags - and was simply a vast empty space, with streams of dusty light pouring in through the high windows. But he suddenly realised that there was something not quite right about that light. It seemed to shimmer, the whorls of dust slowing down and speeding up in pulsing patterns - it just didn't look natural. Stuart stepped forward to get a closer look.

At that moment his body convulsed in pain and he doubled up in agony. Was he having a heart attack? God knew, he deserved it, after three decades of abusing his body. But no, it was much worse than that. He knew with a hideous certainty that he was feeling an agony he hadn't experienced for over thirty years. Not a physical illness at all: his entire life was being torn apart, bit by bit, second by second, moment by moment. He sank to the concrete floor, screaming soundlessly, his hands clutching at the empty air.

What was happening to him? He could hear the Doctor's voice, distant and distorted, but he couldn't answer...

As if through glass: 'Stop!' bellowed the Doctor. 'Don't move - either of you.' Not that Stuart could.

He felt the Doctor reach out and grab his arm, pulling him out. Stuart stumbled before he regained his footing. The pain had gone, but it had been replaced by something else. Something good. He felt... different.

'What happened?' Even his voice sounded strange to him, as if he hadn't heard it in years. He was aware that both Paul and the Doctor were looking at him oddly.

The Doctor was rubbing the arm he had reached out to Stuart with. But there was something wrong. He looked clearer, sharper, than he had done before.

His face coloured by discomfort, the Doctor waved the sniffer-outer in their faces - but Stuart couldn't help noticing that Paul was still staring at him. The Doctor continued. 'I've worked out what the Master's up to. This entire place is rigged as a trap.' He scanned the warehouse with the sniffer-outer. 'It's split into dozens of irregular zones, each one running at a different time.'

He went to put his arm around Stuart, but stopped and started to rub it again. 'Even thirty years makes a difference to a Time Lord,' he muttered.

'What do you mean?' asked Stuart, a strange suspicion beginning to grow in his mind.

The Doctor took a step back, and pulled something out of his pocket. 'When we last met, Kronos stole sixty-odd years of your life. Thankfully, you got them back. This time, the Master has given you back at least thirty. The dark gift of the Time Lords.' He held the mirror to Stuart's face.

It was the face of a young man.

'I don't understand...' Stuart muttered.

The Doctor waved his hand around the warehouse. 'The moment the door to the warehouse was closed, the Master's TARDIS generated a jigsaw of temporal boundaries. Within the regions created by those boundaries, the flow of time differs from the norm. In some, it is frozen. In others, it is running hundreds, thousands of times faster. And in others still it is running backwards. You, Stuart, had the good fortune to stumble into one of the regions in which it was running backwards, as well as the good fortune for me to pull you out of there before you unaged back to an embryo.'

Stuart shook his head. 'You mean I'm twenty-five again?'

'At a rough guess, yes.'

'Will it last?' Although the idea that he was physically thirty years younger - but still with the maturity of his fifty-five-year-old mind - was almost intoxicating, Stuart didn't want to feel complacent. What if it was all taken away from him again?

The Doctor shrugged. 'I'm sorry, Stuart - I just don't know.'

Stuart sighed. Whatever happens, I'm going to make the most of this, he decided.

'I presume that the only way we can get out is to reach that police box?' asked Paul.

'According to the readings, the Master's TARDIS has set up a temporal standing wave. There's nothing I can do with this -' the Doctor held up the sniffer-outer, 'to disrupt it.'

'Doctor - you managed to reach into one of the regions and rescue Stuart. Can't you make a run for the Master's TARDIS? You are a Time Lord,' said Paul.

The Doctor shook his head. 'Yes... and unfortunately no. We Time Lords live incredibly long lives, but we are still subject to the laws of time. We are usually immune to the collateral effects of temporal distortion - I had no problem getting through the field that TOMTIT set up when the Master operated it - but this is different. My arm was affected by the region - it's currently about thirty years younger than the rest of my body and it's playing merry hell with my physiognomy. If I tried to run through all of these zones, the temporal stresses would almost certainly trigger a regeneration at best.'

'And at worst?' said Stuart.

'At worst, it would tear me to pieces and destroy me.'

Stuart started speaking before he even knew what he was going to say. 'Doctor - I've been given an extra thirty years. I don't mind giving it up to get us out of here.'

The Doctor shook his head. 'Even if I were willing for you to sacrifice your new-found youth, there's still the problem of the temporal stresses. You'd stand even less of a chance than I would.'

'Then we are stuck,' said Stuart dejectedly. 'Stuck in a cement warehouse while the Master is up to God knows what.'

'Maybe not.' The Doctor reached into his pocket and retrieved an extremely small screwdriver. He started to unscrew the back of the sniffer-outer. 'Possibly a few adjustments to the microhelmic circuits...' An alarming whine began to issue from the device. Stuart could see the needles on the twin dials spinning round at an incredible rate, virtually a blur, while the little LED flashed hysterically. The whine was now almost ultrasonic - and to Stuart's younger hearing, very painful.

The Doctor held the sniffer-outer away from him for a second before hefting it in his hand and throwing it as far from him as he could, an arc of stops, starts and reverses as it passed through the time zones.

It exploded in the air about three metres away, the flame, smoke and debris moving apart at different speeds as they entered different time zones. Even the sound reached them at different times, a distorted scream that echoed back and forth throughout the cavernous warehouse.

The Doctor, Paul and Stuart watched as the burnt fragments of the sniffer-outer dropped irregularly to the concrete floor.

'Oh well,' the Doctor said sadly. 'I suppose we're stuck in a cement warehouse while the Master is up to God knows what.'

Unhindered by security - as far as they were concerned, they saw a venerable old professor on his after-lunch constitutional - the

Master strolled through the corridors of the university, only stopping to allow the odd gaggle of students to pass by. The pursuit of knowledge, indeed.

He compared their undisciplined behaviour, their raucous laughter and outlandish clothing, with the peace and ordered calm of the Academy on Gallifrey, where he and the others of the Deca had debated the profound wisdoms, questioned the Ancient Covenants and extended their belief systems. The ten of them had believed they could change the universe... And in many ways, they had.

But with the power of the Lux Aeterna, the Master wouldn't simply be able to change the universe; he would *be* the universe. What would the others of the Deca say? The Rani, with her biochemical experiments; Mortimus, crossing and double-crossing the CIA; Drax, with his infernal tinkering; and the Doctor himself... They and the surviving others would have to acknowledge him as their Master.

He touched Arlene's proximity card to the sensor and pushed open the double doors into the chrome and marble of the TITAN suite. He would never admit it openly, but he admired humanity. However many times it was overpowered, beaten, brought to within an inch of extinction, it always found some way to fight back. Its wonderful inventiveness and ingenuity always triumphed.

TITAN was a magnificent piece of temporal engineering - indeed, the Master doubted that he could have done better. Paul Kairos had taken the original TOMTIT concept and brought it to the next level: a level that would give the Master what he wanted.

As he approached the chrome console - as good as new following Arlene's repair work - he decided that it was time to check up on a few of his other projects. He tapped a button on his wrist unit and waited a few seconds until a small holosphere bled into focus next to him, resolving into a three-dimensional image of the warehouse. After a brief glimpse at the Doctor, Hyde and Kairos pinned down in his temporal trap - what had happened to Hyde? - he turned his attention to his little harem.

Excellent. Professor Cole and Ms Whitefriar, clearing his path to godhood. He watched them building and programming for a moment, reassuring himself that they were carrying out his orders, before returning to his first order of business.

TITAN.

The holosphere, now bobbing just above the chrome surface of the console, continued to run as the Master began to interrogate the quantum computer. His experience of quantum computing was sadly limited: the Lurlak incident had given him a good grounding, but he had to admit that he lacked Paul Kairos' expertise. Upgrading the software had been a mechanical process, but anything else was outside his experience.

His knowledge of mathematics and theoretical physics was second to none, but at the quantum level all the old rules and regulations simply didn't apply - and to the Master that simply wasn't right, whatever the Academy might have taught him. And there was more than that, another reason why he needed the humans.

To calculate the correct penetration envelope, one which would breach the sanctity of the Lux Aeterna, wasn't just a matter of bits and bytes, but a matter of faith... Another example of human ingenuity alien to the Time Lords.

His fingers darting across the keyboard, the Master began to run the definition series that would culminate in the final program: the key to the Lux Aeterna. As he entered the increasingly complex functions he concentrated on the end result, allowing the image of the wave envelope to actually generate the parameters of the envelope. Cause and effect reversed, thanks to the insane physics of Calabi-Yau Space. Catastrophe theory mingled with Shrödinger's wave equation, Rassilon's eighth precept crossed swords with Heisenberg's Uncertainty Principle... Disparate branches of physics combining to create the key to the Master's apotheosis.

Something tugged at his subconscious. Even though breaking off the defining sequences now would mean he would have to start all over again, his instincts told him to stop. He looked at the holosphere... and immediately realised why. Anjeliqua was whispering to Arlene.

'There's something I just can't put my finger on,' her image was saying. 'Everything he's told me sounds convincing, but I'm just not sure...'

Oh, my dear Anjeliqua, you have been naïve. Did she really think she could double-cross the master of the *double jeu*? Did she? Filing the event away for future reference, he started the defining sequence, all over again.

'You are kidding?' Paul watched with concerned amusement as the Doctor and Stuart carefully carried moth-eaten chairs, a hat stand, and assorted pieces of bric-a-brac from the edges of their temporal zone. He was also aware that the Doctor had been gingerly reaching into the neighbouring zones, and had winced in sympathy as he had suffered the pain of being in two time zones at the same time. How much pain could a Time Lord take?

'Not at all, Paul,' said the Doctor breathlessly. 'There is a method to all this madness.' He started to pile one chair on top of another. The hat stand toppled over. 'Trust me,' he added wryly.

'Doc... is this what I think it is?' asked Stuart as he hefted the hat stand back into position. Paul still found it difficult to reconcile the grouchy old professor who had taught him the finer points of temporal physics with the person who now appeared younger than he did. Temporal theory was one thing, but temporal practice was quite another.

The Doctor was placing another chair on top of the hat stand. Amazingly, it appeared to balance. 'That depends on what you think it is, Stuart.'

'It's just a load of junk,' said Paul. 'What's it meant to be?'

'It's not meant to be anything,' began the Doctor.

'It just is,' said Stuart.

The Doctor broke into a broad grin. 'You remember!' He turned to Paul. 'You're a temporal physicist. You must understand the fundamental relationship between different molecular bonds and shapes?'

Paul nodded. Of course! 'Then you're saying that this is a time-flow analogue?'

'Exactly. The Master and I used to build these at school to

disrupt one another's time experiments. Let's see whether I've still got the knack.'

The assemblage of junk was complete. Three upside-down swivel chairs in a triangle; a hat stand balanced at the centre; another chair delicately sitting on top of the hat stand. It wouldn't have looked out of place at the Tate Modern.

'Here we go!' The Doctor span the top chair round, as if he were spinning plates.

The chair fell off.

'Astounding, Doctor. Quite astounding.' Paul shook his head. 'I take it that wasn't the point of this little exercise?'

'Hmm.' The Doctor picked up the chair and placed it back on top of the pile. 'There's something missing.'

'Tea?' asked Stuart. Paul raised an eyebrow. 'It was the missing ingredient when the Doctor last made something like this.'

'You're right, there is something missing!' exclaimed the Doctor. 'But not tea... this is the heavyweight version. It needs something a little stronger...' The Doctor frowned. 'An organic bond, perhaps. The valences might generate the right torsion in the matrix, complete the crystalline structure of ratios. C_2H_60 might suffice...'

'Alcohol?' Stuart grinned. 'I might be able to help out there.' He reached into his pocket and brought out the silver hip flask that he took with him everywhere. Paul remembered when Ruth had given it to him for his fiftieth birthday. 'A drop of single malt, Doc?'

'That will do nicely.' The Doctor took the flask and emptied the contents all over the assembly. Paul caught the pained expression on Stuart's face.

'Let's have another go, shall we?' The Doctor span the top chair around.

This time, it didn't fall off. Instead, a burbling tone issued from the pile of rubbish. Simultaneously, the hat stand started to glow, pulsing in time with the burbling.

'I know this is a stupid question, but what's it doing?' asked Paul.

The Doctor smiled. 'It's creating a still point, Paul. A point where time and space don't exist. And if you create one within the field of a temporal device, such as TOMTIT, or even a TARDIS, it should disrupt that field... Ah. This might be it.'

The burbling had reached a higher pitch. At the same time, the hat stand was positively fluorescing. But Paul could feel its power reaching out, flooding the warehouse...

'Paul - grab that sack of cement and hurl the contents into the centre of the warehouse,' yelled the Doctor.

'Why?'

'Just do it!'

Paul obliged, ripping open the top of the nearest Blue Circle bag and throwing the contents up into the air. He watched as the cement dust scattered and settled. In some of the time zones, it danced a slow minuet; in others it hurled itself around in a wild frenzy. But along a single, thin corridor, from the zone the Doctor, Stuart and Paul were trapped in straight through to the mocking blue double-cube of the Master's TARDIS, it fell normally.

'That's it!' The Doctor grabbed Stuart and Paul and propelled them down the newly formed corridor. 'Quickly - the time-flow analogue isn't going to last for ever!'

Paul could feel the pressure on them. Surrounding the corridor, time was going backwards and forwards, ebbing and flowing, waxing and waning. It was unnatural, and he felt physically sick. But he carried on running.

'The corridor is collapsing. Run!'

Paul sensed the imminence of the collapse - past, present and future hurtling towards him. He ran faster, Stuart and the Doctor in front of him. Behind him, the time zones closed in, whispering to him, beckoning him... what did it mean?

The Doctor and Stuart reached the Master's TARDIS as the corridor collapsed.

Paul wasn't so lucky.

He felt the waves of time engulf him. The Doctor was reaching out for him, but the time vortex was summoning him, welcoming him home...

The Doctor's hand grasped his wrist and pulled him out of it. Paul stood in front of the police box, panting. And aware of a tremendous sense of loss.

'We've done it!' shouted Stuart. 'We've done it, we've done it, we've done it!'

'Simmer down, Stu,' said the Doctor. 'You must learn to control your new-found youth, to govern your passions. We still aren't in the clear. Let's see whether this works.'

He took a key from his waistcoat pocket and inserted it into the lock of the police box.

The effect was immediate. The police box began to wheeze and groan, an elephantine roar that echoed around the warehouse, as its substance faded away. At the same time, the remaining cement dust showed that the time zones were vanishing, dissolving... As the Master's TARDIS dematerialised, the warehouse returned to normal.

Whatever that was.

The Doctor shrugged. 'Time to phone a taxi?'

Paul nodded, but all he could think about was the feeling he had had when the temporal disturbance had engulfed him. A feeling of going home.

Mel felt the dematerialisation in her bones. Where were they off to now? With a sinking feeling, she realised that she couldn't stay in the Master's library indefinitely: she had to put herself in a position where she could escape and warn the Doctor. Assuming that the Master hadn't already embroiled the Doctor in one of his Machiavellian schemes.

She carefully opened the heavy wooden door and crept into the dim twilight of the corridor. She had to find an alternative exit from the Master's TARDIS - there was no way that she was going to confront him in his own console room. One TARDIS couldn't be that different from another, could it? So there had to be alternative exits from the Master's TARDIS. She just had to find them.

Surely it couldn't be that difficult. *I mean, there are only an infinite number of rooms to choose from.*

The Master smiled as his TARDIS reappeared in the TITAN suite, its chameleon circuit disguising it as a mirror image of the Deutsch 3270 quantum computer on the far side of the room.

Its return meant that the Doctor and his associates had either perished in the trap - sadly unlikely: if three so-called experts on temporal theory couldn't rustle up a time-flow analogue they didn't deserve the name - or they had escaped, and were on their way back. Unfortunately, with his TARDIS now here, he had no way of checking up on them. That gave the Master about fifteen minutes to complete the final adjustments to the TITAN Array and make good his escape.

He heard the doors swing open behind him, and was pleased to see Anjeliqua and Arlene dragging the device into the suite. The man-sized framework of chrome wiring and Whitefriar Lattice was the key to the next stage of his plan. It was the means by which he would draw the power of the Lux Aeterna into himself.

'Take it into the TARDIS and wait for me there,' he ordered, touching his wrist unit to open the doors. As the women carried out his orders the Master made the final adjustments to TITAN, ordering it to disconnect from both the university power supply and the processing power of the Grid. He wouldn't need either of them where he was going.

'Don't move!'

The Master slowly turned from the console, his hands raised in surrender. The Doctor, Hyde and Kairos were standing in the doorway. The Doctor was pointing something at him. No - at the console. A gun of some sort.

'I wasn't expecting you so soon, gentlemen,' said the Master. 'No traffic on the A4?'

Mel reassessed her logic. She knew that there was an exit through the power room. She also knew that the deeper within the TARDIS you went - and she was still assuming that the Master's was basically the same as the Doctor's - the deeper it felt, the indescribable pressure weighing down on her that she was currently experiencing. And the deepest that she had ever been in the Doctor's TARDIS had been the dynamorphic generators when they were trying to correct the damage caused by the rogue Bandrils.

And the dynamorphic generators were right next to the power room.

Pleased that her logic was holding together, Mel continued her progress deeper into the Master's TARDIS.

'Oh, my dear Doctor, do you really mean to use that? Guns were never your style. Unlike me!' Gunslinger fast, the Master's tissue-compression eliminator was in his hand and aimed squarely at Stuart Hyde. 'It would be a pity if your new-found youth were to be wasted so soon, Professor Hyde.'

'It isn't a gun, Master.' The Doctor's aim didn't waver. 'It's the quantum cache from the master console. Without it, TITAN simply won't work. So it's actually a bit more than a weapon.'

The Master looked more carefully. On closer inspection, the object looked less like a weapon and more like a component: Whitefriar Lattice here, holographic storage there... And stealing vital components from each other was an important part of the Doctor and the Master's ongoing game. The Master had a feeling that the Doctor wasn't bluffing.

'Hand it over, or Professor Hyde will have the shortest rebirth in history. Literally!'

'Drop the TCE, Master, or I'll crush the cache.'

'Do you really think I wouldn't be able to duplicate that primitive technology? I'm a Time Lord!'

The Doctor grinned. 'I don't think you have any alternative. If you're willing to go to all this trouble to attack the Chronovores, that suggests desperation. What happened? Did they pay you a night-time visit? Threatening death and destruction?'

'I am the Master - nothing frightens me.'

'Ooh. Big words. But I happen to know that quantum computing isn't your strong suit. And I'm gambling that you just don't have the time to spare.

'Am I right?'

The Master glared at him.

It felt like she was at the bottom of the deep end of the pool. An unyielding pressure that made her sluggish, confused... Mel stopped and tried to centre herself. The corridor was almost totally pitch-black, but she could still make out a huge metal door, about five metres high. It was embossed with the swirling pattern that the Doctor had once referred to as the Omniscate - the seal of the Time Lords.

Exactly the same as the door to the dynamorphic generators in the Doctor's TARDIS.

She pushed the centre of the door. Slowly, agonisingly, it creaked open.

The Master realised that the Doctor was in danger of gaining the upper hand. It was time to even the score, and the Master always had an extra card up his sleeve. In this case, literally. 'Perhaps this will make you see reason?' Tapping his wrist unit, he indicated his TARDIS. A second later, Arlene came out. Her face was blank.

'As you can see, she is completely in my thrall.' Another tap. 'Completely.'

The Master relished the horrified looks on the faces of the other three as Arlene reached up and placed her hands around her neck.

'As you know, there is a reflex in humans which prevents them from strangling themselves. My control systems ensure that such reflexes can be overridden. Give me the cache and I will let her live. Continue this standoff and I will allow you to watch her kill herself.'

'You bastard!' Paul went to move forward, but the Doctor restrained him.

'Don't do anything that might endanger Arlene.' His head slumped. 'Here.' He held out the quantum cache, unwilling to meet the Master's eyes. 'You really are a devil.'

'A compliment, coming from you.' The Master grasped the cache.

'Let Arlene go!' shouted Paul.

The Master smiled. 'Ah, now that would be both foolish and detrimental to my plans, Professor Kairos. I will release Arlene at a time and a place of my choosing.' He tapped his wrist unit; Arlene's hands dropped from her throat as she returned to the Master's TARDIS.

'Doctor?' It was Stuart Hyde.

The Doctor's face was bleak as he replied. 'Endgame, I'm afraid.'

Defeated. Yet the Master could have sworn that there was a trace of defiance in his voice. What did the Doctor have up his sleeve?

The room that housed the dynamorphic generators - if you could call something like this a room - was identical to the one in the Doctor's TARDIS: at least a mile high, and stretching off into the distance in all directions. It was a room without walls. Even the door through which Mel had entered was nothing more than a freestanding square of gunmetal grey.

But it was far from empty. Every few yards, a thick pillar of emerald crystal reached upwards from the stone floor, its interior flickering with tiny stars of golden light that flowed upwards towards the distant ceiling, vanishing in the dark thunderhead clouds that hung far above. Trachoid time crystals, the Doctor had called them. All of them. Millions of them. And every few seconds, a storm would erupt amidst the dark clouds, its thunder booming through the room, lightning glittering off the pillars.

In many ways this was the heart of the TARDIS. If the power room was the circulatory system, if the mysterious telepathic computer was the brain, the dynamorphic generators were the heart. From what the Doctor had told her, the generators took the primal energies that gave the Time Lords their power, energies that were both beamed from the original Eye of Harmony on Gallifrey and generated by the perfect copy of the Eye that lay at the heart of each and every TARDIS - although the Doctor had always been reticent about showing it to her - and converted it into the titanic energies necessary to propel the TARDIS through time and space and maintain the machine's dimensionally transcendental interior.

She couldn't help but look up, feeling dwarfed by the huge pillars that were channelling more energy than she could comprehend. It was at times like this that she remembered the Doctor wasn't just her mentor, he wasn't just an intergalactic schoolboy... he was a member of an alien race that had solved problems humanity wouldn't even encounter for thousands, millions, of years.

Another thunderclap from above reminded her that she had a mission: to find the door into the power room. To find a way out.

Mel started looking.

With his TCE still trained on the Doctor and that brace of professors, the Master backed into his TARDIS.

'What are you planning to do?' asked Paul.

'Professor Kairos, I'm going to put your invention to good use.'

'Deadly use, more like,' muttered Stuart. 'After what you did with TOMTIT...'

The Master raised an eyebrow. 'Professor Hyde, you know me too well.'

'What about Arlene?' said Paul quietly.

It was obvious that all the fight had been taken out of him. Which was good: with his staggering intellect, he was possibly the most dangerous of them all. 'Your partner will be returned to you. On that, you have my word.'

'Your word?' hissed the Doctor. 'For what that's worth.'

Still the overconfidence. It made the Master uneasy. 'That's all you have, Doctor: you should learn to live with it. Now, goodbye, Doctor!' He walked backwards into his TARDIS, the doors closing a second later.

Mel was puzzled. According to her photographic memory, the door to the power room should have been in front of her.

It wasn't.

A creeping realisation came over her. What if the Master's TARDIS really was that different to the Doctor's? What if there wasn't a way out through the dynamorphic generators? Swallowing down her panic, Mel continued her search through the emerald forest.

The moment the doors of the Master's TARDIS closed, the Doctor turned to Stuart and Paul. It was going according to plan! He beckoned them closer.

'We haven't got much time,' he whispered. 'Paul - set up the resonance wave I told you about. TITAN can still do that without the quantum cache.'

'But not without power. Or the Grid!' Paul pointed to the chrome console, obviously reading the displays. 'He's disconnected both of them.'

'Oh.' For a moment, the Doctor frowned in concentration. Then he saw the solution - it was obvious!

'Not a problem, Professor Kairos. Use the ordinary power supply for your calculations. I can broadcast both the processing power and the energy that you need from the TARDIS.'

'Is that going to work?' asked Paul.

'Just do it, man! I have to reach my TARDIS!' With that, the Doctor ran out of the door. The Master was just about to discover that he didn't hold quite all of the cards.

Arlene and Anjeliqua were standing obediently by the transference device, their faces blank - the limbo atrophier had proved to be a most versatile addition to the Master's armoury. That left him able to concentrate his efforts on the console as he prepared to dematerialise. And it was an effort. He was holding this body together with the last of his willpower, and he wasn't sure how much longer he could do it. But he refused to return to that rotted, ephemeral form. And this would solve all of his problems.

He returned his attention to the console. This wasn't a normal dematerialisation: the Master was taking considerable excess baggage with him - not so much the weight, but the dimensional resonances inherent within that baggage. He manipulated the controls on the console as if it were a battlefield, setting his armies against the armies of the time vortex, fighting for the parameters that would extend the time field beyond the confines of his TARDIS. Satisfied that his configurations were correct, he slammed his hand on the vortex primer. With a concussive boom, the titanic engines cut into life, his time rotor banishing the shadows with its luminescence as it began its rise and fall.

It stopped.

With a distorted, stuttering roar, the time rotor ground to a halt, the glass column half in and half out of the console, its interior flickering erratically. The regular susurration of the console room became an accusatory hiss.

His TARDIS had stalled!

Snorting in anger, the Master checked the readings on the console. According to them his TARDIS was being assaulted on two fronts. Firstly, the TITAN Array was generating a temporal disruption field: he glanced up at the scanner and saw Paul Kairos hunched over his own console: no doubt he was running interference and making the time vortex as turbulent as a hurricane. Under normal circumstances, that would be nothing more than an irritation: his TARDIS had flown through a quasar without so much as a scratch.

But these circumstances were far from normal. The second - true - problem lay with the Doctor's TARDIS: he had placed a time lock on the TITAN Array, boosting its reality quotient above one and embedding it deeply into the space-time continuum. The Master's TARDIS would normally have been more than capable of reaching into the continuum and grappling it free, but not with the current distortion from the TITAN Array. Together, the two fields were disrupting his TARDIS's operation and making achieving his intentions problematic.

Time to pull another card from his sleeve.

Over the centuries, he had made many, many adaptations to his TARDIS. He had even stolen another from Gallifrey, only to watch it burn and die on Traken. But his original Ship was full of all manner of ingenious improvements, as the Doctor was about to discover.

The Master entered a series of commands. That would show him.

Within his own TARDIS, the Doctor kept looking back and forth from the console to the screen and back again. The screen showed the TITAN suite; the console showed the Master's progress in tearing the suite away. Paul's disruption field was helping, but keeping the temporal lock on the Array was paramount. As the Doctor had surmised, the Master was after the Array - with the Doctor's temporal lock in place, it was now one TARDIS against another.

And he knew the Master had made quite a few changes to his TARDIS that weren't in the handbook. The Doctor boosted the temporal fields, increasing the depth of the time lock to a reality quotient of three; at the same time, he instigated a graviton matrix, flooding the structure of the TITAN Array with wavicles of pure gravity. The lights in the console room dimmed as he diverted power from the dynamorphic generators.

There. That would show him!

The Doctor had no intention of giving up.

The Master stroked his beard in concentration. A graviton matrix? Ingenious, very ingenious. The Doctor was playing a very dangerous game, but the Master was more than willing to increase the stakes. All he needed was more power - a fitting description of his entire life.

Many years ago the Master had engineered the Doctor's regeneration, before setting trap upon trap to defeat him during his regeneration crisis.

He had failed, much as it pained him to admit it.

The Doctor had seen through the play-acting on Castrovalva, and had torn it all apart. The matrix of block-transfer computations that comprised the city of Castrovalva had dissolved, and the Master - and his TARDIS - had only just escaped. However, the dimensional collapse had caused serious damage to his dynamorphic generators. The link between his TARDIS and the Eye of Harmony had been disrupted, and the Master had used the last of his machine's strength to seek out a new power source. And he had found it on Earth, 140 million years into human prehistory, when his TARDIS had led him to the Xeraphin. When it had all gone horribly wrong.

It was a period of his life that he really didn't care to remember. Was it really any wonder that the Source of Traken was now a dying fire, given all that he had endured at the hands of that schizophrenic race?

Following that, however, he had managed to repair the damage, rebuilding and reconfiguring the infrastructure of his TARDIS to free him completely from the tyranny of the Time Lords.

And now his dynamorphic generators were far superior to the standard design - such as those in the Doctor's TARDIS. His dynamorphic generators could draw on far more than any version of the Eye of Harmony could offer: they could tap any power source in the immediate vicinity. Such as the European power grid and the West London University main generator.

He boosted the output one more time...

Mel had guessed that something was up - activity in the emerald forest had increased significantly over the last few minutes, with the trickle of energy flowing up the crystalline pillars growing to a torrent - but nothing could have prepared her for this. The floor itself was beginning to resonate, a deep thrumming that she could feel through the soles of her feet.

And the torrent had become a blinding flood, the pillars now burning shafts of green light. Mel squinted through the brilliance: was that dark, square shape the door to the power room, about thirty metres away? Closing her eyes against the blinding emerald glare, she set off for what she hoped was the door, before stopping and straining to keep herself upright. She felt so weak! It was as if time were expanding and contracting... time...

Temporal radiation! That had to be it! The Master must be using full power, and that power was flooding through the time crystals. And she was stuck in the middle of it. With the last of her strength, she dragged herself to the metallic square of the door, so close, so very close...

Mel slumped to the cold black marble floor, her fingers inches away from the doorframe.

The Master laughed maniacally as the extra power surged through his TARDIS, shattering the graviton matrix and destabilising the temporal lock, the disturbance field becoming nothing more than a distraction. TITAN was his! His time rotor resumed its even rise and fall as the burbling roar of dematerialisation filled the console room.

'*Au revoir*, Doctor!' he yelled, punching the vortex primer.

'No!' bellowed the Doctor, darting around the console even

though he knew it was far too late. The Master had counteracted with more energy than the Doctor's TARDIS could muster, destroying both the time lock and the graviton matrix. A couple of small electrical fires erupted from the console as the Doctor tried to minimise the feedback to his own systems, but there were other things for him to think about.

The Master had won. And the consequences of that were too terrible to contemplate.

'Paul - something's happening!' Stuart Hyde pointed at the curdling, rippling shape of the Master's TARDIS as it fought against the Doctor and Paul's traps and countertraps. For the last five minutes, the thin silver shape of the Master's TARDIS had been fading in and out, in time with unexpected yet threatening pyrotechnics from the TITAN Array. Paradoxically, it was both fading and gaining definition. At the same time, the lights in the TITAN suite dimmed to virtually nothing.

With a sickening feeling, Stuart realised exactly what was happening. The Master had overcome their defences, and was now dematerialising.

At the same time, the TITAN suite filled with a warbling, groaning noise which echoed around the marble and chrome edifice of the Array.

An edifice that was itself fading out of existence.

'No!' screamed Paul, running over to the master console. But he was too late. By the time he reached it the console had gone. As had every bit of crystal, chrome and circuitry that had comprised the TITAN Array.

Paul stumbled through the newly emptied chamber, unable to accept what he saw. But he had to.

The Master had stolen the TITAN Array.

Chapter Five
Two Out of Three Ain't Bad

Seconds after TITAN had dematerialised, the Doctor came skidding into the empty suite. As soon as he came to a halt, Stuart could see that he had assessed the situation.

'Damnation!' the Doctor spat, running his hand through his curly blond hair.

'What happened?' asked Stuart pointlessly. Sadly, it was only too obvious. The Master had won.

'He found an extra source of energy - probably the university generators, maybe even the European Grid. He was able to shatter the graviton matrix, and the time lock, *and* the disturbance field. And now he's who knows where!'

The Master stepped back from the console. All elements of the TITAN Array were now time-locked to his own TARDIS, being tractored through the time vortex to their new resting place. Where they would stay until he could assure himself that he was secure.

The Master had needed a place near enough to Earth to lure the Chronovores, but far enough from it to prevent immediate detection. And it also needed to be cavernous enough to house the Array.

Initially, he had thought of Mars. There were enough abandoned Ice Warrior cities buried deep below the permafrost to serve his purpose, but the remaining natives might not take too kindly to his plan. And all that ancient Osiran technology might not mix and match with the TITAN Array.

Then it had come to him. Somewhere he had discovered centuries ago, thanks to a clue in the Matrix. Somewhere perfect for his plans...

Everything he had ever cared about was gone. Arlene, TITAN, his career, his belief in himself... All taken from him during a game played by gods. Paul felt sick.

Arlene a prisoner of the Master. Stuart had told Paul the stories, about the evil megalomaniac and his knowledge of time travel, but Paul had dismissed them as the boastful ramblings of an old man. Yet Stuart wasn't an old man any more, was he?

Paul and Arlene were getting married at Christmas: three days of celebration with a traditional English wedding, a traditional Caribbean wedding and a traditional Greek wedding - three ceremonies to appease every one of their joint societies, and every one of their gods.

And now she was gone.

But Paul also worshipped another god, the god of science. Ever since he had learnt to read he had been fascinated by inventions, by stories of new technology and progress. As a quiet, introspective kid living in north London he had progressed from *Ladybird* books to *Look and Learn*, *The Boy's Encyclopaedia of Science*... and to American superhero comics.

When Paul had been younger - although not that much younger - he had been a great comic fan, spending his time seeing machinery the size of whole star-systems created by godlike beings from before the dawn of time. With TITAN, he had been paying homage to his heroes, building a machine worthy of the name.

He had had an image in his mind when he designed it. A four-colour picture of a machine imagined forty years ago, in the pages of a comic book. TITAN - chrome, marble and ruby crystal - was a virtual replica of the Chronal Guardians' Heart of Time from the pages of *The Sensational Six*, back in 1966. OK, so he had indulged himself... but it had looked good, hadn't it?

And now it was gone, stolen so that a being from a race of unimaginable beings could use it to destroy everything.

It was enough to make Paul cry.

'Of course!'

Paul looked up to see the Doctor virtually dancing on the spot. 'You said it yourself, Stuart!'

'Did I?' Stuart looked confused.

'"Son of TOMTIT." That was what you said, wasn't it?'

When Stuart caught Paul's glare, he blushed. 'Paul based TITAN on certain aspects of TOMTIT, true,' he said, 'but how does that help?'

The Doctor gave a knowing smile. 'It might be our only hope. Come on - we need to get to the TARDIS.' With that, he headed out of the door, Stuart following closely.

Paul waited for a moment. He missed Arlene. His missed the TITAN Array. Together, they meant everything to him. Together, they defined him.

So why did he miss that moment in the time corridor even more?

Hundreds of millions of years ago, gods had walked amongst the stars. They had graced countless worlds, influenced cultures, altered societies, changed the course of history.

Now the majority had gone, their time over, their existence all but forgotten.

But they had left traces.

The Time Lords, destroying Minyos, colonising Drornid and Trion, interfering with Planet 5; the Osirans, completing their millennia-long hunt for the renegade Sutekh on Earth and Mars; the Jagaroth and the Daemons, both meddling with human development...

And then there were the ones whose names had been lost. Whether that was because they had chosen to be forgotten, or because the universe desired to forget them, was a question that remained unanswered. But they had left their mark. Artefacts, languages, cities, planets.

They had gone a couple of hundred million of years ago. All except one race, a race that stubbornly refused to accept that its time was past.

The builders of the Midnight Cathedral.

Carefully manoeuvring both his machine and its precious cargo, the Master materialised his TARDIS within a small section of an enormous underground cave-system, one that was far from natural: the Midnight Cathedral had been carved from the ancient rock a hundred and fifty million years ago, when Earth Reptiles had still ruled the blue world above them. It had been abandoned soon after, but even the Matrix hadn't known why. All it had on file was that the Constructors of Destiny had been persuaded to leave the galaxy, leaving the Midnight Cathedral as a memorial. A forbidden, sacrosanct place.

It was perfect for his needs.

Stuart looked around with amazement. Even though he had realised from his last encounter that the Time Lords hid their miraculous space-time vehicles from mortal sight inside utterly pedestrian objects, he hadn't been prepared for this: what he gathered was the dimensionally transcendental interior of the Doctor's TARDIS, all packaged up in a blue Metropolitan police box standing round the corner from his study.

Funnily enough, it had looked right at home.

'I've run a complete scan of a sphere one billion light years in radius, looking for the characteristic energy signature of both TOMTIT and the TITAN Array, but there's no sign of the Master,' said the Doctor, leaning over the hexagonal console that sat in the middle of the huge white room. 'He must be shielding himself. However...'

'He's gone,' said Stuart. 'With one of these he could have gone anywhere.'

'However...' said the Doctor

'Not if he's trying to attract the Chronovores,' said Paul, standing in a doorway in the white, roundelled wall.

Stuart's surprise at Paul's comment was surpassed by the Doctor's expression.

'Go on,' said the Doctor slowly.

Paul seemed momentarily embarrassed at the attention he was getting, but he continued. 'You said it yourself, Doctor: he wants to lure the Chronovores into the open. Just using the TITAN Array at a random location might not be sufficient bait. But if it's being used in the vicinity of the Earth - a planet that has already inconvenienced the Chronovores - then they might take notice.'

'That's what I've been trying to say,' said the Doctor. 'However...'

'What is it?' asked Stuart, none the wiser. 'Come on Doc, spill the beans!'

The Doctor's face was like thunder. 'I have been trying to "spill the beans", as you so quaintly put it, for the last five minutes. If I might have the floor?'

Stuart grinned. 'Of course, Doctor. Spill away.'

'However... the TITAN Array is based on the principles of TOMTIT! TOMTIT - and TITAN, come to that - has limited access to the spatial dimension of the time vortex, but unlimited access to the temporal one. If the Master is still within this solar system, and if I can reroute the TARDIS sensors through the TOMTIT paracybernetic circuits, I might be able to search for the Master through the TOMTIT gap!'

Now Stuart did understand. 'So you'll need TOMTIT?'

The Doctor raised his eyes to the heavens. 'What do you think?'

'Can't you teleport it?' asked Paul. 'Like the Master did with the TITAN Array?'

The Doctor shook his head. 'Materialising around TOMTIT wouldn't do the old girl any good.' Stuart assumed he meant the TARDIS. 'TITAN has better shielding, and I imagine the Master's TARDIS has enough stolen technology hooked into it to materialise around a star without worrying. So come on!'

'What?'

'Let's go and get TOMTIT!'

As the Doctor and Stuart walked through the great white doors neither noticed Paul leave the console room through the interior door.

Mel blinked, once, twice... the blinding light had gone. And so had the emerald forest. Instead, she was lying on grey, compacted earth, looking up at what appeared to be the interior of a nineteenth-century steel mill. Even if it didn't have a ceiling. Or walls. Or any recognisable boundaries.

She had a dull recollection of the dynamorphic generators burning like tall stars, and of her efforts to pull herself up and through the heavy metal door just in front of her, but that was all.

Dirty brickwork, gusts of red-hot air, black iron machinery

thumping away and the acrid stench of coal and metal in the air. In the distance, a stream of molten metal split the gloom, red and yellow pouring hundreds of yards into a waiting vat.

This was the Master's power room? The Doctor's was far more prosaic: huge bellows, brass engines, steam-driven contraptions...

But it wasn't real. The Doctor had explained that the power room reflected the mood of the TARDIS, which in turn reflected the mood of its occupants. The Heath Robinson/Jules Verne hybrid suited the Doctor; these dark satanic mills were obviously the Master's personal peccadillo. But a power room was a power room, and it had to have a door...

During the Doctor's previous encounter with Stuart and TOMTIT, he hadn't had time to have a close look at the machinery itself. It turned out that his memory of a collection of boxy devices had been both right and wrong.

There had been a collection of boxes, it was true, but most of them had been recording instruments or the devices the Master had used to drain the crystal of Kronos. TOMTIT itself was a green unit, about five 1.5 metres long, one metre high and 60 centimetres deep. And, thankfully, it was on wheels.

As the Doctor and Stuart pulled TOMTIT from its hiding place in a broom cupboard before manoeuvring it down the corridor towards the TARDIS, the Doctor had a chance to put his thoughts in order.

The Master had stolen the TITAN Array, planning to use it to lure the Chronovores into their Higher Place. And then, presumably, he would employ one of his devilish schemes to destroy all of them.

The consequences of that didn't bear thinking about. Did the Master really think that the upper echelons of the cosmic hierarchy would stand by and allow part of their pantheon to be annihilated? Earth would simply be the first casualty: the Doctor screwed his eyes up to vanquish the image of the First Phalanx of the Eternals swooping down and then away, leaving the surface of the Earth a sea of molten lava; the Great Old Ones taking advantage of the disarray to make another of their bids for universal domination; and finally the Guardians working in metaconcert to ensure that humanity never had and never would exist.

He had to stop him. The Doctor started to push TOMTIT even faster down the corridor.

Paul had been wandering down the corridor for hours. Or had it been minutes? Time seemed meaningless inside the roundelled white tunnels that led away from the impossibly large control room.

It also seemed all-important.

This machine, this wonder, should have been so far beyond Paul's comprehension as to be madness, and yet he felt an affinity with it. He wasn't walking aimlessly - he knew where he was going.

Somewhere called the power room.

The Master coughed. And again. He continued coughing, steadying himself over the console until the attack subsided. Finally he was able to grab his breath, wheezing as he waited for his hearts to stop pacing. The power of the source was dying - and so was the Master.

And he was well aware of Anjeliqua's eyes boring into his back.

'The time has come to explore our new home.' He smiled at Arlene. 'It may not be the TITAN suite, but I'm sure that you and your paramour would find it fitting for your magnum opus.' Pulling the red door lever, the Master waited for the great doors to glide open.

'Care to join me?' he ordered.

The Doctor and Stuart just about managed to edge TOMTIT through the doors of the TARDIS, raising it over the police-box step like a shopping trolley, pushing it through the black interstitial void and then into the brilliance of the console room. The Doctor grimaced every time the boxy unit bumped into the pristine white doors and walls.

Finally they pushed TOMTIT through into the light and against the hexagonal console. The Doctor adjusted it slightly so that it was abutting the console panel that dealt with the sensor systems... so he said.

So far, so good, thought Stuart, but TOMTIT didn't run on batteries, and he didn't see a plug socket anywhere near. 'So, how do we hook it up, Doc?'

The Doctor frowned. 'Stuart: I understand that your body and mind have undergone a significant shock, and that the events of the last day have come as something of a surprise to you, but will you kindly refrain from calling me *Doc*?'

'Sorry, Doc... tor,' said Stuart. 'But seriously... I can't see how this TARDIS of yours can handle 240 volts and a 13 amp fuse.' He smiled at an image in his head. 'Unless you have a really universal adapter.'

Groaning, the Doctor shook his head. 'And I thought Peri had the market in poor jokes. Watch and learn, Professor Hyde, watch and learn!' The Doctor took the power cable and the data feed and touched them to the six-sided base of the console. Instantly, their connectors melted into the grey pseudometal.

Beats changing the plug, thought Stuart, before his attention was drawn to something he had never expected - never wanted - to see again. But it was the most wonderful thing in the universe.

TOMTIT lit up. Flashing telltales and glowing dials burst into life as the knowledge and the power of the TARDIS flowed into it. A vibrant hum threatened to overwhelm the background noise of the TARDIS. TOMTIT lived.

'Now all I need to do is reroute my sensor array through the gap your little box of tricks is going to generate, and then...' the Doctor grinned. 'Then it's your turn, Professor,' he said brightly, rubbing his hands together. 'But first, the bit I'm going to enjoy.'

Mel carefully picked her way through the Master's power room, narrowly avoiding the jets of steam and the blasts of scalding air that came from the grimy monstrosity. The sooner she was out of there, the better: there was an air of all-pervading evil that Mel found almost nauseating, but finding the door was proving problematic.

Then she saw it. Far beyond the three furthest brick stacks, a glint of metal. The same metal from which the door into the power room had been constructed.

The way out.

Mel climbed over a pile of clinker and headed towards her only means of escape.

Paul looked around the power room, still underimpressed. For one of the most important rooms in one of the time ships of the gods, it had a decidedly lacklustre feel. No depth. *No substance*. A glittering matrix of pearly light, the room had no floor, no ceiling, no walls. It was nothing but a frame of time-light with a central shaft of primal energy piercing its very centre.

And it was talking to Paul.

'It's beautiful.' Arlene stood at the centre of the Dusk Nave of the Midnight Cathedral, trying to comprehend what she was seeing. It was so alien that ordinary terms of reference just didn't work. But with the Master at her side, it didn't seem strange at all.

The structure was about one hundred metres high and three hundred across, with a vast, domed and vaulted ceiling of unearthly blue stone, every inch covered in detailed inlay - she had seen those details just after she had left the Master's TARDIS, now a blue marble altar lying between two of the supporting arches.

Angels and devils, fighting and uniting, committing acts of unspeakable atrocity and unbearable good. The images should have moved her in some way, but Arlene simply couldn't connect with emotion. It was as if her body was an ill-fitting spacesuit, rendering everything once removed. Unsettled by this, but unable to act upon it, Arlene had walked away from the Master's TARDIS and joined him and Anjeliqua at the very centre of the Nave, where she could see so much more.

From her new perspective, she could see that the blue pillars of the dome eventually became huge sapphire arches which formed a vast birdcage of blue stone and crystal. And, just in front of her, here at the very centre of the chamber, a huge statue reached from the polished blue marble floor to the very apex of the Nave: crucified through its angel wings, its hands begging for supplication. Yet it bore the face of a devil: horns, cruel slitted eyes and a fanged mouth. Arlene shuddered, but whether it was because of the satanic visage or the overwhelming feeling of loss and regret that seemed to fill the chamber, she didn't know. Even more puzzling was the smell: the fragrance of roses was everywhere.

'I must agree with you, my dear.' The intruding thought vanished at the sound of the Master's voice. 'It is beautiful. The Midnight Cathedral is one of the very wonders of the universe. And the Dusk Nave is but one chamber amongst countless hundreds.'

'Who built the Cathedral?' asked Anjeliqua.

'That, Ms Whitefriar, is a cosmic mystery. From my sources I gather that the Constructors of Destiny built their works across the entire universe, but that this is the only one that survived. Perfect for my purpose.' He smiled that smile, his eyes glittering, glowing...

'Return to my TARDIS and bring out the device.' He raised his hand. 'Actually, wait: I believe you deserve to see this. It's time to retrieve the TITAN Array from the time vortex.' With that, the Master tapped his wrist unit.

The same twisted, groaning bellow that Arlene had heard inside the Master's TARDIS bounced across the Dusk Nave, growing into a thundering roar. At the same time, a hail of glitter appeared around them, like fake snow...

The dome and archway of the Nave were suddenly decorated with the chrome circuitry of the TITAN a.rray, its topology intact but its geometric integrity surrendered to the curved, vaulted architecture. The TITAN core, that scintillating ruby at the heart of the Array, materialised in the hands of the demon-angel, fulfilling its entreaty to some unknown god.

The TITAN Array was now an integral part of the Midnight Cathedral.

'Come, my dears. We have a lot to do and so very little time.' With that, the Master returned to his TARDIS, Anjeliqua and Arlene following.

Arlene knew that what she was doing was wrong; she knew

that the Master was evil. But there was nothing that she could do. Not with her body feeling like an ill-fitting spacesuit.

Paul looked around the power room, trying to locate what it was that had summoned him. Then he saw it, looming through the cat's cradle of neon light. A being of fire and ice, beckoning him...

He knew he should have been terrified, but he wasn't. If anything, he felt reassured. He drew closer to the shining figure.

'Is this really going to work?' asked Stuart, passing yet another bundle of Whitefriar Lattice to the Doctor. An earlier series of explosions from the console after the Doctor had switched the power on hadn't exactly been reassuring. And Stuart still wasn't happy about the plume of smoke that had drifted out of TOMTIT.

'Of course it is,' snapped the Doctor, looking rather affronted. 'It's just that different time machines get a bit... temperamental when they're first introduced to one another: it's a bit like stage fright. Trust me, Stuart. I'm just about to instigate the greetings protocols –'

Part of the console exploded. Again.

After what seemed like hours of clambering across grey slag, Mel finally reached the door. Gunmetal grey, marked with the Omniscate, it was identical to the door through which she had entered the generator room.

And identical to the door in the Doctor's power room.

Mel pushed it open, allowing a better quality of light to filter through. Especially when she noticed the chrome circuitry embedded in the stone. Circuitry? Remembering Anjeliqua's description of Paul's invention, she could only come to one conclusion. The Master must have stolen the TITAN Array!

She peered through the gap in the doorway. And gasped. Wherever she was, it virtually defied description: an alien cathedral of stunning beauty and majesty. Polished blue stone and sapphire, it reminded Mel of a great kingdom she had once known.

Dragging her attention away from her stunning surroundings,

Mel tried to get her bearings. The door from the power room exited at the rear of the Master's TARDIS, which was currently disguised as a ornately carved altar. Quietly, she crept round the side until she could see what was going on.

Arlene and Anjeliqua were dragging a coffin-shaped cradle of circuitry over to the base of a huge statue with a devilishly evil face; of the Master, there was no sign. Mel knew there was no point in trying to talk to either of her friends; the Master's mind control was more than even her hectoring could overcome. She decided that retreat was the better part of valour, and looked for an exit.

There! A beautifully embossed doorway, a light blue arch in the bright blue marble, stood about a thirty metres away, leading into a dimly lit corridor. Sparing a last glance at Anjeliqua and Arlene, Mel sprinted over to it.

There! The Doctor stepped back from the console with a proud smile on his face. 'There you go, Professor Hyde - one fully integrated TARDIS/TOMTIT assembly!' He waved a hand over the angular green bulk of TOMTIT. 'My TARDIS is now configured to peer straight through the TOMTIT gap into the time vortex and thence... thence to the Master.' He grabbed Stuart by the shoulders. 'What do you think?'

Stuart tried to feel reassured, but the scorch marks, on both TOMTIT and the TARDIS console, from their earlier attempts did little to help.

'Are you absolutely sure, Doctor?' Even though he was thirty years younger, he had retained his cynicism. Linking up the TARDIS to TOMTIT was a sensible move, but they were dealing with the Master! He looked around for Paul, but he was nowhere to be seen.

'Sure? Sure? Sure?' The Doctor thumped the console. And then yelped in pain. 'Of course I'm sure,' he said quietly. 'Would you care to do the honours?' He indicated TOMTIT. 'I mean, it seems only right.'

Stuart reached over to the ancient dials and levers. It was like coming home.

* * *

Paul nodded. It was so very clear to him now, and he knew exactly what he had to do.

The shining figure smiled in approval. All would be as it should be.

The Master held back another coughing fit and examined the read-outs on his console. He knew he couldn't evade the Doctor for ever - grudgingly, even he had to admit that the man was far too resourceful. But he wanted to know the exact moment that the Doctor tracked him down. Because he didn't want to miss a thing. If the Doctor was living up to his reputation, he would have conscripted TOMTIT by now.

For a moment, the Master wondered whether he really could pull it all together. There were so many elements, so many points of potential failure... But his very life was at stake. He would succeed, whatever the cost.

He smiled in anticipation, before checking his wrist unit for another element in his plan: one that he knew he could rely on to blunder around. She had escaped from his TARDIS, so where was the delectable Miss Bush?

Mel continued to run down the gloomy corridor, trying to ignore the ever-present carvings of demons and angels on either side of her. All she wanted to do was find the Doctor - he had to be around here somewhere! All this was too much for a simple girl from Pease Pottage...

Which she wasn't. All those years ago, when she had helped out the Doctor with that business with the Usurians, she had had no idea that it would lead to an intergalactic odyssey which would take her to the edge of the universe and back. She wasn't the same Melanie Bush who had stowed away on the TARDIS - she had seen too much!

From Stalagtrons to Heracletes, from Vervoids to Quarks and their giant wasp servants, from SénéNet and the Nestenes to the Valeyard and then Maradnias... Mel had had enough. It had changed her, and she wanted to be changed back. She wanted her life back!

That's when she came to her decision. She would tell the Doctor what she had found out about Anjeliqua - it might be of some use - and then get as far away from him as she could do. And then she would be free. She carried on running down the corridor.

The light became even dimmer - almost pitch-black - as Mel reached the junction. She had three choices: left, right or straight ahead. Three more marble tunnels to run down.

She chose straight ahead.

'Isolating matrix scanner,' advised Stuart. 'TOMTIT gap opening now.' He turned the handles on the dials, feeling his way into the equipment. Even after thirty years he could still remember the exact operation of the device. He felt the steady thrum beneath his fingers as the needles on the dials edged from the green to the amber zones. 'Four five, five oh, five five...' Stuart adjusted another control. 'TOMTIT gap open, Doctor.'

The Doctor nodded his understanding. 'Activating sensors... now!' With a flourish, he tapped out a series of commands on the console.

The scanner screen suddenly erupted into a vista of static.

'Something's coming through...' muttered the Doctor, as a mottled grey globe began to resolve on the screen. 'The TITAN Array is about 250 million miles from Earth...' He slapped his forehead. 'How could I be so blind!' he exclaimed.

'Doctor?'

The Doctor pointed at the scanner; the image was now instantly recognisable. 'The Master's on the moon! Somewhere on the dark side...' He scratched his curly blond hair. 'Of all the infernal arrogance!'

'What?' Stuart wasn't exactly happy about being reduced to the role of sounding board.

'The Master's TARDIS is on the western edge of the Midnight Cathedral - anywhere between the Dusk Nave and the Twilight Transept.' The Doctor chewed his bottom lip. 'The idiot! He knows it's out of bounds!'

'What is it, Doctor?' Sounding board again, but what else could he do?

The Doctor turned from the scanner. 'The Midnight Cathedral was built on the dark side of your moon about one hundred and fifty million years ago by a mysterious race of godlike aliens called the Constructors. Even the Time Lords have no idea who or what they were, only that their entire species was wiped out by some unimaginable horror - something even the Time Lords fear. The Midnight Cathedral is the only one of their great works to survive - and we keep well away!'

Stuart scratched his chin. 'So the Master, Arlene and Anjeliqua are on the moon? How do they breathe?'

'The Midnight Cathedral possesses artificial gravity and an osmotic atmospheric barrier, Professor Hyde: one of the Constructors' party pieces. Lack of oxygen is something they don't have to worry about.' He grinned. 'And neither do we. Time to put an end to the Master's little party, don't you think?' He began to set the coordinates.

Mel reached the end of the corridor. Beyond the carved marble archway was what appeared to be a dusty grey cave-system, with no visible design or direction. It looked as if she had reached the limits of the strange alien church - perhaps something outside its environs would give her the chance to find out what was going on. She forged ahead.

'I'm going to make an educated guess that the Master has landed in somewhere in the vicinity of the Meridian Altar. Only that and the Dusk Nave have enough space to house the TITAN Array.' He frowned. 'Where is Paul, by the way?'

Stuart shrugged. 'I haven't seen him since we went to get TOMTIT. Why, is it important?'

The Doctor shook his head. 'No, just wondered. Didn't want him to miss the fun.' His hand hovered over the materialisation switch. 'Then again, I'm hoping that we can slip in without the Master noticing.' He indicated TOMTIT. 'That's the beauty of old technology - understated.'

Deep within the antiquated circuitry of TOMTIT, a technology which held more in common with the TARDIS began to stir. Techno-organic nanites began their fractal multiplication, reaching out through the prehistoric motherboards and transistors until they found what they were looking for.

A link to their home technology.

A TARDIS. The TARDIS.

Flowing up the cables like cybernetic salmon, the nanites escaped the confines of TOMTIT and broke free into the TARDIS's primary systems.

A faint chime issued from the Master's wrist unit. He didn't even need to check - everything was proceeding perfectly. But a second bleep did pique his curiosity. When he saw the reason, he couldn't help but laugh. 'This is excellent!'

'Master?' asked Anjeliqua, busy at the converter cradle.

He laughed. 'I thought that I had planned the perfect trap, but good fortune has rendered it infinitely more satisfying!'

'That's odd,' muttered the Doctor, stroking his chin. 'Most peculiar. Positively bizarre, you might say.'

Stuart was standing behind him. 'A problem?'

The TARDIS was encountering a cloud of time spillage churning up through the portion of the vortex just below them.

'She's acting a bit... sluggish. As if...'

The Doctor didn't finish his suspicions. The TARDIS tipped by forty-five degrees, accompanied by a torn screaming, her normal tones ripped and broken. By the time the Doctor had managed to haul himself upright and over the console, the TARDIS was level, but something was terribly, terribly wrong. He could sense that the Ship was crying out in pain, as if something were tearing her apart. Seconds later he had the awful confirmation: the Cloister Bell began its mournful tocsin, warning of imminent destruction.

'What's happening?' shouted Stuart over the noise.

The Doctor looked up from the console. 'It would appear to be some kind of external interference.' He looked back at the console. 'Hang on... that isn't external...' He examined the

monitors frantically, desperate to find a clue. Any clue.
The Cloister Bell continued to chime.

Mel licked a finger and held it up to the breeze. Which proved rather pointless, really, since there was no breeze. The air was cool, clean... and perfectly still.

She was standing in a domed cave, a junction with five tunnels branching off in front of her. All of them equally uninviting. 'Oh well, only one thing for it. Here goes nothing,' she announced, taking a deep breath and trying to feel braver than she did. She stepped into the rightmost tunnel.

And stumbled. She suddenly felt light, as if... as if the gravity had been reduced! She tried to adjust, taking a deep breath...

She reached for her throat, unable to breathe. Panic rising, she realised why. There wasn't just a lack of breeze, there was a lack of air. She had stumbled into a vacuum! With no sensible gravity and definitely no air, she sank to the dusty ground. Not again, she though desperately.

She tried to crawl back into the domed cave, but her strength was draining from her. She clutched the ground, but her fingers couldn't get any purchase in the silky dust. Seconds later blackness began to enclose her, creeping in round the corners of her vision and driving her into unconsciousness

One metre from the osmotic barrier.

'Having trouble, Doctor?' The Master's gloating tones floated through from the scanner. The Doctor spared a second's attention, partly to confirm that his nemesis was playing his usual, boastful game, but mainly to get some clue as to his precise location.

Listening to the Master's tired cant and seeing the carved blue marble of the Midnight Cathedral, the Doctor succeeded on both counts.

But there were more pressing matters. According to the readouts over half the TARDIS's systems were under attack, causing them to malfunction. But they were being attacked internally. And the rate of increase was exponential. Almost as if...

He suddenly realised what was going on. 'It's a virus!' he yelled.

The Master's tone was almost congratulatory. 'Well spotted, Doctor. A virus - and a particularly vicious one at that. I hid it inside TOMTIT thirty years ago, just in case you chose to use the machine against me in Atlantis, but it's taken you that long to trip it. Sadly, it also means that you won't reach me in time to prevent this!' The image on the scanner swam and re-formed into a shot of Mel lying in the grey dust, clearly gasping for air.

'She's outside the osmotic barrier, Doctor,' the Master whispered malevolently. 'Vacuum-packed, you might say.'

'You fiend!' The Doctor redoubled his efforts around the console, transferring power from all but the most essential systems into the TARDIS's internal defences. But it was useless: virtually every system - including the internal defences - had already been compromised. The lights began to flicker and at the same time the Doctor realised that it was getting colder - much colder. But given the rate at which the air was thinning, hypothermia was going to come a close second behind asphyxiation.

Then he felt it, somewhere within his soul: a scream in five dimensions. It was a sensation that few Time Lords ever survived. Because it was the feeling passed through the symbiotic link from TARDIS to occupant when a TARDIS was entering the most dangerous, the most fatal, manoeuvre possible.

Time ram: one TARDIS materialising at the same point in space and time as another, where two TARDISes matched temporal frequencies and materialised at exactly the same point in each and every one of the eleven dimensions of space and time, every particle of one TARDIS coinciding with every particle of the other.

Cosmic blasphemy. Such a move had an inevitable consequence: the complete and utter destruction of both TARDISes. The outer plasmic shells ruptured, the conditional pathways were aborted, the relative dimensions evaporated. And the occupants died, of course.

And it was happening here, now... with one fundamental difference.

The Doctor's TARDIS wasn't time ramming another TARDIS - it was time ramming itself, ramming a version from mere nanoseconds in the past. A hypothetical proposition put forward by some dusty old Academy cardinal, one greeted by disdain by the rowdy audience of students. *Eigen-Ram*.

Only it wasn't hypothetical any more. And the Doctor regretted being a rowdy student and not paying much attention. Momentarily stunned by his discovery, he could only watch as the time rotor darkened: the lattice of diamond and ruby turned into a cylinder of pure ebony, as the time fields of the TARDIS and her twin began to overlap. He turned to the scanner, where the prone form of Mel twitched one final time before becoming still.

'Mel,' he whispered. 'I'm so sorry...'

The time ram began to tear the TARDIS apart.

Chapter Six
Bat Out of Hell

Was nothing sacred to the Master? Violating the Ancient Covenants, trespassing on the Midnight Cathedral, and now daring to use the Profane Virus of Rassilon? What was he planning next? A fist fight with the Guardians?

As the Doctor darted round the console, realisation had dawned with a fatality and a finality: he recognised the symptoms that were crippling the TARDIS. And he clearly remembered the physical sickness he had felt when he had first discovered the existence of the Profane Virus.

At his coronation.

The moment that the circlet had been placed on his head his mind had swooped into the Matrix, enveloping the data streams, encompassing the infinity and eternity that was the essence of the Time Lords. He had soared through the excitonic pathways, revelling in the freedom that the Matrix provided - a freedom that he had never felt before and would never feel again.

He had accessed the Matrix before, of course: as a student, it was a training aid; as a Technician, he had relied on its data. But as President, his access was both total and immediate. And precise.

He had found the wall within moments. Most Time Lords would have seen it as a minor inconvenience, something to be bypassed, but the Doctor, trained by the Mind Monks of Darron to see beyond the obvious, saw it for what it was. A barrier. A wall.

He broke down that wall.

And saw it. All of it. The Slaughterhouse revealed in all its malignant glory.

The Profane Virus was just one of a whole armoury of theoretical weapons in the Slaughterhouse, stockpiled by the CIA and stored in the Matrix, its sole aim to destroy Time Lord technology, from a native Gallifreyan to a TARDIS to the Eye of

Harmony itself. Mutually assured destruction.

Did the Time Lords fear their technology being stolen by others? Or did they fear the consequences of a civil war?

Whatever the reason, the weaponry had been there, and the Doctor had had but the briefest of moments to study it... before the Vardan invasion force had hurled him from the matrix, leaving him unconscious on the cold floor of the Panopticon. It was information that the wisdom of Rassilon had once denied him - but subsequent events had unearthed it, unearthed a darkness that he would have to live with for the rest of his lives.

And now, to save his Ship, he had seconds to trawl through that darkness and retrieve whatever information he had about the virus before the time ram was complete. Thankfully, both the TARDIS and its past self were valiantly fighting the infection, trying to drag their time fields apart. But with the virus's hold getting stronger by the second, the outcome was inevitable.

Only two Time Lords had ever survived a time ram: the Doctor and the Master. The *same* time ram. *But that time we had the help of the Chronovores. This time, I'm on my own.*

He continued to try to devise a countermeasure, but the wave of warning lights and the cacophony of alarms made it clear that his attempt was futile.

How can it be futile? he screamed to himself. I am the Doctor! I give monsters nightmares! Then another set of memories overcame him.

'You've killed them.' Mel's eyes had been red with crying, her voice spilling over with pent-up despair. But there was another emotion there, fighting to get out. And at that moment in time, that was the last thing the Doctor wanted. All he wanted to do was set the coordinates and get as far away from Maradnias as he could. Only then could he begin his own mourning.

'All of them.' Mel's blame, her hurt, her anger... it was all focused like a laser, burning into him, burning into his resolve. But what was he supposed to say to her, to sweet Mel, who had stood by his side these many, many years?

'What happened?' Mel's voice was quiet, but the pain was

obvious in her voice. With that pain, there was no way that the Doctor could look up from the console. He just couldn't look into her eyes!

'I miscalculated,' he murmured to whatever gods were listening. Whatever gods cared now. But there was a logical argument: perhaps that would calm Mel down, and give him long enough to understand and accept the magnitude of what he'd done.

'I didn't realise how strong the anti-Federalist faction was, or that they'd be idiotic enough to use their nuclear stockpile. I –'

Mel didn't let him continue.

'You miscalculated?' she screamed. 'This isn't an exercise in mental arithmetic, Doctor! Billions of people have died because of you; billions of innocent lives - all gone, all because you miscalculated!'

Logic had failed - thankfully. There was nothing logical about Maradnias. It was time he faced the fact.

'Don't you think I'll carry the blame for this for the rest of my lives?' he implored. But who was he imploring? Mel, or some higher power? He had engineered the destruction of a planet, for Rassilon's sake!

Mel's immediate response cut him to the core. Forget Daleks, Cybermen, even that shard of evil he had once played chess with. Humans held the monopoly on true emotional warfare.

'No, Doctor, I don't. Who knows what Time Lords feel? What you feel? You go on about the Daleks, the Cybermen, the Vervoids - creatures that you blame for spreading untold misery and destruction - if you ask me, you want the universe to be filled with evil! Those creatures only seem to exist to justify your own crusade. If it wasn't for them, you'd have no moral high ground to preach from, would you? And that wouldn't suit the Doctor, great and glorious righter of wrongs, would it?'

The image of Mel faded, but the reality of the situation was still there. He had done wrong. He had miscalculated. And now, there was nothing he could do.

The Doctor stepped back from the console, his mind flooded

with the psychic pain of the TARDIS, his body racked with the infernal radiations of the time ram. But his soul was flooded with Mel's accusations.

She was right. It was time to accept his punishment. Pulling his mind away from the TARDIS, the Doctor finally accepted defeat.

It was over.

Captured in the iridescence of a holosphere, the Doctor's TARDIS was pitching and reeling in space, the light on its roof flashing erratically. It was clearly in a lot of trouble.

The Master watched with glee, his smile broadening as a ghost image of the blue police box overlaid itself on the original... although, in terms of absolute age, this afterimage was the original, of course.

The time ram was taking far longer than he had anticipated; perhaps the Doctor had made a few improvements to his battered old capsule since the Master had last broken into it. But he suspected this had more to do with the Doctor's legendary luck than any technical prowess. No, the results of time rams were as inevitable as death and taxes.

And all of us pay our taxes in some way.

No, this was a trap the Doctor couldn't possibly escape - even with his TARDIS at stake and his gaggle of innocent humans in tow, he couldn't escape a time ram. He didn't have a Chronovore to help him this time!

Before he could even check his wrist unit, it chirped to inform him that Miss Bush's life signs had fallen into the critical zone. So, now it was time to deal with the lesser concerns.

Although the girl meant nothing to him - apart from being a hyperactive irritation - she would provide a useful hostage if the Doctor did manage to escape, and some light entertainment if he didn't. His wrist unit was fully integrated with the environmental systems of the Midnight Cathedral: he extended the osmotic barrier so that it flowed over her inert body, and noted with approval the spasmodic jerks that immediately racked her as she took breath once again.

'Ms Whitefriar... please be so good as to escort Miss Bush to the

Dusk Nave and the hospitality of my TARDIS? You'll find her in the fifth north-east corridor, on the far side of the Infinity Font.'

Anjeliqua nodded, but the Master could sense the resentment from her. Not to worry - knowing one has an enemy was the first step in defeating them. He returned his attention to the Doctor's TARDIS, now listing in space as its external features began to melt and blur.

Excellent.

Paul's hands were firmly enmeshed in the pearl-strewn web of the power room: one nervous system routed into another, one mind touching another. There was a comfort in that.

But there were also drawbacks. As Paul and the TARDIS met on a level that Paul couldn't even have dreamt about a couple of hours earlier, he felt everything that she felt.

Everything.

He could feel her pain, he could feel the virus eating into her. He could feel the other TARDIS, confused, scared, alone, unable to comprehend what was happening to it. And he could feel the Doctor, pulling away, just when his mind - his soul - were needed.

Pulling away, and unreachable.

But he could also feel the virus itself, nanoscopic specks fleeting down excitonic circuitry and artron conduits, wreaking havoc and destruction in their wake, specks which grew and multiplied and hurt the TARDIS. Indeed, which hurt the Doctor. But, more importantly, they hurt time.

Not any more.

Throughout the infinity and eternity of the TARDIS, a dead hand fell: from the bottomless depths of the dynamorphic generators to the dizzy heights of the observation towers; from the sterile contemplations and reflections of the cloister room to the gossipy whispers of the library; from the eternal minaret to the jade pagoda, the nanotech virus was grabbed by that dead hand and twisted out of existence. One minute it had infested the TARDIS's entire infrastructure; the next, it had passed through the highest of the higher dimensions. There wasn't even a trace. The TARDIS was cleansed.

Paul - and his new friend - just hoped it was enough.

With one last chime from the Cloister Bell, silence fell. The lights and the rest of the life-support infrastructure began to function again. The TARDIS slowly stabilised.

The time ram was over.

Trying to make sense of the confusion, the Doctor peered at the only surviving monitor on the only surviving panel. 'That can't be right.' He scratched his head. 'That suggests the virus has somehow gone and the TARDIS - TARDISes - are trying to re-establish the time flow. But given the current temporal potential in the vortex, that would mean a catastrophic artron backlash -'

The Master folded his arms in preparation for the denouement. The two time-shifted TARDISes had done their best, but the Profane Virus of Rassilon had been tailored by Erkulon himself, the greatest nano-engineer Gallifrey had ever known. Even the Master had marvelled at every aspect of the virus, from software and hardware to firmware and wetware. The creatures were simply staggering in their complexity.

And the Doctor's poor, battered, antiquated wreck of a Type 40 TT capsule was simply no match for them -

The holosphere whited out in a blaze of actinic light. As the glare slowly diminished, the Master checked the sensors. According to his readings there had been an artron explosion just beyond the Earth L3 LaGrange point, some one hundred and fifty million miles from the moon.

Exactly where the Doctor's TARDIS had been.

'Go on, Doctor, get out of that one!' His smile became a grin. They had been taught the concept of Eigen-Ram - a TARDIS time-ramming itself - at the Academy, but to see it in action was a delight. Still grinning, he turned his attention to the cradle of wire and circuitry that lay at the base of the curious statue.

Even though the information in the Matrix had been hazy, it had revealed that the mysterious Constructors had worshipped this angel-demon - indeed, the Midnight Cathedral was dedicated to it.

'Superstitious fools,' the Master muttered, taking a closer look at the control panel. With the Doctor out of the way, it was time to move on to the main event.

Apotheosis.

'Ow!' The Doctor rubbed his head, his faced screwed into a grimace of pain. 'That hurt!' he yowled in the manner of an aggrieved schoolboy.

'Is everyone OK?' Paul helped Stuart to his feet before assisting the Doctor.

'Where have you been?' demanded Stuart. 'Do you have any idea what's just happened?' Then he realised that he didn't have much idea either. He shot the Doctor an entreating glance.

'The TARDIS was infected with a nanotech virus tailored to attack TARDISes. And you saw who was responsible!'

Stuart nodded, but any response was muted by what he saw next to the rather singed control console. TOMTIT. Or rather, all that remained of TOMTIT. The metal frame was twisted and melted; the pea-green fibreglass of the control panels shattered into fringed shards and cinders, tattered fragments of Whitefriar Lattice smouldering around it.

'Oh,' he said sadly. Whether he and Ruth had created TOMTIT from scratch, or simply modified the Master's designs, there was a precious part of Stuart invested in the machine. And now, thanks to the Master, TOMTIT was nothing but a smouldering pile of broken, melted crap. He felt a hand on his shoulder.

'I'm sorry.' The Doctor's expression was one of sadness, almost matching Stuart's own. 'I know how much TOMTIT meant to you. But it did save our lives.'

'Save them?' Stuart shook his head. 'TOMTIT was the cause of all of this. You heard the Master - the virus was inside TOMTIT...' He trailed off as the implications of that became clear. 'That bastard infected TOMTIT!'

'Something held at the last minute, that's for sure,' said the Doctor, his eyes scanning the one intact monitor on the console. 'The TARDIS was within seconds of converging with her former self. Even with the mysterious disappearance of the virus, it was inevitable, inescapable... And then this TARDIS somehow managed to get a message to that TARDIS, through the TOMTIT gap, persuading it to change time frequencies. Without TOMTIT and the TOMTIT gap, we would have been utterly annihilated.' An interesting argument, but Stuart couldn't help catching the curious glance the Doctor shot at Paul.

'Anyway, let's see how badly we've been hurt.' The Doctor cracked his knuckles and returned his attention to the console.

Mel could feel that she was lying on something soft, rather than the hard dusty ground on to which she had collapsed. But she was making every attempt to stop consciousness returning: she knew she wasn't going to like what she saw.

Consciousness won, and she gingerly opened her eyes.

And realised, with a feeling of total horror, exactly where she was. The walls were white and roundelled, but it wasn't the Doctor's TARDIS. The sinister whispering all around her proved that she had been captured by the Master.

'Mel - you've woken up!'

The voice was far too familiar. Anjeliqua! That traitor was sitting next to Mel's bed, her face a picture of concern. Hypocritical cow!

Mel sat up. The room was a perfect cube of roundelled walls, empty save for the bed and a polished wooden table with a brass orrery on top. But even a cursory glance showed that the model wasn't of Earth's solar system: not with twin-ringed gas giants orbiting one another, it wasn't.

'Woken up to find I'm a prisoner!' she argued.

'You're not a prisoner, Mel.' Anjeliqua patted her on the hand. 'The Master knows what he's doing. Once he's completed his plan, we'll all have everything we've ever wanted.'

Mel sat up. '"Everything we've ever wanted?" Anjeliqua, it seems to me that all you've wanted to do for the last couple of years is humiliate Paul. Well, that's your concern. But to hook up with the Master to do it...'

'The Master is very important -'

'He's pure evil, Anjeliqua!'

Anjeliqua's voice grew quiet. 'Mel... you don't understand.' So she started to explain.

And that's when Mel got really frightened.

'So how far from the moon are we?' asked Paul, even though he was sure he knew the answer.

'Hmm,' murmured the Doctor. 'Too far. It would appear that the artron backlash from the aborted time ram threw us millions of light years across space and billennia across time. I'm trying to get a fix at the moment, but the time ram has shaken the old girl up a bit.'

'This is a time machine, isn't it?' said Stuart.

'Of course it is.'

'Then just get us back to the moon before we were thrown across the universe. Surely that can't be too difficult?'

The Doctor gave an irritated sigh. 'I thought you were meant to be a temporal physicist, Hyde? Haven't you read the works of Aaron Blinovitch? The laws of time and causality just don't work that way. Our timelines and those of the Master and the TITAN Array are irrevocably linked. Any attempt to subvert that could lead to disaster. I'm afraid we're going to have to do this the hard way.' He turned back to the console and began his calculations.

'Mel... if you want an answer to all of this, remember what Professor Norton used to tell us.'

With that, Anjeliqua closed the white door behind her, the brief neon flare around the frame indicating that Mel was still a prisoner.

As she got up and looked around the room for some means of escape - a remote possibility, true, but better than lying there moping - Mel thought about her erstwhile friend. How could Anjeliqua even consider that course of action? Didn't she realise how dangerous it was? Despite her new-found attitude problem, Anjeliqua was still one the most intelligent, level-headed people Mel knew. What she was proposing was insanity.

Mel had to get out of the Master's prison - and she had to stop Anjeliqua.

* * *

'I trust Miss Bush is conscious and aware of her captivity?' asked the Master, as Anjeliqua came out of his TARDIS. He knew very well that she was. He had monitored the entire conversation between Anjeliqua and Miss Bush, and the humans had a phrase for it. 'Give someone enough rope...' The Master had given Anjeliqua more than enough to hang herself with.

'She still doesn't see the error of her ways, Master, but I'm sure she'll learn.' The Master caught her glance towards the converter. Did she really think he was that stupid?

'I'm sure she will.' He nodded towards the casket of cabling and circuitry; huge trunks of Whitefriar Lattice connected it to the TITAN console, the quantum computer and the Master's TARDIS. Arlene, newly awoken and terribly keen, was just closing a small panel on the side of the console.

'What's the status of the converter?'

'Fully integrated into the TITAN Array,' Arlene answered.

'Ready to go when you are,' echoed Anjeliqua.

The Master smiled. This was where the fun started.

'Any joy, Doctor?' asked Stuart, bored out of his skull. It felt like hours since the Doctor had first started messing about with star charts, dividers and, at one point, a ludicrous device he called an 'astral map'.

The Doctor sighed. 'Finally, yes. We are becalmed in the vicinity of the constellation of Virgo, fifty million light years from Earth and close to the Abell 3627 galactic cluster. Too close.'

'Is that a problem?' asked Stuart, immediately realising the absurdity of the question. Of course that isn't a problem. We're stranded in an impossible space-time machine, captained by a lunatic time traveller, drifting in space millions of light years from Earth. No problem at all. But the Doctor's expression suggested that there was far more to it than that.

'The Virgo cluster is also the home of the Great Attractor, Professor Hyde. I realise that astronomy probably doesn't fall under the remit of temporal physics, but you must have heard of it, man!'

It was Paul who answered. 'An enormous gravitational mass in space. The Milky Way is being drawn to it at the rate of a million miles an hour.' He shot an inquiring look at the Doctor. 'I've always wondered what it actually was.'

The Doctor's tone made it quite clear that there were some things mankind was not meant to know. 'The home of something I pray we never encounter,' he whispered. 'But the immediate problem is that the gravitational flux in this region of space is going to play merry hell with the TARDIS's navigation systems.'

'But you know where we are,' Stuart countered. 'Why is it a problem?'

'Because', began the Doctor, with the tone of voice of someone talking to a five-year-old, 'I can't guarantee that we'll end up at the point I'm aiming for - I can't guarantee that we'll end up anywhere, come to that. With the local gravity as it is, the time vortex is going to be prey to random gravity lenses, quantum mirages, substrate diversions... We're trapped in a gravimetric lattice, I'm afraid.'

'There has to be something we can do!' shouted Paul. 'The Master's got Arlene, TITAN, Mel... Doctor, you have to do something!'

The Doctor frowned. 'I am well aware of that, Professor Kairos. But the TARDIS isn't a 22 bus to Putney Common! And besides, she's been damaged by the time ram. I have to think carefully about our options!'

Paul grabbed his shoulders. 'You have to get us to the moon!'

'I fully intend to,' snapped the Doctor, breaking away from him and returning to the console, which was almost completely unscathed once more - some kind of autorepair gizmo, Stuart guessed. Shame it couldn't help TOMTIT. 'Unfortunately, this is one of those occasions where "kill or cure" is an apposite epithet.'

Stuart couldn't help but shudder at the utter finality of the Doctor's statement. 'What do you mean?'

'The only way we can break free from this situation is to find something to hang our hats on and then pray that we can fling ourselves out of this gravitational mess. The TARDIS can see where we want to end up, but not the route. Therefore, I have to home in on something and hope for the best.'

'The Master's TARDIS,' muttered Paul. 'You're going to match temporal frequencies and attempt to materialise near it.'

The Doctor broke off from his ministrations at the console to stare at Paul. 'Very good, Professor. Very good indeed.'

Stuart was still trying to understand. 'A bit like a lasso, Doc? Lassoing the Master's TARDIS and pulling ourselves free?'

'Got it in one. However, to do that I have to match temporal frequencies perfectly until the very last moment.'

To Stuart, that sounded familiar. Too familiar. 'You're going to time-ram the Master's TARDIS!'

The Doctor nodded. 'Got it in one, Professor, but it's our only hope. I just have to make sure we break off just before the time ram occurs: the closer to ram we get, the closer to the Master's TARDIS we arrive. Now let me set the coordinates. The sooner I can get started, the sooner we can rescue Mel and Arlene.'

Stuart wasn't happy about this. He wasn't happy about this at all. He just didn't fancy the idea of them getting that close to the Master's TARDIS.

Beneath the shadow of the giant statue, Anjeliqua closed the final panel on the master console and got to her feet. 'Everything's complete, Master. We're ready to activate the TITAN Array at your command.' Anjeliqua was definitely ready. She was rapidly tiring of this servile act - the sooner she could show the Master who was in control, the better.

'At my command? Really?' The Master's voice was even silkier than usual, silkier - and suspicious. Anjeliqua felt a chill on the back of her neck. Surely he couldn't suspect?

'Of course, Master,' she replied.

'Oh, I apologise. I was under the impression that all of this was to satisfy your own desires and caprices, Ms Whitefriar.'

'I don't understand...' she muttered. What did he know?

'Credit me with some intelligence, woman!' The Master tapped his wrist unit. A holosphere materialised between himself and Anjeliqua. Another Anjeliqua, talking to Mel inside the Master's TARDIS.

I've rigged the device, Mel. When the Master tries to tap the power of the Lux Aeterna, it will surge. He won't be able to control it - it will burn him out.

The Master was icy cool. '"Burn me out"? What an eloquently vile turn of phrase. And so very inaccurate. I could have built this device myself: my people mastered such technology when your ancestors were primeval slime fussing around on beaches, trying to work out how to divide. I simply used you and the Cole woman as slave labour.'

He shook his head. 'Your pathetic attempts to sabotage my godhood were dismantled moments after you installed them. Did you really think I wouldn't notice something as fundamental as your interference? Did you?' He grabbed her throat with a black-gloved hand. 'I have to admit I was both disappointed and impressed,' he stated calmly, tightening his grip. Anjeliqua was finding it hard to breathe. 'I didn't think you were that technical,' he whispered into her ear.

'I remembered the patent application for that one,' she gasped. The game was up, and she had no need to act as the simpering little woman any more.

The Master removed his hand and let Anjeliqua fall gasping to the cold blue marble floor. 'You insect! You dared to stand in the way of my apotheosis? You dared to deny me the Lux Aeterna?' He turned his back on her, rubbing his hands together. 'But you can still be of service. Even without your puerile meddling, I always knew there was a chance that the flow would prove too great. I do need to calibrate the device - and the effect of the Lux Aeterna on the human form will provide a perfect chance for that calibration.' The Master snapped his fingers at Arlene. 'Make Ms Whitefriar comfortable within the framework.'

Anjeliqua glanced towards the doorway, but realised that she had nowhere to hide. As Arlene grabbed her she struggled, but Arlene's strength appeared to be almost superhuman.

'No!' she screamed. 'Not now - I was so close!'

'As they say on Earth, Ms Whitefriar: close but no cigar.' He took a puff of his Cuban and laughed as Arlene brutally shoved Anjeliqua into the coffin-shaped framework of wire and circuitry, snapping the restraints over her.

Unable to move, Anjeliqua just hoped that Mel had found the clue in time.

The Doctor stood up from the console and addressed Stuart and Paul. 'I've located the Master's TARDIS, and I've set my TARDIS to home in on it.' He looked round at Stuart. 'And yes, we will effectively be time-ramming the Master's TARDIS. I'll monitor the time frequencies and perform a temporal bounce-back at the moment of full ram.'

'Sounds wonderful, Doc,' growled Stuart. 'Can't we fly through a couple of supernovae and dive-bomb a quasar on the way? Just to ease the boredom?'

The Doctor arched an eyebrow. 'Don't be funny. This is an extremely dangerous manoeuvre, and not one that I relish. But if we're to rescue Mel, Arlene and Anjeliqua Whitefriar, and stop the Master from fulfilling his diabolical plans, it's our only choice.' He tapped the console; a whirring noise issued from one of the roundelled walls. Two padded couches flowed seamlessly from the wall.

'Strap yourselves in, gentlemen,' said the Doctor cheerily. 'This is going to be a bumpy ride!'

Mel had searched every inch of the horrid, whispery room. Nothing! She sat back on the bed, trying to look at the situation logically. What was it Anjeliqua had said? *Mel... if you want an answer to all of this, remember what Professor Norton used to tell us.*

Professor Norton had been their lecturer for Project Management: First Principles, sharing the duties with Professors Martin and Parncutt. And the first thing he had taught them was to build everything from the floor up. From the floor up... Mel dropped from the bed and started searching the warm, white floor of the Master's prison.

She found it in moments. A small brown ball. Like a planet... Anjeliqua must have left it there.

The orrery virtually shouted at her.

She rushed over to the table and sought out a gap in the brass model. There it was! Mel inserted the small moon and was rewarded by a neon flare around the doorframe.

Now all she had to do was reach the console room.

The Doctor gripped the ridged edge of the console. With one hand, he gingerly reached out and pressed the vortex primer.

As the familiar noise of the time engines flooded the console room, he considered his actions. This really did have to be the most stupid move he had ever attempted, up there with tractoring that neutron star away from Chloris and trying to take on the Eye of Harmony, but he really didn't have any alternative - not if he was going to save Mel and the others.

The smooth roaring of the engines began to falter. 'Hang on!' he shouted to Stuart and Paul, strapped into their seats. 'This is where it gets really hairy!'

But even the Doctor hadn't expected the TARDIS to do a 180 degree turn on him.

Hanging on to the console as it suddenly ended up above him like some Art Nouveau chandelier, the Doctor's main thoughts were about Mel. Had she survived? And if she had - could she forgive him?

Thanks to her earlier explorations, Mel found her way through the Master's TARDIS with the minimum of effort, although the dark, hissing corridors gave her a severe case of the willies. She just hoped she would be in time to stop Anjeliqua from doing anything stupid.

She opened the door to the console room a crack, praying that it was empty.

It was. But it was still black, still steeped in shadow and still whispering. Swallowing down her fear, she darted inside and over to the console, and located the scanner switch.

And immediately wished that she hadn't.

Anjeliqua was strapped into some kind of iron maiden, a coffin-shaped device made of gold and silver circuitry. Mel guessed that this was the conversion device Anjeliqua had been speaking about. But it was clear that the Master was calling the shots: he was ordering Arlene around, and Anjeliqua didn't look too happy about being strapped into the device.

But of course she wouldn't - it was the same one that she was supposed to have booby-trapped! Mel looked for the door lever.

The console room finally righted itself, throwing the Doctor into an undignified heap on the floor. He scrabbled to his feet, casting a glance at the distinctly green Stuart Hyde and a strangely oblivious Paul Kairos strapped into their chairs, before checking the readings.

The TARDIS had cleared the Great Attractor - with a touch of the high dramas, in the Doctor's opinion: the old girl loved to grandstand, and pulling herself out of a gravitic well was as good a chance as any - and was now in the vicinity of Earth's moon.

And the very close vicinity of the Master's TARDIS. The temporal frequencies of the two TARDISes were converging at an alarming rate, and the Doctor had to ensure that he broke the time ram off at the exact moment of convergence. It wasn't even something he could leave to the automatics: that close to time ram, TARDISes tended to panic and the automatics went all over the place. No, this needed the captain at the helm. He touched the telepathic circuits, calming and reassuring the ship as he prepared for the materialisation.

He didn't expect to be thrown across the console room. Or slammed into the wall.

The Doctor shook his head and tried to work out what was going on. The psychic shock had been unbelievable - as if the TARDIS had done it deliberately. Then he realised: she *had* done it deliberately.

The TARDIS could be many things - wilful, temperamental, flirtatious even - but she had never attacked him before. He staggered to his feet and made his way back to the console.

'What's going on?' shouted Stuart above the laboured grind of the time engines.

But the Doctor wasn't listening. Because he suddenly understood.

The old girl was terrified. She had just been infected with a debilitating virus, been within nanoseconds of time-ramming herself, only to have to leap blindly out of the gravitic well of the Great Attractor.

Bracing himself, he again made telepathic contact. The emotion was now clearly fear, pure terror flooding the circuits. But the Doctor held on, fighting the pain, pouring his support... his love into the console. He owed it to Stuart and Paul, he owed it to Mel and Arlene, he owed it to the TARDIS... But above all...

He owed it to himself.

And, according to the readings, it was now or never. He twisted the helmic regulator, breaking off the ram. It had been close, very close, too close...

That was the moment when the Doctor realised that something just wasn't quite right. The console room was echoing to the sound of materialisation, but there were also the subtly different harmonies of a dematerialisation...

The wall to the left of the great doors faded out of existence, revealing another console room behind it. A console room with something of the night about it.

As the time engines came to a halt with a thud, the Doctor ran through the newly opened gap, knowing exactly where he was.

'Doctor!' The shriek came from behind him; he turned to experience a diminutive redhead throwing herself around his neck. 'I'm so glad to see you!' she cried. 'I've got so much to tell you. Anjeliqua was planning to sabotage the Master's energy converter, but it looks like she's been found out. He's planning to pour the whole of the Lux Aeterna through her body!'

Lux Aeterna? Who had Mel been talking to? But there were more important items to attend to. He returnd to his own console room and pulled the door lever.

And nothing happened. It was as if the outer plasmic shell was still in the vortex...

'Of course!' he yelled. 'The TARDIS hasn't emerged into the space-time continuum! Our only link to reality is through the Master's TARDIS. Quickly, you three -' he pointed into the dark-mirror console room - 'Through there!'

* * *

'Professor Cole, you are familiar with the procedure?' asked the Master, indicating the TITAN console.

Arlene gave a loyal nod. 'Of course, Master.'

It was nothing more than a series of instructions: Professor Cole had learnt them immediately. 'Tell me.' He just wanted to be certain, and he would be far too busy to pay attention.

'I will run the TITAN program,' Arlene intoned. 'It will access the Lux Aeterna and bleed a small amount of the energy into your TARDIS, activating the force field geometries. Once the Chronovores are cut off from the Lux Aeterna, its full power will be siphoned and fed through the converter frame into Anjeliqua. The biometric systems in your TARDIS will calibrate the flow rates based on your Gallifreyan-hybrid physiognomy. As soon as the analysis is complete, TITAN will automatically halt the flow, enabling you to remove Anjeliqua's remains and take your place within the frame.'

Arlene didn't even blink at the procedures she had just described, procedures which would almost instantly reduce Anjeliqua to a pile of ashes. The Master knew his control over her was possibly the most powerful he had ever accomplished. But he was asking her to betray everything she believed in; for that, he needed to be totally sure of her. It was a strain, but what choice did he have? He glanced at his hand; the skin was already blistering and flaking. Without TITAN, without the converter, without the Lux Aeterna, he would be nothing.

Ever.

'Excellent. Run the program!' The time was so very, very near and so very, very short...

As Arlene's hands darted across the polished surface of the console, urging the black-light converters imbedded in the marble dome of the Midnight Cathedral to fluoresce with their unholy neon, the Master couldn't help but feel a touch of unease. It was all too simple. Where was the Doctor and his self-appointed righteousness? Where?

He dismissed the thought: this plan had been meticulously calculated to the nth decimal place - nothing had been left to chance. The Doctor was dead, blown away by the time winds, and there was nothing to stop his own ultimate evolution.

Arlene called across to him from the TITAN console. 'Accessing Lux Aeterna in three, two, one - access!'

The TITAN core burnt with a red incandescence that defied description. It was the blood of gods, reflecting off the carved and vaulted dome in a dappled inferno of purples and scarlets, as the majesty of the Lux Aeterna washed over the Dusk Nave of the Midnight Cathedral.

'Force fields activating.'

From across the Cathedral, the blue altar of the Master's TARDIS momentarily blurred and faded, accompanied by the faintest of materialisation noises.

'Force fields in place. Transferring Lux Aeterna to the converter in three, two one. Full transfer achieved.'

The Master allowed himself a small sigh of relief and turned his attention to the converter attached to the base of the statue's pillar. For a moment, there was nothing: Anjeliqua, strapped into the frame, was rigid with fear, her face white.

The metallic filigree of the Whitefriar Lattice suddenly flared through the spectrum, from red to gold to a Cherenkov blue, while the titanium-shielded processor frame started to hum with the energy throughput. The entire converter began to burn with the purity of the Lux Aeterna. But it wasn't confined to the converter for long.

A second later, the energies arced into Anjeliqua's imprisoned body, arcs of blue and white and gold which lit up her skin, her tissues, her bones. Energies that no human could ever have imagined, let alone experienced.

Anjeliqua screamed.

Perfect, thought the Master. Let the meretricious cow burn. It was a necessary sacrifice on the route to his immeasurable glory.

'Calibration forty per cent complete,' Arlene yelled above the duet between Anjeliqua's screams and the howl of the TITAN Array, its entire assembly turned from chrome to crimson. The TITAN core was now an incandescent bloodstone, rendering the winged statue a vivid red. *Soon you will be turning your supplications towards me,* thought the Master. *And I will find your vaunted Constructors, your worshippers, and punish them for their neglect. When I am a god.*

A shout echoed around the Nave. 'No!'

The Master span round at the familiar voice. 'Too late, Doctor!'

The Doctor was standing in front of the Master's TARDIS, the newly rejuvenated Hyde and the surly Kairos behind him, the irritatingly indestructible Melanie Bush at his side. How homely. And how pathetic.

'You have no idea what you're doing,' said the Doctor, striding towards him with his little family in tow. 'None.'

The Master was glad the Doctor was there to witness his apotheosis, but his spurious morality could become so very wearing. 'I have every idea what I'm doing, Doctor: I am finally taking my rightful place amongst the pantheon of gods. Time? Pain? Death? Eternity? They will be my brothers and my sisters. The Guardians of Time? They will thank me for ridding the multiverse of their bastard children, the Chronovores. The Eternals? Perhaps I can take part in their games, risk everything for a taste of Enlightenment?' In one smooth move, he drew out his tissue-compression eliminator. The Doctor - only a couple of metres away - gave it a contemptuous glance, while Miss Bush and Professor Hyde looked on in horror. Only Professor Kairos seemed unperturbed: he had closed his eyes.

'But I choose to be a benevolent god, Doctor. Don't interfere, and I will spare you - for now. But, with the imagination of a god, I feel sure I shall have no problem devising a suitable fate for you.' A telltale flashed on the master console. The biometric readings were complete: the flow dams would now cut in. 'Time to remove the warm-up act, Doctor - and prepare for the grand finale.'

But the flow from the Lux Aeterna didn't stop. If anything, the glare from the converter increased. He looked over at Professor Cole, who was staring at her erstwhile friend in the converter. The Whitefriar woman was haloed in gold and screaming, straining against her bonds and burning in the agonies of the Lux Aeterna. It was a suitable punishment for betrayal, but immediacy dragged him from his satisfaction.

'Professor Cole - raise the flow dams manually!' he yelled over the wailing that echoed around the Nave.

At his command she darted over to the console. She dithered over the controls and finally looked up.

'I can't, Master.' There was sheer terror in her eyes - but it wasn't terror of him. It was if she had seen something in Anjeliqua's wild eyes that had scared her half to death. 'Something's happened,' she stammered. 'Some kind of link between the Lux Aeterna and Anjeliqua!'

'What?' The Master dashed over to the converter, but the wall of sparks he encountered knocked him back.

'A problem, Master?' asked the Doctor in his predictably sarcastic tones.

'A force field?' the Master muttered incredulously. Then it came to him. They were stealing his power! They were taking his birthright from him! That was why the Doctor was here! 'No - I will not allow it!'

Anjeliqua's delightful screaming had stopped, but she was still writhing in soundless agony. And something else was happening. Her body was beginning to glow, from gold to yellow to white. She was stealing what was his by right!

The Doctor was shouting at him. 'The human body isn't designed to absorb the fundamental force of the cosmos! Every *cell* in her body will rupture under that sort of influx. She'll die!'

The fool! 'Don't you think I don't know that, Doctor? I have to release her. Help me!'

Help me fulfil my own destiny.

The Doctor hesitated - but for the barest of seconds. If he helped to free Anjeliqua, the Master could take the Lux Aeterna for himself. And, unlike Anjeliqua, a hybrid Gallifreyan-Trakenite body - augmented with the powers of the Eye of Harmony, the Source of Traken, and goodness alone knew what else the Master had stolen on the way - might very well be able to absorb those energies.

But there was a person's life at stake, and he could deal with the Master when the time came. The Doctor ignored his gibbering and ran over to the console. Taking in the readings at a glance, he looked up at Anjeliqua. She was now motionless - a still point in the ever-brightening fire that flickered over her body. A fire that could ignite the universe.

The Doctor just hoped she wasn't already dead.

But the readings from the console told an even more horrific story. 'She's bonded with the Lux Aeterna! Unless we can free her there will be a rupture in the space-time continuum. A vortex rupture! Surely even you can't countenance that degree of damage to the web of time?'

It was at this point that the Doctor realised the Master had visited madness and gone straight through to the other side.

'I will *be* the web of time, Doctor.' The Master knocked the Doctor out of the way and threw himself on to the console, his hands pathetically clawing at its chrome panels, his whole body hugging it maniacally. 'I will disconnect her. I will. I will!'

The Doctor tried to drag him out of the way, but it was impossible: the depths of the Master's insanity and desperation were giving him a strength that even the Doctor couldn't match. But having seen the readings, he suspected that disconnecting Anjeliqua was pointless, anyway. She and the Lux Aeterna seemed to be coexisting on some level that the TITAN Array simply couldn't touch.

He tried to look at her, but it was so difficult now. It was almost impossible to make out her figure at the centre of the golden incandescence: she was just a couple of charcoal strokes in the flames, a smudge in a bonfire.

Forces beyond his control - beyond his comprehension - were at play here. It was time to get the innocent bystanders out of the way. Then again, how innocent were any of them in this current situation?

'Mel, Stuart, Paul - get back to the TARDIS! You'll be safe there.' Safe? Even the invulnerability of the TARDIS couldn't be guaranteed where the Lux Aeterna was concerned. The fundamental force of the cosmos against the mathematical arrogance of the Time Lords? But what else could he do?

The explosion almost knocked the Doctor over, a dull woomph just behind a blinding light.

He skidded over the blue marble floor of the Dusk Nave, and just about managed to maintain his balance before he knocked into Paul, Mel and Stuart as if he were some kind of multicoloured ten-pin bowling ball. Regaining his dignity, he found himself facing what was left of the converter: a tattered pile of grey and glitter. But above it...

Deep within the Doctor's psyche was the knowledge that the Time Lords were not the pinnacle of existence. There were others, far beyond the poor vision of old Gallifrey.

Gods.

With a shriek of triumph, she announced her presence to the universe. Magnificent wings of fire burnt behind her as she emerged from the embers of the explosion.

It was Anjeliqua.

Redesigned as a god.

Her eyes sparkled with the wisdom of universes, her hair was a wild fiery mane, tossed by the winds of time. As for her face... It was still Anjeliqua's face, but it shone with the authority of ages.

Her figure was no longer that of the comfy, dumpy Anjeliqua Whitefriar; the Lux Aeterna had transformed her into a tall, striking woman of incandescent white, naked and yet clothed in fire. But, more importantly, the change went further: it was clear that her mind boiled with an intelligence and a strength that scared the Doctor to death. She was one with the Lux Aeterna! So what had she become?

'Hear me, Time Lords.' Her voice, like a chorus of angels and the tortured scream of devils entwined, penetrated his mind. 'I am no longer the woman you knew. I am now life and fire incarnate.' Her wings extended, flooding the entire Dusk Nave with golden incandescence.

'I am the Quantum Archangel. And nothing will ever be the same again.'

Magnificat

Chapter Seven
What Have I Done to Deserve This?

'No!'

Arlene dragged her attention away from Anjeliqua at the shout. It was the Master, his face contorted in terror at the apparition, as though he were looking at the devil. Then she caught a glimpse of the same expression on the Doctor's face. Was this something out of Time Lord mythology? Or some shared nightmare they had once faced? She suddenly realised that her blind obedience to the Master - something that had felt so natural - had evaporated. She was her own woman once more... and very, very angry. He had stolen her free will!

Before she could consider further, the Master made a run for it. Knocking a dazed Paul Kairos out of the way, he darted across the Dusk Nave towards the squat blue altar of his TARDIS.

'Stop him!' yelled the Doctor. 'He's our only way out of here.' But it was too late. The Master skirted round the back of the marble altar and was gone. Moments later, modulated grinding and roaring filled the Midnight Cathedral as his TARDIS dematerialised, leaving nothing to show that it had ever been there.

'He's taken my TARDIS with him,' the Doctor groaned.

'All will be well.' The unnerving voice echoed in their minds. The creature that had once been Anjeliqua had been watching the Master's escape impassively; it now turned its haughty attention to the four who remained.

'Who are you?' asked Mel nervously. 'What happened to Anjeliqua?'

'Dear, sweet Mel,' came the reply. 'Your concern is unjustified. Nothing has happened to Anjeliqua. Nothing bad, that is. Part of me is still Anjeliqua, but I am much, much more. The fundamental force of the cosmos runs through me like lifeblood. I have become a goddess.' Her face was calm and unemotional - if only Arlene could have felt the same. 'But I am still your friend.'

Unsurprisingly, that did nothing to reassure Arlene. Someone as spiteful, petty and bitter as Anjeliqua with the powers of a god? It didn't bear thinking about.

'Calm yourself, Arlene.' It was Anjeliqua again. 'Such concerns are now beneath me.' *She read my mind!* 'With the power I now wield, nothing is impossible. But with such power comes a great responsibility - a responsibility that I intend to uphold.'

She threw her arms outwards, as if to embrace the Dusk Nave. Her wings began to flare, expanding until Arlene had to avert her eyes. They filled the Nave, washing over Arlene, the Doctor and the others. But the light didn't burn; if anything, it calmed Arlene, reassured her...

For a moment, she was elsewhere. The beginning of time to the end of time, spread across the universe... Then she was whole once again, racked with an overwhelming sense of loss.

It took her a couple of seconds to adjust to her new surroundings. The ubiquitous blue of the Midnight Cathedral had gone, to be replaced by a more familiar white. She was in the TITAN suite!

The chrome of the Array was back to its rectilinear configuration, the core at its centre. The quantum computer and the master console were where they had always been. She looked round for the others, and was reassured to see that Mel, Paul and Stuart were standing behind her, although why Stuart was looking so young was a mystery to her. But where was the Doctor?

He was standing on the far side of the TITAN suite, a satisfied expression on his face. He was staring at the incongruous shape of an old-fashioned police box, which Arlene assumed was his TARDIS.

Anjeliqua had brought them all home.

'The Midnight Cathedral is an old and revered temple to gods long since departed.' Anjeliqua was hovering above them, her wings caressing the steel beams of the Array. 'It should be left in peace.'

The Doctor appeared to have recovered his composure. 'Thank you for returning us to Earth, Anjeliqua. What's next on your list?' There was an arrogance born of fear in his voice.

'Ah, Doctor. You know so much, yet understand so very little. Anjeliqua Whitefriar is only a small part of me now. She is the moral compass of the Quantum Archangel; I will use her to guide my actions.'

Why didn't that reassure Arlene?

'What actions? Anj... Archangel, you possess the ability to bend reality to your will. In the wrong hands, that could prove catastrophic!'

The Quantum Archangel - it was difficult to think of the brilliant figure as Anjeliqua, and even the creature seemed to be referring to Anjeliqua as a different person - held her hands out and seemed to examine them for a second. 'But these are not the wrong hands, Doctor. I intend to make things better.'

'Better? Better for whom?' demanded the Doctor.

'For everyone.' She beat her wings, blinding them all for a second. When Arlene's vision cleared, the Quantum Archangel was nowhere to be seen.

The Doctor's voice barked out. 'All of you - into the TARDIS.'

A few moments later they were standing in the Doctor's console room. Although it was virtually identical to the Master's, there were none of the sinister shadows, no creepy whispering. It was white and comforting.

A rhythmic burbling suddenly filled the room. The Doctor turned from the console. 'There - I've activated the TARDIS force field. It probably won't last for a fraction of a second against the Quantum Archangel's powers, but it's about all I can do at the moment.'

'Perhaps you might like to explain what the hell is going on?' asked Stuart. 'With subtitles for the hard of thinking?'

The Doctor sank back into the red velvet chaise longue that stood by one of the roundelled walls, and held up his hand. 'Professor Hyde, this needs subtitles for Time Lords, I assure you.' He drew a deep breath. 'The person we knew as Anjeliqua Whitefriar has been completely subsumed by the Lux Aeterna.'

'Doctor, subtitles for Mel, please. All I know about the Lux Aeterna is from what Anjeliqua told me. Something very powerful?'

The Doctor elaborated. 'The Lux Aeterna is the energy lattice that underpins the entire multiverse: not just this universe, but any and every other one that could ever possibly exist. It is infinite power, but without form, without reason. Somehow - thanks to the Master's ham-handed attempt to access it - it has bonded with Anjeliqua. Her sentience has given form and reason to the Lux Aeterna.' He flung his arms out. 'Somewhere - out there! - is a sentient being of unimaginable power. She - it - can split a quasar in two with the merest thought. Create entire new realities fashioned to its whims. Destroy Gallifrey just because it suits it!'

'It said that Anjeliqua was its moral compass,' said Mel. 'I could handle that if it had been the old Anjeliqua: she was very different when we were at university, wasn't she?' she asked Paul and Arlene.

'Right up to the point where she stole the patent to the Whitefriar Lattice,' Arlene replied.

'I think you ought to look at this,' said the Doctor. He was holding up a burnt clump of silver circuitry - Whitefriar Lattice - which he had taken from the base of the charred hulk of TOMTIT. 'Take a look.' He thrust it forward.

Arlene took it from his hands and looked at it. And realised what the Doctor meant. Whitefriar Lattice resembled a silvery Brillo pad, but with small spheres every now and then - the processing nodes. Each of them had the patent information printed on to it in tiny white script: ® Whitefriar Lattice. Except that this bundle of Whitefriar Lattice didn't. Instead, each node bore the legend: ® Kairos Lattice.

'Kairos Lattice,' Mel said. 'Anjeliqua has changed history.'

'She's making everything right,' said Stuart. 'That's what she said she was going to do.'

The Doctor ran a hand through his hair. 'Make everything right? That's the worst thing she could do!'

The Master's TARDIS was now far away from Earth and its constellation, hurtling through the time vortex as fast as its time engines could take it.

He had failed!

That woman had managed to execute the perfect foil to his plans; not only had she denied him the Lux Aeterna, but now she embodied it! Dumpy little Anjeliqua Whitefriar, now with the powers of a god! Powers that should have been his! But seeing that figure soaring above him had filled him full of primal terror, driving him to the safety of his TARDIS.

As if he stood the faintest hope of escape.

With the activation of TITAN and the rape of the Lux Aeterna, the Chronovores couldn't help but have noticed. Their revenge must be hot on his heels, and it was most definitely in his best interests to get as far away from the source of the incident as possible.

The Master tapped another course change into the console, and was horrified to see his hands. Rather than the healthy pink flesh he was used to, they were rotted and decayed, skin corrupted back to tendons and muscle. He raised those hands to his face, and realised that he was feeling sinew and bone rather than skin. The Source of Traken was finally burnt out, and his physical form was rapidly decomposing into his Gallifreyan body, exhausted beyond its regenerations into nothing more than an animated cadaver. Even the pain seemed to be fading, as if his nervous system was simply giving up. It was all melting into a single dull ache that consumed every part of him.

He was dying. All his hopes, his plans, his schemes were for naught. Within a matter of hours he would be unable to maintain his mind within his dead physical form, and the Master would be no more.

He would not give up. He would not surrender. He was the Master - he would survive.

He pondered his options. The deathworms offered a degree of immortality, as did the living planet of the Cheetah People -

His TARDIS lurched to one side, the attack cutting through the Farquazi shields as if they hadn't even been there. Barely clutching on to the console with his withered hands, he looked up at the scanner, unable to stop himself but well aware of what he was going to see.

The roiling blue and gold of the time vortex was obscured by the beating of a million actinic wings: the Divine Host of the Chronovores, swooping up from the Six-Fold Realm through the channel he had created for them. One Chronovore could destroy his TARDIS. So how would he stand a chance against the entire Divine Host? Running was no longer an option: that number of Chronovores was creating a natural jamming field which made dematerialisation impossible. And it wasn't as if his TARDIS had any weapons so that he could stand and fight.

A peculiar feeling swept over him, a disturbance that only those with a special relationship with time would have sensed. For a second, it was as if there were two of him, two alternate Masters from alternate realities, subtly yet importantly different. Then they combined, with an inevitability not that dissimilar to the materialisation of a TARDIS.

Instinctively he turned to the console, not noticing the wholesale changes that had made it more regimented, more military. As far as the Master was concerned his TARDIS was as it had ever been: a fully armed space-time machine.

At his command, one of the panels on his console reconfigured into the weaponry grid; he activated the offensive array, priming the Klypstrømic warheads, arming the artron cannon and initiating the vortex lance. The Divine Host of the Chronovores might be all-powerful, but the Master's TARDIS was armed to the teeth. He might not survive the encounter, but he fully intended to put up one hell of a fight.

As the first wave of the Divine Host descended with the beat of a million wings, he fired the artron cannon.

'She's altering reality,' said the Doctor, examining the charred Kairos Lattice as if it were a valuable antique. 'In this universe, I suspect that Anjeliqua never stole the patent. It was always credited to you, Paul.'

'But if she's changed reality, how come we remember the Whitefriar Lattice?' asked Stuart. 'Surely we should always have known it as the Kairos Lattice?' Alternate universes and parallel realities were covered in the temporal mechanics course - he had taught enough of them - but as theoretical models they were nothing more than a set of mathematical absurdities, and he had never expected to see them proved to him. Then again, when he had woken up with a hangover this morning he hadn't expected to take part in a time ram, visit the Great Attractor and end up in a hidden cathedral on the moon. Nor had he expected to end the day thirty years younger.

'This has all the hallmarks of an incomplete reality shift.' The Doctor scratched his head. 'I suspect - I hope - that she's still learning about her powers. The Lux Aeterna may be omnipotent but it's dependent upon Anjeliqua's intelligence, and that's a limiting factor.'

'As much as it pains me to say it, Anjeliqua isn't exactly stupid, Doctor,' said Arlene.

'And the Lux Aeterna is ultimate power,' the Doctor continued. 'Even a genius cannot comprehend it in its entirety. But that doesn't give us any room for complacency: the fact that any part of the reality shift breached the TARDIS at all is a clear demonstration of just how powerful she's become. But she hasn't quite mastered the intricacies yet. A reality shift has to occur on a near-infinite number of levels simultaneously for it to be seamless. That we still remember the Whitefriar Lattice suggests she hasn't yet learnt how to completely separate the new reality from the old.'

'But if she can't control her powers, we haven't got anything to worry about, surely?' asked Arlene.

'My dear Professor Cole, we have everything to worry about. With every passing second she will gain more and more control. Until the entire cosmos becomes her plaything.'

She had been there for an eternity. Then again, what was eternity to the Quantum Archangel?

Stars could burn and die, galaxies could collide, timelines could converge and collapse... but the Archangel would wait, wait out her long silent vigil in the depths of the darker strata. She knew she would be undisturbed there.

The infinitesimal yet vital part of her that was still Anjeliqua

Whitefriar was experiencing a degree of confusion. What had brought her here? And why did it feel so familiar?

It was familiar because it was part of the consciousness that she shared with the Lux Aeterna: its life was her life, its past was her past. So she knew that she was deep within the time vortex, a shunned and disowned part of that realm that the Chronovores and the Eternals had wiped from their collective memories. She could feel the horror that had confronted the ancient races, the collective shame that had led them to take the ultimate action: involving the Six-Fold-God. Anjeliqua even understood the complexities of the politics and relationships, the allegiances and subterfuges that were being presented to her: memories from the Lux Aeterna that it had never before had the intelligence or the emotion to remember. She was remembering for it.

But she had another set of memories: memories of Professor Anjeliqua Whitefriar. As she floated in the void, allowing the currents of the time vortex and the breezes of the time winds to gently buffet her, she finally had the tranquillity to reflect on what had happened to her. What she had become. And the resources of the Lux Aeterna allowed her to see and feel the experience as if it was happening all over again...

Strapped into the converter, Anjeliqua could only watch as the Master brought the TITAN Array online. All her plans, her revenge... a failure! And Anjeliqua was not used to failure.

But she knew there was no way out of this particular situation. She was strapped into the assembly of titanium steel and Whitefriar Lattice. Hah! Whitefriar Lattice! Poetic justice, she supposed. Just her luck to be killed by the patent that had made her millions.

As the thrum from the TITAN Array increased, Anjeliqua had braced herself for the influx of energy: after all the work she had done on both the converter and the Array, she was well aware that the Lux Aeterna was power beyond imagining. The regulators and transformers in the Array could have dampened down a million nuclear reactors; but even with those regulators and transformers in place, a human body simply wasn't designed to absorb the minutest fraction of that power: the moment it flooded into the converter, she would be like a moth to a flame, a sacrificial victim to the Master's arrogance. And to hers, she suddenly realised. What on Earth had possessed her to behave that way?

And then the Lux Aeterna was upon her.

As the first arcs of searing energy burnt into Anjeliqua, she screamed. But it wasn't with pain - it was with revelation. She knew why she had behaved that way!

Before she could even consider what she had learnt, the energy altered subtly: now it seemed to have a purpose, a direction. It was exploring her! She could feel it travelling through her nervous system, examining her muscles and organs. There wasn't an intelligence, but an instinct. It was curious! And then it found her brain, her mind, her soul...

It read her. All of her.

She felt the satisfaction that coloured the energy as it finally understood her, understood what it could offer her and, more importantly, what she could offer it.

In her mind she could sense it holding out a hand to her, offering to save her, to remake her, to give her access to the secrets of the universe and beyond...

It was an offer she simply couldn't decline. And at the moment she admitted that to herself, the full force of the Lux Aeterna had surged through the TITAN Array, into the converter... and into her.

It had existed since before the dawn of time, formless, meaningless, inexhaustible, unlimited power without desire or reason. But with Anjeliqua, it now had meaning, it had reason, it had desire. She felt it enfold her, welcome her, become a part of her... And she became a part of it.

And so the Quantum Archangel was born.

Borne on wings of fire, she had become something so very much more than the sum of her parts. The impotent human and the aimless, godlike energy source, suddenly combined into a goddess.

She was whole! She was the Quantum Archangel!

It was time to survey her new kingdom.

What had once been only marble and chrome became something quite different. She could see the ebb and flow of time through the TITAN Array. And what once been an ancient monument was now full of thoughts and memories.

It took her less than a fraction of a second.

She could see Stuart Hyde, Paul Kairos, Melanie Bush and Arlene Cole as smudges of intelligence, those nodes of knowing that gave the universe meaning. Precious intellects that she was now sworn to protect.

And then there were the Doctor and the Master, members of a race that had taken the first steps towards understanding the deeper mysteries of time. Both from the same race; so alike, and yet so very different. The Master had sworn to steal the Lux Aeterna and had been prepared to sacrifice Anjeliqua to achieve that, but the Quantum Archangel was not a vengeful goddess: the Master's actions had led to her birth.

As for the Doctor... a man of good with the seeds of such unimaginable evil lurking within him. She could feel his memories of Maradnias, but they were only the gloss on a patina of self-doubt and uncertainty. Words and images flooded through her: the Valeyard, time's champion, the champion's sacrifice... Such doubt and fear within someone who had saved the universe countless times over.

It was enough! Both of them would learn that life would be so very much better under the wisdom and guidance of the Quantum Archangel.

But her new reign could not yet dawn. She had already discovered that. Her first attempts to right those wrongs that beset the cosmos hadn't been completely successful: she had tried to repay Paul Kairos for the wrong she had committed as Anjeliqua and given him back the ownership of his great discovery, but she hadn't been able to complete the weave. And she had given the Master the chance to defend himself, but the tapestry still remained unfinished.

Some of the threads of reality were obvious, and she had rewoven them easily. But the subtler ones had been beyond her abilities, left as loose ends flailing about, spoiling the perfection of the warp and weft.

She had the power, she had the intelligence... but omnipotence eluded her. No, it wasn't omnipotence, it was omniscience. The sheer calculating power necessary to rewrite creation and balance all the probabilities was beyond her grasp.

She needed an ally... something, someone, who could provide the calculations. Who could provide –

'The processing power!' yelled the Doctor. 'Of course – that's it!'

'Processing power?' asked Mel. 'But I thought the Lux Aeterna was all-powerful?' She Mel still couldn't get to grips with the idea of Anjeliqua having godlike powers. Even the old Anjeliqua, with her crusade of the week and passion for lost causes, would have been bad enough, but the manipulative, spiteful woman she had become?

The Doctor started waving his hands at her. 'But don't you see, Mel: that's the point! The Quantum Archangel has the intelligence and the brute force, but no way of combining them. It's simply a question of mathematics.'

Mel had a different image. 'Or of computing,' she countered. 'She's got the processor and the hard drive, but no memory or cache. She hasn't got anywhere to actually perform the calculations.'

'Exactly!' said the Doctor. 'So we have to predict where she's going to go to find it. Out-think a god.'

Paul interjected. 'You mean she needs a computer? What about the quantum computer in the TITAN suite?'

The Doctor put a hand on his shoulder. 'Paul: she needs more processing power than this planet has seen or will ever see. To her, your all-singing, all-dancing Deutsch 3270 is nothing more than an abacus. She's going to be looking for...' He looked over at Mel. 'Mel – hurry off to my study and fetch some paper and a pen.'

Mel stared at him in puzzlement. It was as if the events of Maradnias had never happened and their relationship hadn't changed. But she also realised that there was a greater threat to be overcome. If the Doctor's implications were even only half-correct, the destruction of Maradnias would be nothing compared to the havoc that Anjeliqua could wreak – whether she intended to or not. Her thoughts and feelings about the Doctor would have to wait.

She dashed out of the console room to his study.

After a carefully executed sequence of vortex jumps, the Master had managed to shake off a large number of the Chronovores. There were still tens of thousands of them on his tail, but they were no longer quite the threat they had been, thanks to the weaponry hidden in his TARDIS.

His sustained assault on the host had torn enough holes in its ranks to allow dematerialisation: even with the Chronovores' mastery over time, a point-blank artron pulse was more than sufficient to tear their ethereal forms to fading tatters, whilst a spread of Klypstrømic warheads irradiated the vortex itself, poisoning them and leaving them weak and broken.

At that point he had decided that a strategic withdrawal was undoubtedly the course of action with the best chance of survival, and had instigated the vortex sequence. But how could he hide from the Divine Host for ever? Launching another wave of Klypstrømic warheads, he began to calculate another series of jumps. It was all he could do.

The Doctor spread what appeared to be a large sheet of off-white vellum over an Edwardian occasional table that Paul had dragged from one of the rooms just outside the console room, and wielded the large, lacquered fountain pen that Mel had brought him.

'Right,' he announced. 'Anjeliqua will be looking for processing power. The bigger, the better...' He frowned. 'At the top of the list, we have to have the Matrix.'

'I wouldn't disagree,' said Mel knowingly.

'Why are we wasting time compiling shopping lists?' demanded Stuart. He had felt the power of the Chronovores in the most direct way possible. If Anjeliqua possessed all their power, she had to be stopped.

He could sense the tension in the Doctor's voice: he obviously shared Stuart's worries. 'Professor Hyde – I understand your concerns. Left unchecked, Anjeliqua poses one of the greatest threats to this cosmos I have ever encountered. But that same cosmos is a very large place. Even with the TARDIS, we haven't got the time to go blundering around aimlessly. Which is why I'm trying to narrow down the search.' He licked the nib of his pen and wrote a name on the vellum with scratching strokes.

'What's this Matrix?' asked Arlene.

'The amplified panatropic neural network, also known as the Matrix of Time - one of the ultimate creations of the Time Lords of Gallifrey. It has more than enough excitonic processing power for her needs.' He shook his head. 'Although she'd be foolish to attempt it. The psionic framework of the Matrix is powered by the souls of the dead. Anjeliqua isn't going to have the strength of will to overcome them, and the Lux Aeterna doesn't have any will anyway.'

'Perish the thought that the Time Lords might be vulnerable,' snapped Stuart, although he tailed off under the Doctor's withering gaze. 'So, what next?' He wasn't sure he wanted to hear about technological achievements that made his researches look like cave paintings, but he had to agree with the Doctor's logic. 'Some superabacus on the edge of the galaxy, hovering inside a black hole? Or the slide rule of time in the Great Attractor?'

The Doctor gave him another look. 'Given that I seem to have a marvellous knack of tracking down mad supercomputers and blowing them up, the universe is surprisingly lacking in them. There's always the Conscience of Marinus...' He scribbled it on the vellum. 'Mustn't forget the God of the People, and then there's Xoanon, I suppose...' scribble, scribble. 'The Emperor Dalek has access to the Dalek galactic webwork...' His eyes were suddenly sad. 'And Logopolis would have been perfect...' He stopped and looked at Stuart quizzically, as if an unbidden thought had just popped into his head.

'What did you say?'

'When?'

'Just now.'

Stuart strained to remember. He might be thirty years younger, but his brain was still getting used to it. It was like spending your life driving an old rustbucket, only to be given the keys to a Ferrari. 'About the abacus?' Why was the Doctor getting so agitated about a bit of sarcasm?

'That's it! You said: "Some super-abacus on the edge of the galaxy, hovering inside a black hole? Or the slide rule of time in the Great Attractor?".' The Doctor leant back against the carved woodwork of the chaise longue. 'Mustn't forget to put that one on the list. It is supposed to be inactive, but we can't be too careful.' If Stuart was deciphering the Doctor's scrawl correctly, it said 'Mad Mind of Bophemeral'. Then again, it might very well have said 'Sad King of Bovril'.

Stuart glanced at his watch, before realising the uselessness of the act. But even if he didn't know the exact time, he knew it was very quickly running out.

Meanwhile, the Doctor added yet another name to the list.

Even though the Quantum Archangel knew she should wait until she had full control over her powers - a problem she still had to solve - she felt uncomfortable simply resting in the darker strata. Even if she couldn't carry out all the calculations necessary to form an entirely new universe, she could still explore the alternatives. Her wings spread outwards, once again lighting up the murk of the vortex. But her mind turned back, back to the past of Anjeliqua Whitefriar.

To her old friends.

The list contained about fifty names, supercomputers the Doctor reckoned could give the Quantum Archangel what she needed. But what does she need? thought Mel. More importantly, what does she want?

'I'm going to input the coordinates of this little bunch of cybernetic horrors into the TARDIS's navigational system.'

'How will that help if we don't know where she's going?' asked Stuart, peering over the Doctor's shoulder. The Doctor waved him away.

'The TARDIS is capable of both active and passive scans, Professor. Active scans are exhaustive, but the range is severely limited: we would only be able to cover about one-tenth of that list. But the passive scan can just about encompass that distance in time and space, although a couple of the entries are at the very limits of detection. At the first sign of a disturbance – '

'Such as the power of the Lux Aeterna flying past,' interrupted Stuart.

'Such as the power of the Lux Aeterna flying past,' repeated the Doctor through gritted teeth, 'the TARDIS console will light up like a Christmas tree.'

'Neat,' said Stuart. Mel couldn't help but laugh at the banter between the Doctor and Stuart. It wasn't that difficult to reconcile the Stuart who had taught her in 1985 to this decade-younger version: still as enthusiastic, as opinionated... in many ways, the Doctor and Stuart were now evenly matched. Both of them far older than their physical appearance and experience...

She felt divided. No, duplicated. Two versions of her, combining, becoming one, becoming...

Mel looked over the top of her glasses at the minister in front of her. 'This report is wholly unacceptable, Lynne. You still haven't addressed the real problems of the inner city homeless.'

Lynne Thomas MP, Secretary of State, shook her short brunette bob. 'But with all due respect...'

Mel was back in the TARDIS, a momentary shiver of loss and separation running up her spine. What on Earth was that? She was suddenly aware of a strident whooping from the console.

'It's started again!' bellowed the Doctor. 'Surges of time spillage, washing across the TARDIS – washing across the Earth, come to that.' He darted around the console, examining the read-outs, his expression growing more severe by the second. 'It's peaking at nearly 1,000 on the Bocca scale... massive reality disruptions...' He sighed. 'It's over.'

'Will somebody kindly explain what the hell is going on?' Mel turned at the unfamiliar voice, to see an elderly woman – early sixties? – wearing a white lab coat, standing by the console. Her hair was a silver-white bob, framing a lined yet mischievous face. Then there were two of her, one old, one much younger...

A woman in her late twenties, dressed in a baggy jumper and

jeans, had replaced her. But they were the same woman...

'Ruth?' whispered the Doctor. 'Ruth Ingram? What are you doing here?'

The woman frowned, before looking at each of them in turn. 'Mel, Paul, Arlene: what is the Doctor talking about?'

Mel remembered the name, although she had never met the woman before. Ruth Ingram had been the scientist who had helped Stuart - and the Master - to build TOMTIT thirty years ago. So what was she doing here? And, more importantly -

'Where's Stuart?' Arlene was looking around the console room. 'He was here a second ago.'

'Stuart?' asked Ruth Ingram. 'Why would Stuart be here? He's up in Cambridge.'

'What's he doing there?' asked Paul, looking extremely pale Mel thought. As if he'd had a shock. Perhaps he'd seen something as well.

'Where else would he be?' said Ruth. 'He's director of the Newton Institute for Temporal Research. Anyway, what has Stuart got to do with any of this?'

The Doctor tapped away on one of the console keyboards, reading the result off the monitor before sitting on the chaise longue, his head in his hands. 'The Archangel's effects have been far more widespread this time. According to *Who's Who*, Ruth's right. Stuart Hyde was made director of the Newton Institute nearly thirty years ago, after he successfully demonstrated a method of transferring matter through interstitial time. And Ruth became Emeritus Professor of Physics at West London University.' He looked at Mel, Paul and Arlene. 'According to this, she taught all three of you ...'

'Of course I did. What is all of this?'

The Doctor raised an eyebrow. 'Did anyone else experience anything?'

Mel remembered how she had felt a few minutes ago. 'I did have this really strange sort of vision just now. It might have been...' It sounded so silly, but she had been so sure... 'I might have been an MP.' Yes, it did sound silly.

'Anjeliqua wanted to make everything right for all of us,'

muttered Paul. 'She's started to explore those parallel universes which have the strongest possibility of giving us what we've always wanted.'

Anjeliqua's words came back to Mel. '"I intend to make things better." That's what she said. But me as an MP? Where did she get that one from?' Then again, hadn't she considered a career in politics once? When she had been a student she had been passionate about injustice – almost as passionate as Anjeliqua. She had wanted a career in which she could help people...

The Doctor stood up. 'Paul's right. She is learning to alter the prime reality. This universe now has the Kairos Lattice and Stuart as director of the Newton Institute. It also has us teaming up with Ruth from the very start. And Ruth experiencing the temporal reversion in the warehouse, I might add. Far more than enough to attract attention, unfortunately.'

'For heaven's sake, can't you just tell us what's going on?' It was obvious that, like Stuart, Ruth didn't take kindly to stupidity or procrastination.

'Very well, Doctor Ingram. I have to assume that you are familiar with everything that has happened to us over the last couple of days? Yes? Good. Anjeliqua is now acting as the intellect behind the Lux Aeterna. She has decided – reverting to her basic moral code, it would seem – to make everything right for all of us, which I would guess involves changing reality to give every single person on Earth their most heartfelt dreams and ambitions.'

'But surely that can't be possible,' countered Ruth. 'There are seven billion people on this planet. How can she create a world that pleases seven billion people?'

'She can't,' said Mel suddenly realising where the Doctor's reasoning was leading. 'So that's why she needs the processing power. She needs a supercomputer that can realise not just seven billion people, but the lives of every single being in the cosmos.' She looked over at the Doctor. 'Is that really possible?' Unfortunately, she knew the answer.

'Sadly, yes. We're talking about computers where the basic engrams are inscribed on the fabric of the space-time continuum itself. Where the memory can be an eleven-dimensional self-referential lattice or a pocket universe. Where processing occurs faster than the speed of light - faster than the speed of time. Supercomputers such as the ones on my list,' he said proudly, glancing at the console. 'Thankfully, there's no sign of activity anywhere within the detection grid. And I would imagine that she's going to have to approach her target directly - I doubt she'll be able to take the processing power without going there physically.'

'But she's demonstrated what she can do!' shouted Arlene. 'Mel thinks she's an MP, Stuart and Ruth have swapped places, and Paul has invented the most popular piece of hardware on the planet! What next?'

The Master swung his TARDIS through the time fissure, ignoring the screams from the console as he pushed the machine so far beyond its capabilities that he fully expected it to disintegrate around him. His tattered windpipe hissed a shriek of relief as his TARDIS flew from the fissure into the open spaces of the vortex. But he wasn't alone.

The Divine Host was much diminished, but there were still enough Chronovores to tear his TARDIS apart. If they got the chance he was dead... if he didn't kill himself first, of course, he noted, guiding his protesting ship through an avenue of vibrating superstrings that crisscrossed the vortex like some insane spider's web.

As he and his TARDIS performed leaps of unbelievable calculation in navigating the superstrings, the Master knew it was time to think of an alternative. If he was honest with himself, the machine was falling to pieces, he was falling to pieces and his chances of living through this were nothing more than ashes blowing in the wind. He glanced at the scanners, watching as the first of the Chronovores burst through the fissure before accelerating towards him.

One last trick.

The Doctor was apparently increasing the sensitivity of the detection grid. 'I thought we had more time... time until she found the processing power. But we're already in danger!'

Arlene was getting more confused by the second. 'You keep talking about this great danger we're in. I realise that, for the sake of cosmic bookkeeping, having all these parallel universes springing up must be a bit of a chore, but if it's giving everyone the most perfect world they could imagine, what's wrong with that?' She thought of Stuart and his director's position: how could that change be wrong?

'It's more than a question of "cosmic bookkeeping", Arlene, although I will admit that parallel universes do require an awful lot of paperwork.' The Doctor turned from the console.

'The universe is an ecosystem so complex, so interrelated, that it is almost beyond comprehension. Avatars of reality itself stalk the heavens, deciding whether civilisations are worthy or not. Courts of law stand in judgement over the gods themselves. Silent witnesses observe every single act of kindness or cruelty across all of time and space.'

Ruth held up her hand. 'Very poetic, Doctor. Ever thought of taking up writing as a hobby?'

'Do you want an explanation or not?' he snapped. 'Imagine the multiverse - the totality of all possible universes - as a garden. The multiverse has to be tended, nurtured... and pruned. Parallel universes are a fact of life - quantum uncertainties lead to Jonbar hinges and then the universe diverges, buds. But the overwhelming majority of these buds rapidly rejoin their primary universe, nanoseconds later. However, there are occasions when buds diverge from that primary reality very quickly. They possess enough dimensional momentum to achieve escape velocity - they become *important*.

'These parallel universes branching off from the primary are considered to be weeds in the garden, an infestation that must be cleared.'

'Why?' asked Mel. 'Remember, I'm the only nontemporal scientist in the room, Doctor. What harm do they do? It's not as if they're going to run out of space, is it?'

A good point - and Arlene was a temporal scientist. She could just about remember listening to Stuart's entertaining lectures about parallel universes. Except that they had been Ruth's lecture, hadn't they?

The Doctor smiled warmly at Mel. 'No, but there appears to be a possibility that they will run out of reality.' He held up his hands. 'And I'm not sure how or why, either. But these parallel realities are considered to be a threat, and, like weeds, they are pruned, weeded out.

'And the Chronovores are the gardeners.'

The Quantum Archangel threw her head back and laughed into the void. It was so simple!

Even without the power she needed to fulfil her destiny, she could still make a difference. After her initial fumblings, it felt natural now: she could see the endless possibilities in any given moment, and she could use the one that she knew was the right one. She could see virtually all the levels of existence and alter them in a harmony of life and fire.

She could make the new reality important, and that gave it its freedom.

Already she had given Paul his birthright back and Stuart what he had always wanted, serendipitously provided Ruth with the adventure she craved, and soon Mel would feel the favour of the Quantum Archangel. But they were just a handful of the thousands - tens of thousands - of realities she had already altered and given form to as her consciousness expanded across the face of the Earth. Just imagine what she would be able to do when she found her necessary ally!

But some of these new universes demanded more personal attention. She reached out for the Master and saw him, felt his fear and anguish. She saw the Divine Host, its vengeance searing across the vortex - and she knew that the Master needed her help.

The Quantum Archangel would not countenance his death at the hands of the Divine Host. So she took his reality and improved it.

The Master's TARDIS shot from the funnel of superstrings seconds before the Divine Host. The Chronovores immediately split into two legions, obviously trying to create a pincer movement to trap him.

For a moment, he shuddered as the console room blurred around him - another of those dimensional effects that he suspected were caused by his pushing his TARDIS so far beyond its operating parameters.

Shaking his head to clear the afterimages, he looked up at the holographic scanner that dominated one side of the battle chamber. He could see the Chronovores re-forming behind the bristling sphere that was his Type 94 WarTARDIS: two shining crescents closing in for the kill.

The Master didn't intend to give them the chance.

Furiously operating the sleek black hemisphere of the weapons console, he considered his options. He needed something to distract the Divine Host for the fraction of a second it would take to escape, but what to choose? Klypstrømic warheads and the artron cannon were small fry to the Chronovores, and the vortex lance had already proved ineffectual. Even seeding the time vortex with Earthshock bombs would be nothing more than an irritation.

No, it was time to bring in the big guns. Indeed, the biggest gun of all. He placed a black-gloved hand on the trigger that flowed from the hemisphere at his command.

'Let's see how well the Chronovores cope with the full power of the Eye of Harmony, shall we?' he hissed.

Before he could squeeze the trigger and direct the full might of Rassilon at the Divine Host, the scanner momentarily flared with light and fire, blinding his now sensitive eyes. When his sight returned he realised that the scanner was empty of images. The Divine Host had gone.

Barely believing his luck, but desperate to make the most of it, the Master turned to his WarTARDIS's navigation console and quickly took flight.

'Anjeliqua's desire to "make everything right" is going to generate more and more parallel universes,' explained the Doctor. Mel could see the concern - even a trace of fear - in his eyes: things were bad if he was this worried.

'According to the TARDIS sensors, tens of thousands of minor reality shifts have already occurred - and that's before she has full control of her powers. Some of the shifts will achieve full independence from this universe, while some of them will exist as a minor alteration in the prime reality, such as Stuart and Ruth's transposition.

'But the truth is, the Earth is now teeming with probabilistic effects, inverted causalities and the beginnings of complete parallel realities.'

'Which means?' asked Arlene.

The Doctor's face was ashen. 'Chronovores subsist on the power of the Lux Aeterna - which has been denied them.'

'So they're hungry?' asked Paul.

'Ravenous!' the Doctor exclaimed. 'But the key word is "subsist". That's their diet of gruel, Professor Kairos. A living timeline, such as the life of a human being, is a tasty snack. But a parallel universe is like a gourmet banquet - seven courses and a very good wine.' He sighed. 'And the Earth is now the site of thousands of parallel realities. Under normal circumstances, only a small number of Chronovores patrol the universe - their Higher Place - at any given time. But thanks to the Master, they now all have access.'

Paul shook his head. 'But how?'

'The Master has opened a passageway for them - by the very oldest of laws, once created such a passageway will continue. They can come and go as they please - and with no food in the Six-Fold Realm...' The Doctor pursed his lips.

'It's feeding time for the Chronovores. With Earth as the main course.'

As if on cue, the TARDIS began to rumble. At the same time, one alarm after the other started to erupt from the console. The lights flickered as the burbling of the TARDIS force field grew louder.

The Doctor tried to dampen down the alarms, but as soon as one bleep stopped another chime, screech or wail sprang up in its place. It was clear to Mel that whatever the Doctor had been dreading was now coming to pass.

'The Chronovores?' she asked.

The Doctor nodded gravely. 'By the look of it, it's the Divine Host - the Chronovore equivalent of shock troops. They've started to devour the parallel realities.'

'In which case we have nothing to worry about,' said Mel. 'From what you've said, that's a good thing. Isn't it?' She steadied herself on the console. A wave of dizziness overcame her... a wave of dizziness like the last time. But this time the wrenching, the dislocation, was far more acute. She squeezed her eyes closed, trying to stop the pain...

'Are you all right, Prime Minister?' Mel's eyes snapped open. The woman with the dark bob and the large eyes was sitting in front of her. In the Cabinet Room in Number 10.

Prime Minister?

The Quantum Archangel smiled. Dear sweet Mel. What wonders would she now be able to achieve? Such human imaginings as hers could move entire worlds!

But with an aching sadness she also knew she had reached the limits of her own achievements. Hundreds of thousands of people - friends, friends of friends, friends of friends of friends - were living the best of all possible lives, but it just wasn't enough! There were seven billion people on Earth, but the Earth was just one planet amongst the countless trillions of worlds that needed her help and guidance. She could achieve nothing more until she allied with the processing power that would furnish her with unlimited room for imagination...

Drawing her wings around her in a shining caul, the Quantum Archangel threw her consciousness across the vortex like a fisherman's net, seeking the one thing that would make her complete. As she did so, she remembered one last debt that needed to be honoured. Even as her mind expanded throughout existence, a single command darted backwards to the Earth.

For a moment, the Doctor simply stared at the empty spot where Mel had been standing. Obviously she had vanished, but it hadn't been like a transmat or a dematerialisation where, to the elegant senses of a Time Lord, there was always an afterimage, a suspicion of what had just left. It was as if she had been surgically excised from reality.

Because she had been.

'Mel?' It was Arlene, her voice trembling. The Doctor was vaguely aware of her turning to Paul and grabbing his hands. 'What's happened to her?'

The Doctor checked the TARDIS databanks. Thanks to some incredibly clever programming of the force fields, he had made sure that one section of the databanks contained all the facts and figures of the world outside the TARDIS's doors.

A world with no trace of Mel. Melanie Jane Bush had never been born to Alan and Christine Bush in Pease Pottage. She had never attended West London University. She had never encountered the Doctor in Brighton in 1989.

She had never existed.

In this universe.

'Now we are in trouble,' he groaned.

'Where's she gone?' asked Ruth.

'Into her own private universe,' muttered the Doctor.

'So she's still alive?' Arlene looked positively relieved. A shame that the truth was going to make that relief short-lived.

'Remember what Mel asked me, just before she vanished?'

Arlene frowned for a second. 'About why wiping out these parallel universes was a bad thing?'

The Doctor nodded. 'It's a bad thing because each of these completely separated universes is fuelled by the timeline and the imagination of the person whose "perfect world" it is.

'When that reality is consumed by the Chronovores, so is that person. Like a boa constrictor eating a rabbit - fur and all!'

That was the last thing Arlene heard. She had her own universe now.

Looking out at the packed auditorium, she took the microphone from its stand and launched into her third encore. As the rapturous applause filled the Albert Hall, Arlene - no surname necessary - with ten platinum discs and a recording career that made Madonna jealous, couldn't think of anything she would rather be doing.

* * *

The Master's WarTARDIS accelerated straight through the heart of the time spiral, deafening alarms filling the black-and-gold of the battle chamber. An explosion came from behind him - from the screech that issued from the navigation console and the acrid stench like burning flesh, he guessed the primary-shield generator had just gone off-line - but there wasn't time to do anything about it. The temporal stresses were tearing his WarTARDIS to pieces. But what option had he?

By navigating this treacherous route, the Master hoped to reach his destination without another encounter with the Chronovores. Given the state of his WarTARDIS - over forty per cent of its systems were currently either destroyed or in self-repair mode - there was no way he could survive even the most minor skirmish: not with one Chronovore, let alone the Divine Host.

Concentrating on the navigation console, he could see he was just about to exit the time spiral. Another explosion made him wince. If he had calculated correctly, he should materialise in orbit above the Earth.

With a wounded roar, his WarTARDIS materialised. The Master looked across at the holographic scanner, but was momentarily unable to accept what he saw.

The space-time continuum in the vicinity of Earth was alive, a teeming mass of wings, claws and beaks, shining predators ripping, tearing, gorging. Parallel universes and alternate realities, consumed in an instant.

The feast of the Chronovores had begun.

Chapter Eight
It's a Sin

Was it bravery? Or bravado? Or simply blind panic? The Master would never know. Indeed, he would never care to know.

Without hesitating, his hand descended on to the black trigger and squeezed.

For the briefest of briefest moments the outer plasmic shell of his WarTARDIS became a wormhole, linking a small point in orbit around twenty-first century Earth to another point, in another time and another place.

The Eye of Harmony.

As the Master's WarTARDIS felt the first warmth of the Eye's majesty, its topology twisted once more, forming a five-dimensional lens that focused the unstoppable might that instantly flooded through the wormhole.

An actinic spear arced out across both the space-time continuum and the time vortex - and hit the precise centre of the Chronovores' vicious flock.

The reaction was immediate. A few Chronovores effectively evaporated under the onslaught, their polydimensional matrices shattering under the impact; many more were caught in the edges of the blast and left injured or dying, their once perfect bodies deformed and broken. But the remainder saw the folly of remaining: with the last vestiges of their dignity wrapped round them like their wings, they took to the time vortex as a single body, a razor-tipped cloud of ivory-and-gold hatred vanishing into another realm.

But the Master knew they would be back. A cursory inspection of the environmental console showed that dear Anjeliqua had been very busy, with parallel universes and no end of causality violations popping up like weeds. The multiplication of realities appeared to have ceased for the moment, but the Chronovores would have to come back. The Earth was now nothing more than an irresistible feeding ground - and without the Lux Aeterna it was their only hope for survival.

It had been the Master's intention to bring them all through the channel between the Six-Fold Realm and the Higher Place, but only if he had the power to defeat them. Even the full force of the Eye of Harmony wouldn't dissuade them for long.

All the more reason to hurry. He dragged his aching, rotting carcass across to the navigation console and entered a complex series of instructions. If this was to work, he had to be accurate to a million decimal places.

But he was the Master. He would not fail.

Sir Stuart Hyde, director of the Newton Institute of Temporal Physics at Wootton, looked around his study and gave a contented sigh: the accumulated rewards of three decades surrounded him. Leather-bound copies of his researches, researches which had made him and the institute famous across the world. Awards for cracking the fundamental mysteries of time. Piles of journals by academics half his age who were desperately trying to catch up with him and failing.

At the age of fifty-five, Stuart Hyde was a very happy man. He picked up the silver-framed photograph on his desk and stared back into his past. It showed him as a bright, hopeful graduate, his mentor Doctor Ruth Ingram at his side, ready to take on the universe.

And they had done. She was now indulging her first passion, teaching: thanks to her, West London was now producing the highest calibre of temporal physics graduates outside of Cambridge and Warwick.

Sitting back in his comfortable leather armchair, Stuart couldn't help grinning. It had been a good life. Indeed, he couldn't have hoped for anything better.

'I can't do any better than that,' said the Doctor. For the last fifteen minutes, Paul and Ruth had stood aside while he had wheeled one box of tricks after another out of the depths of the TARDIS and proceeded to hook them up to the console. Paul assumed that they came from another time or another place, or both, and definitely had no idea of their purpose: a clotheshorse made of tiny sapphires, a gold jellyfish in a fish tank, a purple dodecahedron with ruby vertices... He just hoped the Doctor knew what he was doing.

More importantly, he just hoped they could get Arlene and Mel back. Arlene's loss was tearing him apart, but he knew that anger or panic wasn't the answer. He had to hold himself together, keep a tight focus on his mind. It was the only hope. And, worryingly, it was far easier to accomplish than he would have thought.

'What are you doing?' Well, he had to ask. A day ago, he had been one of the most respected professors of temporal physics in the world; today, he could only stand by as an alien from a race for which the TITAN Array was a child's toy made him feel like an imbecile.

Now he knew how Stuart had felt.

But it was more than that. He felt distanced, cut off. There were gaps in his memory, discontinuities that disturbed him. Then again, with all of this going on, it was hardly surprising, was it?

'I'm attempting to bolster the TARDIS's force fields. We have to stop Anjeliqua, but we won't be able to do that if we're off enjoying our own private universes, will we?'

'Hasn't she stopped for now?' asked Ruth.

'It's a shame she didn't stop sooner,' muttered Paul angrily.

The Doctor strode up to him. 'Professor Kairos, I can understand your distress. But let's not forget Mel has also gone as well, and as for Stuart... Let's just hope she has stopped for now. Her action - or rather, inaction - suggests she's going to set off my detection web at any second. And once she finds the processing power she needs, that'll be an end to everything - unless I can ensure that we're in a position to stop her.' The Doctor laid a hand on the clotheshorse. 'This is a psionometric isolator, powered by Metebelis crystals. It should prevent the Quantum Archangel from reaching into our minds and working out our ideal worlds in the first place. The dodecahedron is a reality inhibitor, boosting the TARDIS's reality quotient to about ten. That should make the formation of parallel universes a bit tricky, even for her.'

'And the jellyfish?' asked Paul.

The Doctor pursed his lips. 'This jellyfish, as you so quaintly put it, is an aquatic invertebrate from the water moon of Kaesov.'

'As I said - a jellyfish.'

'Professor Kairos,' said the Doctor patiently. 'The marine Owse is from a planet on the edge of a temporal rift. It reacts to any sign of a reality shift.'

'A jellyfish with an early warning system. Nice.'

'I'm depending on it -' The Doctor stopped as the console room filled with the now-familiar sound of a TARDIS materialising. Paul looked round for the source of the noise, and saw a portion of empty space begin to darken, to thicken.

'Of all the damned cheek!' shouted the Doctor. 'Materialising without an invitation.' He turned to the console - obviously trying to stop the materialisation - but it was too late. A police box was forming in the corner, but it was nothing like the Doctor's TARDIS. It was larger - about half as big again - and black and gold. Paul had to admit it looked quite impressive.

'Show-off,' muttered the Doctor. 'Then again, envy is the beginning of all true greatness, I suppose.'

A few moments after the Master's TARDIS had solidified with a thump, the door opened.

Paul almost threw up.

The creature that stepped out was dressed in an elegant black suit, almost like morning dress, perfectly tailored and edged with silver. But the thing that was wearing it... It was like looking at an animated corpse. The face was decomposed and rotting, with glistening brown flesh, decomposing sinews and twitching muscles. The eyes bulged from decayed sockets, surveying the console room. It raised a spavined hand.

'I need your help,' it gurgled. 'The situation has gone too far, Doctor.'

With a sudden sense of confusion, Paul realised that this zombie was the Master. What had happened to the suave, handsome man who had held Arlene and Anjeliqua in his thrall?

The Doctor's expression was also one of sheer horror. Horror mixed with something else. Was it pity?

'You've exhausted the Source of Traken, haven't you?' It was pity. Despite everything that had happened between them, despite the Master's machinations, it was obvious that the Doctor somehow cared about him.

The Master gave a pained shrug. 'I will find another way of living, Doctor. But all of that is moot unless we can stop the Quantum Archangel. She threatens everything.'

'I have to agree with you.' The Doctor indicated the console. 'As you can see, I've put a few defences in place.'

The Master's egg-like eyes glanced at the array of equipment arranged around the console. 'Inventive. Ingenious.'

He looked back. 'Doctor Ingram! A pleasure, as always. You don't look a day older than when we last met.' He reached out a skeletal hand to her, but she turned away in disgust.

Paul couldn't blame her.

The Master pulled himself back to the console. 'Your defences will be inadequate, Doctor. You know that,' he hissed. 'We must work together to defeat her.'

For the briefest of moments a look of anger clouded the Doctor's face. Then resignation took over. 'You're right.' He held out his hand. 'Together, then?' He shook what was nothing more than a collection of bones covered in rotting flesh.

'You can't be serious!' shouted Paul. 'That bastard hypnotised Arlene - he took her over! He caused all of this in the first place. How can you possibly trust him?'

'After what he did to Stuart thirty years ago, Doctor - he's the devil incarnate!' spat Ruth.

The Doctor held his hands out. 'We really have no alternative, Professors. Anjeliqua - the Quantum Archangel - must be stopped. And the best chance we have is if the Master and I team up.' He glanced at his new-found partner. 'Although involving this person does not please me.'

The Master stepped forward. 'Joining my efforts with the Doctor would not have been my first choice, I assure you. But Anjeliqua Whitefriar has become a threat to the entire universe, Doctor Ingram. You must understand that.'

'What choice do I have?' she spat.

'Where is the Anjeliqua hybrid now?' It was obvious that the Master considered the debate over.

'I don't know yet.' The Doctor beckoned him over to the console. 'I set this up earlier.'

'A detection grid. A sensible move. But how did you derive the pattern of the grid?'

'I compiled a list of supercomputers and plotted the grid from there. You must have worked out that she lacks sufficient processing power to fulfil her aims?'

The Master's mouth formed a brittle rictus. 'I have been busy with the Divine Host, Doctor, but yes, it had occurred to me. May I see the list?'

The Doctor snatched the vellum from the table and handed it over. The Master grasped it in his decayed hands and scanned the entries, the paper trembling in his tattered fingers.

After a second he looked up. 'An exhaustive list, Doctor, including a small number that I do not know. Although I would have added the Star Abacus of Beta Pheonii 9 and the spectacular ArcHive of the Cyberlords in the hundredth century.' His staring eyes transfixed the Doctor. 'A simple oversight, I'm sure.'

The Doctor raised his eyebrows. 'The Star Abacus was infected with the Paragon virus which wiped out the computing systems of the Andromeda galaxy in the year 87 BC, and the ArcHive... well, I wouldn't back Anjeliqua's chances against Emperor Brandt and the Cyberlords. And I'm not sure that she has that much control over her temporal location.'

The Master gave a gracious nod. 'Perhaps not. But I am concerned about the Matrix. I notice you virtually discount it from your list.'

'So?'

Despite his rotted face, the Master somehow managed to look guilty. 'There is a back door. One I have used to my advantage over the years.'

'Close it!' said the Doctor as he reached into the pockets of his jacket, his voice as hard as steel. 'Now!' He held his hand out to the Master: he was holding a stack of white squares. The Master grabbed it from him and began to link the squares together.

'What's he doing?' asked Ruth to Paul.
It was the Doctor who answered. 'He's instructing the Time Lords to find and close the back door that he's been using to plunder the Matrix. Aren't you?'
It wasn't a question.
The Master held up the completed white cube in the palm of his hand. 'Is this sufficient for you?' The cube vanished, accompanied by a tiny dematerialisation noise. 'Gallifrey now knows about the breach. The Quantum Archangel will think twice about attempting to access the Matrix.' Even through his distorted voice, the resentment was clear.
The Doctor turned away from him. 'I suggest we get started.'

The Great Attractor. Fifty million light years from Earth, in the constellation of Virgo, on the edges of the Abel 3627 galactic cluster.
By the early twenty-first century, it was still a relative unknown to mankind. Scientists knew that it was a tremendous gravitational source; they knew that the Earth's galaxy was hurtling towards it at over a million miles an hour. But that was all. Another of the universe's mysteries, out there to be solved.
Unfortunately, it was about to be solved, far sooner than anyone could have hoped. Or feared.

The Quantum Archangel formed from the quantum foam, her physical being solidifying from the eleven-dimensional nothingness like a brand-new star. Throwing out her wings, she announced her presence with a scream of triumph, her flames illuminating dust clouds that had been dark for aeons.
It had a been a long and difficult quest, but to the Quantum Archangel time and space were nothing: to achieve her goals, she would have searched the entire universe. But that hadn't been necessary. It was there, in front of her. She had found her ally.
The Great Attractor. And it was beautiful.
To the Quantum Archangel, it was an elegant ballet of cosmic forces, gravity and electromagnetism dancing a stunning minuet to the counterpoint harmonies of the weak and strong nuclear

forces, their voices soaring at the speed of light, their dance moving at the speed of time.

To Anjeliqua, it was a vision in blue and gold, a swirling maelstrom into which planets, stars, even galaxies, spiralled to their deaths, hurtling into an accretion disk that then accelerated into the event horizon of a black hole a billion, billion, billion times heavier than the sun. Nature at its most vicious, most brutal... and most glorious. A poetry that she wished she could have described.

But the Great Attractor was anything but natural, and the Lux Aeterna knew that. Anjeliqua was learning that the Quantum Archangel was the only way that the Lux Aeterna could satisfy its desire to understand.

Since the dawn of time, the Lux Aeterna had passively observed the cosmos unfold, every second, every aeon, for billion of years.

It had watched Event One fill the multiverse with new matter, new energy, new life. It had stood by as the Old Ones from the revenant universe had continued their ages-old war; it had remained impartial as the primal evil had shattered into an infinity of shards that spread across space.

It had watched, observed, stood by. Yet it had been incapable of understanding - until now. All that the Lux Aeterna had seen, the Quantum Archangel now knew. And with Anjeliqua's living mind, the Quantum Archangel could now finally understand the truth about the Great Attractor. As Anjeliqua watched the black hole spin in its halo of fire, the Lux Aeterna knew and the Quantum Archangel remembered...

The given name of the race had been lost. Some say deliberately.

If any remnants of them still survived, it was as the Constructors of Destiny. They had reigned a billion years ago, gods walking amongst the stars with the other gods, seeding the new worlds with their essence, instructing the lesser races as to their roles in the universe. These were the first races to discover the gift of sentience, and they felt indentured to honour that debt.

The gods saw the unfolding cosmos as their responsibility, their birthright: there were too many forces at large which desired chaos. Above them, the ancient gods still played out their tired stratagems; beneath them, the shards of original sin still tempted beings with their corrupted games.

The Constructors of Destiny would be better. They would act as gods. They would guard and nurture sentience in all its myriad forms.

On prehistoric Gallifrey, they had moulded the ape neanderthals towards their destiny; on Earth, they had subtly manipulated the developing strands of DNA to allow noncollective intelligence, before spinning a counterpoint Earth into orbit, beyond the planet's sun, for a control.

They were a pantheon of great works and high ideals.

Too high. Too great.

Then came a time when there was dissent amongst the gods. Unlike the others, the Constructors of Destiny sought to understand. And to that end they planned the greatest of their great works: a calculating engine that could understand the universe and all its works.

The Constructors of Destiny told their brethren what were trying to accomplish, proud of their aims and their plans, assuming that the great pantheon would act as one.

They were wrong.

War broke out in heaven.

The most ancient of ancient races, terrified by what one of their number was proposing to create, fought the idea for a million years. They tore up the vortex, ripped the time spiral apart, created tsunami in the quantum foam. But for naught: the idea was stronger. Finally, realising the damage they had caused, and the Armageddon that they could cause, the Constructors of Destiny admitted defeat.

In a single moment, they abandoned everything. Hoping that they had taught their children well, praying to their own gods for forgiveness, they departed for their own higher realms, never to return.

Alone now, the Constructors of Destiny dismissed their fellow gods' short-sightedness. Their magnificent engineering project was the culmination of all they had desired, and if the others couldn't understand that, then the loss was theirs. Bophemeral would be their legacy to the children – the ultimate tool to understand the ultimate truth.

They fulfilled their own destiny. They built. They constructed.

It took them a million years to encode the operating system, and another ten million to build the physical machine to run that system. It was a feat of engineering the like of which the universe would never see again.

Thankfully.

The operating system was engraved into the very fabric of the space-time continuum, its engrams patterns in the quantum foam.

Billions upon billions of tons of strange matter were cast into a motherboard that plated the interior of the event horizon, an eternal mirror that would both serve and protect.

Quintillions of light years of superstring material were woven into the strange matter matrix to render Bophemeral invulnerable to the ravages of time, as well as giving it a defence against those races that, one day, might attempt understanding before they were ready for it.

Finally the Constructors of Destiny created the memory, a standing wave that oscillated across the event horizon like a tide of time. It was memory that could contain both every event and every possible event in the cosmos.

After eleven million years, the physical framework was in place. But the titanic black hole was simply the host. It was time to go beyond simple construction. It was time to bring new life into the cosmos.

They initialised the processor matrix, an Array of a billion dwarf suns, a starscape that dotted the ebon interior of the black hole. The suns flared for a second, illuminating the emptiness.

It lived. But it still did not think. The Constructors turned their attention to the silent golden hoop that orbited the singularity, the interpreter core that housed the soul of their great creation.

The Mind of Bophemeral.

Their child: it would understand. It would understand everything.

One hundred and fifty million years ago, the vast armada of the

Constructors of Destiny surrounded what would eventually be known as the Great Attractor. The last of the gods, waiting to give life to their surrogate child.

But other gods had taken notice. Before the Constructors could bring life to the mind, three visitations descended upon the fleet. Three opinions - but would the Constructors listen?

From the far future, a single Time Lord - one of a race that the Constructors of Destiny themselves had nurtured - warned them that the Mind of Bophemeral would bring nothing but pain. He was dismissed to far Gallifrey - let him learn the price he would pay for defying gods.

From the present, the Xeraphin lectured the Constructors as to their folly, telling them the universe wasn't there to be understood. They were sent back to Xeraphas, where the punishment for their audacity would await them.

But from the past...

The Constructors thought themselves gods, but the final visitation was beyond even their imaginings. Omnipotence and omniscience together, demon and angel combined, it told them that the Mind was vital for the future. Their great work would form one of the cornerstones of the universe; they were its architects.

It gave them its blessing, and in remembrance the Constructors even raised a temple for it on a distant barren moon. It had shown them the way, it had given them approval. It had proved them right, against the judgement of the other gods.

Satisfied, they knew that it was time: time to give life to the Mind of Bophemeral. Their child, their hope for understanding. As a race, they reached out and gave birth.

The golden hoop began to spin around the singularity as the greatest engineering project in the universe was born.

It was utterly, utterly mad.

Within nanoseconds, the Mind of Bophemeral had discovered the nature and purpose of the Constructors and annihilated their armada - patricide and deicide in one. A second later, it derived block-transfer computation from first principles and built itself an army of metallic drones. As its robotic servants swarmed across the cosmos it began to research quantum mnemonics, learning the arcane language that would permit it to mould reality to its liking.

It would become God.

The children of the gods saw what was happening, and knew they had to stop it. But without the gods to help them, where would their saviours come from?

They came from the most unlikely places. Races were forced to grow up faster than they would have liked, and to accept the mantle of responsibility that had been passed to them before their time. Alliances were forged between the oldest of enemies; ancient friendships were torn asunder by death. Over a thousand races united to build the greatest war fleet - and the greatest alliance -the universe would ever see.

To save that universe.

With the Mad Mind's robotic servants teeming across creation, the newly forged alliance had to act quickly. The forces of over a thousand worlds mobilised and engaged the mind at every point and at every level.

The Millennium War had begun.

After the spectacular opening victory at the Rift of Perseus, where the Daemons used their mastery over matter to put paid to the Mad Mind's plans to harness a dark matter-cloud, the alliance fleet was spurred on to even greater victories.

Within the Horsehead nebula, the Osirans used their vaunted technology to lase raw starfire at the Mad Mind's artificial minions, narrowly preventing them from creating a wormhole that would have killed quintillions.

The Euterpians and the Greld, cloaked by the battle shroud of the Semquess and wielding the Omnethoth, showed the Mad Mind why they were the most feared races in the Virgo cluster when they detonated an entire galaxy - simply to take out a thousand of the Mind's fleets.

But there were also failures. Too many failures.

Eldrad's Kastrian fleet was utterly destroyed and their planet laid waste when the Mad Mind turned their own computers against them, leaving shattered silicon blowing in the icy winds of now-dead Kastria.

The Exxilons and the Uxariens combined their energy-draining devices and doomsday weapons to ambush the Mad Mind's robotic fleet in Andromeda, only to discover that they themselves were caught in a trap: one which would leave both races in a social and technological decline from which they would never recover, and ignite the Crab nebula as a testament to their failure.

United for the first time in a thousand millennia, the Sontara Warburg and the Rutan Host combined their impressive fleets and their complex battle stratagems, constructing a four-dimensional pincer movement to attack one of the Mad Mind's drone factories. The combined fleet and its pincer movement was smeared across the event horizon of a nearby black hole within a second.

A tactical psionic attack by the Grey Hegemony and the Influence of Light was anticipated by the Mad Mind, and met with horrific feedback. Both races were left altered by the experience.

However hard the alliance fought, the Mad Mind always eventually found a way to triumph. Its infinite intellect and total control over artificial intelligences - the existing robot races were taken over immediately - meant that one race after the other either fell or was forced to retreat.

Take time forward a thousand years. With defeat now not only possible but probable, the remaining races made a final stand at the Great Attractor itself. They had nothing to lose except the universe itself. The gods had gone. So who could they pray to?

Which was when those forces watching on the sidelines realised that their time had come.

With the threat of another God, the People broke every clause of their nonintervention policy and revealed their existence. The early Time Lords, seeing their future's end in the Matrix, travelled forward in time and materialised en masse, their time fleet commanded by Rassilon himself. The Masksmakers of the Pageant, the Faction Paradox and the Ministers of Grace - the last returning from the very end of time to ensure the universe's survival - emerged from their hiding places to offer their assistance. Life from the very beginning to the very end of time, ready to save everything in between. And not a moment too soon.

The Mad Mind was only seconds away from deriving the first axioms of quantum mnemonics and becoming God, its fleets and armies crumbling into rust as it concentrated its resources. Within the fortress of its black hole, it began its apotheosis.

Choreographed by the People and assisted by the survivors, the new gods mounted their final assault.

With covering fire from the Osirans, the Nimon used their black-hole technology to fire ten million quantum collapsars into the Great Attractor itself. As the event horizon momentarily destabilised, the fledgling Time Lords - with the knowledge they had gained from Omega's sacrifice, as well as assistance from the god of the people - generated a time loop within the singularity itself. With less than a nanosecond remaining before the Mad Mind declared itself God, time within the event horizon compressed into a fraction of a fraction of a fraction of a second, a single chronon condemned to loop until the end of all days.

The battle had been won, but at what cost? Countless races annihilated; whole galaxies laid waste; incalculable promise squandered.

The survivors held an agonised postmortem, their representatives meeting in the Midnight Cathedral, that monument to the folly of the Constructors of Destiny. For the first and last time, Osiran sat with Daemon, Time Lord with Uxarien, Nimon with Grey, the God of the People in judgement.

It was agreed. The Millennium War against the Mad Mind of Bophemeral would be forgotten. Totally, utterly. All that would be permitted to remain was the knowledge that the Great Attractor and the Midnight Cathedral represented the ultimate in recklessness. The universe wasn't there to be understood.

But the survivors needed help to accomplish that. They needed gods. True gods.

With the unanimous agreement of the war council, the God of the People called out, demanding fulfilment of the Ancient Covenants.

And the Six-Fold-God responded. The Council of Guardians manifested in the Midnight Cathedral, filling the Dusk Nave with their wisdom and glory. Structure, Entropy, Justice, Equilibrium, Dreams and Life: white, black, red, azure, crystal and gold.

Six voices spoke as one to every single life form that had engaged in the Millennium War, a chorus of thought and song that spanned the galaxies.

YOU, THE YOUNGER RACES, HAVE DONE WELL. YOU HAVE EARNED YOUR INHERITANCE AND WILL HAVE YOUR REWARD.

IGNORANCE.

A single spinning cube of crystal formed in the centre of the Nave, drawing a gasp from even the most restrained of the representatives. A whisper rose from the assembly - the stuff of myths and legends, there in front of them. Truly a magnificent sight.

The Key to Time, the focused totality of the Guardians' powers.

SO BE IT.

The Six-Fold-God gave its command to the cube: one word, a word that entered the universal consciousness to be remembered for ever.

FORGET.

And they did.

Even with the Lux Aeterna supporting her, Anjeliqua reeled at the intensity of the memory. Gods had walked the cosmos, fighting a war for existence itself. Breathtaking!

But the Quantum Archangel knew that she too was a god. A god who would not make the same mistakes as the misguided Constructors. Reaching out, her wings caressed the impenetrable event horizon, a barrier of time and matter, energy and thought. It had withstood a millennium of attack, from particle weapons to psionic cannons, and had only been breached by the combined might of the new gods.

The Quantum Archangel flew through it as if it were a light summer breeze.

Within the event horizon, everything was as the Lux Aeterna remembered: the ultimate computer formed from the ultimate in matter and energy. But it was dead, the mind that should have been driving it trapped in a moment of time. She considered the singularity, a point of sheer nonexistence impossibly close to her and yet infinitely far away. But the insane physics of a black hole meant nothing to the Quantum Archangel: her mind reached out and saw the thin ring of shining gold fixed around the singularity. But she knew it wasn't fixed: it was spinning backwards and forwards, reliving the same instant of time for ever - a single chronon, the motion only visible to one such as the Quantum Archangel.

She needed it. And what the Quantum Archangel wanted, she would get.

The Time Lords arrogantly thought themselves to be masters of all, but their time loop was nothing more than an inconvenience to her. They understood time, but she was time - time and space, matter, energy and thought in one. With a single command, she shattered the chains that imprisoned Bophemeral, allowing time to resume as it was meant to. For the first time in a hundred and fifty million years, the golden hoop span continuously once more.

The Mind of Bophemeral lived - and the Quantum Archangel could finally be whole. Fuelled by anticipation, she relocated her essence to inside the interpreter core.

Her physical form materialised within the arcing gold corridor that ran through the central processor, the fire from her wings illuminating the funereal calm like a new sunrise.

How fitting. A sunrise for the universe.

But she was no longer within the gold hoop. Anjeliqua recognised her surroundings as her bedroom at her parent's house in Guildford, even down to the copies of *Ecology Today* strewn across the carpet. The Lux Aeterna had the vaguest impression - filtered through Anjeliqua's consciousness and understanding - of Event One. For the Quantum Archangel, she was flying through the darker strata - somewhere that meant home.

Illusions. She was still in the interpreter core. But it was somehow reassuring to accept the illusions rather than stand in a cold gold corridor.

'Welcome to Bophemeral.' In all three scenarios, the voice was barely above a whisper, tightly restrained with only the barest hint of emotion.

Another presence.

To Anjeliqua, it was a small thin man in a tailored grey suit. Indeed, a tailored grey body - it was clear that this was simply a construct, a focal point for her to address. To the Lux Aeterna, it was a current in the Event One maelstrom - unremarkable, common. To the Quantum Archangel, however, it was her perfect mate: a solid, muscular, golden humanoid, his wings as impressive as hers. A Quantum Consort.

The part of the Quantum Archangel that was Anjeliqua tried to concentrate on the grey man. The rest was just too distracting.

He looked at her with his pinched, ashen face, his hair thin and plastered to his scalp. His hands were clasped in front of him. 'I am the Mind of Bophemeral.' His eyes glittered through steel-rimmed circular glasses. 'Welcome to my home.'

A strident alarm sounded from the console. 'The detection grid! We've found her!' exclaimed the Doctor, furiously inspecting the monitors. But his voice was grim when he turned round to face them.

'She's found the Mad Mind of Bophemeral,' he whispered. 'Oh no.'

'Is that bad?' asked Ruth, feeling guilty that she actually felt quite glad something was finally happening.

'Bad?' said the Doctor. 'Bad?' He slammed the console. 'Bad? The Mad Mind is an abomination! Spawned for the most misguided of reasons, defeated in the greatest war this cosmos has ever seen? Of course it's bad!'

'The Mad Mind of Bophemeral?' gurgled the Master. 'I'm not familiar with that.' He didn't sound comfortable dealing with something outside his experience, but the Doctor didn't seem particularly comfortable himself with the Master's ignorance.

'Not familiar? Not familiar? But the war, for goodness' sake!'

'What war?'

'The Millennium War, man. Every civilised race in the universe, fighting together one hundred and fifty million years ago to defeat the Mad Mind?'

The Master's egg-like eyes blinked once. 'Doctor, I assure you I know of no such war. And given my proven intelligence-gathering abilities, I doubt that I would have missed something like that. It simply didn't happen.'

The Doctor shook his head, frowning in puzzlement. 'This is not the time for an argument, but I assure you there was a war. Anyway, the Mind of Bophemeral was the cause of that war - an insane intellect that was eventually defeated by the Time Lords. They looped it - and my guess is that the Quantum Archangel has broken that loop. And that makes matters a thousand times worse.'

'How can this make anything worse?' asked Paul. 'A computer is a computer, surely? It gives her the processing power she needs - surely that's bad enough?'

The Doctor glanced at the Master. 'Whether my... associate remembers or not, the very name should clue you in. Bophemeral is utterly, utterly insane. That insanity coupled with the infinite power of the Quantum Archangel simply doesn't bear thinking about.'

'There are gaps in my memory lattice,' whispered the Mad Mind in all three environments to all three aspects of the Quantum Archangel. 'Elements of my history have been excised with surgical precision,' it continued. 'Your handiwork?'

The Quantum Archangel needed the analytical engine that was the Mad Mind to fulfil her destiny. The Lux Aeterna wanted to use it to remember and understand its existence. But Anjeliqua Whitefriar knew that a Mad Mind, resentful of its defeat at the hands of the new gods, fully in command of the reality-altering abilities granted by quantum mnemonics, would prove catastrophic for the universe.

And so she had altered its memories, tweaked its perceptions. She could have altered its past, but the consequences of the Millennium War still echoed aeons later, and she couldn't yet calculate the consequences of such a change.

It was true that, allied with her, it would have access to her own omniscience, but that omniscience would be under her absolute control. There was nothing to fear from the Mind of Bophemeral.

'It was necessary to heal you,' she explained. 'All will be well.'

The grey man nodded. The Quantum Consort flexed his wings. The turbulence became a standing wave. 'I live. I think. I am the Mind of Bophemeral. Naturally, all will be well.'

'How quickly can we get to this Mad Mind?' asked Paul. There was a determination in his voice that puzzled the Doctor. True, Paul was worried about both Arlene and Mel, but there was more to it than that. Indeed, he had seemed distracted since they had first entered the TARDIS.

Something for another time, the Doctor decided. 'Hopefully, not as long as it took us to escape it the last time.' He gave Ruth a knowing look, assuming that, since she had replaced Stuart in their little escapade, she would understand.

She did. 'The Great Attractor?' She gave a deep sigh and shook her head. 'You plan to take us back there after what it took us to get away? And helped by the thing that put us there in the first place? Anyway, who in their right minds would put a supercomputer so close to a supermassive black hole?'

'My dear Doctor Ingram, the Mad Mind of Bophemeral is the black hole. Its event horizon is the memory, an array of supercharged blue dwarfs its processor. And its interpreter core orbits the singularity.'

She snorted. 'Do you really expect me to believe that?'

'I don't care whether you believe it. The fact is – '

'Fact?' The Master stepped forward and supported himself on the console. 'Intergalactic wars at the dawn of time? Supercomputers built from black holes? And you plan to take this decrepit excuse for a time machine into the heart of the Great Attractor?' He thrust his decaying face into the Doctor's.

'Do you really expect me to believe this ridiculous farrago of cretinous drivel? A supercomputer that no one's heard of, a war that never happened? You're insane!' Dragging himself away, the Master made for his TARDIS. 'I'd rather take my chances on my own.'

'On your own? The Quantum Archangel might have given you a souped-up TARDIS, but how far is that going to get you? Admit it, Master – you need me.' The Doctor closed his eyes. 'And I need you.' *Don't make me say please.*

The Master turned away from his TARDIS. 'It seems that I simply have no alternative,' he gasped, looking across at the Doctor with his staring eyes. 'I will help you to reach the Great Attractor.' He staggered over to the console: whether to support himself or to plan a course of action, the Doctor wasn't sure. 'From what Doctor Ingram has said, I gather that your escape from the Attractor wasn't without incident.'

'It's the most massive object in the cosmos, Master,' said the Doctor, arching an eyebrow. 'I doubt that even your augmented TARDIS, with all its bells and whistles, will be able to cope with that.'

The Master didn't even bother to look round. 'I seem to remember that my grades in cosmic science at the Academy surpassed yours. Furthermore, my... experiences have taught me much that was missing from Cardinal Sendok's banal curriculum.' He indicated the panel which governed the chameleon circuit. 'May I?'

'Liberty Hall,' said the Doctor dismissively. True, experience counted for much more than dry and dusty lessons, but it wasn't as if the Doctor had been sitting around doing nothing for the last six hundred years, was it?

'Have you ever heard of the Cla'tac'teth?' asked the Master, his bony fingers tapping away at the panel.

'No,' the Doctor was forced to admit.

'The Cla'tac'teth is an insectoid race that will live just before the heat death of the universe. Their home is a neutron star orbiting the Great Attractor.'

'So?' asked Ruth. 'The TARDIS was almost destroyed pulling itself out of that gravity well: I don't exactly relish the thought of going back there. And I can't see what a planet of creepy-crawlies has to do with it.'

The Master continued programming the chameleon circuit as he replied. 'Doctor Ingram, I see that neither age - or the lack of it - have improved your deductive abilities.'

Seeing the look on Ruth's face the Doctor decided to intervene, simply to stop an argument. He still didn't understand what the

Master was getting at, but he felt it his duty to explain. 'At the heat death of the universe, the universal constants such as gravity will lose their bite.'

'If you subscribe to the concept of the universe succumbing to entropy', Ruth snorted, 'which I don't, by the way - then that event won't happen for hundreds of billions of years.'

The Doctor couldn't resist proving her wrong. 'The universe reached the point of heat death about twenty years ago, with an emerald wave of entropy sweeping across the universe.' An emerald wave that had destroyed so much: Metulla Orionis, Oa, one-third of the Shi-ar empire... So much tragedy.

'The last time the Master and I joined forces, we helped to set up a series of exit points for that entropy.'

'Arrant nonsense,' Ruth replied, her confidence faltering. 'Entropy isn't green anyway. Is it?'

'The universe was suffering from what you humans would call "premature ageing", Doctor Ingram,' explained the Master. 'Thanks to a tailored virus, entropy was increasing at an accelerated rate and, twenty-two years ago in your time, concerned parties took it upon themselves to cure it. But there is an alternate universe in which that event did not occur. In that parallel universe, matter and energy are infected with the entropy virus - its waste products are emerald green, for your information - which reduces all of creation to a dull red glow. The coordinates of that particular Hades are hardwired into the navigation circuits of my TARDIS.'

'Hold on just one second!' The Doctor stepped forward. 'Wait just one minute! A parallel universe? With all those Chronovores out there?' He held his hands out. 'What are we going to do - give them indigestion and then persuade them to give up?'

The Master forced himself to stand upright. 'That will not be an issue, Doctor. We will only be in the parallel universe of the Cla'tac'teth for the briefest of moments. But it will offer us a short cut to the Great Attractor in this universe, and the chance to stop this Archangel gestalt from assimilating it.'

The logic might hold together, but the Doctor still didn't like it. Chronovores or not, parallel universes were nasty things and did nasty things to TARDISes. But unfortunately, their options were limited and their time was short. Once again, he found himself facing the most uncomfortable of decisions: no choice.

'Very well. How do you propose to accomplish this little parlour trick of yours?'

The Master's tone was almost patronising. 'I have used my chameleon circuit and the functioning parts of yours to bond the outer plasmic shells of our TARDISes together. My TARDIS - with its more advanced navigational systems - will navigate us into the realm of the Cla'tac'teth. Given the weakened state of the sidereal barriers due to the Chronovore incursion, and the combined power of our dynamorphic generators, we should have no problems in reaching the Great Attractor in this universe.' His thin lips pursed to reveal yellowed stumps of teeth. 'Satisfied?'

'No,' replied the Doctor, 'but we don't exactly have much choice, do we?'

'I am important to you,' said the three aspects of the Mad Mind to the three aspects of the Quantum Archangel. 'I can see the desire, the need, the want.' And then it asked a vital question. 'Why?'

The Quantum Archangel was impatient to begin, and saw no harm in sharing her great plan with the mind. Besides, it would be easier if it co-operated.

'The universe is imperfect. I have the power to make it perfect, but I lack the comprehension. That is what you will provide.'

'You wield the powers of the Lux Aeterna, embodied in a frail human form,' it murmured. 'While the Lux Aeterna was able to re-create your body as eternal and inviolate, it has no concept of mind. The limited intellect of a human has shown it a fraction of what it can achieve. With the boundless processing power that I can provide, the Lux Aeterna will truly understand.' It considered its words for a second: the grey man stroked his chin, while the Quantum Consort's wings flared up and down the spectrum. The turbulence at event one was momentarily becalmed.

'I was created to understand the universe,' the mind finally concluded. 'But it was to have been a passive understanding. With you at my side, I could understand the universe in a way that my creators could never have foreseen.' It nodded. 'Together we shall understand the universe in all of its aspects. Together.'

In the middle of Anjeliqua's room, the grey man shook her hand. The turbulence at event one surged in a tsunami.

And within the event horizon of the Mad Mind, the Quantum Consort's wings enfolded the Quantum Archangel, and brought his face close to hers. Then he kissed her, deeply, passionately.

'The linkages are set, and your navigation circuits are now slaved to mine,' said the Master, obviously relishing the word 'slaved'. 'We are ready to begin.'

It was clear to Paul that the Master's decay was continuing; his gnarled hands and face were now more bone than flesh. How much longer could he survive?

'Very well,' muttered the Doctor.

'Would you care to do the honours?' wheezed the Master, indicating a flat, circular button. 'A simple push on the vortex primer will do it.'

'I'm well aware how to operate my own TARDIS, thank you very much.' The Doctor stepped over to the console and placed his hand over the controls. 'And may she forgive me for what I'm about to do.'

Anjeliqua, the Lux Aeterna and the Quantum Archangel welcomed the addition of the Mind Of Bophemeral to their gestalt, its processing capabilities interlacing with them at every level.

What had been two combined as one became a trinity and a chorus: the sheer force of the Lux Aeterna and the naked humanity of Anjeliqua, all enhanced by the greatest pure intellect the universe had ever seen. Three separate life forces, bound together in a single soul: the raw passion of the Quantum Archangel.

The reborn Quantum Archangel burst free from the confines of the event horizon, her consciousness instantly encompassing all of space and time. Her outstretched wings were billions of light years across, sweeping majestically through nebulae, galaxies and quasars. Her hair trailing behind her like a comet, she threw her head back and laughed, a laugh which echoed throughout eternity.

It was time to begin. Countless lives, countless planets, countless possibilities... The Quantum Archangel - mind, memory and power, all in one - reached out across the universe.

Punching through the sidereal barriers which separated parallel realities was never easy. With the Master having withdrawn to the sanctuary of his TARDIS, giving the excuse that he needed to monitor the journey from there, and Ruth and Paul strapped into the couches, the Doctor was left grabbing the console.

As the temporal energies such transitions caused forced their way into his TARDIS and resonated within the symbiotic nuclei in his body, the Doctor couldn't help being reminded of his trip to the dying Earth of the Inferno project, and the agonies he had only barely withstood. Then again, that had been using just the console; at least now he had the protection of the TARDIS.

Not that it felt like it as his nuclei burnt like hot needles.

Perhaps it was because the Inferno universe had only diverged from the primary reality about fifty years before the Doctor attempted the transfer, rather than the millions of years of divergence for the Cla'tac'teth reality, but this journey was proving to be almost as bad as the escape from the Great Attractor! Not for first time since the this whole sorry affair had started, the Doctor's hearts went out to his poor, suffering TARDIS.

Don't worry, old girl. When this is all over, I promise I'll make it up to you.

He held on even harder as another wave of turbulence battered against the TARDIS exterior. The walls appeared to buckle and melt, the roundels warping into melted ovals, while the TARDIS engines laboured against the assault, screaming out in pain.

Straining against the time fields that were buffeting him, the Doctor glanced round at the Master's TARDIS, and was shocked to see it fading in and out, the huge pearl that stood in for a roof light almost too bright to look at.

Obviously the Master was having trouble maintaining the linkage between the two time machines. The Doctor reached out to the chameleon circuit panel to offer assistance, but a wave of dizziness overcame him.

He was on Gallifrey, studying his dry and dusty lessons, whilst dreaming of what lay beyond; he was on Gallifrey, following a bronzed coffin through the darkened corridors; he was facing the greatest affront to human dignity he had seen, a patchwork battlefield of innocent victims that he had to help; he was on Gallifrey, standing before the judgement of the High Tribunal, facing exile to Earth; he was on Earth, unconscious in an Essex wood...

The Doctor shook his head to clear the far-too-vivid images and looked up at the scanner: they were rapidly approaching a wall of blue fire, the sidereal barrier between this universe and that of the Cla'tac'teth. Once through that, things should get easier. Maybe not plain sailing, but certainly a more gentle passage.

With a blow to the TARDIS that knocked the Doctor on to the floor, the roundels flared in azure as the TARDIS - TARDISes - hit the barrier.

And stalled.

The blue grew deeper, brighter, blinding the Doctor as he scrambled to his feet and stumbled over to the console. The Master's desperate voice issued from a speaker. 'Doctor - you must boost your matter gain to the outer plasmic shell! The structural integrity of both our vessels is collapsing - we cannot breach the sidereal barrier!'

The Doctor's hand reached for the requisite controls -

He was on Gallifrey, studying his dry and dusty lessons, whilst dreaming of what lay beyond; he was on Gallifrey, following a bronzed coffin through the darkened corridors; he was facing the greatest affront to human dignity he had seen, a patchwork battlefield of innocent victims that he had to help; he was on Gallifrey, standing before the judgement of the High Tribunal, facing exile to Earth; he was on Gallifrey, pardoned by his peers. He was on Gallifrey, accepting the Matrix circlet, the Rod and the Sash of Rassilon; he was on Gallifrey, convincing his people they could be a positive force for the universe; he was on Gallifrey, preparing to lead the Time Lords on a final jihad...

'A fourth Enemy fleet has just broken through the substrate, my lord. What are your instructions?'

The Lord President Admiral frowned at his adjutant. 'How are the other Enemy fleets responding, Cardinal Commander?'

The commander checked his status board. 'They are manoeuvring to form the vertices of their tetrahedron around us, my lord. I advise we withdraw while we still have access to the vortex and can rejoin the fleet.'

The Lord President of the Time Lords, Admiral of the Fleet, the Keeper of the Legacy of Rassilon, Sash-Bearer and Ka Faraq Gatri, ran a hand through his curly blond hair. The time dreadnought *Righteous Fist of Rassilon* was the flagship of the First Imperial Gallifreyan Fleet. Its loss would be a severe blow to Time Lord morale... but with four Enemy fleets around them, the opportunity to strike a decisive blow for the Time Lords was irresistible.

The Lord President Admiral cast his gaze across the emerald-and-black command deck, at the Time Lords manning their positions, Prydonians all. He owed it to them, he owed it to the Time Lords on Gallifrey, he owed it to the universe.

'Cardinal Commander: order the fleet to emerge from the vortex!'

'My lord?'

'Do it!'

Four Enemy fleets against one fleet of Time Lords.

He felt sorry for them.

The Master waited for the Doctor to boost the matter gain, well aware that both TARDISes were collapsing under the onslaught of the sidereal barrier. Unless the Doctor complied to the request in a few seconds, it would all be over. He diverted one of the monitors to the interior of the Doctor's TARDIS.

The Doctor was gone.

The joint integrity of the outer plasmic shell of the two TARDISes was disintegrating, and there was no one in the

Doctor's TARDIS to assist: it wasn't as if Kairos or Ingram knew how to do it, was it? Perhaps he could get out there and boost the matter gain himself? No: he couldn't leave his TARDIS. Not only did he have to monitor and adjust, but outside his console room his physical form would almost certainly dissolve: only temporal grace was holding him together now. Could he control the Doctor's TARDIS remotely? It wasn't as if he hadn't managed it before.

Another jolt rocked his TARDIS; the Master hung on to the console, glancing at a monitor as he did so. And realised that the situation was worse than he could have imagined.

According to the readings, the Quantum Archangel had begun to spin her parallel universes once again: this time at an exponential rate. In response to this harvest festival, the Divine Host of the Chronovores now felt brave enough to descend, followed closely by the rest of their brethren, driven by hunger. How much worse could it get?

He looked up at the scanner. And realised that it could always get worse.

Framed against the electric blue of the sidereal barrier the Quantum Archangel shrieked in triumph, her body aflame. Wings of brilliant fire swept out behind her, incandescent gold against actinic blue. For a moment, another figure, similar but male, flew next to her, his wings entwined with hers. And then they were one, talking to him, their voices like fire in the abyss.

All will be as it should be, Master.

The Master's withered hands descended upon the console, but he knew it was useless. The Quantum Archangel had reached the barrier first. She knew his plans, she knew how to stop him.

There was nothing he could do.

Hear me now, Time Lords. I am no longer the woman you knew. I am life and fire incarnate!

The wings of the Quantum Archangel enfolded the Master and the Doctor's TARDISes. Wings of unimaginable possibility...

Chapter Nine
Opportunities

'For goodness' sake, Lynne, can't you give me a straight answer to a straight question?'

It wasn't often that Melanie became exasperated with her Home Secretary, but the Homeless Act was the cornerstone of her government's policies - indeed, it was the cornerstone of Melanie's moral beliefs. And she took any apparent failure in the act personally.

When she had been elected to the position of First Lord of the Treasury, it had been because she had known what had to be done. People needed to be helped. And the 2008 Homeless Act (Rehousing and Retraining) was designed to give every single one of the underclass a chance to reclaim their lives. Accommodation, food, training... all of it funded by the People's Lottery.

And unfortunately, like too many of her electorate, it simply wasn't working.

Lynne Thomas was a slim elegant woman in her late thirties, with a boyish face and brown hair cut in a fashionable bob. She and Melanie had known one another for years, and Melanie knew that Lynnne shared her views on the subject, which made it all the more annoying when the papers - tabloids and broadsheets alike - became obsessed with the story of seventeen-year-old Ben (no surname) who had 'slipped through the net', just one of the many emotional euphemisms that kept cropping up. A lurid saga of drugs, rent boys and eventual suicide - or was it murder?

The fourth estate was having a field day.

'Melanie - the facts speak for themselves,' said Lynne defensively. 'A seventy-eight per cent reduction in the number of homeless. Eighty-four per cent employment rate for those who make it through the programme. Impressive success in drugs rehabilitation. This Ben is just a glitch.'

'A glitch?' Melanie took to her feet. 'A young man is dead, and we are responsible. I hardly consider that a glitch!' She sat down again and rubbed her eyes. It had been a very long day.

'I'm sorry, but even one failure... Lynne: launch an investigation into what happened - and I want the report on my desk in three days. Let's see whether Ben's death helps us to tighten up our procedures.'

'Yes, Prime Minister.' Lynne recognised the dismissal and stood up. As she reached the door that led out of the Cabinet Room she paused. 'Your scientific adviser is waiting outside for you - shall I send him in?'

It was nearly midnight, and all Melanie wanted to do was climb the stairs and go to bed. But her scientific adviser never bothered her unless it was important - and she knew from experience just how vital he was to the security of the United Kingdom.

'I suppose so. Is Steve still hanging about?' Steve Christian was her taciturn defence minister.

'Isn't he always?' Lynne laughed. It was widely known that Steve had a bit of a thing about his Prime Minister.

'Then send him in too.'

A century ago, defence of the realm had meant defending it against the build-up of the German military machine; fifty years ago, it was the Russians and the Cold War. But in 2010, it was something quite different from either: threats from beyond. And there was no one better able to spot them than her scientific adviser, and no one better to understand the magnitude of the threat than Steve, veteran of over a dozen extraterrestrial incursions.

'Mel?' Steve was the only person who still called her that. He was framed in the doorway: tall, stocky, with short, iron-grey hair. Even though he was wearing a charcoal suit he still managed to make it look like a uniform.

'Steve, take a seat.' She indicated his chair round the Cabinet table. 'I gather that the Doctor is hovering around.'

'What a charming analogy, Prime Minister. You make me sound like some kind of exotic bird.' The Doctor was standing right behind Steve, tugging a cuff of his frilled shirt. The jacket was the usual velvet, with blue the day's colour of choice. He ran a hand through his coiffured white hair. 'Sadly, I think that today I'm going to be more of an albatross than a peacock.'

Mel couldn't help smiling. 'Doctor, please sit down. I gather you wanted to talk to me.'

'Quite correct, Melanie.' The Doctor sat next to Steve. 'I have discovered something which worries me immensely.'

Melanie had known the Doctor for twenty-three years - exactly half her life. She had been introduced to him by her tutor, Ruth Ingram, back in her university days, but even now she still didn't know very much about him. He was an alien. He was virtually immortal. His mysterious race had exiled him to Earth forty years ago. And he had sworn to serve his adopted race.

In the five years since she had taken office, he had been invaluable. And she gathered from the missing sections of UNIT records that he had been helping mankind for a lot longer than that.

'This is an image from the Hubble II Array, in orbit around Ganymede.' He laid a brilliantly coloured photograph in front of her. It showed an irregular, glowing nebula, burning in green and gold. 'The telescope has standing orders to photograph this region of space once every three days.'

'And don't I know it,' Steve muttered. 'You weren't the one who had to negotiate with the Pentagon.'

'My good chap, your internal politics can wait.' The Doctor stabbed a long finger against the picture. 'Compare this with the equivalent photograph taken last week.' He withdrew it from the tooled-leather folder he had brought with him.

Melanie tried to spot the difference, but it was late and she could hardly keep her eyes open, let alone focus.

'I'm sorry, Doctor -'

'There, Melanie!' He was pointing to the top-left corner of the image, on the fuzzy border of the nebula. 'An area of increased luminance: six million candela! And given the spectrographic readings from that area, its precise location, and the distance, it's just as I've feared.'

'Which is?' asked Steve.

'Invasion! The spectrograph alone confirms it; the location...

irrefutable proof. That glow is the emission wake from a Cyberman BattlePhalanx - presumably one that escaped my little trap in 1989. It'll be within firing range of Earth in approximately five days, given the distance, the speed of light, and a rough guess at the speed of their hyperdrive.'

Mel couldn't believe what she was hearing. 'An invasion?'

'Invasion or sterilisation - it depends upon what the Cybermen consider to be the most logical course of action.' The Doctor looked at Steve. 'And our survival depends on what you and your fellow warmongers can do.'

'No chance of negotiation?' Steve asked.

'None. We are facing the cold steel of pure logic, General Christian. What are your chances?' Mel could see the seriousness in the Doctor's face. She had seen him defeat Daleks, Ice Warriors, Yeti, Quarks... and yet she had never seen such fear in his eyes before.

Steve snapped to it. 'We can invoke the Third Enabling Act and mobilise all the remaining nuclear arsenals. The strategic orbital defence platforms are at eighty per cent completion. The lunar-surface directed particle weapons are ready for immediate deployment. Is that enough for you, Doctor?'

The man who Melanie had considered their last best hope against anything slowly shook his head. 'If that's the best you can do, then I'm afraid mankind doesn't stand a chance.'

Stuart placed the report on his desk and frowned. As director of the Newton Institute of Temporal Physics at Wootton, he didn't really have time to follow every single project that the institute funded. He gave a wry smile - as a temporal physicist, time should have been the least of his worries. But this particular project was turning out to be more than problematical.

For one thing, he wasn't exactly sure what they were doing.

Oh, he knew what they were supposed to be doing: the research team from Munich University had made a fascinating proposal to the board, talking about exploring the application of temporal resonance as an archaeological tool. Husband and wife Lügner and Hündin were obviously a gifted couple, whilst their assistant, Schurke, had a knack of building all their equipment from scratch. As for Magier... Stuart had to admit that his grasp of temporal theory was as good, if not better, than Paul Kairos'. He'd even built a small version of the TITAN Array, simply as a research tool.

But the list of purchase orders in front of Stuart suggested they were up to one hell of a lot more. One hour's use of CERN - five million pounds. Six Deutsch Quantum computers, and all the gubbins for a 216-way processing Array - one hundred million pounds. An archaeological dig in Santorini to test their theories - half a million. The institute wasn't exactly strapped for cash, but this was ridiculous.

So what the hell were they doing? And why did it need so much money? To the professors who had signed off the budget increases, it had obviously made sense. But now that the Munich team's demands had exceeded the professors' authority, it was up to Stuart. And as far as he was concerned, Lügner and Hündin were spitting in the wind.

The eighteenth symposium of the World Council for Temporal Research had proved that the LeFabvre paradox was insoluble, and yet Lügner and Hündin were claiming that the proof was nothing but a corollary of their findings. Over in Moscow, Aaron was demonstrating the concept of closed loops in time, while Magier's mathematics apparently showed that time was, by its nature, incapable of such an action.

It just didn't make sense.

Stuart decided it was time to look at the Munich team's experiments a little more closely. Before their fanciful schemes bankrupted the institute.

Arlene hated the winter. Especially when it was raining, her car hadn't arrived and she was due on stage in three hours.

She had tried her PR and her PA, but neither was responding. She'd phoned the theatre, but had only managed to reach their booking service. She'd even tried the local cab firms, but not a single car was free: even for Arlene Cole.

Then again, what else could she have expected on Christmas

Eve? Her only option was to try to hail a black cab, but she knew from experience that Islington - especially the avenues and cul-de-sacs around her house - wasn't exactly on the main drag as far as they were concerned. So she had pulled on her overcoat, grabbed an umbrella and started to walk towards the main road, hoping that she could find a cab that would brave the West End on Christmas Eve.

Thankfully, her wardrobe - and, as importantly, her dressers - would be waiting for her at the theatre. Even after a couple of minutes, she felt sure she looked like a drowned rat: her long grey mac was soaked, even with the umbrella. Not exactly the image a number one recording artist wanted to present.

She was so preoccupied by being angry that it didn't occur to her until about five minutes after she had started walking that this probably wasn't the most sensible thing she could have done. Although she made every effort to preserve her privacy, her fans could be persistent; far too many letters arrived at the house rather than at the office. And the contents of some of them were rather… disturbing.

She shook her head. Get a hold of yourself, woman. Arlene had grown up in Islington - it wasn't as if she didn't know the streets, didn't remember the long walks back from the bus stop at four in the morning. She knew Islington like the back of her hand.

Arlene had read the articles: why, with her huge business empire, her homes on the East and West Coasts, the chateau in Normandy and the mansion in Buckinghamshire, did she still mainly choose to stay in her modest six-bedroom house in Islington?

Because she didn't stay there - she lived there. She stayed at the other places.

A noise!

She didn't turn round. She didn't even break step. But her heart began to beat even faster. There was someone behind her - she knew it!

She was about three minutes from the tree-lined alleyway that led to Holloway Road. If she could just hold herself together for three minutes… but down an alleyway? In the pitch black? She thought about phoning her PA again, but what would the person behind her do when he saw her getting out her mobile?

There was no one there, she told herself. The rainswept streets were empty. Cold and empty –

'Arlene?' said the voice from behind her.

Arlene almost screamed. She turned round. 'Yes?' She tried to sound calm, brave – God alone knew whether she did, since all she could hear was the sound of her heart thumping.

'I'm sorry to startle you.' He was standing in the dim orange pool of a street lamp – a man, in his twenties, a baseball cap pulled down over his eyes to ward off the rain. His face was sad, with large brown eyes and a wispy ginger goatee beard. In the rain he looked like an abandoned puppy. His voice was quiet, diffident. 'I wondered if I might trouble you for an autograph.' He thrust out a leather-bound autograph book and a pen.

A fan. Wanting an autograph. She almost laughed. 'Of course.' She took the book from his hands, trying to work out how she was going to sign it without the page getting soaking wet.

'Would you mind holding the umbrella, Mr…?'

'Mark. Just Mark. Of course not.' He moved close to her and took the umbrella from her. 'I've been here every night for the last month,' he continued. 'I've taken at least ten rolls of film.' He tapped the expensive-looking camera swinging round his neck.

Arlene opened the book and gave the other autographs a cursory glance. Soap stars, sporting heroes, musicians… nothing out of the ordinary. But as she began to sign her own name, something came to her. There was something about one of those names, something from the news…

'I've got lots of really good pictures,' he said enthusiastically. 'With the telephoto lens, I can see straight into your bedroom. And your bathroom.'

At that point she remembered the name. Liz McCarthy, the soap star. Murdered on the way back to her flat in Mayfair.

Her killer had never been caught.

Arlene threw the book away from her in disgust. The man was no longer a puppy-like fan. He was a seriously sick piece of work.

'Get away from me!'

'I only want to get to know you better.' The diffidence had been replaced by a sinister, wheedling tone. 'I feel I know you already.'

Arlene began to back away, but the man started to advance.

'Don't you want to know me better? You and me... well, think how good it would be. You're so important to me, Arlene.' He dropped the umbrella and reached out to her. 'I know you feel the same way, Arlene. Admit it. Admit it!' His face twisted into a deranged leer. 'I used to be in the army – I don't think you'll be disappointed by my body. I'm still very fit.'

Arlene's flesh crawled with revulsion. Her worst nightmare, here on the streets of her childhood home. She had walked through LA, through New York, but she had never felt as scared as she did now.

'The army didn't understand me,' he continued. 'They said I was schizophrenic. But I knew they were wrong. I knew my friends would understand me. Friends like you, Arlene.'

That was it. Abandoning any thoughts of reasoning with him, she started to run, but she knew she didn't stand a chance. Arlene, singing diva in heels, versus an ex-army psycho?

But she didn't exactly have a choice, did she? The alleyway was just a few metres away. If she could only get through that, she'd be on the main road. Even her stalker wouldn't be so stupid as to attack her so publicly, would he?

He was still shouting to her, but Arlene blotted it out. All that mattered was the alleyway, the alleyway –

Her heel snapped, sending her sprawling on to the wet pavement. Ignoring the pain from her ankle, she looked up to see Mark leaning over her. 'Arlene,' he hissed. She could smell the alcohol on his breath as his face grew closer and closer.

'Arlene!' The gruff familiar voice barked out through the winter night. Mark jumped to his feet and started to run away from her.

She recognised Gerard, her driver, six feet two of Mancunian muscle. He helped her to her feet. 'Are you all right?'

Arlene winced as her sprained ankle touched the ground. 'I've been better.' She realised that she was shaking, and allowed Gerard to give her a comforting hug. People like Mark should be locked up – or worse.

'Do you want me to go after him?' asked Gerard.

Arlene didn't know what she wanted. No - she did. A long, hot shower. Her schizophrenic stalker could wait. The police would know what to do.

'Get me to the theatre, Gerard,' she groaned. 'I've got a show to do.' Spoken like a proper trouper. It was just a shame that she felt like a frightened little girl.

The four Enemy fleets - thousands upon thousands of jet-black saucers acting as one - completed their tetrahedron, an enclosure one thousand miles a side. There was a slight shudder in its invisible lines as the final adjustments took place, before each fleet made contact with the other three, breathtaking beams of purple neon cutting through the blackness. Within the tetrahedron, access to and from the time vortex was impossible.

The good news was that the Time Lord fleet had managed to ascend into space-time seconds before the enclosure had completed.

The bad news was that it would have to stay there until the Enemy was defeated - or face annihilation in the process.

On the command deck of the *Righteous Fist of Rassilon*, the Lord President Admiral watched the progress on the main holoscreen, a starscape that covered the entire ceiling.

They were trapped: but they had both might and right on their sides. They would cleanse the universe of the Enemy presence - or sacrifice that universe trying.

The full might of the First Imperial Gallifreyan Fleet was an impressive sight to behold - not that aesthetics mattered one jot to the Enemy's calculating tin minds, of course.

Six white-and-gold time dreadnoughts, each one a mile-high monolith like a Gothic cathedral, with vaunted arches and flying buttresses sweeping up to the single needle that surmounted each one like a spire. The dreadnoughts had to be that huge: along their central axis, hundreds of miniature Eyes of Harmony generated the titanic forces that the dreadnoughts wielded. Time destructors - each one capable of taking out an entire star system.

Flanking the dreadnoughts, thirty-six destroyers - smaller and less powerful, but more manoeuvrable, vessels - flew in formation, while a cloud of over one thousand WarTARDISes darted in between the fleet and in and out of the black-and-silver bulk of the TARDIS carrier, protected at the very centre of the fleet.

Although they were outclassed in terms of sheer numbers, the Lord President Admiral knew that the odds were actually far better than four to one. A critical mass of Enemy saucers had to remain in formation at each of the vertices of the tetrahedron, otherwise the vortex jammer would fail. And the Enemy wouldn't dare risk further materialisations by the Time Lords - their battle-computers simply wouldn't allow the possibility.

It put the odds closer to two to one. But that still wasn't good.

'Cardinal Commander - patch me through to Castellan Captain Andred on *The Glorious Aspect of Omega*.' The commander, Tortheth, was a veteran of nearly a dozen campaigns, and the president's right-hand man. He was pleased to see that Tortheth had already opened a channel before he had spoken.

The president could imagine the Enemy battle-computers calculating the strategies and tactics, working out the precise formation necessary to take out three of the six dreadnoughts - their standard response. A minimum of four dreadnoughts was necessary to run sufficient interference to give the WarTARDISes a chance to demonstrate their prowess. At least, that was what the Matrix predictions indicated. But they were predictions - the president himself had succeeded with two dreadnoughts. It was not an experience he particularly wanted to repeat.

Although the temporal grace that protected the Time Lord fleet extended what were nanoseconds for the Enemy's battle-computers into minutes for the Time Lords, time - ironically - was of the essence. Thankfully, the Enemy's lack of imagination allowed for considerable second guessing.

'Lord President?' Andred's mannered tones filled the air around the president's head.

'Andred - we need to knock out one of the nodes. Despite the pasting we gave them in the Arcturus sector, I doubt that the Enemy have learnt of the improvements we've made to the dreadnoughts.'

'My thoughts exactly, Lord President. Permission to requisition the *Sacred Might of Gallifrey*?'

'Permission granted. I'll be travelling in my ship. And before you say anything, Andred, you will not persuade me otherwise.'

'I know.' The resigned tone made it clear that Andred had lost this battle too many times to argue. The Lord President Admiral always led the WarTARDIS attack: he would never ask a fellow Time Lord to take a risk he would not take himself. 'Good luck – may Rassilon's will be with us.' The channel closed.

'Cardinal Commander: have my TARDIS ready for immediate dematerialisation. Instruct the WarTARDIS commanders to execute attack pattern theta sigma.'

Tortheth nodded.

If they could take out a node, the vortex jammer would go off-line. And then the technical improvements made to the dreadnoughts' armouries could come into play.

The president nodded at his two chancellery guards in their red-and-white livery. One stepped in front of him, the other fell into step behind him, as they left the command deck and headed for his quarters. And his ship.

The regimen of the WarTARDIS carrier had never really suited his TARDIS – it found it too formal and, besides, the newer models tended to be rather haughty, always whispering amongst themselves. But there was another reason why the Lord President Admiral kept his ship close to him. His years of experience in the field had taught him that he could never know when he might need an escape route.

Outside a battle situation, he could have used an intraship time ring to reach the staterooms. But in the fleet's current predicament, every ship was flooded with a soft icaron field to prevent the Enemy using any of their diabolical – and stolen – temporal weaponry against them. Unfortunately, that left the president only one way to get to his quarters. On foot.

The main corridor that led to the staterooms ran along the spine of the dreadnought, parallel to the time-destructor manifold. Walls, ceilings and floors were transparent: a complex matrix of perpetually regenerating solid energy. Even if the dreadnought were destroyed, the corridor would probably survive.

Far beneath the clear floor, the president could see the dynamorphic generators, each one slaved to one of the countless block-transferred copies of the original Eye of Harmony.

Once, at the dawn of the first age of the Time Lords, Rassilon had decreed that all Gallifreyan technology would be powered by the Eye that lay buried below the Panopticon as a symbol of the might of the Time Lords. However, over the subsequent millennia, it had become clear that this was both inefficient and potentially dangerous: missions to the edge of the Time Lord noosphere ran the risk of drifting beyond the range of the eye. Despite protests that it was blasphemous, all TARDISes later than Type 25s carried perfect block-transfer computations of the prime Eye.

And the Gallifreyan time dreadnoughts manifested that achievement in abundance. Clamped on to the thin mirrored barrel of the destructor, hundreds of perfect copies appeared as a spiral of tiny black spines, each Eye housing a raw singularity torn from the heart of a quantum black hole.

Beyond the other three sides lay the rest of the bulk of the dreadnought: a vastness lit in opalescence, filled with floating geometric shapes of varying sizes linked together in a network of access tunnels and energy feeds, strung across the emptiness in a glittering spider's web.

Each of the shapes represented a different function: the dodecahedra were the mess rooms for the chancellery guards, while the spheres contained the ground assault vessels, their designs culled from a thousand worlds and times. Spheres, isocahedra... if a geometric body existed, the Time Lords had a use for it: monitor rooms, APC terminals, the rotating tetrahedra of the cardinal captains...

And alone among them, the sedately spinning cube in the middle distance was the stateroom of the Lord President Admiral.

As he strode towards it, he hardly noticed the deferential bows and nods from the assorted ranks of the Time Lord hierarchy - a gold usher here, a surgeon-general there, the scurrying figures of the Propagandists. The war had taken many casualties, but Gallifreyan formality was one that the President would miss the least. All that pomp and stuffiness, the ancient ritual and cant – luxuries that a capitol on a war footing could hardly afford.

The corridor opened up into a miniature version of the Panopticon. Fashioned from marble and aeternium, scaled-down versions of the six statues of the founders of Gallifrey sat in silent judgement. How would they feel, given the current situation? Would they be proud that their children were fighting for justice and morality, for the freedom of the cosmos? Or would they have preferred Gallifrey to remain inviolate, aloof from the lower races?

Whatever they would have felt it was irrelevant, the president tried to convince himself as he walked through the silent chamber. Gallifrey was at war, and there was only one possible outcome. Annihilation. Annihilation for the Enemy, or for the Time Lords, or for the universe – but annihilation, none the less. He was grateful to leave the Panopticon, grateful to leave the heavy gaze of the six stone founders. He simply didn't feel worthy of them. Not after the atrocities that had been committed in their name.

Long minutes later, he reached the smooth glass junction which led from the spinal corridor to his stateroom. Dismissing his guards, he walked the final few metres to the door alone. Alone save for his thoughts – and they weren't the best thoughts he had ever had.

He waited patiently as the security devices confirmed his identity. Forget access codes, retina scans, even genetic analysis; after the horrifying loss of the *Arcane Mystery of the Other*, there was no guarantee that the Enemy weren't employing another of their temporal duplicates. Only a full quantum scan could ensure that he was the right president from the right universe.

With a series of clicks, the doors to his stateroom slid open. As they closed behind him, he sank heavily into the anachronistic red leather armchair, just one of the eccentric items of furniture dotted around the circular white room, and finally allowed the facade to drop. Within the sanctuary of his stateroom, he didn't have to be brave, he didn't have to be fearless. He didn't have to be the one who scared the monsters away. He could simply be the Doctor again. For what it was worth.

He rubbed his eyes with the palms of his hands. The knowledge he was carrying was sometimes too much - even for the President of the Time Lords. Even for a race to which secrecy was second nature, the Lord President was privy to a secret that would rock Gallifrey to its foundations.

Forget the information broadcasts, forget the propaganda fed to the less-informed races; far from the Time Lords being on the brink of glorious victory over the Enemy, the war was going badly for them. Extremely badly.

For a mighty war fleet consisting of vessels calling themselves such vainglorious names as the *Righteous Fist of Rassilon*, the *Glorious Aspect of Omega*, the *Sacred Might of Gallifrey* and the *Blind Visage of the Pythia*, its performance was anything but glorious - it was an insult to Rassilon, Omega, Gallifrey and even the Pythia. The Enemy now outclassed, outranked and outgunned it at almost every turn.

It hadn't always been so. At the beginning, the success of the jihad had appeared to be a certainty. Despite the Enemy's greater numbers, despite their fearsome fire power, the Time Lords had had the edge. Millions of years of temporal superiority had led to victory after victory. As the war spread across the cosmos, the Enemy's defeat had grown closer and closer.

But soon after the Doctor had been persuaded to return home and accept the heavy mantle of presidency, things had started to go very, very wrong.

The third and fifth fleets had cornered an Enemy task force close to the Greater Magellanic cloud, only to simply vanish. It was as if they had been taken out of time...

The Time Lords' greatest allies, the Cyberlords, suddenly changed sides - in the middle of battle. It was as if their history had been altered...

Using the latest sentient TARDISes, Chancellor Morbius had attacked one of the Enemy's most strategic strongholds. But the stronghold wasn't there - it never had been there. It was as if time had been rearranged...

These, and other similar incidents, had led to the formation of a special task force, run by the CIA and answerable only to the Lord President. A task force to look into this run of so-called 'bad luck'.

Twelve hours ago, the President had taken delivery of the report. And nothing could ever be the same again.

Sighing, he stood up, feeling every second of his many lives. He reached around his neck, locating the key beneath the heavy gold links of the sash. It was time to go. Across the room, a blue Metropolitan police box waited patiently, as she had done on so many occasions.

Within the TARDIS, all was as it had ever been. The white, roundelled walls, the hexagonal console, the reassuring hum. But nothing could reassure him after he had read the task force's report.

His hands deftly operated the controls, but it was all second nature: skill and strategy would only be needed once the WarTARDIS fleet was timeborne. His TARDIS began cycling, trickling power through all the systems in preparation for war. But the President's mind was elsewhere. He glanced over to the corner of the console room: set upon a bronze podium engraved with old High Gallifreyan script, a perfect crystal sphere stared back at him like some baleful eye. A crystal ball, foretelling the future. A perfect description of the Matrix.

Linked to the APC net on Gallifrey through methods the Enemy could never comprehend, this child of the Matrix ensured that the President alone knew of the latest developments. Such as the report from the CIA.

Soon after the war had commenced, the High Council had considered the unthinkable. Genocide. If they could find the Enemy's world of origin, they could prevent the war ever occurring. Of course, there would be unfortunate temporal side effects, but they were Time Lords, weren't they? Nothing that couldn't be cleaned up afterwards.

The argument had dragged on for an age. The CIA had stuck its oar in, urging direct action, while the High Tribunal endlessly discussed the legal ramifications. The High Council sat in judgement, knowing that the war had to be stopped but unwilling to compromise the very constitution of the Time Lords. Finding a middle ground was anathema to all of them.

Finally, however, they were all in agreement. If the Enemy's homeworld could be located, they would strike. And end this war for ever.

Despite the ruling, the Lord President had been uneasy: article seven of Gallifreyan law, which forbade state-authorised genocide, dated back to the Vampire Wars and was countersigned by Rassilon himself. Did the president have the right to suspend it? But there really had been no alternative: not if this terrible war was to end. His hands tied, he gave the necessary order.

But over the following decades, the decision had become increasingly irrelevant. The location of the Enemy homeworld had eluded them... until Mortimus of the CIA elite executive, on an undercover mission, had made his way further beyond Enemy lines than anyone had previously done. And there he had discovered the awful truth.

The Enemy no longer had a homeworld. Indeed, they had never had a homeworld. All the evidence suggested they had employed sophisticated dimensional engineering techniques to loop their worldline, rendering it inaccessible to Time Lord attack.

So what did this mean? Gallifrey itself was protected by even more complex temporal defences, its worldline twisted and warped through all eleven dimensions to hide it from Enemy attack. It was the home of the Time Lords, the legendary masters of time. Surely the Enemy lacked the level of knowledge to manipulate its own worldline?

On Gallifrey, the temporal theoreticians had had a field day. It had been millennia since they had faced such a conundrum, and the President suspected they had deliberately made heavy weather of their investigations to boost their self-importance.

But they were Time Lords. The mysteries of time were theirs to uncover, and uncover them they did.

They uncovered the unthinkable.

The Enemy had time travel.

Of course, the Enemy had always had access to the basics of time technology, rudimentary time corridors and travel machines to name but two. But the theoreticians were suggesting they now had control over time to a degree that had always been the sole province of the Time Lords: temporal manipulation, the ability to rewrite time to their own design.

The task force's conclusion was that the Enemy had either developed or stolen the secrets of the Time Lords. The edge that had swung the balance of the war in Gallifrey's favour no longer existed. And Matrix predictions suggested that the Enemy's greater numbers, their inexorable logic, underpinned by their new-found temporal abilities, would inevitably lead to an Enemy victory. In what should be the Time Lords' epitaph, it was only a matter of time.

With that knowledge eating away at him, the President looked up at the scanner. The WarTARDIS fleet was ready, thousands of shiny black spheres, orbiting the massive carrier. And he was ready to lead it.

If an Enemy victory was inevitable, then so be it. But the Time Lords would fight until the bitter, bitter end.

He pressed the vortex primer, allowing the grinding and groaning of the engines to wash over him. *An Enemy victory? That'll be the day.*

Seven billion parallel Earths. Seven billion alternate worldlines. A feast for the Chronovores.

Through the channel the Dark Lord of Time had created between the Six-Fold Realm and the Higher Place, the Chronovores had descended, the lure of the rarest of delicacies irresistible. Without the Lux Aeterna, food had been scarce. Now they could feed for ever.

The selfsame being who had denied them the Lux Aeterna had provided them with sustenance beyond measure: never before had there been so many parallel universes, screaming for their attention. Each alternate worldline was an endless banquet, something to tease and gnaw at, a chance to relish the exquisite flavours of the different, the unusual, the strange.

Their hunger was great, but they knew that devouring the worldlines completely was short-sighted: better to drain them bit by bit, parasites not carnivores, rather than consume them wholesale. That way, they could draw out their feast for an eternity, feeding on the alternates until each worldline was finally extinguished, a guttering candle brought to a forced yet natural end.

Somewhere, deep below their primal urges, the Chronovores knew the effect their feeding was having on the alternates. It pleased them.

As they feasted, the reality of each alternate darkened and corrupted, blossoming with the fruits of its self-destruction - but that simply added a nuance, a delicate flavour, a spice, to the consumption. It was the way of the Chronovores. It was, and ever had been. Since the Great Old Ones had spawned them so very, very long ago, the Chronovores had roamed the cosmos, spotting the alternates as they formed and then devouring them. So very, very few alternates... until now.

Now was their epiphany, their greatest triumph. After an eternity, the Chronovores could dine on a banquet of realities never before seen in this continuum. Knowing their past, anticipating their future, they feasted as they had never done before.

The Divine Host tore at the carcass, while the lesser hosts were permitted to toy with the remains. After aeons of the bare, poor sustenance of the Lux Aeterna, these new universes were to be savoured, devoured.

One at a time.

'Oh, come on!' Lynne Thomas looked up from the screen. 'Surely we can do better than that?'

Her undersecretary of state - who didn't look old enough to shave, let alone be in government - gave her an apologetic sulk. 'I'm sorry, Minister. Those are the latest reports from Geneva.'

Lynne shook her head. 'There's an entire battle fleet above our heads, and the UN is still quibbling? This is ridiculous!'

She looked round as the door to the Cabinet Room flew open. The Prime Minister hurried in, followed closely by Steve Christian.

'Update, Lynne?' Melanie, in a navy-blue trouser suit, pulled her chair round to face her Home Secretary before sinking into it. She indicated that Lynne and Steve should do the same. Lynne could see how tired Melanie was: the bags under her eyes, the tone of her voice. Then again, Lynne hadn't slept for three days either, and she doubted that Steve had.

'The secretary-general thinks we should attempt negotiations with them. And our dear friend President Dering is saying the same!' Lynne slammed her folder on to the cream leather blotter. Were they the only ones who understood the severity of the threat?

'I would have thought Tom would have known better than that after his experience with the Quarks and the giant wasps in Central Park,' Melanie sighed, running her hands through her mane of red hair. 'We have less than three days before the Cyberman BattlePhalanx arrives, and every power on this planet is running about trying to pretend that it's not there!' She looked across at Steve. 'Any sign of the Doctor?'

Her defence minister shook his head. 'Not a thing, Melanie. It's as if he simply vanished into thin air...' Steve trailed off, and cast his eyes heavenwards. 'You don't think -'

Mel jumped to her feet. 'No, Steve, I don't think. The Doctor has served this country - this planet - for the last forty years. The idea that he might even consider betraying it is beneath contempt.'

Lynne tried to defuse the situation. With an interplanetary invasion fleet breathing down their necks, it wasn't surprising that tempers were running high. But a schism in the Cabinet wasn't going to help, was it? 'Melanie... I'm sure Steve wasn't implying anything. But you have to admit, we really could do with the Doctor at the moment.'

'You're right,' Mel sighed. 'Steve - I'm sorry. Lynne: any word from the Russians yet?'

Lynne opened her mouth to answer, but before she could say a word the Cabinet Room was filled with a raucous trumpeting. The source of the disturbance became obvious about a second later: just in front of the main double doors, against the twin white Corinthian columns, the air swam aside to allow a large blue box to materialise. Lynne immediately recognised it from its description in UNIT files: an old-fashioned Metropolitan police box, housing the Doctor's fantastic space-time machine.

The Doctor! Forget the orbiting defence grid, the land- and moon-based nuclear deterrents; mankind's last best hope came giftwrapped in a police box.

Melanie, Steve and Lynne leapt to their feet as the blue doors creaked open. And Melanie's hand leapt to her mouth when they saw who - what - came out.

The white curls and the velvet finery were the same, but half the Doctor's face was missing, replaced by shiny silver and circuitry, a single, black hole for an eye socket. One of his hands was now a three-fingered cybernetic claw, clutching mechanically.

'Melanie.' Only the faintest traces of the Doctor's lisping, aristocratic voice remained; it was now overwhelmed by an emotionless, robotic burr.

'Doctor?' Melanie's own voice was now a horrified whisper. 'What's happened?'

The Doctor stepped out of the TARDIS doorway. And at that point they all realised he wasn't alone. Three more figures stepped out of the darkened box and formed what appeared to be a guard of honour around him. Two metres tall, clad in silver, their faces were skull-like masks of impassion. Lynne remembered the pictures from one of their earlier incursions.

Cybermen.

The Doctor moved over to the table. 'I realised the futility of fighting the Cybermen, Melanie. They are a cleaner, better breed than mankind. Superior, immortal - they are the rightful heirs to the universe, Melanie, metal and flesh conjoined as one. They have given me my freedom and I have given them time travel. I have given them the secrets of the Time Lords and they have shown me completion. Together we will cleanse this cosmos of the imperfections of base organic life. Together we will educate the lesser races in the purity of the man-machine synthesis.'

'You bastard!' screamed Steve. 'You've sold us out to these... these robots!' In a single smooth movement, he pulled out his service revolver and fired.

The bullet struck the Doctor's chest. And bounced, with a metallic clang.

'That was foolish, General Christian. Foolish.' The Doctor raised his metal claw. 'Subdue him.'

One of the Cybermen turned in Steve's direction and nodded towards him, almost respectfully. But the effect was anything but respectful. Lynne couldn't help screaming as a pulsing white electrical discharge leapt from the third eye atop the Cyberman's helmet and burrowed into Steve's head. Soundlessly, he sank to the floor.

'You've killed him!' shouted Mel, vaulting over the Cabinet table, sending blotters and lamps flying. She scrambled to her feet and knelt at Steve's side.

'He has been subdued,' the hybrid Doctor intoned. 'Killing him would be a waste of his military potential. Killing any humans would be a waste of raw material.' He strode over to Mel and grasped her wrist in his claw, pulling her face towards his. 'You are the leader of one of the most powerful political blocs on Earth. With your help, this planet's transformation can be achieved more rapidly.'

'Never!' Mel tried to pull away from him. 'I'd rather die than sell my people out to these creatures!'

'Death will not be necessary. Once you have become like us, you will think like us. That is the way of the Cybermen. We will survive.'

Lynne caught the look in Melanie's eyes. It wasn't fear: it was an expression of complete and utter incomprehension. One of the Cybermen came over to join the Doctor, and took Mel's arm with a gentleness that belied its size. Without resisting, she allowed herself to be taken into the Doctor's TARDIS.

Lynne felt the strength drain from her as the other two Cybermen approached. One lifted the unconscious Steve as if he were a baby; the other stared at her with the empty holes that passed for eyes, its silver hands reaching for her.

That was the last thing that Lynne remembered.

As a human being, that is.

Stuart looked at his watch and growled. It was over an hour since he had asked - demanded - that Lügner and his associates meet him in his study, but there was still no sign of them. Typical of their arrogance.

Their most recent request had been their most audacious: three hours' use of the heavy particle accelerator at MIT. Didn't they realise how much that would cost - it was even more expensive than CERN. There was no way Stuart could authorise nearly eight million pounds of institute money for their harebrained schemes - schemes that every other temporal scientist on the planet was ridiculing. The Newton Institute was becoming a laughing stock! Apparently, even mad old/young Aaron was referring to them as the 'funny farm'.

Checking his watch for a final time, Stuart stormed out of his study. He had been patient until now. He had let the German scientists hide behind their legally binding contract of secrecy. But no more. He was the director: he had a right to know what was going on.

The Germans' laboratory was behind a pair of badge-locked titanium doors in the west wing of the institute. But as director, it hadn't been difficult for Stuart to pull a few strings with the facilities people. If Mohammed wouldn't come to the mountain... well, Stuart felt sufficiently mountainous to come to them. Especially with the institute pass card in his hand.

Finally reaching the solid doors that led to the laboratory, Stuart swiped the card through the reader and waited for the little light to turn from red to green. As the lock clicked, he threw open the doors and strode through the annex into the main laboratory.

'Now look here, Lügner -' Stuart froze at the scene revealed before him.

The last time he had seen the laboratory, the German scientists' equipment had been in crates. Now it had been assembled.

In the centre of the lab, a green-grey pillar stretched from floor to ceiling. But it didn't look manufactured; if anything, it appeared to have been grown. It didn't have the smooth texture of metal; instead, it seemed fleshy, organic. There was even the faintest hint of phosphorescence, like mould. As Stuart watched, he could have sworn that it pulsed - as if it was breathing...

Cables - or were they tendrils? - snaked away from the base of the pillar, linking it to more familiar equipment. Stuart recognised most of this from the requisition orders he had signed for the scientists: a nuclear magnetic resonator; a bank of quantum computers, a more common-or-garden number-crunching array.

But he certainly didn't recognise the plain grey box against the wall, with three thick cables entering it through a square hole of unimaginable blackness. He stepped over for a closer look.

'Ah, Director. You really shouldn't have.'

Stuart looked round, but he was still alone in the lab. That had sounded like Lügner - almost. But there had been no heavy German accent.

Another black gap appeared in the grey box - this one was more of a door. Lügner and Hündin stepped out. Yet there was something different about them: they had eschewed their familiar white lab coats for clothes of a far more ornate design. Lügner was dressed in a black velvet frock coat with silver edging, while Hündin wore tight, brown leather trousers and a revealing silk top. Light years away from the traditional image of a scientist, thought Stuart.

'I thought I'd save you the effort and come and see you,' he said sarcastically.

'No, Professor Hyde: you misunderstand me,' said Lügner. 'I meant, you really shouldn't have.' Without seeming to move a muscle, he was holding a stubby black cylinder, aiming it at Stuart.

'If only you hadn't been in such a rush to see us,' said Hündin, her voice similarly unaccented. 'We're virtually finished with your miserable little world.'

'Who are you?' whispered Stuart, even though a terrifying suspicion was growing in his mind.

'My dear Professor Hyde - has it really been that long?'

He was younger than he had been, but wasn't that a Time Lord gift? 'The Master?'

'The recognition of old friends is always a delight,' Lügner said silkily. 'And my attractive colleague here is popularly known as the Rani.'

'Another Time Lord?'

'Don't forget us.' At the sound of the gruff voice, Stuart turned to see the thuggish Schurke and the fey Magier standing behind him.

'I'm Drax,' said Schurke, now in a shiny black jump suit.

Magier, in a floor-length hooded black robe, gave an elaborate bow. 'Mortimus, otherwise known as the Monk. I must thank you for the generosity that you and the institute have shown our little endeavour. We could never have managed this without you.'

Stuart looked at the atrocity that was growing in the centre of the lab, at the self-satisfied smiles on the faces of the Time Lords. After the Master had fooled him as Professor Thascales, Stuart had sworn that he would never again be the unwitting, unwilling puppet of these 'higher' beings.

And now he had discovered a whole nest of them, under his very nose, feeding off him and his institute. He felt sick.

'What are you doing here?' he asked quietly. 'An invasion?'

'An invasion?' laughed the Rani. 'You humans have such limited imaginations. Nothing so mundane, Stuart.' She inclined her head towards the Master. 'This is supposed to be one of the greatest minds on this benighted mudball?'

The Master smirked. 'Pathetic, isn't it?' He waved his hand around the lab. 'Come now, Professor - you signed off all of the purchase orders. Surely you can make an educated guess?'

Stuart pointed at the pulsing malignancy that towered over them. 'I certainly never authorised that!'

The Master graciously held his hand out. 'My dear Rani, I do believe that the professor is admiring your handiwork. Perhaps you would care to share its secrets? The Rani is one of the greatest geneticists and bioengineers to grace this galaxy,' he added conspiratorially.

'The DNA recombinator is probably my crowning glory,' crowed the Rani, striding over to its mouldlike bulk. She stroked it affectionately, as if it were some bastard child in the attic. 'Conceived by the processing array, gestated under the sunlight of your nuclear reactor and given birth by particle accelerator, the recombinator simply needs one final element to reach adulthood. And thanks to the archaeological expedition you so kindly financed, we now have that element.' She nodded at Mortimus. He reached within the folds of his cloak and withdrew an object that glittered in the artificial lighting.

To anyone else, it was simply a remarkably pure quartz crystal. But to Stuart...

'The Crystal of Kronos?' he gasped.

'The very same,' said the Master proudly. 'Or rather, another part of the original trident so diligently tended by dear Dalios and his priest-king ancestors. If anything, its crystal lattice is even more suited to our current purpose. My dear Rani - the honour is yours.'

The Rani nodded.

'But what does it do?' Stuart was almost shouting in a combination of fear and anger.

The Rani tutted. 'You really are a microcephalic insect, aren't you, Hyde? I told you. It is a DNA recombinator. Once primed with the reality-altering abilities of this shard of the Kronos trident, it will search out every last strand of DNA within a given region and rework it into its new matrix.' She inserted the crystal into a dilating pustule.

Stuart struggled to understand this madwoman. Reworking DNA? Surely she didn't mean what he thought she meant? 'But that will kill every living thing!' he protested.

'Don't think of it as death, Professor,' said Mortimus, tending the processor array. 'Think of it as a noble self-sacrifice to serve a far higher cause.'

'Our cause,' growled Drax, checking the quantum computers.

'Once the recombinator is activated, all life based on deoxyribonucleic acid will become greater than the sum of its parts, an organic gestalt of unimaginable physical and psionic potential. A living weapon that we shall use to bring the cosmos to its knees!' proclaimed the Master. 'Now, Rani!'

'No!' screamed Stuart, leaping over to the Rani and trying to pull her away. But she too possessed superhuman strength: she shrugged him off, sending him sprawling to the floor. As he caught his breath, he tried one last tack. 'It'll kill you as well,' he hissed.

'The triple helix is the legacy of Rassilon,' the Rani replied. 'Our birthright will protect us.' With that, she slammed the crystal home. Stuart watched as pulses of blue and yellow joined the green phosphorescence, shooting up and down the monstrous device. The sound of a thousand trees being blown in the wind filled the laboratory as its hellish energies reached outwards, tugging at Stuart's very genetic structure...

And the crowd went wild.

Arlene made her final bow, trying to ignore the calls from her adoring public for yet another encore. She had given them three already - what more did they want? Being impromptu just wasn't her style. Not any more. Especially not after what had just happened.

Waving, she backed offstage and made her way to her dressing room, clutching at the bouquets that were thrust towards her, trying to get out of earshot before the cheers from the audience turned into disappointed catcalls. She went through the motions - thanking her fans and signing the odd autograph, her face a mask of gratitude - but her entourage knew that, this time, she simply wanted to be left alone. The incident in Islington had shaken her more than she had thought.

Which was why she was less than happy to find Sidney sitting in her dressing room, leafing through the latest edition of *Mojo*. Arlene wanted to take off her iridescent red dress, have a shower and slip into a pair of jeans and a sweatshirt - not have a conversation with her accountant.

'What is it, Sidney?' Sidney was a tall, frosty Scandinavian in his mid-thirties, all muscles, blond hair and blue eyes, and never one to mince words. He had been the financial comptroller of her huge business empire for the last five years: dependable, efficient - and straight to the point.

Like now.

'I have learnt what occurred and I am sorry, but the business is in trouble,' he stated flatly. 'Serious trouble.' He thrust a sheaf of papers at her. 'This is the overview of the financial audit I ordered. There are huge gaps all over the place, Arlene. We are talking hundreds of millions of dollars.'

For a moment, she couldn't understand what he was talking about. In the last ten years, after buying out her own contract and going it alone, Arlene had turned Cole Productions from a single recording studio with the rights to her face into a worldwide record label and merchandising organisation representing over half of the top forty artists in any given week. Of course, Cole Productions was now far too big for any single person to know exactly what was going on, but that was why she employed people like Sidney, for God's sake!

Ten years was hardly meteoric – she remembered packing boxes of T-shirts to send out to shops when all she had was an office above a knocking-shop in Soho – but she had still rated the odd cover on *Newsweek* and *Time*, as well as winning Businesswoman of the Year on three occasions. So what the hell was Sidney talking about? She extracted the papers from the plastic folder and gave them a cursory scan. Financial gobbledegook, of course, but she understood enough to know what was Sidney was talking about.

Huge portions of Cole Productions had been mortgaged off into junk bonds. There were bottomless pools of debt in virtually every arm of the company and in every country. A line of creditors queuing up to foreclose on loans. Financially, her company was falling apart.

'How did this happen, Sidney?'

He shrugged. 'Whoever is responsible has systematically gone through the company over the last year, and crippled it financially. They knew exactly where to look.'

'How long have we got?' However bad it appeared, at least she now knew about it. Carefully handled, and with the right people in place, Arlene felt confident that she could restructure the company.

The expression on Sidney's face was even graver than usual. 'Technically, Cole Productions is already bankrupt. I have stalled the larger creditors, but we have run out of time. You will have to liquidate at least seventy per cent of the company to pay off its outstanding debts.'

Arlene gasped. This just wasn't happening! She took a series of deep breaths, trying to formulate a plan. There had to be something she could do? Her voice was controlled as she spoke.

'Call an EGM at the LA office for the twenty-eighth. Start working on a recovery plan that will at least give us a breathing space: look towards selling off everything outside our core business.' As panic subsided, she started to use the business acumen that had made her so successful – and that she knew would save her and her company.

Without even a knock of warning, the door to her dressing room was thrown open. Two men stood in the doorway: a younger one, looking vaguely disinterested, and a shorter, older man, with a bald head and a world-weary expression. Two of Arlene's people were trying to stop them, but she recognised that determined body language before either of the strangers could say a word.

Police.

'Miss Arlene Cole?' As she nodded, the older man flashed a badge in her general direction. 'Inspector Burgess. This is DS Stanton. We're with S06: the fraud squad.'

'Fraud?' Obviously the news had already slipped out; even Sidney's meticulous attention to detail was sure to have triggered alarm bells at Companies House. Still, it was soon going to be household news; the sooner she had the fraud squad's help, the sooner they could identify whoever had decided to rape her company.

Burgess came a couple of steps closer. 'We'd like you to come down to the station. You're not under arrest yet, but serious irregularities have come to light regarding some of the companies you own.'

'What do you mean, "not under arrest yet"?'

She was totally unprepared for Burgess's next line. 'The evidence we have amassed so far indicates that you're the one responsible.'

With this second shock in the space of minutes, Arlene simply didn't know what to say. She looked back at Sidney, just in time to catch a knowing look pass between her financial comptroller and Burgess.

And in that moment, she understood what was going on.

'You bastard, Sidney!' she screamed, her hands reaching out to grab him, to tear at his face. 'Why?'

She was still screaming as Burgess and Stanton dragged her out of the theatre.

The Master staggered. For the briefest of moments, it was as if he had been elsewhere. Not just elsewhere, but lots of elsewheres, spread across realities like a series of ghosts. He steadied himself on the console. Even with every defence his WarTARDIS could muster, the flaming wings of the Quantum Archangel were penetrating the outer plasmic shell, waves of time spillage battering the vessel like some cosmic storm.

He had to reach the Doctor's TARDIS. He had to boost the matter gain to the outer plasmic shell and restabilise the two time machines before the Quantum Archangel tore them apart. His clawed hand pulled on the door lever. As the doors opened, he could see the lights dipping and fluttering in the Doctor's console room. But he could also see a shadowed figure at the console itself.

The Doctor?

Still staggering, the Master slowly made his way through the doors.

The battle was going badly. Fully one-third of the WarTARDIS fleet had been either destroyed or incapacitated, while the *Glorious Aspect of Omega* listed in space, venting time spillage through a gaping hole in its hull. Watching the carnage from his TARDIS, the president could only close his eyes in pain. Life-sign readings were dropping - it looked as if the breach was terminal.

'Andred, this is the President!' he bellowed through the telepathic circuits. 'Andred - your hull integrity is falling below critical!' But only psychic static answered him. Every fibre of his being demanded that he help Andred, but he knew his place was here, on the front line. Pain striking him like a dagger, he knew there was nothing he could do for the captain.

Somehow, the Enemy was wielding a directed temporal weapon

which could cut through outer plasmic shells, energistic matrices and gravitic hulls as if they simply weren't there. Where had that come from? There was no evidence that the Enemy had ever deployed a weapon anywhere close to that level of sophistication.

The battle was approaching the point of no return: the President didn't need the battle-computers or the doomsaying of the Matrix to tell him that. Wrecked TARDISes to the left and right, the crippled bulk of the *Glorious Aspect of Omega* behind him...

He couldn't see how they could win this one without recourse to the final sanction. Losing the flagship simply couldn't be countenanced - not least because they needed to tell Gallifrey about the Enemy's new armaments.

Firing a volley of Klypstrømic warheads at a squadron of Enemy saucers, he managed to avoid the violet spear of their mysterious new weapon as the TARDIS hurtled towards one of the struts of the tetrahedron. He slammed the all-stop moments before his ship would have collided with the impenetrable barrier, and took advantage of the brief respite. There was enough interference to momentarily hide him here.

'This is the President to the *Righteous Fist of Rassilon*,' he barked. And then he gave the order that he had prayed he would never to have to issue.

'Break open the Slaughterhouse.'

'What are you doing?' rasped the Master as he left his TARDIS. A glance to his left showed that Ruth Ingram was unconscious. But in front of him...

Paul Kairos was standing over the console. Paul Kairos was boosting the matter gain. Paul Kairos was saving their lives. But how? He was nothing more than a human!

'Outer plasmic shells recalibrating,' Paul answered. 'I've set up a modulating resonance field between the two TARDISes; she shouldn't be able to breach that for a while.'

The Master would have narrowed his eyes, had he had eyelids any more. 'But how?' Even given Paul's temporal knowledge, a

TARDIS wasn't just a machine; it was a living extension to the power of the Time Lords. No human could master the complexities of the manoeuvre that Paul had just accomplished!

Before Paul could answer, the Doctor's TARDIS was hit by another shock wave. The Master made a grab for the console but failed to reach it, and was slammed to the floor.

'She's managed to breach us!' shouted Paul. 'Hang on!'

But the Master had nothing to hang on to. Not even reality...

The President frowned as an insistent bleep came from the console. He had been expecting Tortheth, but he was being hailed on an Enemy frequency. From a WarTARDIS! Had they managed to capture one?

The image that suddenly appeared on the scanner made everything horrifyingly clear.

'Ah, Lord President, we meet for one final time. As you have learnt, my forces now have the upper hand. Surrender, and I shall be merciful.'

The erstwhile Chancellor of the High Council of the Time Lords. A man the President had called *Friend*.

'Your forces?' This just wasn't possible. The Master had always been the staunchest of allies. At the start of the jihad, he had been one of the first exiles to return home and offer his services. He had even commanded the *Arcane Mystery of the Other*, until its unfortunate loss. The idea that he could not only change sides, but lead them as well, was unthinkable.

Unfortunately, given the presence of the enemy standing behind him in his WarTARDIS, it was obviously true.

As was the reason for the enemy's new-found superiority. No wonder no one had ever discovered the final fate of the *Arcane Mystery*. Its remains were probably lying in an enemy shipyard, its secrets dissected, analysed and re-engineered into the Enemy fleet.

'You gave them our knowledge,' the President hissed. 'You've sold us out.'

'Sold you out? No,' came the answer, dripping with wounded feelings. 'I simply realised the truth of Darwin's theories, old friend: survival of the fittest. My colleagues recognise true leadership, Lord President. The age of the Time Lords is over - you must see that. Our way is the right way. Only through force can this sad and sorry universe be united. United as never before!'

The President felt sick to his stomach. How could someone who had been his trusted friend for so many, many years have betrayed them all so utterly?

'I'll stop you,' he hissed. 'I'll stop you if I have to bring down the entire cosmos in the process!'

The Master's bearded face broke into a broad grin. 'Brave words, Doctor, but are you prepared to follow them through?' He turned to one of his metallic associates. 'End this,' he ordered.

The moment of reckoning, thought the President sadly. Time Lord against Time Lord, friend against friend, brother against brother. *End this*, the Master had said.

The President really had no alternative.

He pressed his hands against the telepathic circuits. 'Tortheth, this is the President. Give me access to the Armageddon Sapphire.'

'Lord President?'

'Just do it, Tortheth. In Rassilon's name.' He looked up at the chancellor and his voice was low and cold. 'I cannot allow you to do this, Master. I would rather destroy all of creation than allow it to fall to you and those monstrosities.'

The Master threw his head back and laughed. 'Destroy all of creation? Just try it, Doctor. You don't have the stomach for it. That's the problem with the Time Lords - you start a jihad but you simply cannot follow it through.'

The Enemy, led by the Master, with access to the secrets of the Time Lords. They would plunge the universe into hell. Better a swift end than an eternity of their metallic rule.

'Armageddon Sapphire slaved to your TARDIS, Lord President,' came Tortheth's voice, quiet and terrified. With good reason.

The Doctor's voice was also quiet, but shot through with a firm resolution. 'Goodbye, Master. May whatever gods you still have forgive you for this. And may whatever gods I have forgive me.'

The Doctor's hand reached for the switch that would activate the Armageddon Sapphire.

The Armageddon Sapphire was the darkest of dark secrets, buried so deeply inside the Matrix that it had taken technicians a thousand years to even prove its existence, let alone discern its function and purpose.

Born from Rassilon's darkest moments and his most terrible fears, it combined everything he had learnt about the fundamental nature of reality into a single device. Forget time destructors, forget particle disseminators, forget the de-mat gun; the Armageddon Sapphire simply tore reality apart, agitating Higgs bosons to the point where the space-time continuum collapsed into Calabi-Yau Space like a house with its foundations gone. Theoretically, the universe could eventually re-form from the chaos. But it would take billions upon billions of years, and would bear no resemblance to what had gone before.

A total rebirth. The only thing that would stop the Enemy. The only thing that would stop the Master. And once activated, it could never be stopped.

The Doctor's fingers touched the button.

Chapter Ten
Always on My Mind

Despite the chaos that reigned around him, Paul's mind was wandering. Wandering into different dimensions, to be brutally frank. His hands gripped the console, his mind gripped that of the TARDIS. And that of the Master's TARDIS.

Fight her. Both of you. Together. Now.

Blue flame began to ripple around him, tearing at his physical form. Paul Kairos groaned in pain, but no matter - it wasn't as if it was real, was it? All that mattered was his mind, reaching out across the alternates, seeking the correct ones amongst billions. The ones that he would need if this was all to come to pass as planned.

There!

With a concussive explosion that defied even the warped physics of dimensional transcendentalism, his mind breached the boundaries of the TARDIS, breached the boundaries of the current universe, and found itself somewhere else.

The universe that he was looking for.

'Doctor! Don't!' he screamed across the console room. The same console room, yet different. A different universe.

The Doctor, dressed in white and gold, with a heavy gold sash around his neck, span round from the console, his hand hovering above an insignificant-looking button. 'Who the hell are you?'

'A friend,' said Paul. 'Take your hand away from the control, Doctor. If you activate the Armageddon Sapphire, you could set off a dimensional cascade that even I couldn't stop. There is a better way.'

The Doctor shook his head. 'This is a trick. Something the Enemy's rustled up...' He returned his attention to the console. 'I have to stop the Enemy. If I don't -'

Paul grabbed his wrist, and was surprised at how pleased he was at the Doctor's expression when he realised he couldn't move. 'This isn't reality – it's fantasy.'

'Fantasy?' The Doctor tried to pull away once more, but to no avail. 'You're mad!'

Paul gave the Doctor an understanding smile. 'Somewhere, in an alternate dimension, a composite being called the Quantum Archangel has taken the worldline of Earth and is giving every sentient life form on the planet its own universe. You may be a Time Lord, but you still attracted her attention.' He nodded at the screen, where the Master and his cyborg servants watched and waited. 'As did he.' He let go of the Doctor's wrist.

'I... I believe you.'

'I thought you might,' said Paul cheerfully. 'Some Time Lord gift or other, no doubt. But you just got a bit carried away by it all, didn't you?'

'But if it isn't real, what's all this about?' The Doctor looked around the TARDIS, his expression puzzled, sad even.

'A final victory against an old enemy. The knowledge that you and the Master have an intertwined destiny. The desire for respect from your Time Lord peers.' Paul shrugged. 'You choose.'

'Whatever,' said the Doctor dismissively, although it was obvious that Paul's words had had an effect. 'How do we get back to reality, then?'

Paul held out his hand. 'It's actually quite simple, now that you understand.' He glanced up at the scanner. 'The same goes for you, Master.'

The Master raised an eyebrow. 'As much as it pains me to admit it, young man, I too believe you. Better to fight the Doctor in reality than to battle him in fantasy.'

'NO!' A metallic screech came from behind him. 'He is the Ka Faraq Gatri. He must be exterminated!'

Paul clapped his hands together. 'I think it's time we went home, don't you?'

After three hours, Arlene was climbing up the walls. For the last ten years, all she had known were luxury hotels and fawning waiters, so a ten by ten by ten cell in Charing Cross police station was the closest to hell she had ever known. Looking at the graffiti-scrawled walls, the stained mattress and the grey metal door, it was all she could do not to burst out crying.

'Hello, Arlene.' The dark-haired, bearded figure grinned at her, and held out his hand.

'Paul?' Somehow she knew him...

'Time to go home.'

Arlene didn't know what Paul meant, and she cared even less. Anything was better than this hellhole. She took his hand.

'The process will be painless, Melanie,' droned the Doctor. 'Your intelligence is amongst the highest on this planet. Once you have joined us, you will see the wisdom of our actions. You will understand the necessity of our cause. You will have earned your place in our supreme command.'

'Your cause? Your supreme command? You're just a pathetic bunch of impotent hybrids who've outstayed your welcome.'

Mel strained against the metal bindings that pinned her to the hard, flat couch, fighting the drug that had been injected into her.

'Melanie?'

Through the pain and the fog the voice was familiar, although she couldn't place it.

'Come along, Mel. Time to go home.'

With a click of metal and a feeling of waking up, Mel found she could sit up with a clear head. The monstrous form of the half-man, half-machine Doctor appeared frozen in place, as did the other six Cybermen around her. But the figure leaning over her was completely human: olive-skinned, goatee-bearded, his smile warm and reassuring. 'Paul?' She took his hand.

'No!' Stuart screamed as the DNA recombinator tore at his genetic structure, trying to absorb it into its new, enslaved collective. All his life, he had fought for his individuality. He wasn't going to surrender it now.

'Come on, Professor.'

Stuart forced his eyes to open against the bilious glare from the recombinator. A young man was standing over him, his hand outstretched. 'Who –'

'A friend. Now hurry!'

In the environs of the Great Attractor, fifty million light years from Earth and close to the Abell 3627 galactic cluster, two vessels from a civilisation that had fought a terrible war there one hundred and fifty million years ago fought the battle once again. This time, the eternal enemy was joined by the fundamental energy source that underlay the cosmos, backed by the revenge of a human, merged into a composite of unimaginable power: the Quantum Archangel.

It should have been unbeatable: omniscient, omnipotent. But the two TARDISes were holding their own. Both machines had been reworked again and again since their birth in the TARDIS cradles, with countless improvements from countless civilisations. And for the first time since they had both left those same cradles, they were on the same side.

The Quantum Archangel was losing.

The two TARDISes, fighting as one, broke through the sidereal barrier, knocking the Quantum Archangel away as if she were no more than an irritation, rearranging their artron wakes into whips and knives to keep her at bay. As she flailed in the vortex, a flaming figure in distress, the TARDISes reached the parallel universe of the Cla'tac'teth, found that race's planet orbiting a dead neutron star orbiting a lifeless version of the Great Attractor...

... and passed back through the sidereal barrier to another Great Attractor, leaving the Quantum Archangel on the other side.

Both TARDISes shuddered to a halt around the gargantuan black hole, unsure as to what to do. This Great Attractor was far more dangerous than the one they had left behind, and their respective masters were elsewhere; free will wasn't exactly something they were used to. Tentatively, apologetically, they parted company, one dematerialising out of the other and subsequently keeping its distance. Alone - for a scant few seconds.

Then their masters returned.

'What the hell was that all about?' Stuart Hyde looked around the TARDIS, patting his body to make sure all of it was intact. DNA recombinators and a quartet of evil Time Lords - where did that all come from? And how old was he? Fifty-five, twenty-five, fifty-five again? He'd experienced all three in the last day, and just didn't know any more. He touched his face, but couldn't tell whether there were wrinkles there or not. And the TARDIS wasn't exactly brimming with mirrors, was it?

'And what about Ruth and the Master?' asked Mel.

The Doctor's reply was quiet.'Given Stuart's presence, I would guess that Ruth is back where she was meant to be, and that the Master is back in his own TARDIS.Well, it isn't here, is it?'

'Alternate universes? That's what it was, wasn't it, Doctor?' Mel went over to him and put her hand on his.'Doctor?'

He looked at her with distant, empty eyes. 'What might have been, Mel.What might have been.' He span round and pointed an accusing finger at Paul.

'Who are you? *What* are you?' He walked over to him.'You saved the TARDIS from a Gallifreyan virus.You saved both mine and the Master's TARDISes from the Quantum Archangel. You reached into parallel universes and saved us all, just before the Chronovores devoured us. And don't deny it - she told me!' He flung his arm back at the console, presumably indicating the TARDIS.'Who are you, Paul? What are you?'

Professor Paul Kairos took a step back and shrugged.'I suppose you deserve to know the truth. But the fact is, I only learnt it myself a few hours ago.' He threw his arms open, as if greeting old friends.'The truth is... there never was a Paul Kairos.'

'What?' shouted Mel and Arlene together.

'But I taught you for five years,' muttered Stuart.'You built the TITAN Array.What are you blathering on about?'

'You taught a construct, professor. A being spun from thought and imagination. A being that came to Earth to serve one single purpose.' A blue aura began to form around Paul at the same time as his face and body began to blur and distort.

'Kairos,' muttered the Doctor through thin lips. 'Of course, I should have realised.'

'What do you mean?' asked Arlene.'Will someone tell me what's going on?'

Stuart's voice was a whisper as he answered. 'The Greeks had two words for time, Arlene. Kairos meant "the moment". But time itself...' Stuart's stomach did a somersault. 'You're kidding.'

Paul's physical form was now engulfed in blue flame, illuminating the console room in flickering azure fire.

'Kronos,' stated Mel. 'In Greek, time is... oh my God.' She looked at Paul, her eyes wide with horror. 'You can't mean...'

'Many have called me such, Melanie. Both Kronos and god.' Of Paul, there was now no sign. Instead, a figure of blinding brilliance stood in his place, but it was difficult to concentrate on its exact form. One moment there appeared to be a white, birdlike figure within the radiance; at another, a man made of blue fire, a burning crown on his head. Another moment, and a young woman stared out. There were others, but Stuart stopped trying to concentrate on them. It was giving him a headache.

Arlene stepped forward. 'Where's Paul? Where is he?'

'Arlene... Arlene. I am Paul. I have always been Paul. But I have always been Kronos. I was born within him when the time was right.'

Arlene turned away, her arms clasped around her chest. 'He's gone, isn't he?' she asked Mel. Mel simply grabbed her and gave her a hug. For the next few seconds, all that could be heard was the sound of Arlene's sobbing.

'This all began when Kronos threatened the Master,' said the Doctor. 'But none of that makes sense - not if you've been helping us. So what has been going on?'

Paul, Kronos, whatever - the brilliant creature looked into each of their eyes, filling their minds with images from somewhere unimaginable.

'Watch. Perhaps you will understand.'

The entire Council of Guardians, six burning figures of wrath and vengeance, of power and unimaginable majesty. A Six-Fold-God. A Six-Fold-God for a Six-Fold Realm.

YOU HAVE TRANSGRESSED THE ANCIENT COVENANT, they said, six voices as one. YOU HAVE BROKEN THE VERY LAWS OF THE CONTINUUM.

YOU WILL ALL BE PUNISHED.

Elektra and Prometheus remained silent: there was nothing to say, nothing to do. Together, the Guardians could bend reality, fashion space and time to their whims. To them, a Chronovore and an Eternal were insects - less than insects.

And then Elektra realised what they meant - what they intended to do. She screamed her defiance, her cries tearing through the vortex, powerful enough to shred matter down to the quark level. But to the Council of Guardians, it was nothing more than a summer breeze.

They had decided. Now they would act. Without further discussion, they handed down their sentence.

Prometheus was the first to be punished for his sins. Acting in metaconcert, the Council of Guardians was the most powerful force in the universe. In many respects, they were the universe. Effortlessly, they took Prometheus' timeline and unravelled it, string by superstring, back and back. Elektra could do nothing; even if she had dared to defy the Council, its massed energies were freezing her in stasis. She could only observe as her lover, her partner, her mate, was unpicked from the fabric of space-time.

She could feel Prometheus' mind convulsing in agony, reaching out for her in a single long moment of need, before he ceased to exist. Before he ceased to ever *have* existed. The time vortex turned inside out as it came to terms with its fundamental nature being disturbed, before finally calming down into the blackness of the darker strata.

Painfully, Elektra's attention turned from the nothingness that had been one half of her life, anger igniting within her. Even though Prometheus had never been, his memory - his seed - would live on within her. Avatar. Even the Guardians could not rob her of that.

CALM YOURSELF. YOU WILL NOT BE HURT.

YET.

IT IS THE CHILD WE WANT.

No!

AVATAR.

She was still screaming as the First Phalanx of the Eternals, her family, descended from their hiding places and took her away.

They say she never stopped screaming.

Even after the Avatar was born.

The Council of Guardians seized the child at the moment of its birth. It was an abomination, a violation of the very laws the Council had imposed on the cosmos. It too screamed. The scream of a monster.

Yet they could not kill it. Abomination or not, it embodied the best and worst of the Guardians' own children: the empty longings of the Eternals and the depraved appetites of the Eternals. They had entered this universe with a debt to repay, and this throw, this child, this avatar, was the repayment for that debt.

They would not kill it. They would imprison it until the time came when it would serve its purpose.

Six Guardians agreed as one. They span the Key to Time, and with it they wove a prison. A trident, a crystal jail that would last until the time was right. A jail to hold the mewling hybrid until the time was right.

But even gods have gods.

You must name it. Even one such as this deserves a name.

Even the Council of Guardians deferred to their elders. Great Old Ones had even Greater Old Ones, and their word was law.

WE HAVE A NAME, A NAME FOR THIS BASTARD ABOMINATION. WE NAME IT KRONOS. AND THUS SHALL IT BE KNOWN FOR THE DURATION OF ITS IMPRISONMENT.

And thus was the trident thrown into the time vortex, to land where it would. A perfect prison for a being the universe should never have spawned.

'You're Kronos?' Stuart staggered backwards. 'You!'

The blinding figure nodded. 'I understand your feelings, Stuart. But I am here to help you.'

'How can you say that? How?' Ignoring the blinding light, Stuart stepped forward. 'Thirty years ago, you stole my life. Simply because I was in the wrong place at the wrong time. And yet you say you're trying to help us!'

'A life that has been returned to you, Stuart. I have given you those years once again.' For a moment, Stuart garnered a glimpse of himself, standing in the console room. He was still young!

'Five thousand years ago you destroyed Atlantis, Kronos. Another act of benevolence?' the Doctor queried.

'My crystal prison has been hidden on many worlds, Doctor. Travellers brought it with them on one of their many visits to Earth, one hundred thousand years ago. They knew that the crystal contained forces that beggared even their comprehension. As part of one of their experiments on humanity, they explained some of the crystal's secrets to the priest-kings of Old Atlantis.'

'Experiments?' muttered the Doctor. Then he nodded. 'Of course: the Daemons.'

'The priest-kings learnt a rudimentary form of communication with me. They learnt to harness my powers for the most benign of purposes: weather control, fertility, crop growth.'

'But they wanted more, didn't they? They tried to release you.'

'Not all the priest-kings were as far-sighted as Dalios. One ancestor sought dominion over his neighbours, and to achieve that, sought dominion over me. He deciphered the sacred words of the Daemons, just as the Master would, five millennia hence. But only enough of them to release me. He ignored the coded warnings.'

'Warnings that you were barking mad, no doubt,' snapped Stuart. How could they hold such a civilised conversation with a creature that had robbed him of his life, his hope?

'Exactly, Stuart. The Six-Fold-God had designed my prison down to the last detail. It understood that a time would come when my release would be necessary: a time when balance would be off kilter. But release before that time would be accompanied by madness and a thirst for destruction: the baser instincts of my father writ large. My moment of freedom sounded the death knell for Atlantis; for that, I shall be forever guilty.'

'I still don't get it,' said Mel. 'If you were imprisoned - well, how come you're free now?'

'After the destruction of Atlantis, I was once again trapped in my crystal prison: the magicks of the priest-kings were brief in their effect. But that scant experience of freedom had occurred in two time periods. A temporal bridge had been created between them.'

'The Ancient Covenant!' shouted the Doctor. 'Even the Guardians couldn't prevent that one!' Stuart saw Mel tug at the Doctor's sleeve for an explanation: of course, she hadn't been there when the Doctor explained it earlier.

'According to the rules that govern the Chronovores, once a link is forged between two regions - be they spatial, temporal, dimensional, whatever - Chronovores are free to pass between them. Hence what's happening at the moment with the timelines - the Master created a link between the Six-Fold Realm and here, the Higher Place.' His eyes widened. 'Hang on - the Master created the link between Atlantis and thirty years ago as well.' He chewed his bottom lip. 'Oh no. I detect a paradox coming on.'

'After the Master's actions, I was free to traverse time and space across those five thousand years, although still trapped within the crystal. Thirty years ago in your terms, at the latter terminus of my travels, I detected the mind of Stuart Hyde and saw the means of my eventual escape.'

Stuart took a second to register that the glowing figure was talking about him. 'Me? What did I do?'

'You built TOMTIT, Professor Hyde. Without you, it would never have worked. And I would never have been freed.'

Stuart gasped. He did create TOMTIT! It was one thing to hear that from the Doctor, but from a being such as Kronos... He swallowed down a lump in his throat.

'Your temporal knowledge was unique on this world, Stuart. It lured the Master here. I lured the Master to the crystal. And TOMTIT released me.'

'I knew it,' said the Doctor huffily. 'A time paradox.'

'I share the heritage of two races for which the rules of time are simply guidelines, Doctor. We are beyond the Time Lords as you are beyond the humans you care for.'

'Really,' the Doctor replied, obviously unused to being put in his place. 'But that still doesn't explain what's going on. Why were you pretending to be a human scientist?'

'I wasn't pretending, Doctor. I was Paul Kairos. It was important to my plan that I become a human.'

Arlene shook her head. Stuart could see she was crying. 'I loved you, Paul. We're supposed to be getting married. And you're trying to tell me that you weren't even real?'

'Arlene: the love that Paul felt for you was real. Unfortunately, Paul wasn't. The depth of your feelings is unknown to me, but I can sense his love.'

'That isn't good enough!' screamed Arlene. 'Who are you to play God?'

'I am a god. Accept that.' Kairos, Kronos, whoever and whatever he was, held his hand out towards her. 'Even for beings such as us, time is of the essence. Forget now. I shall ensure that you remember.' Arlene's eyes rolled back into her head before she started to collapse. Mel caught her and gently laid her on the chaise longue. 'What have you done to her?'

'I am aware that my deception has damaged her. If we survive, I will make reparations.'

'Reparations? She's -' Mel began, before the Doctor put his hand on her shoulder.

'Hush, Mel. I promise you we'll get to the bottom of this.' He grasped his lapels. 'The universe is being eaten away by those creatures you call kin, Kronos. Just explain what you think you're up to!'

'Revenge, Doctor. Revenge against the Chronovores. I want them to suffer for their actions.'

'Why the Chronovores? Why not the Eternals, or the Guardians? It seems to me that they're all to blame.'

'There is more to show you.' Kronos' mind reached out yet again...

It will be an abomination, anathema to the Ancient Covenants, protested Lillith, matriarch of the Chronovores, as she presented her petition to the Six-Fold-God. Elektra watched silently, body and mind bound by the godlike forces that swirled all around them.

It will be a living being. It already is a living being. Sadok, patriarch of the Eternals, turned his back on them all. He knew the Chronovores could be creatures of unimaginable cruelty, but this was evil, even for them. *How can you dismiss this child so easily?*

Child? Lillith sneered. *Monster. Our peoples are separated by rules that predate this cosmos,* she continued. *You cannot break those rules, even if Prometheus is your son, Sadok. Elektra and Prometheus have breached –*

And Elektra is your daughter, Matriarch. Elektra and Prometheus expressed a primal urge. The offspring of that urge –

The offspring of that urge is an abomination. It must be destroyed!

Sadok could sense the power building in the Chronovore matriarch, the power to destroy even one of her own daughters.

IT WILL SURVIVE.

The Six-Fold-God had spoken. Lillith and Sadok fell silent.

WE HAVE LISTENED TO YOUR PETITIONS. WE HAVE WEIGHED YOUR OPINIONS. AND WE HAVE DECIDED.

What have you decided? demanded Lillith. *You cannot suffer this bastard to live.*

THERE WILL COME A TIME WHEN THE CHILD OF THE ANCIENT ENEMIES WILL BE NEEDED. HAD BOTH RACES AGREED TO SUFFER IT TO LIVE, WE WOULD HAVE FOUND ANOTHER WAY. BUT THE PROTESTS OF THE CHRONOVORES CANNOT BE IGNORED. IT WILL LIVE. BUT IT WILL NOT HAVE ITS FREEDOM UNTIL THE MOMENT FALLS ON THE UNIVERSE.

IT WILL REMAIN IMPRISONED WITHIN A CRYSTAL OF OUR DESIGN, ONE FASHIONED FROM THE PRIMAL MATERIALS FROM WHICH WE FORGED THE KEY AND THE JEWEL. IF ANY ATTEMPT IS MADE TO RELEASE IT BEFORE THE MOMENT, THE ABOMINATION WILL ENTER THE UNIVERSE IN MADNESS.

And thus did the imprisonment of Kronos begin.

'You see? Even the Six-Fold-God was merciful. Yet the matriarch of the Chronovores condemned me for an eternity, locked in a crystal prison that it would have been madness to escape. You saw Atlantis, Time Lord, you saw the madness they visited on me.

'I shall have revenge for that madness. I shall be revenged on the whole pack of them.'

'By destroying the Earth?' The Doctor shook his head. 'And not just the Earth. Bonded with the Mad Mind of Bophemeral, there's no limit to what the Quantum Archangel can achieve. Once the Chronovores have left the Earth a desiccated husk, where next?

Wherever she creates these alternate realities, the Divine Host will follow.' He threw a hand in the air. 'Skaro, Telos, Gallifrey, even. This has to stop.'

'It cannot be stopped. No one in this reality can stand before the Divine Host and survive.'

The Doctor darted over to the console. 'If we can separate Anjeliqua and the Lux Aeterna from the Mad Mind, we limit both the destruction and their source of power. With them weakened, we might be able to do something.' He started flipping switches and pulling levers. 'If I can breach the event horizon of the Great Attractor – '

'My plan has failed. This is not how I predicted it.'

'What?' The Doctor stopped what he was doing and slowly turned to look at Kronos. 'All this destruction, this carnage, this damage to the space-time continuum, and it isn't how you predicted it? What did you predict, Kronos?'

'It was not the Chronovores who appeared to the Master in his TARDIS, it was I. I led him to think that the Chronovores desired revenge for his dominion over me.'

The Doctor frowned. 'But why?' Then realisation dawned on his face. 'You wanted him to steal the Lux Aeterna, didn't you? You wanted the Master to absorb it, become like that... that thing out there, and then he'd destroy all the Chronovores when they emerged into our reality. That was your revenge, wasn't it?'

Mel stepped forward. 'Of course. You did it, didn't you?'

'I do not –'

'Anjeliqua.' Mel stroked her chin. 'I came to Earth to see a dear friend. Instead I found a spiteful, manipulative witch who bore no resemblance to the Anjeliqua Whitefriar that I'd known. So I did a bit of research, trying to found out when and why it happened. I found out the when – but not the why.'

Stuart remembered the moment only too clearly. 'Just after Paul developed the Kairos Lattice. One minute she was talking about marketing it, making Paul another Bill Gates or Larry Ellison. The next, she'd stolen the patent, cut Paul out of the deal and taken bitching lessons from Joan Collins.'

The shining figure nodded. 'Everything had to be right. Paul could not abandon his researches into the Six-Fold Realm. Anjeliqua would have taken him from that path. Furthermore, I needed Anjeliqua to aid the Master in his revenge. The subconscious part of Paul that still knew itself to be Kronos influenced her.'

'Influenced her?' shouted Mel. 'You corrupted her, altered her entire personality. And now look what's happened!'

'But you never expected her to become the Quantum Archangel, did you Kronos?' said the Doctor calmly. 'It was always meant to be the Master, who would have channelled the power of the Lux Aeterna into anger and revenge. Not a human woman whose basically someone who wants to help people, to help them make the best of everything.'

'I assumed that the human form would be unworthy of the Lux Aeterna, incapable of withstanding its majesty.

'I was wrong.'

'And that has to be the understatement of the century,' muttered Stuart.

Kronos' hand reached out and touched the Doctor's temple. 'Perhaps now you will understand.'

The Doctor's eyes widened for a second. Before he collapsed.

Curled on the black floor of his TARDIS, the Master took a rattling breath, fighting for air. He had a vague memory of a different TARDIS, a WarTARDIS, and a war, an endless war... But there were other memories, memories of the Rani and that bumbler Drax, and of that oleaginous Mortimus...

And in both sets of memories, he had been whole again.

Unlike now. The Source of Traken was extinguished. There was nothing within him that could renew him. His regeneration cycle was exhausted, and only the vaguest trace of Tremas' genetic structure was still bonded to his Gallifreyan triple helix. Most of his flesh was gone, leaving withered sinews which only just covered his bones. Thankfully, his nerves were now virtually cauterised, or else he knew the pain would have been unbearable. As it was, every part of him screamed in agony.

He was dying.

He had failed.

He managed to raise his head and look at the scanner through unfocused eyes. He recognised the Great Attractor, that pit of darkness that they had tried so hard to reach, but what was the point? The battle - all his battles - was over. For the briefest of moments he considered begging the Doctor for help, but even at the point of death the thought was unbearable.

Once, a long, long time ago, he had been a noble, respected Time Lord, preparing to assume the highest of offices. Now, despite his manifold crimes, despite his scheming and manipulation, he would die with the same nobility.

'You will not die today, Time Lord.'

He had a brief vision of fiery wings enfolding him, healing him... and then he was elsewhere.

'Where am I?' There was now a glimmer of strength within him. Not enough to rejuvenate or regenerate, but enough for him to stand unaided, to breathe without struggling. Enough for him to close eyes which could now focus - but on what?

'You made me, dark one. For that you have my gratitude. The humanity of Anjeliqua Whitefriar, the limitless intellect of the Mind of Bophemeral, the unimaginable majesty of the Lux Aeterna, combined in one as the trinity of the Quantum Archangel.'

The Master realised that he was standing in the time vortex, its butterfly-blue colours swirling around him. How was that possible without a vortex shield?

But he knew it was possible because of the figure that hovered in front of him.

'What do you want with me?' He tried to colour his voice with defiance, but wasn't entirely sure that he had succeeded.

Her voice changed. After lifetimes of experience, the Master recognised the twist in her tone. It was madness.

'Want with you? What could I possibly want with you? A creature of such flawed nature, driven by the darkest of purposes? I suppose I could use you as a plaything, pushing you closer and closer to the moment of death before restoring you once more. Indeed, it would be fascinating to push you beyond death, and see if I can retrieve you.'

This wasn't Anjeliqua. But there were two minds at work in the Quantum Archangel now: Anjeliqua - bitter, resentful, but basically sane; and the Mind of Bophemeral. Utterly, utterly mad. It was clear that the integration between the two wasn't complete. Which meant the Master was dealing with a being of limitless power and insane appetites.

Good. He was on familiar ground.

'Your plaything or your associate, Archangel?' he countered at his most persuasive. 'Your dreams of perfection for the universe are being corrupted by the Chronovores. I can help you to stop them.'

'You? A member of that same race that condemned me to exile? A pitiful worm on the edge of death? How can you help me?'

'I once enslaved a Chronovore. Kronos - greatest of the Chronovores. I deciphered the ancient texts of the Daemons and learnt the words of power to bring Kronos under my thrall. With my knowledge, we can defeat them, send them back to the Six-Fold Realm and allow your great work to unfold!'

'You could help me?' It was Anjeliqua's voice once more. 'Help me to fulfil the universe's destiny?'

The Master nodded reverently, bowing as he did so. 'I would be honoured to serve you, Quantum Archangel.'

A smile played upon her lips. 'And serve us - me - you shall. Let us return to the beginning, Lord Master.'

The time vortex vanished around him, replaced by a vaulted blue dome far above his head.

He was back in the Midnight Cathedral.

The Quantum Archangel stood in front of him, floating a few inches above the marble floor, her wings wrapped around her. 'The final testament to the Constructors of Destiny. A fitting locale for the transcendence of the Mind of Bophemeral.'

Her wings arched backwards, washing the Cathedral with fire. The Master closed his eyes for a moment; when he opened them, the cathedral had been redecorated with the chrome of the TITAN Array and the coffin shape of the converter. His TARDIS - back in the disguise of an altar - stood against the far wall.

'Destroy the Chronovores, Master, and your perfect reality will be an eternity of your own personal heaven. Imagine conquest and dominion without end; that can be yours if you rid me of my demons.'

She was gone, a faint afterglow the only indication that she had ever been there.

It worked! He had life - limited, but enough. More importantly, he had access to the TITAN Array, the converter, and the buried secrets of the Constructors of Destiny.

Plaything or accomplice? He would be neither. He was the Master - and always would be. He set to work.

'So how did Anjeliqua survive?' asked Mel. 'If this Lux Aeterna is so powerful, why didn't it consume her, as the Master thought it would?' The Doctor was busying himself at the console, worlds away after his brief moment of unconsciousness.

It felt strange, talking to this burning figure with many faces, especially since one of them looked like Paul. Paul Kairos, her best friend. An imaginary friend.

'When the part of Paul that was Kronos realised that Anjeliqua's life was in danger, I acted. I would rather have given her the power of the Lux Aeterna and see my plans collapse than allow an innocent person to die due to my miscalculations.'

Mel thought of Maradnias - and the Doctor. True, this crisis was on a cosmic scale, but she had never seen the Doctor appear so driven. Perhaps he thought the same way. Indeed, ever since he had recovered from whatever Kronos had done to him, he had shown an almost frightening intensity.

'So you protected her?'

'I augmented her physical form with a portion of my power - power initially derived from the Lux Aeterna. It was sufficient to make her the perfect vessel for its ascent into the Higher Place.'

'Got it!' yelled the Doctor. At the same time, the TARDIS filled with the wheezing and groaning of dematerialisation.

'And what precisely have you got?' asked Stuart, trying to peer over his shoulder before the Doctor swatted him away.

'During the last five minutes, the energy signatures of the

Quantum Archangel and the Master's TARDIS both vanished. Thankfully, I was able to track their wakes.' The Doctor gave a sheepish grin. 'Back to the moon, I'm afraid.'

'The Midnight Cathedral?' asked Mel.

'The very same.'

'For God's sake, Doc,' snapped Stuart. 'After the effort it took to get away from the Great Attractor, and the effort it took to get back here... what are we? Some kind of galactic yo-yo?'

The Doctor arched an eyebrow. 'Very droll, Professor, very droll. This time round, we weren't flung here by the Quantum Archangel, nor is she around to prevent us passing through the sidereal barrier. I can retrace our steps with ease.' He tapped a button on the console. 'See?'

Ten seconds later, as she pulled herself to her feet, Mel couldn't help smiling at the Doctor. 'With ease?'

The base of the angel-demon statue was a cylinder about 1.2 metres tall and 2.4 metres across.

It was also hollow.

The Master may not have known about the great war that led to the imprisonment of the Mad Mind of Bophemeral, but he knew a lot about the Constructors of Destiny. According to the Matrix, their great works always contained a cache, a hidden collection of some of their great secrets, passed on to their children.

The Constructors were considered gods. And the Master would need the knowledge of gods if he was to pull this off. He had already used some of their discoveries: their understanding of block-transfer computation exceeded even that of the Logopolitans, and had been vital in his control of that world and the creation of Castrovalva. But they had also been masters of energy transfer.

With the information carved into the crystal matrix of the blocks of aeternium that had lain hidden in the base of the statue, he was now close to perfecting the converter. He hadn't dared attempt it before, even though he had deciphered the blocks long, long ago: the Constructors' methods were of the all or nothing variety. Their science and technology were based on the rules of probability - maybe it would work, maybe it wouldn't.

And at the time, even fleeing the vengeance of the Chronovores, he hadn't wanted to take the risk of being incinerated if the dead hand of the Constructors threw the dice the wrong way.

He stood back, allowing himself the luxury of admiring his handiwork. The converter now boasted a second skin of components from his TARDIS, duplicating the research of the Constructors. In its new form, the converter could possibly destroy him: the cut-offs and fail-safes had all been disabled as part of the redesign. But so could the Quantum Archangel. Besides, he was dying anyway.

Moving over to the TITAN console, he entered the sequence that would override the barriers he had placed between the Chronovores and the Lux Aeterna. A gap that would open for the minutest of moments: but more than sufficient for him to either ascend to godhood, or die trying.

'Step away from that.'

He looked round. The Doctor was standing next to the Master's TARDIS, accompanied by that annoying Miss Bush and Stuart Hyde - obviously returned from whatever parallel universe the Quantum Archangel had flung them into.

'Why should I? I have nothing to lose, Doctor.'

'Help us send the Chronovores back to the Six-Fold Realm,' said the Doctor. Was he pleading? The Master hoped so.

'My dear Doctor: in a few moments I shall have access to the same power as the Quantum Archangel. And my first act as God will be to shall squash the Chronovores beneath my heel.'

'You idiot!' The Doctor strode across the Dusk Nave towards him.

'Stay back, Doctor.' The Master brandished his tissue-compression eliminator at him. 'I may be dying, but all it would take is a little pressure.'

'Go ahead,' said the Doctor. 'And see how far that gets you.'

The Master was momentarily fazed. But the Doctor was standing in the way of his immeasurable glory. Even more importantly, he was standing in the way of his very survival.

Almost instinctively, he fired.

The modulated beam of gravitons and Pym particles hit the Doctor squarely in the chest... and scattered in a soundless display of lilac flame.

'I didn't come alone, Master.' The Doctor indicated the statue. 'You never knew about the Millennium War, did you? Not really surprising, since the Guardians wiped it from the universe's collective memory. But it was restored to mine - thanks to Kronos. They were an interesting race, Master. They designed, they built, but they were also a god-fearing race, in their way. They especially feared the god they found buried on their homeworld, buried beneath the earth and imprisoned within a crystal trident.

'Kronos.'

'What are you talking about?'

'This entire cathedral was a monument to Kronos. He spoke to them through the crystal, encouraged them to build the Great Attractor and compile the Mind of Bophemeral. Kronos wanted it built - for you. Even you would have needed the additional processing power.'

The Master couldn't begin to understand what the Doctor was talking about. And he told him that.

And the Doctor told him of Kronos. Of his origin, and of his plan. And how it had gone so very wrong.

The knowledge that he had been manipulated, directed, used... The Master leant on the TITAN console for support. 'No. I will not believe it. I will be a god!' The Master activated the converter. 'I will rule, I will live!'

'I gave you your freedom and your life once before. Accept the gift again. A more than sufficient reward for your perfidy.' An incandescent figure materialised next to him, blazing for a moment before darkening into a familiar form.

Paul Kairos.

'I think this is mine,' Kairos said, indicating the console and the Array. Then he punched the Master in the face, sending him sprawling. 'Now, Doctor.'

The Doctor ran over to the converter and climbed into it. He looked over at Mel and Stuart. 'Here goes nothing.' He gave a thumbs up sign to them both.

As the Master struggled to get up, he watched while Paul Kairos entered the final sequence. The converter began to flare with the primal flame of the Lux Aeterna, its brilliance consuming the circuitry before moving on to the Doctor.

'I don't understand,' whispered Mel. 'You're killing him!'

Paul's body melted into a figure of fire. 'To fight gods, Melanie, one must become a god. The Doctor must endure this.'

The Master could only watch as the Doctor embraced the fundamental force of the universe.

And became a god.

Chapter Eleven
Domino Dancing

The Doctor came to his senses. All of them. He had always felt a combination of guilt and superiority about the way he perceived the universe compared with his friends on Earth, but now it was his turn to be overawed. With the Lux Aeterna flooding through him, he could experience aspects of the universe he had never known existed. The scent of matter, the taste of light, the texture of space... He knew he was still using his own terms of reference, but he didn't actually have any others, did he? He began to wonder how long it would be before the otherworldly senses of the Lux Aeterna began to integrate fully with his mind. He might have the powers of a god, but he was still a Time Lord. He was still the Doctor.

Wasn't he? With the Lux Aeterna irradiating every cell, he knew that might not be true very longer. Best to take care of Anjeliqua as soon as possible and get back to reality - before reality stopped having any proper meaning for him.

He momentarily wondered what he looked like, only to see the image immediately pop into his mind. He still looked like the Doctor, his Doctor, but a version of himself that had been amplified, augmented. His light brown hair was a shining golden mane, while his eyes were piercing, their blue-green irises like precious stones that could see all the way through the to the centre of the universe. His physique was solid, muscular - just the sort of Olympian ideal Mel had been trying to mould him into with all her talk of exercise and carrot juice. But who needed carrot juice when you had the Lux Aeterna? He was dressed in a black tailored suit with a neck-high collar - not unlike the Master's favoured attire in an earlier incarnation - but there was an impression of dark fire all around him. The Doctor chose not to examine the significance of that - there simply wasn't time.

Another presence soared towards him through the scintillating blue of the time vortex.

'You have joined us. I had hoped that you might.' The Quantum Archangel swooped down through the turbulence of the vortex. 'The Master promised subservience, but intended conquest. But you, Doctor - you have a rare and exquisite mind. You are worthy to share in this epiphany.' She held out a shining hand. 'Join us.'

'Worthy? Worthy? Worthy?' The knowledge that he could now bend reality and fashion it to his whims did not sit comfortably with him. 'No one is worthy of this, Anjeliqua.'

'But Anjeliqua is just a part of what I have become, Doctor,' sang the Quantum Archangel. 'I am now so very much more.'

'Indeed you are,' the Doctor replied. 'You're also a limitless source of cosmic energy and a mad supercomputer. Getting a bit crowded in there, is it?'

'Do not fight me, Doctor. I am a god.'

'No you aren't. You're the result of a billion-year-old plan that went horrifically wrong. As you stand now, you're nothing but a doomsday weapon, threatening all of creation.'

'Threatening? But Doctor, I will bring peace to the universe. I will bring harmony. I shall ensure that all life forms achieve the pinnacle of their possibility.'

'For how long, Archangel?' The Doctor made a gesture that was supposed to indicate the rest of the universe; what actually happened was a plume of black flame erupted from his hand, staining the vortex like a vapour trail. He ignored it. Almost.

'Until the Chronovores consume that possibility? Until they leave every planet, every worldline, every timeline a dead, exhausted husk? Because that's what's happening, Anjeliqua. Destruction on a cosmic scale.'

'The Chronovores are unimportant.' The voice was different now; thinner, harder, brittle, even... The Doctor guessed that the Mad Mind of Bophemeral was now in residence. 'I could vanquish them without a second thought.'

'And disrupt the balance of this universe? I don't think so. The problem with you, Archangel, is that only two of your trinity are actually blessed with intelligence. The most powerful of you, the Lux Aeterna, is simply along for the ride. It's watching through your eyes, but not making any of the decisions.'

'Then it will not interfere with my wisdom.'

The Doctor took a gamble. 'Really? When it realises that you are threatening the balance it underpins? Threatening ancient laws and covenants that have prevented this universe becoming a blood bath? Thanks to the insensate authority of the Lux Aeterna, a war between the primal forces has never occurred. But if you force it to destroy a whole layer of the cosmic food chain... don't you think others might notice? The Eternals? The Guardians, even? Have you got enough power to face up to the Six-Fold-God?'

The Quantum Archangel laughed. It wasn't a pleasant sound. Especially as the Doctor could now see that the laugh extended into all eleven dimensions and generated a whole raft of exotic particles which he could taste and smell. The Lux Aeterna's influence was increasing.

'Even the Six-Fold-God will prove impotent in the face of my majesty,' cackled the burning figure. The Quantum Archangel shouted to the heavens: 'I challenge you! I laugh in the face of the ancient strictures! Confront me if you dare!'

The last thing the Doctor wanted was to be caught in the crossfire between the Quantum Archangel and the Guardians. And he didn't think it would do the universe much good, either. Time to be a little more direct.

'You aren't the only one wielding the power of the Lux Aeterna, you know.'

'Ah, yes... you too have drunk from the divine source,' replied the Quantum Archangel - and it sounded as though Anjeliqua was back in control, thankfully. 'But the Quantum Archangel is one with the Lux Aeterna - you have simply bathed in its essence. You are of no consequence, whether Time Lord or fledgling god.' To demonstrate her superiority, she swatted the Doctor with an incandescent wing.

He didn't move. The brilliance of the wing splintered into a million shards of light.

It wasn't that he had tried to stand his ground. He had simply decided not to allow the Quantum Archangel's strength to affect him. Or had that been the Lux Aeterna's decision?

He decided to go on the offensive. 'Very impressive. What do you do for an encore?'

'Are you mocking me, Doctor? Would you dare?'

The Doctor laughed. 'Oh, I think I can dare that.'

'Insect!'

They were no longer in the azure realm of the time vortex. The Doctor and the Quantum Archangel were floating in space, within an ancient, lifeless solar system.

'If you will not join me, you will be crushed underfoot.'

'So much for the harmonious new order of the Quantum Archangel.'

'You threaten that new order, Doctor.'

'You sound like every other dictator I've ever met. What's today's little cant? The end justifies the means?'

The Quantum Archangel's voice hardened. 'Perhaps that is a cant to which you subscribe?' A hole opened up in space, a window to another part of the universe. Another solar system. She waved a wing in its direction.

'What of Maradnias, Doctor? What of your good intentions and philanthropic actions there? A planet lies dying because of you.'

The Doctor closed his eyes, trying to ignore the pain. 'It wasn't meant to happen like that,' he whispered.

'Nor does it have to.' The Quantum Archangel's tone was silky, seductive even. 'Watch.'

The poisoned brown seas suddenly lightened to blue; the ugly green radioactive haze evaporated. The dark scars of thermonuclear reaction healed and blossomed with life.

Maradnias was whole once more.

'This is the true beauty of the Lux Aeterna. Nothing need ever go wrong again. Mistakes can be rectified, miscalculations put right. This is an illusion, Doctor, but what it shows is within your gift. Free yourself of the guilt of Maradnias and join us.'

'No!' The Doctor's anger boiled over. Without thinking, without caring, he shot a shining black stream of force towards the Quantum Archangel. She too stood her ground, but was visibly shaken by the assault. 'Living with the consequences of our actions is what makes us alive,' he said. 'What is the point of the universe if we cannot make mistakes? Mistakes have to be made – that's how we learn.'

'Mistakes which cost billions of lives, Doctor?'

'Even mistakes which cost billions of lives, yes,' he replied sadly. But seeing Maradnias as the shining jewel it had once been, before his interference, was heartbreaking. 'The Time Lords learnt early on that with great power comes great responsibility. Minyos, the Vampires – even the Millennium War. Dreadful mistakes happened, countless lives were lost. But we refused to simply "put everything right".'

'For fear of damaging the underlying fabric of time, Doctor, fear of interfering with your great works. Not because of any higher ethical consideration. Admit it!'

'No, I will not admit it. Maradnias is dead, and I killed it. I just hope I've learnt my lesson.'

'Pitiful. Absolutely pitiful.' Mel's face was in front of him. 'You've just been given the chance to save all those lives and you refuse – because it affronts your morality. Where was your morality when the bombs were going off? When the seas were dying and the forests were burning? Answer me that, Doctor.'

He knew it wasn't Mel. Mel had cried endless tears over Maradnias, but she knew the rules. She knew that they couldn't go back and change things.

'You could have saved me, Doctor. Just a few seconds back in time, and you could have rescued me from the freighter. But you refused. Why, Doctor?' Adric?

'I trusted you and you killed me. Why?' Kamelion's silver face hovered in front of him. 'I only wanted to serve.' Other voices pleaded with him: Katarina, Sara, every last and lost soul on Maradnias...

'Stop these parlour tricks!' he demanded.

'I, Doctor? You too have access to the Lux Aeterna. Who's to say that these voices are not your conscience? For the conscience of a Time Lord is a terrible and ancient thing.'

'No!'

'Six lifetimes of consequence, Doctor. How many lost lives will it take for you to learn, Doctor? How many?'

With the instincts that came with limitless power, he reached out and hurled the nearest object at the Quantum Archangel.

The nearest object was a moon.

The Quantum Archangel defended herself with a scattering of gold-white radiance; the moon disintegrated harmlessly before it even came close to her.

'That's it, Doctor - listen to your emotions. They are your true moral compass.'

He was throwing moons at her. But he couldn't stand by and watch her destroy everything. Even if she had the power to put everything right, it meant nothing. Every life-form in the universe would simply become an actor in an endless, eternal set of rehearsals. Don't like the performance? Change the actor. Don't like the costumes? Get a new designer. Lighting not right? Ignite another supernova.

He would not stand by and let her turn the cosmos into a puppet show for gods.

Before he could react, the red giant behind him swelled, faster than nature would ever have allowed. The cool burning photosphere and chromosphere washed over him like a summer breeze - then the detonation of the ancient core hit him in the back like a pile-driver. He started tumbling through the void, unable to get his breath, unable to right himself.

'If you will not listen, if you will not understand, then you have no part in this. You will die, Doctor.'

The voice was that of the Mad Mind. If only he could get through to Anjeliqua - he knew with certainty that if she realised the consequences of what she was doing, she would stop. But if the Mad Mind was in control - nothing would stop the Quantum Archangel. Ever.

'Anjeliqua - listen to me,' he gasped. 'Think about what you're doing. Think what it was like before Kronos changed you. How much you cared for your friends. For Paul, and Arlene, and Mel. They're all on Earth, now. They need *you*, Anjeliqua, not the Quantum Archangel!'

'Shut up!' A gas giant, its rings disintegrating as it was propelled through space at lightspeed, narrowly missed him. In retaliation, the Doctor set the region of space around the Quantum Archangel on fire, the quantum foam bubbling and burning. She screamed in pain - hopefully that would weaken the Mad Mind's hold.

It didn't. If anything, it made the Quantum Archangel even

angrier. A rip in space-time opened up underneath the Doctor, threatening to drag him down into the substrate. It took all his strength - both strength of character and the borrowed strength of the Lux Aeterna - to prevent himself from falling into the black void.

The plan had failed. His actions had buried Anjeliqua so deep within the Quantum Archangel that he doubted anything he said could reach her.

So much for living with the consequences. He just hoped the others were having more success.

Kronos, a man-shaped figure burning in sapphire and diamond, had been standing silently in the centre of the Midnight Cathedral for over ten minutes, his hands across his chest, his eyes closed in concentration. Mel decided that if a god needed to concentrate that hard, what he was attempting was anything but easy.

She just hoped that the Doctor was having a bit more luck.

The black hole exploded in the Doctor's face, momentarily blinding him. He could feel that something had broken inside him - ribs, perhaps - but there was no time to worry. As the Quantum Archangel got angrier, she was upping the stakes. He could sense through their shared access to the Lux Aeterna that she was reaching out to a distant nebula, drawing its matter towards her.

Come on, Kronos.

The very human form of Paul Kairos materialised in a small open space within a maze of gold and glass. Circuitry burning within the glass flared intermittently, as if it were being called upon to act far beyond its design parameters.

Which it was. The central processing core of the Mind of Bophemeral was supporting actions billions of light years away, but the intelligence was absent.

He sent his mind outwards and saw the battle that was progressing: the Doctor and the Quantum Archangel throwing planets at one another. There was not much time: especially since the Chronovores' feast was continuing unabated.

It was time to get to work. Paul's physical form began to

sublimate, evaporating into blue fire. For a moment, Kronos searched through the corridors and conduits of the interpreter core – then he found what he was looking for.

Even in their rush to build the ultimate computer, the Constructors of Destiny had learnt the necessity of leaving a back door. Unfortunately for them, they had been annihilated before they ever had the chance to use it, but Kronos, even within the depths of his crystal prison, had noticed it. And now he was using it.

Within a nanosecond, Kronos' being had flooded the pathways and circuits of the Mad Mind, swamping the interpreter core. From outside, it looked as if the golden hoop now had a bright blue aura.

The Mad Mind had to be stopped. Things had gone too far now; the plan was in tatters, and Kronos was too old, too intelligent, to attempt to recover it. It was time to live with the consequences, or perish in the attempt.

But as well as a back door, Kronos knew that there was also a weak link, and he searched the interpreter core for it. Unfortunately, he had no idea where or what it was.

'Anjeliqua – listen to me,' wheezed the Doctor. He was in a bad way: broken bones, blood pouring from a dozen lacerations. Although this was his normal senses' interpretation of his situation he knew that the reality, translated into the higher realms of the Lux Aeterna, was no better. Unless he won, he would soon be dead.

'Why? You have proved yourself unworthy.' Still the Mad Mind. A bolt of diamond intensity slammed into the Doctor's chest, sending him reeling once more. He was outmatched, outclassed, outgunned. A red haze was forming at the edges of his vision, and he could feel his consciousness slipping away. One more concerted attack and he would be dead.

And shortly afterwards, so would everyone else. Dead to creativity, to development. A universe of puppets. He watched as the Quantum Archangel garnered her powers for one last assault.

The weak link. In an ideal universe, the topology of the Mind would have been a closed system. But in their haste to reach completion, the Constructors had decided not to devote millennia to solving the abstruse mathematical problem that would achieve this. Instead, they had literally taken a short cut to close the system. One that Kronos could exploit. With a single thought of unimaginable complexity, the short cut was broken. The topology of the Mad Mind of Bophemeral suddenly opened – the equivalent of a human being suffering an epileptic fit.

Now it was time to wait.

The fire gathered around the Quantum Archangel's fingertips, almost too bright to look at. The Doctor tried to move, but he was rapidly losing strength.

'The battle is over, Time Lord. This is your repayment in full for my imprisonment.'

Is this how it ends, the Doctor wondered sadly. Playing God?

The Quantum Archangel appeared to slump; at the same time, the fire harmlessly burnt itself out.

'Doctor?'

As the figure lifted her head to look at him, the madness had vanished from her eyes. It was Anjeliqua.

'Help me,' she begged. 'Help me put things right.'

'It's terribly quiet,' whispered Stuart, unwilling to break that silence. Any more than he needed to.

'I just wish we had some way of knowing what's going on,' Mel replied.

'If the battle were over,' rasped the Master, 'we would almost certainly know it.' Mel gave him a sideways glance. Was it her natural suspicion of the Master, or was he being too calm, too patient?

A sudden crack of thunder rang about across the Dusk Nave. At the same time, the converter framework glowed momentarily.

The Master's wide eyes opened even wider.

'What do you mean, Anjeliqua?' The Doctor wanted to be certain.

'End this. Go home. Please.'

'Take my hand, Anjeliqua.' The Doctor had no idea whether this would work; and even less idea about what state he would be in if they ever got out of this. But too much was at stake. And he was fully prepared to live - or die - with the consequences.

'You are an abomination,' hissed the Mad Mind. 'You were never meant to exist.'

Within the circuitry, Kronos and the mind faced one another, both in humanoid form. Blue fire versus glittering diamond.

'Nor you,' replied Kronos. ' I engineered your creation. I needed you as a pawn in my plan. The universe should never have seen one as twisted as you.'

'But your plan failed. Soon the Chronovores will have brought this universe to the point of heat death, a sea of endless entropy. Before that happens, I will halt it. The universe will be begging for a god.'

'You? As a god? I would rather see the end of all things than that.' Kronos reached out for the mind's throat. 'But I would rather see you dead.'

At the heart and mind of the greatest computer the universe would ever see, two figures fought for its life.

'You must give back the Lux Aeterna,' explained the Doctor. 'As you do so, attempt to set everything straight. The Lux Aeterna should give you the instinct that you need for that.'

The face of the Quantum Archangel looked puzzled - human, even. 'Will it work?'

The Doctor shrugged. 'We'll never know unless we try, will we?' he said kindly. 'And there's no time like the present, is there?' He clasped both of her hands, shining figures of black and gold in the endless firmament, holding on to one another for grim death - or life.

'Time to live with the consequences,' said the Quantum Archangel, smiling. 'And thank you.'

'Nobody ever wanted you in this universe,' hissed the Mad Mind. 'The hybrid bastard of two antiquated races - what purpose do you serve?'

'More purpose than you,' replied Kronos, punching the Mind in the face and knocking his diamond form backwards. 'Why analyse the universe? The universe analyses itself.'

'Does it? Pain, hurt, fear - I can end all of that, with the power that the Quantum Archangel offers.'

'And replace it with ultimate subservience.'

'My intelligence gives me that right.'

'And my birthright gives me the right to stop you.'

The two figures continued their battle.

'Come on, Anjeliqua, just a few moments more. Put everything right.' The Doctor was squeezing her hands tightly. But she couldn't really feel his grip. Forces were stirring within her that felt like nothing she had ever felt before.

'It hurts, Doctor.' Anjeliqua had never known such pain, tearing and grasping deep inside her. But at the same time it somehow felt reassuring: it was as if she had never felt anything for the last decade.

Her behaviour seemed like a bad dream: how could she have hurt Paul and Arlene like that? How could she have trusted someone like the Master? Thoughts ran back and forth through her head as she let the Lux Aeterna flow from her, heading back to where it came from, back to where it belonged...

As the last traces of the Lux Aeterna left her, she made one last change to reality, moulding it back into its original form, before collapsing in the Doctor's arms.

The converter was on fire. Mel presumed the Lux Aeterna was flowing out of the Doctor and Anjeliqua, back to the Six-Fold Realm and into the depths, and that the converter was still in the circuit, somehow.

'Shouldn't you turn off your force field?' she asked the Master over her shoulder, as she watched the converter burn with golden-white energy. From what she had been told by Stuart, who had been told by the Doctor, the Master had used his TARDIS to isolate the Lux Aeterna from the Chronovores. It was all well and good allowing the Lux Aeterna to return, but not if the Chronovores couldn't access it.

There was no answer.

A sudden grinding and roaring filled the Dusk Nave. Mel immediately recognised it: the TARDIS! But no - it was modulated, warbling... As she watched, an obsidian cube briefly materialised over the converter before fading away once more - taking the converter, and the TITAN Array, with it.

'Stuart!' she cried.

'I saw. Probably one last attempt to save himself,' he said in resignation.

'How can you be so calm?' Mel asked. 'The Doctor and Paul still aren't back yet!'

Stuart put his arm around her. 'Unfortunately, Mel, we have no way of knowing whether they ever will be back.' She could see the concern on his face.

But she knew. She knew with a certainty. 'No: the Doctor will come back.'

In the depths of space, with Anjeliqua in his arms, the Doctor held on to the last dregs of the Lux Aeterna. He focused on a single point in all of time and space, the only point he could ever call home: blue and resolute, waiting for its master's return. He made a final bargain with the Lux Aeterna: its freedom for his.

Power without thought, majesty without reason, the Lux Aeterna agreed.

The star-specked void faded into familiar white walls.

The TARDIS.

The Doctor smiled at his surroundings for a moment and lay Anjeliqua gently on the floor. Then he slumped beside her, consciousness drained from him.

The Master's TARDIS hurtled away from Earth, its engines screaming as the acceleration increased. He wanted to be as far away from that particular planet as he could get.

The TITAN Array had been reassembled in his console room, the chrome standing out from the ubiquitous black. The master console was next to... well, the Master console, he thought wryly. One last joke before the end...

As for the converter...

The shining metal cradle was propped against a wall, its circuitry still on fire. Now it was time for the Master to taste that fire.

He didn't want the full power of the Lux Aeterna - he had seen what that could do. Godlike power was one thing, but the Master would always be in control. Always! And he wasn't sure that something like the Lux Aeterna could ever be controlled.

But it could still be forced into unwitting service, one last time. Dragging himself over to the converter, the Master knew this was his only chance. The recent donation of life force from the Quantum Archangel was all but gone, leaving him only minutes from death. His skeletal figure wrestled with the catches to the converter frame, bone fingers and tattered flesh tugging at the burning metal. Finally, the frame came free, revealing the man-sized interior. With all the strength he could muster, he climbed in, then collapsed into the waiting space.

He would either die - or die trying.

Kronos was on the floor, the Mad Mind's fists raining down on him. Of course, the true battle was one of wills, of mind against mind, but Kronos found that he enjoyed the physical manifestation - even if he was being beaten to a pulp by the insane supercomputer's avatar.

Kronos knew his desire for revenge against one half of his family had come to nothing. Which was the way it should have happened. He had squandered what freedom he had been granted, and he was paying the price. It was one that he would pay willingly.

As the Mad Mind exhausted itself, Kronos allowed a fragment of his life to slip away into the universe, searching, seeking...

And found what he was looking for. The Lux Aeterna, trying to find a way home, a way back to the Six-Fold Realm.

Kronos would give it a way home.

He allowed the Mad Mind to pound his physical form to the point of death - it didn't matter any more. All that mattered was setting things right, repairing the damage that he had never meant to cause.

His physical form now dying, Kronos drew all his remaining strength into himself - and allowed it to detonate.

The last thing he saw was the Mad Mind's puzzled expression as it realised that it had been outwitted. The Mad Mind of Bophemeral, the most powerful intellect that the cosmos would ever see, out-thought - out-thought by a mere god!

Chronovores, Eternals, Guardians. Immortals all. But even an immortal can die.

Millions of years in the future, whatever still lives on Earth will see a new star blossom in the heavens, somewhere in the direction of the constellation of Virgo. It will be brighter than the sun and last for centuries. For centuries, Earth will never know darkness, lit by this new morningstar.

And whatever lives on Earth will wonder: what could have caused that? What could have caused the Great Attractor, the largest black hole in the known universe, to explode?

Mercifully, they will probably never know the true reason.

Kronos knew. As the forces of nature ruptured and exploded around him, he had one last thought. As his consciousness evaporated with the event horizon, as his wisdom and will burnt away with the singularity, one last thought was uppermost.

Elektra.

'Doctor!' screamed Mel, running over to him. He had just appeared in the archway of the Dusk Nave - and Mel had to admit that he looked dreadful. Dried blood crusted his face, one eye had been blacked, and his harlequin coat was ripped and torn. 'What happened?'

He managed a thin smile. 'We put everything right.' Mel saw that Anjeliqua was behind him, her eyes tear-stained. And so they should be, after all she'd put them through!

But Mel realised what she was looking at. Who she was looking at. This wasn't the Anjeliqua Whitefriar who had lied and cheated, who had ripped off her best friends in pursuit of money, power and glory. This was the Anjeliqua Whitefriar who had gone on marches, collected money for charity, staged sit-ins at university...

The only Anjeliqua Whitefriar.

Mel pulled her friend towards her and hugged her closely. 'It's OK,' she muttered. 'It's all going to be all right.' Then she glanced at Arlene. She was still unconscious, as she had been since Kronos had revealed the truth about Paul.

It might be all right for us, but what about Arlene? To know that the love of your live was nothing but an illusion?

Mel swallowed as she saw Arlene stirring. What could she say to her? How could they make everything all right for her?

The Master effortlessly pulled himself from the converter and stood upright in his console room. Taking a deep breath, he savoured the strength that burnt within him, invigorating every part. His hands touched his face, feeling flesh and bone, skin and beard, everything as it should be. He was the Master once more.

A new body - at last. The wake of the Lux Aeterna had flowed through that body, through each and every cell, as it fled the Higher Place. And as it had done so, it had latched on to the nucleotides that had once sung with the glory of the Source of Traken and reignited them, giving him back his mortality and immortality.

He threw his head back and laughed. He had won! Against the Doctor, the Chronovores, against Kronos - he had won!

He was still laughing as he activated the scanner. And then he saw what was happening, what was approaching.

A second later, the laughter had turned into a terrified, anguished scream.

'So?' asked Stuart, swigging from his hip flask, refilled courtesy of the Doctor's extensive collection of spirits from across the universe. 'Are you going to tell us what that was all about, or do we just pack up, go home, and say no more about it?'

The Doctor sighed, and sank into the luxury of a leather armchair. The TARDIS was still on the moon - he didn't want to risk travelling through the vortex for a while, not after all of the upheavals - but he had taken them to somewhere a little more comfortable than the console room: the room of chairs, as Jamie had once called it.

The red leather armchair was just one of the eccentric items of furniture dotted around the circular white room: Mel lounged on a beanbag close to him, while Anjeliqua slept on a chaise longue that was the double of the one in the console room. Arlene simply sat on a high-backed Chippendale chair and smiled. All she would say was that Paul was coming back.

The Doctor wasn't exactly sure what could be done for either Arlene or Anjeliqua. One had lost her lover, one had had her personality altered. But Anjeliqua had got her personality back. What about Arlene? To know that the person you loved was nothing but an illusion, a construction sent by the gods? Such emotion wasn't the Doctor's territory, and he was very glad that Mel was around to help him out on that score.

He returned to Stuart's question. 'So, Professor Hyde?'

'I know we're only mere mortals, but it would be nice to know what the hell has just happened.'

'According to the TARDIS's sensors, the black hole that we call the Great Attractor went hypernova about an hour ago, relative time. Its singularity exploded, and the event horizon blew away in so much Hawking radiation. The Mad Mind of Bophemeral is presumably missing in action.'

'And Kronos?' asked Mel.

The Doctor shrugged. 'Kronos tampered with our minds, Mel. He constructed a fiancé for Arlene, a vendetta for Anjeliqua and a knowledge forbidden by the Guardians - the Millennium War - for me. For Stuart, he created self-doubt about TOMTIT and his abilities, for you, he created doubt in me.' He pouted. 'Then again, it didn't take much for that, did it?'

Mel came over to him and hugged him. 'Come on, Doc. I'll never be comfortable with what happened on Maradnias, and I know you won't either. But we have to learn from our mistakes. You taught me that.'

'Yes I did, didn't I?' Dear, sweet Mel. Somehow, it seemed as if she were becoming the moral compass in the Doctor's life. As if he was losing direction... Sweeping the thought aside, he continued. 'But Kronos - I felt him die,' he said quietly.

'How?' asked Stuart.

'The passing of one such as Kronos sends ripples through the cosmos, ripples that those sensitive to time can feel. The gods - Chronovores, Eternals and the like - can will themselves dead. Indeed, that's the only way that they can die. Kronos committed suicide, and in doing so deliberately opened the way for the Lux Aeterna to return to Calabi-Yau Space - the Six-Fold Realm. The passing of that amount of sheer energy disrupted the space-time continuum: that's what detonated the Great Attractor and - hopefully - destroyed the Mad Mind of Bophemeral.'

'How will Anjeliqua be when she wakes up?' asked Stuart, slumping into a huge, black leather sofa. 'She's been through a lot.'

'She'll need your friendship,' the Doctor answered. 'And your support.' He turned to Mel. 'Someone else for you to look after,' he said kindly.

Mel frowned. 'That'll be a bit difficult if I'm a million light years away in the TARDIS, won't it?'

The Doctor frowned. 'You mean...'

'You silly man. You need someone to look after you. Besides, the TARDIS is my home. I belong here.'

'Home.' He looked around the room of chairs and smiled. The old girl had been through so much over the last few days: time rams, viruses, crossing sidereal boundaries... 'You need a holiday!' he announced.

'A holiday?' Mel replied. 'Why would I need a holiday?'

'Not you, the TARDIS.'

Mel grinned. 'Ah, yes: the TARDIS.' Then she looked behind her. 'But what about Arlene? She's convinced that Paul's coming back to her.'

The Doctor didn't know what to say. Loss, pain, bereavement... the Time Lord way was so different. How could he help Arlene?

What is reality, Doctor? A Time Lord, travelling through space and time in a police box? Or a woman in love? Or a planet of billions, burning in space? Kronos was our child, and we have a responsibility. His legacy resides with us.

For a moment, the Doctor was standing before Lillith and Sadok, the matriarch and patriarch.

We understand, Doctor. All will be as it should be.

'Thank you,' he muttered, understanding.

What of you, Doctor?

'What do you mean?'

You have our gratitude. You too must benefit from Kronos' legacy.

'I don't want anything, apart from Mel, Stuart, Anjeliqua and Arlene coming out of this in one piece.'

Maradnias?

'What about Maradnias?'

We can give it life. Restore it. Undo your error.

Or other wrongs that you would right. Tell us. Remember the Ancient Covenant that we sent down to you?

They owed him a favour. And he had to collect.

The Doctor hesitated. He had always played by the rules, even when those rules had cost him so much. Rules that he had been taught, many, many years ago.

Friends had died and he hadn't been able to save them - because of the rules. Friendships had been broken - because of the rules. A planet had died - because of the rules.

He looked up at Lillith and Sadok. Were those rules so immutable? Just for once, could he break them?

'Do what you think is right.'

We will. We always do.

With a crash of breaking rules, he was back in the TARDIS. He looked down at Mel and grinned. Unexpected consequences.

'Paul Kairos was a construct, created by Kronos as part of his plan. And yet he was born in London in 1964, of Greek parents, and grew up in Camden. He went to West London University, where he studied physics until Professor Stuart Hyde took him under his wing and turned him into one of the greatest temporal scientists this world would ever see. He has a birth certificate, a national insurance number, a driving licence - for most places, that's more than enough.'

'Is it?'

'Whether a construct or not, Paul Kairos was real... aren't you?'

On time, the door to the room of chairs opened and Paul Kairos walked in. Arlene's face lit up: within moments she had leapt from her chair and hugged him.

'But Paul's... dead,' muttered Mel.

The Doctor shook his head. 'No: Kronos is. But Paul was always real. He was born, he'll get married, they'll have children, and - eventually - they'll die. Kronos inserted himself into reality, and liked what he saw. Paul Kairos is his legacy.'

The Doctor turned away from Mel. He wasn't sure how she was going to react. But it had to be said. 'It doesn't excuse my actions, but they put everything right.'

'They?' asked Mel. Then she must have read the look in his eyes. 'Maradnias?'

'The gods. The Chronovores and the Eternals.' He grabbed Mel's hands.'We never visited Maradnias. The civil war never happened. The planet is safe...'

'It did happen, Doctor,' said Mel sadly. 'We were just lucky this time.' With that, she walked over to Paul and Arlene.

The Doctor watched as she left him. The worst thing was that she was right. This time, Maradnias had been saved. But the next time, and the time after that? The gods wouldn't be around to save him then, would they?

Stuart sidled up to him.'And the Master?'

The Doctor raised an eyebrow.'Ah, yes, the Master.' He glanced at Stuart's hip flask.'May I?'

As Stuart handed it over, the Doctor shrugged.'I'm sure that his sins will find him out in time.'

On the outer reaches of the Great Attractor, the Divine Host made its way home. The black hole had become a gateway, and that gateway led back to the Six-Fold Realm.

There was nothing for them in this universe any more: the abomination that was the Quantum Archangel had taken back the alternates, stolen their lifeblood... but the Lux Aeterna was now theirs once more, back in the Six-Fold Realm.

It was time to go home, through the doorway that had been opened for them.

As they flocked towards the hypernova that would take them home, they saw a small, insignificant object. A small black box, floating in the void. A mere bagatelle, and yet the construct radiated with the power of the Lux Aeterna.

Sustenance.

For the last time in the Higher Place, the Divine Host prepared to feed.

Because the timeline of a Time Lord, with all of its endless possibilities, was all that they could ever want.

Acknowledgements

When I first suggested a sequel to *The Time Monster*, reactions ranged from incredulity to...well, incredulity. But I've always had a soft spot for the story, and I hope I've given you a fun romp – 'dripping with camp menace', as one wag put it.

I'd like to thank all of those people who made it possible for me to write this book, whether by proof-reading, providing information and advice, or simply for being there in the first place. Apologies if I've forgotten anyone – the names must have fallen into a parallel universe. Firstly, the proofreader contingent: James Ambuehl, Marco Capiello, Mark Healey, Mark Phippen, John Putland and Adam Richards.

The information providers, who answered my cries for help about everything: from a name for 'Son of TOMTIT' to the article of Gallifreyan law concerning genocide, to which races were around 150 million years ago, especially Meddling Mick Gair, whose knowledge of continuity is quite simply frightening. Here's to the rec.arts.drwho community – better than a programme guide, and decidedly more accurate. And let us not forget the valiant members of the Faction Paradox e-group, for both encouragement and controversy. We love it!

And last, but certainly not least, those people whose inspiration and support over the writing of this book – and a lot longer than that – has been nothing short of a Godsend: Peter Anghelides, Mike Burkitt, Matthew Burgess, John Byrne, Colin Cherot, Chris Claremont, Matt Clark, Ian Collier – the inestimable Stuart Hyde!, Branko Djakovic, John Furniss, Andrew Hair, Auntie Joyce, Sîon Keeling-Dean and the Knights of the Round Table of 79CXR, Bonnie Langford, Peter Lovelady, Arlene Martin, my Mum, Paul O'Brien and his wonderful X-Axis, Michael Papangelou, Mike Ramsay, Justin Richards, Gary Russell, Wesley Stanton, Lynne Thomas and the Lexicats, Eddie Thornley, Troy Turner, everyone human at the IT Network, and above all: Gerard Hall. What would I do without you, Ged?

About the Author

CRAIG HINTON was born in London in 1964, and had the good fortune to go to Warwick University with Justin Richards and Andy Lane, and work for IBM with Peter Anghelides and - wait for it - Justin Richards. Having spent 15 years in various parts of the IT industry, he is currently an IT consultant, and tends to spend his time eating, drinking and flying around the world at PR companies' expense. When he isn't freeloading, he collects American comics, and thinks that *Preacher* is the best thing since sliced bread.

The Quantum Archangel is his eighth novel, and his first for the BBC range of *Doctor Who* books.